Read what the critics s

The Tattoo

"A book about the 'sins of the fathers'… A gritty, troubling book and he's done it well. The issues he raises are key to Hawaii today and for future generations."

—The Honolulu Advertiser

"Unforgettable…If McKinney's ultimate achievement is his portrayal of Hawaiian culture in a way that mainland Americans—those who've never seen, nor ever will, anything but the touristy side of Hawai'i—can identify with, then the ultimate failure belongs to the mainland American publishing houses for ignoring the book for so long."

—San Antonio Current

"Rough-and-tumble, rife with fully drawn badass characters and plenty of action, McKinney's novel is powerful and strong."

—Time Out Chicago

"McKinney's very first novel is thought provoking and revealing to say the least. The way this first-time novelist keeps the story moving is a credit to his skill as a writer…We highly recommend this book to those who enjoy contemporary fiction…."

—The Dispatch

The Queen of Tears

"McKinney vividly recreates Seoul during the Korean War from the beat-up cars made of beer cans to the affluent homes lined with fish ponds and grape vines…It's a technically skillful achievement in a story deceptively disguised as a slim, fast read."

—Honolulu Weekly

"McKinney's portrait of a besieged woman within a multicultural, multigenerational family saga poignantly and powerfully dramatizes the troubles women face, the pan-Asian melting pot of Hawaiian culture, and the conflicts inherent in Americanization."
—Booklist

"McKinney demonstrates a talent for restraint and tight pacing."
—*Publishers Weekly*

"Renewing and revitalizing the genre of Hawai'i noir fiction, Chris McKinney tells his tales of Honolulu's lower depth with an insider's authority and the zeal of a real writer. Beyond all that rings true in McKinney's fiction, what elevates it most is the author's unexpected compassion for those at the bottom or in emotional jeopardy."
—Tom Farber, author of *A Lover's Question*

"[An] interesting case of Korean, Korean American, and Hawaiian characters…[McKinney] has a keen eye for details of places and people. The storyline is well developed…McKinney is pitch-perfect on the social and racial climate of Hawaiians, Asians, immigrants, mixed-bloods, and whites…The frequent dialogues are crisp and pointed."

—*Korean Quarterly*

Bolohead Row

"McKinney is exceptionally skilled at imagining compelling characters, who worm their way into the consciousness of even reluctant readers… If his aim is to provoke self-righteous middle-class Islanders into awareness and understanding of the folks who populate *Bolohead Row*, he succeeds. [It] is well written and potentially very important for its ability to reflect…"
—*The Honolulu Advertiser*

"With *Bolohead Row*, McKinney officially establishes himself as the state's young breakout writer, and singlehandedly creates the genre of hardboiled Honolulu fiction."

—*Honolulu Weekly*

"What makes this book work is McKinney's "talk story" approach. He allows the reader to "sit down" and listen as Charlie tells us about his struggles. Through his journey—which includes drugs, violence and even murder—he begins to find a way to let go of the "game" and start concentrating on "life."

—*Hawaii Magazine*

Mililani Mauka

"...*Mililani Mauka* explores new emotional and physical terrain, and promises to grow the Honolulu Community College professor's audience..."

—Ragnar Carlson, *Honolulu Weekly*

"McKinney's brand of dark, underbelly portraits of contemporary Hawaii delves into lives upturned instead of buoyed by Oahu's false suburban promises."

—Christine Thomas, *Honolulu Advertiser*

"McKinney's talent in this book is to bring flawed characters to life and still allow us to make a sympathetic attachment to them."

—Stephen Hong, Asian American Literature Fan

"...In *Mililani Mauka* he [has] created a character who takes revenge in a rather spectacular but ineffectual way on a community that he feels has failed him."

—Wanda Adams, *Honolulu Advertiser*

List of Characters

Boi Rapun, aka "Boi Vise Grip," "Swingman Rapun," and "Boi No Good": Boi is a tough, big-thinking foster child turned beat cop. Driven by envy of his brother, love for a daughter, and hatred toward a changing island that's pushing his people out of existence, Boi sees only two choices: swallow his rage and be a family man or erupt and burn those around him.

Shane Knotting: Adopted by an old money state senator and his beauty-queen wife, Shane's private high school days consist of canoe club paddling and wild parties. While his brother Boi covets his life, Shane yearns to be more than a spoiled prep boy—he wants to be three-hundred pounds of muscle men fear.

Charles Knotting: Shane's adopted father, inheritor of vast family wealth and maybe the next governor of the State of Hawaii. Through the eyes of his son, he sees a Hawaii in need of rescue, and is ready to use all his wealth and executive power to change the face of the islands.

Glory: Older than her two siblings, Boi and Shane, Glory is the only one who ends up stuck with their biological addict mother and barely manages to survive a childhood spent imprisoned in a gutted aluminum tool locker. As an adult, she promises she will kill before she ever lets anyone touch or lock her up again.

Joe Bolosan: Boi's adopted father is a struggling taro farmer. When he's reduced to eeking out a living scraping lead paint and asbestos off renovated beach-front property bought up by mainland transplants, politicians and rich haoles become his enemies. He hopes that his son will soon raise arms against them.

Helen Knotting: A one-time Miss Hawaii and a successful insurance saleswoman, her life is transformed by the adoption of

Shane. She struggles to be a good mother, but her adopted son and his brother Boi may be too damaged to be fixed.

Nina Rapun: Boi's young daughter who lives with her mother in public housing. She is the one person Boi loves unconditionally, but the love is not enough to keep him grounded and it becomes the justification for the crazy things he wants to do.

Patricia Bolosan: Boi's adopted mother. A hula dancer at the Polynesian Cultural Center who is constantly battling her weight, watches helplessly as her husband teaches Boi who to hate.

Chastity Fu, aka "Skank Fu" and "Fu808": A salt-blending welfare queen, Chastity is the mother of Boi's daughter, Nina. Boi fears that Nina will grow up to be just like her.

Boi No Good

Other books by Chris McKinney

The Tattoo

The Queen of Tears

Bolohead Row

Mililani Mauka

Boi No Good

Chris McKinney

Mutual Publishing

The following story is fictional and does not depict any actual person or event. Any resemblance to actual incidents, or actual persons living or dead, is coincidental.

ISBN-10: 1-56647-980-0
ISBN-13: 978-1-56647-980-6
Library of Congress Control Number: 2012946586

First Printing, October 2012

Mutual Publishing, LLC
1215 Center Street, Suite 210
Honolulu, Hawaii 96816
Ph: (808) 732-1709
Fax: (808) 734-4094
e-mail: info@mutualpublishing.com
www.mutualpublishing.com

Printed in Korea

for Morgan

Contents

Acknowledgments

I'd like to thank the following people for their generous contributions. Though this is a work of fiction, the story is set in a real world filled with criminals, politics, cops, safety boards, architecture, and natural disasters. The information, advice, and feedback I received from these experts in their fields was invaluable:

Deputy Public Defender, Craig Nagamine. Supervising Deputy Prosecutor, Kathy Kealoha. Captain, Honolulu Fire Department, Andrew Fukuda. President and CEO of Kobayashi Group, LLC, Patrick Kobayashi. Project Manager at Allied Pacific Builders, Thomas Kim. Author and Publisher/Editor-in-Chief of El Leon Literary Arts, Tom Farber.

My writer's group: Mark Panek, Robert Barclay, and part-timer Alexei Melnick.

Special thanks to author and editor, Don Wallace.

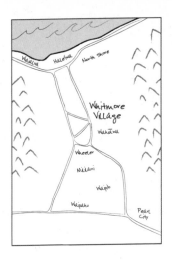

The Wahiawa Circle Island

Unlike most Hawaiian women who wear gold bracelets, each bearing the name of a child or grandchild, Cece Rapun bore ten diamond-cut bands emblazoned black with the names of ancestors, ten generations of mothers and daughters, going back to the time of Kamehameha the Great.

But tonight, propped up eight rows back in a derelict city bus, Cece is down to two. And as her daughter Makana approaches under flickering lights, dressed like a whore as usual, Cece knows she'll soon only have one bracelet left.

She'd named the daughter Makana, "gift from heaven" in Hawaiian. What a joke. Makana, who swipes Cece's social security and disability and spends it on a $50-a-day drug habit, lifts her mother's wrist. She slips a bracelet off Cece's bony hand. Cece struggles to summon rage, to fuel her broken limbs, but nothing comes except a vein she feels pulsing from eye to temple, and a gravelly buzzing in her ears.

"Don't worry, mom," says Makana with her mousy voice, the one she always uses when she lies. "I'll buy them back when I get my shit together. You'll see."

Makana pockets the bracelet. She hussy struts past her three sleeping children, their skinny calves dangling off seats a few rows up. The five of them, Cece, Makana, and the kids, live in the broken bus sitting on a 3,000 square foot red dirt lot in Whitmore Village, Oahu. Ten generations of Hawaiians scrimping, clinging, and busting ass, and all Cece has left is a druggie daughter and three bastard grandchildren crammed in a rusty #52 Wahiawa Circle Island. And now just one gold bracelet. Eventually, it will be headed to the pawn shop, too. Makana's high heels click-clack on metal steps, and the double doors groan as she staggers through the exit.

Cece glances at her wrist. Nina. It had been the last and most difficult bracelet to purchase because she'd hated her mother. After Cece's father had died, Nina donated her land to the Mormon church, which owned over seven thousand acres on the island already. "The spirit of Maroni told me to," her mother had said, wearing a mid-calf black muumuu, solemnly bowing her head. Maroni, the fifth century prophet who left his gospels buried somewhere in Wayne County, New York, whose spirit led Joseph Smith to the holy scriptures. Cece was almost looking forward to death so she could find this Maroni and punch his lights out.

But she'll have to wait. Now, trapped on a busted bus in her busted body, Cece is pure spectator. She's helpless as these grandchildren, Glorya-Maree Ching Kehau Souza-Rapun, Chayne-Marcos Kama Momotaro Nakamura-Rapun, and Boi (just "Boi"), with their ridiculous names, secondhand clothes, and food stamp-nourished, pot-bellied bodies grow wild in this giant lost-and-found metal box.

Boi, the youngest, the one who Cece calls "hee" because his jaundiced eyes resemble an octopus's, wakes. Which one fathered him? The pig-hunting crackhead, the musician crackhead, or the other crackhead? Cece remembers. It was the skinny dead one who fixed cars. Run over by a tour bus last year at three in the morning.

Boi rubs his nose, looks up at his grandmother, and smiles. His stainless-steel-capped teeth remind Cece of the grill on her grandmother's Buick Roadmaster. The four-year-old rummages through a pile of dirty laundry and pulls out a crescent wrench frozen with rust and a dented can of beets capped with pink g-string panties. He tosses the panties and whacks the can with the wrench. It doesn't open. He climbs a seat and raises the can over his head with both hands. He hurls it down. The beets punch a hole through the corroded floorboard. Wide-eyed, he smiles at Cece and howls. Cece would shudder if she could.

Boi steps past the humming gas generator, opens a tiny refrigerator, and pulls out a baby bottle filled with fruit punch. He sucks on the bottle. The juice isn't coming out fast enough. He grabs a steak knife from the pile of laundry and stabs at the rubber nipple with its snapped-off tip. Satisfied, he lies belly-down on a broken, three-wheeled skateboard and pushes toward his grandmother. The half-naked axle screeches on the floorboard. He pulls up to Cece, ducks under her tent dress, and pokes at the feeding tube inserted in her stomach with the knife. "Sore when I touch it?" Boi asks.

It isn't.

Boi gets out from under the dress and climbs on Cece's lap. She blinks hard. The child grins as he shoves the rubber nipple in his grandmother's mouth. "Drink, tutu," says Boi. "It's good for you."

Cece shits her diaper.

Red fructose corn syrup, water, and tears run down Cece's chin as her ears crackle. Her heartbeat quickens as her lungs struggle to take in air. Cece closes her eyes and concentrates, trying to at least force the now blaring sound into pattern, into music, into voices. She filters out static until she can make out faint screaming matches between generations of mothers and daughters about hair-brushing, dead fathers, proper child-rearing, inheritances, bad boyfriends, worse husbands, and dirty bare feet. Her eyes snap open but she sees nothing. She tries to breathe but can't.

Cece's now standing outside herself, watching the broken old woman beneath her, mouth wide open, still, as her grandson tosses the flat-head knife and pounds the bottom of the baby bottle like he's trying to pour ketchup. She spins around as the old bus's starter chokes, the pistons fire, the gears grind. Cece feels the Circle Island inch forward. She grabs a bus pole and steadies herself as gravel crunches under the rolling tires.

The bus picks up speed, bounces over a pot hole, then turns on to the highway. When it hits cruising speed, Cece expects the bus to level off, but it doesn't. She squeezes the vibrating pole as hard as she can as the bus rockets, now moving like a comet past the red dirt fields of Whitmore Village that once grew pineapple for the world. Cece swallows nausea as the bus lifts. Glass jars filled with dead ticks and sparkplugs soaking in gasoline roll past her as the bus climbs over the ocean.

Cece moves from pole to pole, working her way to the front of the bus. She makes it to the driver's seat, sits, and takes the wheel. The windows fog and the bus trembles as it sails higher and higher. Cece wipes the windshield so she can see out. A bell chimes, again and again. Cece glances up at the rear view mirror. Boi is standing on a seat ten rows back, grinning as he yanks the pull cord while his brother and sister, thumbs in mouths, sleep.

She doesn't want to stop.

Cece pounds the gas, eyes the stars, and turns northwest as she wayfinds to oblivion.

2.

A Japanese woman with the face of a model and the body of an aircraft carrier, Mrs. Akamine walks past the charred remains of last week's trash and steps in front of the bus, which sits in red mud on a series of car jacks, cinder blocks, and corroded rims. It's an old model, maybe one from the first fleet of 1971, its rusted, rounded edges patched with spackle and bird shit. Mrs. Akamine frowns at the mailbox by the door and knocks on the glass. No answer. She leans into the double doors, pushes hard, and wedges the doors open. She steps inside, takes one whiff, and gags.

The little girl, Glorya-Maree, paints Cece's toenails while her younger brother, Chayne-Marcos, sniffs gas generator fumes. Boi, straddling the bus seat in front of his grandmother, smiles at Mrs. Akamine as he drops rock candy into a winding toy chute. The candy rattles down the plastic slide like a pachinko ball to drop in Cece's gaping mouth.

"Stop!" Mrs. Akamine screams. The children look up, faces stained with red corn syrup and Cheeto dust. She grasps a steel pole to steady herself. "I'm Mrs. Akamine from social services. Where is your mother?"

The children shrug. Mrs. Akamine hesitates before walking to Cece, who smells to Mrs. Akamine like a colonoscopy bag stuffed with corpse feet. She holds her nose, grabs Cece's cold, bony wrist, and searches for a pulse. She tosses the wrist and steps back, almost tripping over Chayne-Marcos. The gold bracelet slips off Cece's wrist and clangs on the floor. Boi's eyes follow it, and he bounces off his seat. "Where is your mother?" Mrs. Akamine screams.

She pulls Chayne-Marcos away from the generator. "No! Stink!" cries the child, in tears, grasping for the machine, his skinny arms monkey-strong. Mrs. Akamine presses the kill switch on the generator, and Chayne-Marcos goes limp. For a second, she is unsure whether she turned off the machine or the child. She picks up him up, shocked by his lightness, his malnourished body, and hugs him. "Good boy," Mrs. Akamine says. "Be a good boy."

Chayne-Marcos nods.

After removing Chayne-Marcos from the bus and strapping him into her station wagon, Mrs. Akamine heads for Glorya-Maree, who is banging a bottle of nail polish against the floorboard. The girl has a horseshoe-shaped scar under her eye, like she was branded with the top of a disposable lighter.

As Mrs. Akamine snatches the bottle of nail polish, it disintegrates, spraying magenta enamel across the eyes of both girl and social worker. Mrs. Akamine, trying to wipe the polish from her face, yanks the blinking six-year-old off the floor and off the bus.

Out of the corner of her eye, she catches Boi scrambling under the feet of his dead grandmother.

When Mrs. Akamine returns, she finds Boi on his hands and knees, one hand in his pocket. She pulls him off the floor and picks him up. Grinning, he flashes his metal grill. He reaches for her face, smudges nail polish with his fingertips, and draws a dark pink smile.

Mrs. Akamine slaps his hands away as she marches off the bus, Boi slung over her shoulder. He reaches for the small refrigerator.

"Juice!"

His tee shirt rides up his back as they struggle. She feels rows of fresh horseshoe scabs on the small of his back. "Be good," says Mrs. Akamine.

"Go fuck yourself," says Boi.

Mrs. Akamine pulls down his shirt.

"Juice!"

At the station wagon, three children scream for juice, arms outstretched toward the bus like insane sun god worshippers lamenting a final dusk. "I'll get it!" Mrs. Akamine roars. She looks up at the Wahiawa Circle Island, remembering how as a child she used to catch a similar bus from Kaneohe to Ala Moana Shopping Center at five-thirty every morning to attend an all-girls Catholic private school in town. Her father always said she should go to law school. Maybe he was right. This is worse than last Friday night when she had to pick up five kids from the Honolulu Zoo after their addict mother dropped them off while she got high. Gave the oldest five bucks, a fistful of four-ounce formula samples, and a diaper bag. She didn't come back. Mrs. Akamine doubts that the mother of these children will come back, too.

Glorya-Maree, Chayne-Marcos, and Boi, calm now, sucking on baby bottles filled with fruit punch, watch their broken-down bus, fire truck, ambulance, and three police cars vanish as they pass tracts of unused land, the remnants of pineapple fields. The dirt, still fertile, sprouts tall thick roadside weeds. "Where we going?" asks Glorya-Maree, her face a glittered nail-polish mask.

"You're moving out," says Mrs. Akamine. "For good."

Glorya-Maree nods. "I hope I get to live in a castle," she says. "With unicorns."

"Stupid little bitch," says Chayne-Marcos, staring out the window.

Glorya-Maree whips her bottle at Chayne-Marcos. It bounces off his forehead. A small bump instantly rises. She targets the bump and hammers fists on it. Chayne-Marcos covers up and doesn't fight back. Mrs. Akamine pulls to the side of the road, reaches behind, and pulls the girl off her brother. Boi crawls into the front seat.

"No!" After just ten minutes with these kids, Mrs. Akamine feels on the verge of a breakdown.

She's surprised they listen. Her hands trembling, Mrs. Akamine fastens a seatbelt over Boi. She turns back on the road. "Where we moving?" asks Boi.

"Someplace new," says Mrs. Akamine. She looks in the rear view mirror. Glorya-Maree gets up on her knees and waves at men and women in army fatigues passing by in Humvees while Chayne-Marcos closes his eyes, yawns, and falls asleep. Mrs. Akamine turns to Boi, who, now riding shotgun, reaches in his mouth and shakes a loose silver tooth.

"Stop that." Boi rips out the capped tooth and puts it on the dash. It vibrates, doing a directionless dance. The bloody silver tooth falls before Mrs. Akamine can snatch it. Blood dribbles down Boi's lip as he watches, claps excitedly, and laughs. He pops the seatbelt free and climbs in back.

A few miles later, Glorya-Maree is leaning against the door, Chayne-Marcos's head on her lap. Eyes closed, Boi wipes the blood off his lip and wraps his arms around his brother. Their limbs all tangled, they grind their teeth. That's how it is with kids this far gone, Mrs. Akamine thinks. They can only endure affection while they sleep.

PART ONE

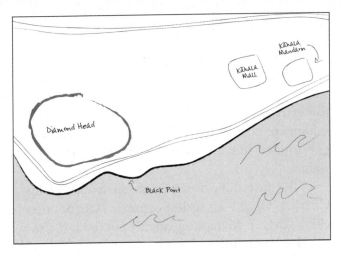

I. Shane Knotting

1.

As they step out of the Department of Human Services with Chayne-Marcos in tow, State Senator Charles Knotting and his wife Helen, matching in head-to-toe Hilo Hattie, look like Lei Day king and queen of the century. A tall, sun-worn blond with a windshield paniolo saunter, Charles smiles and scoops up the child. "I gotta get out of these clothes," he says. "Feel like a giant mango."

Helen twists a pinky ring to turn the engraving of the Aztec wind god out front. "Eighty-fifth percentile in height, but only twenty-fifth percentile in weight."

"This isn't the crack baby one, right?" Charles asks.

"That was the one with the silver teeth."

"The one who tried to bite me when I picked the girl up?"

Helen nods.

Charles looks down at Chayne-Marcos. "We'll have to fatten you up, kid."

The Knottings aren't the usual foster parents. They're not working class people or immigrants horse-trading childcare for a $500-a-month government check. Charles, a descendant of a nineteenth-century shipwrecked whaler-turned-plantation owner, and Helen, the great-granddaughter of a local Japanese who got rich building Oahu's windward suburbs, hardly need the extra money. Charles serves on bank, trust, and land development boards during his downtime from preaching broken government like a broken record. Helen peddles insurance in Kahala.

"The first thing we need to do is change his name," says Charles. "Or at least spell it correctly." Charles tries to tickle the child. Chayne-Marcos, apparently not ticklish, frowns.

"Let's give him a Hawaiian name," says Helen. "He's Hawaiian. His middle name is Kama."

Charles methodically looks for another tickle spot—arm pits, ribs, feet, but the boy does not respond.

Helen shrugs as Charles furls his brow. "We need to go over the paperwork again," says Charles. "Make sure he has his shots."

Helen brushes the bridge of the boy's nose with her fingertip. "His nasofrontal angle is better than mine."

Chayne-Marcos, finally tickled, smiles. Charles sighs, more relieved than satisfied. As the couple steps to their car, Helen opens the back door and Charles hands the boy to her. She secures him in a seat with elaborate straps and buckles. "Look at this thing," says Charles. "What? We're flying him to the moon?"

"How about Kekoa?" Helen says as she tries to untwist a strap.

"Uggh. That's a name you see on a tee shirt next to a spike-collared pit bull."

"It means the brave one."

"He doesn't talk much."

With Chayne-Marcos strapped in, Helen steps inside the car. Charles checks his hair in the rear view mirror, flexes his trapezius muscles, then starts the engine. Helen turns around and smiles at Chayne-Marcos. "You miss your family, Kekoa?" asks Helen, her voice pouring sweet like syrup over pancakes.

"Who's Kekoa?" Chayne-Marcos asks, imitating Helen's tone.

"You are, sweetie. Maybe."

Charles rolls down the window and takes out a cigar and lighter. "Tradition, right?"

Chayne-Marcos, eyes on the lighter, grasps the buckle on his chest and strains to pop the red release button. As the car pulls out onto the street, Chayne-Marcos pounds on the button with his fist but can't get out. "How cute," says Helen. "He's like a little Tarzan."

Charles eyes Chayne-Marcos in the rear view mirror as he lights his cigar. "We need to get him a tutor."

"Put that out," says Helen. "Smoke is bad for the skin."

2.

The Kahala home looks more like a museum than a house. Koa chairs padded with Victorian upholstery; a hutch filled with wooden bowls, china, and peacock feathers; a Thomas Gibson piano once banged on by Princess Kaiminaauao before measles took her at the age of four; and a green sea turtle shell mounted on a wall. It all smells of lemon oil and old money.

And pictures. Lots of pictures. Helen's grandfather breaking ground on a sugarcane field about to turn subdivision. Helen accepting the Miss Hawaii title. Helen straddling a Puuopelu pony. Charles's mother digging into ocean chop from seat one in an outrigger canoe. Charles sliding down twenty-foot waves. Charles shaking hands with past U.S. Presidents at the nineteenth hole.

Chayne-Marcos wanders the living room, careful not to touch anything. The hard wood floor creaks as he approaches the piano and hits a C sharp. "You like music?" asks Helen as she opens French doors revealing a meticulously landscaped backyard. A Micronesian with a back shaped like a question mark rakes leaves and flower pedals. A plumeria-fragranced breeze blows through as the sheer ivory curtains dance.

Helen sits at the piano and struggles through "Moonlight Sonata," one of a half-a-dozen songs she still remembers. Charles steps into the room, carrying bags filled with clothes and toys as Chayne-Marcos watches Helen's clumsy, unpracticed fingers stretch for keys. Charles peels his shirt off his big-wave surfer-body. He tosses his Joe Aloha attire on the polished hardwood floor. "This is morbid," says Charles. "Play something more cheerful." He looks down and flexes his broad, bare chest before grabbing a tee shirt and worn jeans from a laundry basket on the sofa. He puts on the shirt and starts changing his pants.

Helen switches to "Camptown Races."

Chayne-Marcos blinks. "Juice," he says.

"What was that?" asks Charles.

"Juice."

"Juice, please?" says Charles.

"Juice!" the boy screams as he spins in circles and yanks two fistfuls of his long, dark, wavy hair. One foot stuck in a pant leg, Charles hops toward the boy.

"Juice!"

Helen scrambles to the kitchen.

"Juice!"

Charles gets up, takes a toy out of a bag, and rips open the package. Twisted wire straps bind the robotic triceratops in the packaging. Charles struggles to unbraid the wire coils with his big hands as Chayne-Marcos screams. Helen runs in holding a cup of guava juice. She hands it to Chayne-Marcos, who throws the cup at the piano.

"Real juice!"

The boy howls for juice as Charles hands him the triceratops—cardboard, tape, and wire still clung to it. The boy throws it out the open French doors and screams. The Micronesian out back puts down the rake and walks to the front yard. He's dragging one stiff leg like he's trolling for yard fleas.

"You sure this isn't the crack baby one?" Charles asks.

Just as the boy is about to scream again, his teary eyes focus on Helen's wrist—a coiled, silver cuff bracelet. Chayne Marcos reaches for it. Helen glances at Charles, removes the bracelet, and hands it to the child. Chayne-Marcos takes the bracelet, runs to the sofa and lies down. He holds the silver up to his nose as he rubs the band between his thumb and the knuckle of his index finger.

"Wow," says Charles.

Helen ignores him, sits next to Chayne-Marcos, and rubs his back. She spots a mark on his skin and frowns. She pulls up his shirt. Burn scars run up his spine, like the hoof prints of a tiny shoed pony. "What the?" says Charles as he moves closer. Charles touches the scars. The boy flinches as his bracelet rubs quicken.

"Boi! Glorya!" he yells, like a kid who accepts hide-and-go-seek defeat.

"Animals," says Charles, clenching his jaw. "They should be put down. All of them."

Helen tears. "We *are* keeping him," she says.

Charles nods. "Hang them. Wouldn't waste a bullet on them."

Chayne-Marcos mumbles as his eyes get heavy. "Kehau... Alamea... Margaret... Agnes... Rachael... Florence... Victoria... Kalei... Leilani... Nina..." The names of Cece's ancestors roll off his tongue as Chayne-Marcos slips into sleep.

"We'll just call him Shane," says Helen.

"Shane it is."

A breeze flicks at Helen's bare shoulders and goosebumps rise. Charles grabs a washcloth from the laundry basket and squats in front of the boy. He dabs at his sweat-slicked hair. "See this here?" says Charles, still shaking, angry. "This is why I got into *politics* in the first place. Human Services got a line on the mother?"

"Just let it go," says Helen as she carefully tugs the bracelet from the boy's sleepy, once steely, now loosened grasp. "He's ours now."

Charles sneezes. He hands the washcloth to Helen, stands, walks to the French doors and closes them. "Must be the vog."

Helen glances up at the wall of pictures. She focuses on the one of her German mother, an East Asian philosophy professor, shaking hands with the Dalai Lama, the picture that they had put on an easel for her funeral a year before.

The boy sleeps as invisible gas plumes from Kilauea seep through the screened windows, blown two-hundred-miles north by Kona winds.

3.

Every year during the holidays, the shopping center PR department sets up a children's Santa train ride that circles eight-thousand square feet of Christmas decorations. Gaggles of parents run alongside that train, tripping over each other while snapping pictures of their tear-streaked children. Helen Knotting used to consider it great holiday sport to watch these mothers, her age but thirty pounds of flab heavier, run around in circles, toting shopping bags, wearing sensible shoes, stumbling and crashing into the styrofoam snowman display because their eyes were glued to their crying kids. When one mother toppled a lighted, fifteen-foot Douglas fir, it was all Helen could do to not shout, "Timber!"

Helen Knotting had never wanted to have children. And all she had to do was go to the mall during the holidays to remind herself why.

And now, at the mall with Shane, setting him down in the train next to a girl with uneven pigtails and snot dripping to her upper lip, Helen's trying to pinpoint the moment when all that changed, when she'd decided to join this pathetic club of women who regularly attended children's birthday parties, where adult topics of conversation ranged from the durability of inflatable water slides to the latest fitness fad they'd fail to commit to. Now Helen knows a dozen parents like these, parents who parade their kids around like they're the next Thomas Edison or Marie Curie, despite the fact that these children still eat their own boogers. All the while leaving their older kids, the ones who failed to show Edison and Curie potential, to sneak off to their bedrooms to play computer games with avatars named after their favorite TV show characters.

Helen's initiation into this motherhood club started with the death of her own mother. When she died, relatives from across the country flew back to Hawaii to plunder the house. Her older sister, Jenna, who owned her own dotcom startup, took all the jewelry and postmodern giclees. Her younger brother, Michael, a Modesto immigration attorney, took everything else of value that would fit in four suitcases. Which left Helen with the furniture. And the funeral expenses. Because as her siblings said as they tag-teamed her, Helen got the most stuff. But as ugly as that whole business was, the thing that troubled Helen the most was that one day she, too, would be dead. Cease to exist. The world would divvy up her stuff and not skip a beat. Just like that Bruegel giclee her sister took, the one with Icarus falling from the sky. She'd die and no one would notice.

Of course she could not live forever. But it was the first time she felt the dread. Truly imagining the complete loss of consciousness. After the funeral, she thought about it all the time. But she couldn't tell anyone about it, even Charles, who was seven years older than her, because it sounded ridiculous even in her own head. She was thirty-seven. Given her half-Asian heritage and general good health, not even halftime. How could she share her terror with people who were probably closer to death than she was? Besides, shouldn't she be mourning her mother instead of obsessing about her own mortality?

As the train starts, so do the parents. A step forward or two. Then they stop to snap pictures and find themselves several paces behind. Their steps quicken as they try to catch up. Helen resolves to stand perfectly still next to a red-nosed plastic reindeer. Children pass with their arms held out, in tears. One mother lifts out a little girl with cornrows. The girl lubricates her fingertips with spit, then digs her nose. Helen wonders if she was that disgusting when she was a child. No, her mother would never had allowed *that*.

Her mother. Helen sees herself standing in line in front of a smoke-stacked glue factory. The smell of boiling horse hooves fills the air. Her parents are already inside. Helen is next. No one is standing behind her. Maybe she should freeze herself before the time comes. Maybe she can be re-animated a few hundred years later when scientists finally discover the secrets of eternal life.

As the train completes its first lap, Helen spots Shane pointing down at his seatbelt. The snot-nosed girl next to him wipes her hand on his shoulder. Helen takes a step toward the train then changes her mind. No, she won't be that kind of parent. Her mother was like that. Thin, ghostly, long oily gray hair. No jewelry, no make-up, no nonsense. Looked and talked like a witch from MacBeth. She was always hovering, like if Helen weren't under her gaze for a single moment she would disintegrate.

Three months after her mother's funeral, Helen went to her primary care physician to get a complete physical. She was dying. She just knew it. Dr. Papadakis, a Chinese man with a Greek last name, warned her about osteoporosis, which can start as early as what he called "advanced maternal age," suggesting that she was in the midst of this personal era. She walked out in tears as if she was just diagnosed with cancer, passing women in reception whose eyes were glued to open tabloid magazines, an actress on the cover with her Ethiopian kids. Where did the time go?

It was on the drive home that Helen decided she wanted to have a kid. And when Helen got home and told Charles, ready to argue, ready to fight, it was actually Charles's idea to adopt. Take something broke and fix it, he said, rather than buy brand new. He liked the environmental ring to it. She was surprised.

"What about passing along genetic material?" she asked. Weren't men obsessed with that?

Charles shrugged. "What's so good about our genes? Your parents died early. My mom, too. And my father, I love him, but he's a trustfund manic-depressive."

Helen nodded.

"Besides, in the long run, we don't last," said Charles. "It's the name, Knotting, that counts."

As the train circles on its final lap, the parents circling the train full of crying children make a demented carousel. Shane stands up and jumps up and down waving to Helen. He's managed to get out of his seatbelt. The train is so slow, will he even get hurt if he falls? She looks down at the railed wheels and imagines shoelaces tangled around greased axles.

She races to the train, high heels pinching her toes. She's bumping into other parents now, the whole pack moving like a bunch of groupies chasing a rock star while the train sings la, la, la.

Shane leaps out of the train. Helen dives and barely catches him. They're on the ground, and Helen starts to cry, which makes Shane cry. Other kids looking at Helen and Shane wail and start crying too. For the first time in over a year, Helen's thinking about someone else's death instead of her own.

4. _____

On the first day of kindergarten, Shane Knotting is sent home because he kicked Micah Fong in the nuts. Micah looked at him funny when he couldn't tell the class what sound the letter B makes. Three days later, he's sent home again because he stabbed Kiana Schultz with a pencil. Kiana had hugged him because he'd successfully told the class what sound the letter B makes. Two weeks into kindergarten, after Shane tried to open his tin lunch pail with the class mascot—a baby tortoise named Bruce—he's expelled from the private Catholic school. Bruce opened instead of the lunch box, spilling turtle guts on a map of the United States play mat, bloodying Montana.

Today, Helen Knotting pleads with the school, one of the best in the state, the same one she went to as a kid, to take Shane back. She gets kicked up from vice-principal, to principal, to the president, a pasty ex-first baseman from Boston who had been the executive officer of an East Coast Catholic high school that was shut down because of a sex abuse scandal. The top man won't budge. After three days of meetings and ass kissing, this pisses her off. "Noblesse oblige, Mrs. Knotting," says the president. "To whom much is given, much is expected."

"Don't tell me about noblesse oblige," says Helen, who leans over the desk and points a manicured finger in the president's face. "I adopted him, didn't I? Besides, benevolence is expected from the fortunate. Noblesse oblige is exactly what I am asking for."

"Regardless, the safety of the students is my primary concern."

"Didn't your last school have priests running buck-wild buggering altar boys?"

The president stands, about to say something, but changes his mind. Leaves Helen fuming alone in his office. Maybe he's right, maybe Shane doesn't belong here. Two days ago, he pitched a fit in the backseat of the car, opened the door while they were doing seventy on the freeway. Even Helen wanted to stuff him in the trunk for the rest of the ride after that. But no, the boy is fixable. All kids are, right?

It takes the donation of a stained glass window of Father Damien saving the souls of Kalaupapa lepers—the school's third—to get Shane back in class and smooth things over.

5.

The first time Helen sits Shane in the corner for timeout, he leans his head against the wall and falls asleep. The first time she sends him to his room, he crashes for two hours. In fact, with every form of discipline, whether it's rational heart-to-hearts or frustrated screams, Shane nods off like she just double-dosed him with cough syrup. After several months of this, Helen and Charles are just trying to keep the boy conscious.

Every morning, Helen climbs down from the top bunk and wakes Shane up at 6:00. This can take a half-an-hour. Charles makes him breakfast, usually his favorite—sweetbread French toast sprinkled with powdered sugar—while Helen gets ready for work.

Then Helen dresses Shane and drives him to school. After school it's soccer, baseball, or swimming, then the private tutor, then the psychotherapist, then homework, then dinner, then a bath, then a bedtime story at 8:00. When she tries to escape to catch up with work, Shane cries, terrified of the dark. So Helen, on the verge of tears herself, sighs and climbs back on the top bunk.

Every few hours, Shane wakes screaming, bad dreams every night. So Helen hangs her head down from the top bunk and sings to him. She tries to multitask and improvises an isometric ab routine. Sometimes she gets Charles to sub for her. But when he sleeps with Shane, the two end up staying up way too late, Charles speechifying fiscal conservatism while letting Shane pummel him with a plastic tee-ball bat.

On the last day of school, a relieved Helen and Charles attend Shane's end-of-the-year elementary school songfest. He's actually graduating kindergarten. Each class, grades kindergarten to fifth, sings a song while parents click their cameras from the bleachers and applaud with the vigor of home-team fans. And as Helen and Charles sit squeezed between a tattooed local Japanese investment bank drone and a haole Army officer wearing a Brett Favre jersey, Charles looks right then left, flexes his latissimus dorsi, and shifts in his seat.

As fourth graders hit the stage to sing a song about surfing, a teacher wheels out a stunned-looking crippled kid on a strip of blue tarp, a cardboard surfboard glued to his wheelchair. Mouth agape, trach tube sticking out of his neck, the kid drools on his shirt as his vacant eyes fix on the ten-foot paper-mache breaker. Charles leans over to Helen and whispers. "He can stay here until sixth grade. After that, it's my school."

"Can he even get in?"

Charles glares. Dumb question.

Helen raises her camera and focuses in on Shane, who's sitting criss-cross-apple-sauce, front row with the rest of the kindergarteners, all of them wearing blue tee-shirts. When Helen stands up, the parents behind her groan. She ignores them and zeroes in on Shane. Wide-eyed, he stands and points at the crippled kid. "Grandma!" he yells. "He's like my grandma!"

Helen heads down the bleachers toward Shane. Her foot gets caught in a woman's purse strap, and when she tries to kick it off, she sends the purse and a high heel sailing into a sea of third graders. The woman's cursing. Helen keeps going.

A nun moves in to settle Shane down, his voice drowned out by an on-stage fourth grade crescendo. The Army officer in sandbox fatigues turns to Charles. "Used to be you pay fifteen grand a year for a school like this, your kid didn't have to sit in the same class as charity cases."

Charles can imagine the officer's car. Green Bay Packers flags pitched at every corner. Mustang or Camaro. Charles looks at the kid in the wheelchair. "You meant that poor kid?"

The Army guy points to the corner of the gym where Shane, held back by Helen, is trying to sink his teeth into the nun's wagging finger. "No, that one."

6. _____

"Mommy," Shane asks. "Why is there two beds in this room?"

A freshly showered Charles steps into the room, feet squeaking on the hard wood floor. Helen shoots her husband a weak smile. "Because your daddy and I were thinking about bringing home a brother or sister for you one day."

Shane looks up and waves. "I have a brother and sister."

Charles eyes Helen. "Not anymore, kid. Not anymore."

Helen yawns as Charles rubs her arm. She slides off the bunk. "I don't think we're going to bring home another one, sweetie."

"Why?"

Helen pulls off her Mexican silver, each ring slightly tarnished. She hands them to Charles, who pockets them and massages her hands. Charles smiles at Shane. "You're enough, kid. You're enough."

Helen heads to the hallway and throws up a tired wave without turning around. "It's you and me tonight, buddy," says Charles.

Shane crawls out of bed and picks up his plastic bat. "What are we gonna do?" he asks, grinning. He takes a swing at Charles. The red bat cracks and bends as it chops into the big man's knee. State Senator Charles Knotting kneecapped by a crazy six-year-old adopted kid.

Charles squats in front of the boy and takes the now limp bat from him. He eyes the bat as he tries to come up with something to tell his son, something that will resonate, some words of wisdom that the kid will remember all his life. What would his grandfather, a man who spoke four languages, a man who used to surf with The Duke himself, tell a boy like this?

Charles remembers how surprised he'd been when Helen had announced she wanted to have a child. He and Helen always agreed that there were bigger, more important things they could leave behind instead of children. And that having children would hamper their efforts to leave such things. But when Helen asked him what these things were, Charles didn't have an answer. Building things, that was for liberals. Conservatives preserved things. Helen was a member of a group of women who preserved the summer palaces of Hawaiian royalty. Charles, in his capacity as a state senator, tried to preserve the small-government philosophy of early American life, and as an ex-professional surfer, a waterman, he was a staunch environmentalist, much to his party's chagrin. But the Knottings, they didn't make things. And Helen wanted to make something. Eyes wild like a Dr. Frankenstein, she told him she wanted to make a human being.

Charles thought she was nuts, but who was he to stop her? He loved her. Besides, he was at that age where he was feeling ailments once foreign to him (dizziness, tingly joints, and calcium deposits on his elbows), and whenever he was struck with these for the first time, his mind shrieked alerts: CANCER, STROKE, CANCER. He'd been to the emergency room twice in the last year. The emergency room. Charles Knotting, who'd surfed waves so big he snapped at least three dozen surfboards. Charles Knotting, who was once crammed under a coral reef shelf by a twenty-footer and trapped underwater in a labyrinth of coral caverns for four-and-a-half minutes.

But now Charles Knotting was turning into an old man. He understood Helen's crazy idea of creating something new. It was a sort of second life that would extend theirs, as well as slow things down. Time had never moved more slowly for Charles than when he was trapped under the reef fighting coral and blackouts—having a kid would do sort of the same thing. So he suggested they adopt.

Two years later, and even though having a child only made him feel even older, Charles can't imagine his life without this crazy kid. He tosses the plastic bat under the bed. "Do you remember where you lived before you came and lived with us?"

Shane looks down and shrugs.

"Well, let's start talking about it, because soon you're the one who's going to need to know how to talk yourself out of trouble."

Shane nods. "Tell me about where I lived, Daddy."

Charles scoops the boy up and sits him on the top bunk. He tells Shane about drugs, abuse, and poverty and how weak, pathetic souls fold to these misfortunes, like serfs in the face of fire-breathing dragons. But not Shane. He's stronger than that. Charles knew it the moment he laid his eyes on him. He's dragon-slaying material. Shane smiles as Charles's vision of his childhood, a kid too strong to be held down by bad things, replaces his own. What happened to him during his first five years is no longer a story about a damaged boy rescued from doom by blind luck. It's now an epic about a strapping kid too damn tough to drown. As Charles puts it, his biological mother draped him with chains and tossed him in the ocean, but Shane's mighty stroke pushed him up to the surface. All Charles and Helen did was pull him into the boat.

7.

By the time Shane switches to Charles Knotting's alma mater in the seventh grade, to an estate consisting of century-old stone buildings and state-of-the-art air-conditioning that graduated senators, governors, billionaires, professional football players, and movie stars, he wields his first five years like a weapon, though he hardly remembers any of it:

"Where you from?"

"Wahiawa."

"Don't you live in Kahala? Got statues of Chinese lions and shit in front of your driveway?"

"Now. But back in the day, my ice addict biological mother raised me. I not spoiled like you guys. I lived in one frigging bus."

Like Charles had taught him, he throws in a bit of pidgin, the rap of the local working man, for good measure. The guys nod with respect. The girls say, "Poor thing." Shane turns to the teachers and swoops in on them, too:

"Why I got one B Miss Carlson?"

"B means very good."

"I couldn't even read until I was nine. My crackhead mother used to burn me with her lighter whenever I touched her *US* toilet magazines. You cannot cut me some slack? I wasn't raised like you guys."

And B's turn into A's.

Once in a while, when he terrorizes his male classmates with leg trips and headlocks, like Jonah Hines, the heir of a shampoo empire, who, as with many boys at this school, is a product of generations of breeding between privileged eggheads and hungry airheads—he's handsome, but his eyesight and sense of humor are terrible—Shane finds himself in the vice-principal's office, shaking his head apologetically. "Sorry, Ms. Caruso. It's the way I was raised. Mine was one violent household."

Even if he doesn't remember, it really happened, right?

So throughout intermediate and high school, Shane Knotting is known as the local boy, the boy with real island roots, the part-Hawaiian who grew up hardscrabble country, the part-Hawaiian who can scrap (despite the fact no one has ever seen him throw a punch). He's the bad boy with common sense, the guy you'd want with you in the mountains if you got lost (even though the only mountain he's ever been to is Big Bear for snowboarding with Charles). He's the guy you'd want with you if for some reason found yourself in the position of having to gut a pig (the only pig Shane ever touched was at a San Diego petting zoo). And he's the guy you'd want with you if the shit went down, the about-to-get-mobbed by a dozen 300-pound Samoans scenario, because the way he carries himself, chin up, rooster-chested, it just seems like he'd be the guy who'd know what to do, like a man fit to lead an Amazon expedition because he's the only one wearing a safari hat.

By the time Shane is a senior in high school, his classmates bow to him. Cruising around in his environmentally friendly hybrid capped with a watersports rack, picking up barefoot waterpolo queens with anklet tattoos toting $700 handbags, stomping out a clove cigarette before he enters trendy downtown night spots through red brick back alleys and their steel doors, Shane Knotting is King Bull Nuts and no one in his school has the balls to strip him of that title.

And as the end of Shane's senior year approaches, at age fifty-seven, State Senator Charles Knotting announces he's going to make his run for governor. "Time is ripe," Charles tells Shane. It's his favorite cliché, and Shane says it often, too, as if life for him is a climb up a giant jabong tree with plump D-cup fruit hanging from its branches waiting to be plucked. And his father's right. Time is ripe. With the patriarch of the state Democratic party in a coma, other name politicians chasing the vacant U.S. Senate seat, the rest of the country in a Great Recession-spurred, anti-incumbent lather, and Shane almost off to college, if ex-surf champion Charles Knotting can't snatch the governorship now, he never will.

The now-crowded interior of the Knotting residence still resembles a museum with its koa hutches, hand-carved chairs, cherrywood buffet inlaid with mother of pearl tigers and dragons, and polished hardwood floor. They've collected several pieces of new furniture over the years, but the general effect is still the same: do not touch.

They all stand in the living room: bankers, developers, political operatives—kingmakers, the real alii of Hawaii—trying hard not to put fingerprints on anything. Shane, now eighteen, tall and tan, sporting teen-idol shaggy hair and a canoe-paddling champion's build, steps in and drops his backpack on a chair, as Charles, wearing board shorts and a tee shirt, a head taller than the other gray-haired men, stands in front of the group. With his Roman pose and Roman nose, he looks like the King Kamehameha statue outside Aliiolani Hale. "Sorry I'm late," says Shane.

The kingmakers, wearing chinos and Hawaiian shirts, eye a photographer from the newspaper who snaps a picture of Helen while Perry the cub reporter stares in awe at the framed pictures of Charles sliding down jumbo waves. "Why announce here like this?" he asks Charles. "Why not the state capitol?"

Helen steps to Shane, tip toes, and pecks him on the cheek, pau hana malbec on her breath. He glances down at her bare feet, shiny Aztec rings wrapped around each painted toe. Charles smiles at Shane. "I could've announced at a public place, maybe Sunset Beach, where I won my first surf title, or maybe at the capitol, where I continue to fight out-of-control government corruption and spending, but I'm a family man, Perry. This is my hale. I want the people to see where I live and breathe."

Helen had quit her insurance agency to concentrate full-time on her new job, making her husband look good by looking good—forever tweezing, moisturizing, and pouring out sweat on an elliptical to make herself look thirty-five instead of fifty. She fills her wine glass and sips, leaving a lipstick imprint that suggests careful kissing more than drinking. She puts a manicured hand on the reporter's shoulder and brushes off lint. "I love your blog."

Perry glances at her Mexican silver necklace decorated with semi-precious purple stones set over tanned silicone cleavage. He got his start in journalism blogging about the fun things people can do in Hawaii for under thirty dollars a day. Now the next Governor's wife is coming onto him. Helen eyes her husband, his surf muscles and veins poring out of his short-sleeve shirt like fiber optics. "I tried to get him to wear a suit, Perry."

Charles shakes his head. "I don't want to put up any fronts," he says. "This is what I am."

It had, in fact, taken two days and three staffers to find the perfect board shorts and tee shirt. Nothing made by environmentally unfriendly companies. Nothing sewn by Chinese sweatshop workers. Nothing in Hawaiian to upset culturally sensitive Hawaiian-blood voters. Helen almost had to hire a girl to sew the clothes herself. "Don't let the graying blond locks fool you," says Charles, flexing his neck, towering over Perry. "I'm a local boy at heart. Grew up in hardscrabble Kuliouou. Hey, Perry. You meet my son before? Looks like he just got back from school. Always studying, this kid. Off to Yale this fall."

Shane, who had actually just come back from popping ecstasy and finger-banging Lucy Cho in the backseat of his car, trying to convince her to let him stick his entire fist in, wipes his hand on his jeans then shakes with Perry. "Dad thinks he had it tough. I was adopted. My mom was on ice. I lived in a broken-down bus in Wahiawa."

Helen wipes a tear from her eye. Charles throws an arm around Shane as the photographer snaps a picture. The kingmakers nod. "I'll tell you, Perry," says Charles. "This ice thing is out of control. But what isn't, right? We need to clean up state government from top to bottom."

"What programs are you planning to cut, Senator?"

"Tell you what I won't cut. Workers who roll up their sleeves and stick their hands in the dirt every day. By the way, did you know that Hawaii ranks forty-seventh among the states in standardized test scores? Forty-seventh! First thing on my agenda is addressing that issue."

Shane smiles. His father's second greatest political gift has always been a magician's sense of misdirection, the ability to change the topic from some irritating reality hardly anyone understood to something visceral that vexed the majority. He'd once heard Charles change the subject from his hinted opposition to the existence of the Office of Hawaiian Affairs to the coqui frog epidemic, how the deafening nocturnal croaking needed to be put to an end. He said it with such genuine conviction that Shane realized his father's greatest political gift was that he believed every word he said.

Perry thanks the senator, then exits. As Shane picks up his book bag, Charles puts a heavy arm around his shoulder. "Too much?" he asks, as the once-quiet kingmakers chatter about polls, campaign financing, mass transit, and the youthful curl of Helen's hair.

Shane smiles. "You always told me paper beats rock. Rock beats scissors. Scissors beats paper. Bullshit beats them all."

Charles frowns. "I was talking about the other guys."

"Remember what you told me once, about how it feels to get old?"

Charles nods.

"You said when you're young, you wake up and think something exciting might happen. But when you're old, not so much?"

"I remember."

"Is that why you're running for governor? To feel young again?"

As two kingmakers heatedly debate the Micronesian immigrant epidemic and whether they can come up with some kind of legal precedent to ship those Stone Age bums back to their radioactive islands, Helen steps beside Charles. He grabs her hand, she sips wine. In a way, they resemble museum artifacts, well past a half-century-old but still shiny, preserved, and slick. The museum, the kingmakers, the press, the soon-to-be governor, the beauty queen wife—hand Shane a red velvet pillow with a scepter on it—all of this smacks of a coronation more than anything else.

8.

Shane's room, still furnished with a bunk bed, is stockpiled with sports equipment, ghosts of hobbies past. Two surfboards (one long, the other short), a mountain bike, balls, including one for bowling, golf clubs, a canoe paddle, a snowboard, and a rubber-tipped javelin, all lean against the four corners of the room. Shane turns off the light, turns on his flashlight, and dives onto the bottom bunk. He shines a beam of light up, Calculus formulas, shredding surfers, and bikini-clad models are taped to the top bunk's undercarriage. GOVERNOR Charles Knotting. He's going to be a governor's son. He's going to be untouchable. Maybe he'll stop having nightmares.

Still afraid of the dark, but too old to admit it to Charles and Helen, Shane now depends on his flashlight and math problems to send him to slumber. But the bad dreams still come. In fact, he can't remember ever having a good dream. Sometimes he's caged by tattooed savages and held over a pool of lava. On other occasions, Palolo Housing thugs armed with guns break into his house in the middle of the night. Often, he's simply being shamed, confronted by men smaller and weaker than he is, he grovels at their feet. Shane does not sleep for more than two hours straight a night. Upon waking, though, he is instantly comforted by the material world as if unconsciousness is the harsh reality and consciousness is the dream.

While Shane stares at a logarithm, he fantasizes about becoming Honolulu's version of the Dark Knight, his governor father calling him from a secret red phone stashed in his desk drawer at the state capitol. "I need your help, Shane. The sinister stevedores are bringing in a can packed with Korean hookers and meth. My hands are tied. They're holding their votes hostage."

"I'm on it, Dad."

But he can't do the math. Screw Yale. Maybe he should become a cop, vigilante style. Shane thinks about Charles's favorite movie star, that guy with the greasy pony tail. The guy's a sheriff now and has his own reality TV show. Shane can do that. He took three years of aikido.

Shane's flashlight dies. He scrambles out of bed and pulls a plastic container filled with D batteries out from his nightstand. As he reloads the flashlight, his phone rings. It's Fu808. A girl he'd met on Facebook who goes to Kahuku High School. She's sending him a text: log on. Smiley, smiley, smiley.

Shane turns on his computer then locks his door. When he sits, Fu808's smiling face appears on screen. The lighting is bright and blurry with cable access-glare, but the girlfriend-revenge dotcom quality just makes him hornier. Shane hits record and smiles back. "What you doing?" she asks.

"Was just about to crash."

"I have something to show you."

Shane puts his hands behind his head, leans back, and grins. Fu808's image shakes as she stands and re-adjusts the camera on her laptop. She smiles as she reaches inside her tee shirt and pulls out her purple bra. Shane drops his hands and leans forward.

She's the kind of girl he can see himself with. A pretty, hard-looking Hawaiian girl. Dark bushy hair, sticky like bong buds. A neck tattoo, "Kahuku Point Mafia." Fu808 would go a long way to solidify his street cred. He'd never get super serious with her, but for the rest of his life his friends will talk about how he brought her to the graduation party circuit and she put down more beers than all the little Asian boys in the class. How someone called the cops after she'd mounted a townie girl who was flirting with Shane, skirt hiked up to her waist, g-string showing, ground and pounding MMA-style. When Fu808 pulls down her pants, Shane spots a faint horizontal scar under her pierced navel. She have her appendix taken out or something?

Just as Shane is going to ask her about the scar, Fu808's door creaks open behind her. A man pokes his head in and stands the frozen as if he's posing for the cover shot of a horror novel knowing what else to do, Shane raises a fist to his mo' coughs. The man steps in closer. Shane, who for a moment thinks the man is going to reach through the screen and yank him to the other side, rolls his chair back out of arm's reach.

The girl spins around. A hand reaches for her throat. Shane jumps out of his seat. The blurry, shirtless figure pushes Fu808 aside and lurches toward the web cam. It's not a man. It's a kid, about Shane's age. He has a dark, round, buzz-cut head, a veiny neck, and thick-lidded eyes that make him look sleepy. Shane wants to duck under his desk, but instead, he reaches to the corner of the room and grabs his javelin. "I know who you are," the kid says, his flat nose practically pressing against the screen. "I know where you go school. I know where you live."

Shane taps the spear against his desk, avoiding eye contact. He works up a smile. "Listen..."

"Friday," says the kid. "You and me."

Shane looks up. "You and me what?"

The kid smiles then yanks the power cord from the laptop. Nothing happens.

Shane blinks. "You need to remove the battery, too," he says.

"Oh," says the kid as picks up the laptop. The camera shakes then the screen goes black.

Shane leans back in his chair. He grabs his phone, wanting to call the girl. That or 911. He puts the phone back on the desk. He gets up and taps the tip of the javelin on his forehead as he thinks. When he leans the spear against the golf clubs and his aluminum-framed, ergonomic snowshoes, all of it crashes to the floor, his nine iron and sand wedge spilling out of the bag.

Shane replays the video. He pauses when the kid's face pops on screen. A bit of cauliflower around the ears. A terrible nasofrontal angle. No modeling career for him. It's the kid Shane was pretending to be all these years. A hard case, a real Hawaiian O.G.; Shane always imagined himself as an O.G. who was also water polo captain, starting small forward, class president, and salutatorian.

But he had it all wrong. A hard case, a real one, doesn't slam grades, play organized sports, run private school fundraisers, and probably doesn't even know what water polo is. The kid he's looking at wouldn't be caught dead in a rubber cap and speedo. When Shane breathes in deeply and exhales, he lets out a sob. He unlocks and opens his bedroom door.

"Shane!" Helen yells from downstairs. "Can you take out the trash?!"

Take out the trash. It's a chore. Hard cases don't have chores. They don't have curfews. They have gats and tats, not bedtimes.

"In a sec, mom!"

He wants to ask her if she's up to sleeping in the top bunk tonight and singing to him because for the first time he can remember, he's not looking forward to waking up.

But he can't back down. After years of portraying himself as a kid built for trouble, it's far too late to pussy out. Besides, what can the kid do to him? Kick his ass? For Shane, that's the worst-case scenario. And if he really gets hurt, he's comforted by the fact that his soon-to-be-Governor father will have the kid thrown in jail. "Fuck um," Shane mutters. He wraps a hand around a bicep. He has bigger arms than that kid. He stands up and swivels his head. He bounces on his toes and shadowboxes. He eyes the wall. If he can punch a hole through it, he can take this kid. He throws a punch. Despite his resolve, his fist decelerates right before the moment of impact. He better not damage the wall, Shane tells himself. His parents will be pissed. He picks up the phone and calls Fu808. She doesn't answer.

9.

By Wednesday, it goes viral. Fu808 posts "sorry" on his Facebook page, then comments flood in from the Kahuku boys, calling Shane out as a pussy, cyber-bullies full of threats and awful spelling. Before he can de-friend Fu808 and get rid of all the posts, his private school friends chime in. They ridicule the Kahuku boys' word choice, sentence structure, and overuse of exclamation points. They call the boys from the North Shore ignorant, country-ass Internet tough guys. The Kahuku boys say they're (spelled "their") tough (spelled "tuff") in real life, too (spelled "to"), and that they're going to drive into town and show them. Shane's friends tell them to save up bus fare and come on down—Shane, King Bull Nuts, can take on any of them. Now, Shane wishes that he did not de-friend his parents when they forced a math tutor on him early. Maybe they'd see this and stop it.

That Friday, a week before the end of Shane's senior year, word of the impending after-school fight spreads through campus. Shane's best friend, Don, a Korean kid whose senioritis has transformed him into a wannabe rastafarian: dreadlocks; a red, yellow, and green knitted rasta cap; and a pocketed tin can full of spliffs, had a free period after lunch and snuck across the street to take a peek. The boys from the North Shore, who call themselves the Kahuku Point Mafia, are waiting for Shane, five of them sitting in the back of a jalopy pick-up, right across the street from campus.

"What do they look like?" asks Shane.

Don shrugs. "No shirts. Lots of tats. Ghetto, man. Fucking irie."

"That's not what 'irie' means, dumbass."

"You know what I mean."

Shane nods, grim.

"But don't worry," says Don. "Lava-Lava got your back."

Mosi "Lava-Lava," who got his nickname because he wore a traditional Samoan skirt on his first day to school freshman year and was suspended for it, is a six-four All-State defensive tackle who has a full ride to Alabama. "Did Mosi talk to them?" asks Shane.

"Not yet." Besides being the football stud in their senior class, Mosi, who grew up in a big house on the wrong side of the tracks, serves as de facto ambassador whenever his friends run into trouble with the public school kids. Shane, who, like his father told him to, has already begun the process of collecting future ass-kissers, strongarms, kingmakers, and campaign contributors, is glad, especially now, to call Mosi friend. "What you gonna do?" asks Don.

"Go out there and lay them out," says Shane.

Don, in awe, nods. The bell rings and Shane marches outside to the parking lot. A handful of his good friends follow: Don; Mark Prince, a fearless haole motocross junkie; and Mosi, who joins them last. A born-again Hawaiian clique sits on the lawn and braids ti leaves for graduation, ends looped around blond-haired big toes.

"I went elementary with those guys. What you did?" asks Mosi.

"Wasn't my fault!" says Shane, trying to regain control of his voice. "Some girl from Kahuku started sending me naked pics."

"And what? You oofed her?"

Shane shakes his head. "I never even met her. But the kid, he said he knows who I am. But he didn't post anything on my Facebook page. I wonder if he's even with them."

Mosi nods. Shane looks at his other friends. Don and Jonah, with their noodle arms and general maturity, will be wastes of space in a fight. Mark, who broke his neck riding his motorcycle sophomore year and couldn't wait to get back to riding, will be game. Mosi, no question. What about him? What about Shane? The boys pile into Shane's hybrid. "These guys don't have school?" Shane asks.

Don shrugs. "Probably Furlough Friday."

Mosi's Samoan slap-dance ring-tone goes off. He reads a text. "Meet them Chinese Cemetery." He closes his phone. "I hope we no get mobbed."

Jesus, mobbed. Shane didn't even think of that.

As Shane drives past the security guard, his leg shakes, fear charged electric. He thinks about his father's fight stories, how Charles, who'd spent his youth as a private-school haole who loved to surf, had to fight for waves and respect. Shane also loved to surf. But his local look, darker shades of skin color swirled together on a palette, protected him from fights as much as UV rays. Plus, he knew better. Off campus, not around his friends, he was always smiling. How could you hit a kid who looked so damn happy? Even when he'd seen the scariest-looking man he'd ever laid eyes on out in the breakers at Kewalos, his torso shaped like a manta ray, gun-shot scars on his left shoulder, and a face pocked by some disease that was probably cured more than half a century ago, the man smiled at him as if to say, "Hey braddah, you and I are the same, two descendants of ocean travelers from all corners of the earth, out in the ocean just looking to glide upon waves." And Shane smiled back. This was why Charles often said he'd be scared to run against Shane for office.

But as Shane drives through the thirty-four acre Manoa Chinese Cemetery, also known as The Dragon's Pulse, probably because a hundred-and-fifty-years ago some Chinese guy thought it sounded cool, Shane is having a tough time smiling. "Man, look at this property," says Josh. "Prime real estate wasted on dead pakes."

"My dad's been trying to buy this and re-zone it for years," says Mark.

"Shut up, already," says Shane.

Mosi points at a jalopy pick-up and Shane nods. He pulls in several yards behind it and kills the engine. Shane eyes the boys sitting in the bed and smiles, but none of these cats are smiling back. Mosi steps out first and approaches the boys. Shane steps out next and stands next to his car as the Kahuku Point Mafia nod at Mosi, but stare at Shane, stripping him to the bone with their eyes until all that's left is shame and fear, a privileged brat who was given every advantage, his skeleton held together by weak, gold-threaded sinew.

After talking, Mosi nods and heads over to Shane. "One-on-one. Just you and the girl's boyfriend."

So the guy did show up. At least they won't get mobbed.

Shane eyes the five boys. Two don't even look like teens. Bearded and hunched over brown beer bellies, tossing back cans of red and white, they must be older cousins or even uncles. Is that what it means to be local? Sitting around shirtless, unashamed of Buddha guts hanging over frayed waistbands?

The other three, also shirtless, look to be about Shane's age, skinnier and shorter than he is. One, with peroxide hair, has a tattoo that reads "Hawaiian Skin No Brake EZ" scrawled across his chest. Another, probably raised on three squares of rice, processed meats, and ketchup, is so skinny that his ribs protrude from his pigeon chest. And the last, the one who steps out of the truck, passenger side, is a dark, muscular kid. He's the one Shane saw on Fu808's webcam. He seems purposely nondescript, no tattoos or piercings, capped with a flat top, the very picture of a kid who's planned a life of pro crime his whole life and knew better than to mark his body with identifying characteristics. Who knows if this kid has real teeth or even fingerprints.

It's this last one who takes off his slippers and walks to Shane. Shane wonders if they're supposed to bow or shake hands before the fight. Maybe he's supposed to take off his shoes, too. He wants to say something, but is afraid his voice will quiver. The kid is standing in front of him now. He's all wrists, elbows, knees and ankles—he's skinny, but thick at the joints. His meaty hands, cracked, peeling, and oil-stained, hang at his sides. So much for nondescript.

Shane closes his eyes and clenches his fists, trying hard to remember the first five years of his life, grasping at them as if he's a man overboard splashing for a ring buoy. He wants to feel damaged and angry, a kid with nothing to lose, but he can't tap into it. This is his chance to show everyone that he is King Bull Nuts. He opens his eyes and sees Don pointing at the truck cab window. "Man, is that a baby?" Just as Shane turns his eyes to the truck's rear window, a fist smashes against his cheek. Shane takes two quick steps back. The boy holds his hands up, his head bobbing and weaving, and waits for Shane's reaction with blank face. When Shane lifts his own hands and mimics the boy's motion, he's a fraud. He's just copying what he's seeing. At least he now knows he can eat a punch.

And as he moves forward, eat punches he does. His first instinct is to rush the boy, grab him, and throw him to the asphalt. That effort is met with two jabs to the face. His second plan, throwing looping right-handed punches as hard as he can, is met with kicks to the legs that come closer to dropping him than the strikes to his face.

Every time Shane moves forward to throw a punch, the kid never moves back, but is instead suddenly standing at his side, peppering him with two- or three-punch combinations then stepping out. But none of them hurt. Shane, despite the blood on his throbbing bottom lip, knows he is stronger than this kid. His entire body shakes. He's surprised it's not humming. He can take this guy.

Shane glances around him. His friends and the other Kahuku boys have formed a loose circle around them. The one with the "Hawaiian Skin No Brake EZ" tattoo grins while filming the fight with his cell phone, yelling monosyllabic reactions like, "Ho!" and "Mean!" Sometimes he ventures beyond one-syllable words and says, "Automatic!"

Don, cringing, shakes his head. They're going to put this shit up on YouTube. This pisses Shane off.

The boy launches another kick, but this time Shane catches it and throws a punch that smashes the boy's cheek. It feels good, his two big knuckles sending vibrations down his forearm like tuning forks.

The kid spits out blood and smiles for the first time. Now more confident, Shane bulls ahead, swinging away, but he's only connecting with air. Somehow the kid ends up behind him, a muscular forearm wrapped under Shane's neck. Shane is bent back like he's about to do the limbo as the boy squeezes. He tries to pry the kid's fingers open and is surprised he's unable to move them. The boy wraps his legs around Shane's waist and leans back. Just as Shane is about to fall to the ground, he glances at the truck. A little girl with pig-tails and big diamond earrings drops something out the window. She leans out the window and reaches for the now rolling object as Shane tries to rip the forearm from his windpipe. Shane glances at the metal circle that clanks then rattles to stillness at his feet. A gold bracelet inscribed with big black letters.

Nina.

Wide-eyed, Shane stops struggling. They go crashing to the asphalt.

"Boi?"

The kid's arm presses even harder against Shane's throat. Then he lets go. He stands up and brushes pebbles off his bare back while Shane, on his hands and knees, coughs. It's the first time Shane notices they're breathing hard. The kid squats and puts his big hands on his thighs above the knees, taking deep breaths. He turns to Shane, squinting. "About time," he says.

Still a bit light-headed, Shane turns and faces the little brother he hasn't seen in thirteen years. Shock blunts his crushing shame.

"Thought you would be smarter," says Boi, smiling. "Private school and all."

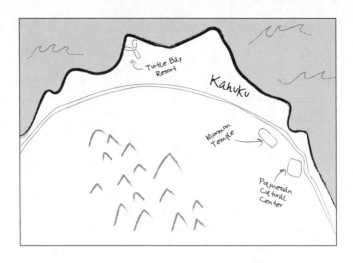

II. Boi No Good

1. _____

Boi Rapun went through three different belt-lashing, wrench-bashing foster homes before he ended up in Kahuku, taken in by a Hawaiian-Filipino organic farmer and his wife. The farm, a clever ecosystem built on a gently sloping hill shadowed by green mountains, was set up so that water from the pig pens up top ran and pooled in the middle of the hill where ducks waded, then streamed to a taro field at the bottom, where the green-leaf tubers soaked in diluted pig and duck manure.

Joe Bolosan, who people called Red Roof Joe after the one-time state loony bin turned community college, had inherited the land from his parents, who'd struggled mightily against golf course and strip mall developers to retain it. By the time Joe's parents died, and the bank was about to take the over-leveraged land, Joe got lucky. He was cleaning a third-story window at the Turtle Bay Hilton and his harness broke. He shattered half the bones in his body. So on his fortieth birthday, Joe handed his settlement money over to the bank, moved back to his parents' house, and decided he'd live off workman's comp and his land. His wife, Patricia, a tour guide and dancer for the Polynesian Cultural Center who couldn't have children and wanted to spend the money on a house in town, struck a deal: if you do this, we will adopt a child or I will walk. Joe agreed.

So when seven-year-old Boi arrived, the farm wasn't resurrected yet. It was mostly just a jungle hill infested with mosquitoes and apple banana trees. At first, Joe, a thin, athletic man who could walk on his hands, even after the window-washing fall, wasn't sure what to do with Boi when Patricia was at work. The kid was a distraction from his real job—building a farm, starting with the laying of a concrete foundation for a pig pen. So he let Boi do whatever he wanted, and the kid wandered, sometimes found roadside a few miles away after dark and brought back by Patricia's Kahuku policemen cousins (she seemed to be cousins with half the island). But it wasn't until Boi crawled into the pig pen one day and got stuck in the setting cement did Patricia finally threaten divorce. When she found Boi stuck in the concrete like a rat on a glue trap and the fire fighters had to bring jackhammers to get him out, she packed her bags and took Boi with her to her sister's house in Laie.

"I never even wanted him!" cried Joe.

"It's not about what you want," said Patricia. "It's about what you got."

So Patricia dragged Boi with her to Laie. She took vacation and shadowed Boi for the next month in Laie, trying hard not to let the wanderlust kid out of her sight. During this time, she discovered three things about him: One, Boi enjoyed building things. In fact, he was incredible at it. One day he spent twelve hours straight making a bus out of toothpicks. Two, Boi could climb. One afternoon he stood outside the house, studying it for a good fifteen minutes. When Patricia went in to grab her cigarettes, she came back out and found Boi, pants down, grinning while peeing off the roof. She had to fight her fear of heights to go after him, and when she finally got up there, Boi was waving at her from the ground, same grin on his face.

And three, Boi was a terrible rascal. Once, on the Fourth of July, when Patricia reached for her cigarettes and lit one, it blew up in her face. Boi had stuffed a tiny firecracker in it. He wanted her to quit smoking.

So it wasn't Joe's begging that brought Patricia and Boi back to the farm. It was singed eyebrows and the knowledge that Boi needed male guidance, otherwise known as the occasional man-sized slap upside the head. And when they got to the farm and saw that Joe had made zero progress on the pig pen, it was Patricia who said, "If we come back, you need to let him help you build it."

Joe frowned at her slightly burnt face. "He's too young. What he can do?"

"He's smarter than me. He's smarter than you."

Joe knew it was true a year later when it was eight-year-old Boi who came up with the irrigation idea for the farm, telling Joe how he knew that shit was a fertilizer and they might as well build a waterfall of it since the farm was on a hill. There might be use for the kid yet. By the time Boi was ten, Joe wondered how the hell he got through life without him, this now white-toothed boy with strange skin that lightened in the winter to an almost haole shade, and darkened to a stain-wood brown in the summer.

2.

On Boi's twelfth birthday, Joe gave his son his most prized possession: Captain Cook's big toe. Joe kept it in a glass jar with a rusty lid: two long and hooked bones that made Boi think maybe Cook had bunions. When Joe told Boi that his great-great-great grandfather, a cousin of King Kamehameha, was the one who'd cut the toe off the great explorer's foot, Boi thought his father was putting him on. "I telling you," said Joe. "He went cut um off."

"Yeah, right," said Boi, looking at the jar. "I wanna see a certificate of authenticity."

"Shit, son. You thinking like one haole. Only haoles think gotta have paper or something never happen. I know because my father told me. And his father told him."

Boi shook the jar. The bones rattled. "This is pretty pilau."

Joe grinned. "Haha, you think that pilau? How's this. After he cut um off, he cooked um and ate um."

Boi shook his head.

Joe winked. "The big toe. That's where the mana is."

Boi looked at his own big toe, which he used to pinch other kids in class to make them cry. Why should his spirit power be stored in such a vulnerable part of his body? Shouldn't such a valuable thing sit under a chassis of bone, like the brain, heart, and lungs?

"I went try take um Bishop Museum one time," said Joe. "They never believe. Run by haoles that's why."

"What haoles ever did to you?"

"Shit, if wasn't for the haoles, I'd be king of Hawaii right now."

These were the kinds of gifts Boi received from his father on birthdays. The year before it had been a koa arrowhead that Joe claimed the great chief Kahekili once used to shoot a huge tiger shark that was terrorizing his people. When Boi pointed out that 1) according to his teacher, the Hawaiians didn't use bow and arrows and 2) his story loosely resembled the plot of some old, famous shark movie with shitty special effects, Joe said 1) Sitting Bull once came to Hawaii on a trip with Mark Twain and gave his bow to Kahekili as a gift and 2) the haole guy who wrote that movie ripped off an old Hawaiian story, because that's what haoles did. "Even the line," Joe said. "Minoaka panopapiki. Fucking haoles ripped um off."

"What's minoaka panopapiki mean?" asked Boi.

"Smile, you son-of-a-bitch."

When Boi would go to his teachers and ask them whether what his father had said was true, the teachers would just smile and shake their heads. "Red Roof Joe," they'd say.

Boi stopped asking after he showed Mrs. Alani the big toe in the cafeteria, and she stood up, all ninety pounds of her quivering as she clenched a fistful of tater tots and told him that the Hawaiians weren't cannibals and that it was yet another racist myth created by haoles.

Boi never asked if his father was telling the truth after that. Not because he finally figured his father was an idiot or lying. He just stopped caring because Joe's stories were better anyway.

3.

Carlton Hookano, one of the last full-blooded Hawaiians in Kahuku, owned the taro farm below Joe's. Carlton was a master grower, a green-thumbed talent who could take orange peel and turn it into a tree. He'd been the one who taught Joe how to plant a loi and told him the mythical story of how taro first sprouted from the buried, stillborn body of a god. After long days in the fields, Carlton would often come over with his sons, sit at Joe's picnic table, eat pupus, smoke out, and drink beer. The two men would share tall tales of old Hawaii while Boi and Carlton's sons shot birds and chameleons with their BB guns.

"Back in the day," said Carlton, "My father caught one white shark in the net. The buggah never have teeth and cried like one baby!"

"Oh yeah," said Joe. "My grandpa told me how my ancestors used to tie up criminals to the reef and wait for the sharks to eat them. Then they would go back, get the bones, boil them, make soup!"

"Shit," said Carlton. "My grandfather used to do that. He said fricking Samoans, tough the meat!"

"Mines too! He said, ho, the Japs and pakes, stringy!"

"Haole meat sweet though!"

The two men would then glance at their sons to see if they were listening, but the stories were often drowned out by snapping pumps of BB guns and gleeful screams as zebra doves dropped dead out of mango trees.

Carlton got too old to farm. When his sons had zero interest in taking over a business that required sign-waving protests to keep the land out of the hands of developers and speculators, he put his lot up for sale and moved to an apartment in Salt

Lake. At the going-away luau for the Hookana clan (too much food, a lot of hugs, not enough beer), Joe couldn't take his eyes off Boi, who, wearing a Tap Out tee shirt and plugged into his MP3 player, was using two rubber door stops and a coat hanger to break into Joe's truck. Patricia sat next to Joe on the picnic bench and kissed him. "I never giving up my farm," said Joe, glaring at Boi.

Patricia turned to look at Boi. "What's he doing?"

"I locked my keys in the truck."

"How he learn that kind?"

Joe shrugged.

"Wonder what he going to end up doing when he grows up," Patricia said as Boi popped open the lock.

"What you mean? He's gonna take over the farm."

Patricia laughed. "Boys no like farm anymore. Not that they ever did. He do all kind stuff, like he get more than two arms. We should've sent him private school."

"No money," said Joe. "Besides, I no like him turn out to be one haole."

Boi looked up at his parents and smiled. He broke into some sort of standing epileptic seizure set to music.

"What the fuck?" said Joe.

"And you afraid he gonna turn into one haole? Worse things to be than that."

"I dunno about that."

"Told you we should send him hula," Patricia said.

4.

Several months later, Peter Patrino, a movie-star comedian, bought the Hookana lot. Landscapers came in with bulldozers to take Carlton's loi apart.

Star of *Hot Chick Management*, *The Wedding Gigolo*, and *Punch Drunk Chuck*, the last a film about a second-rate, glass-jawed boxer who pretends to be a girl so he can become the woman's heavyweight champion of the world, Patrino bought the entire twenty-five acres. If living by a rich haole wasn't bad enough for Joe, the twenty-five acres was also designated as ag land, meaning that the actor, a multi-millionaire, got a huge deal on it and met regulations by planting a papaya tree and buying a horse he named Grover Cleveland. Peter Patrino then began construction on a two-story, six-thousand square-foot monster on stilts that took less than a month to build. The fact that the actor didn't use the land to farm drove Joe to call up all his old protesting buddies, but most of them were already dead. He talked to their sons and daughters, but all of them, either chronics, state workers, or Waikiki hourly wage workers, had no protest in them.

So Joe, all alone, waved protest signs at every neighborhood board meeting for the next three years. Patrino was never at these meetings. In fact, Patrino was hardly in Hawaii at all. After Joe was escorted out of the last council meeting by Patricia's cop cousins, he decided to take matters into his own hands.

It started harmless enough. Joe would ask Boi to do stuff like cut down Patrino's papaya tree or feed his horse laxatives. Joe would sometimes throw pig guts over the wall, but since Patrino was never home, the rotting smell assaulted Joe's nose more than anyone else's. Joe once convinced Boi to help him break into Patrino's house and leave a nest of rats in the kitchen. The rats returned tenfold to Joe's several months later.

After each prank, Joe and Boi would rent Patrino's movies and laugh at how shitty they were. In one, Patrino played a struggling cat groomer who discovered he had a natural talent for surfing and decided to enter the Pipeline Classic and use the prize money to save his floundering business. It was the film that had brought Patrino to Hawaii and made him want to buy land here. To be a child of the land. To be kamaaina, he said in the newspaper. Some of the characters in this movie, including Patrino's, spoke pidgin so badly that Joe would laugh to tears. Joe must've watched that one over twenty times.

One night, the two of them climbed the stone wall with a quarter pound of home-grown weed to try to get Grover Cleveland stoned. They rolled a bazooka joint and stuck it in the horse's mouth. The horse did not resist, but seemed impervious to the smoke, just as it had been to laxatives. Bored, Joe and Boi took hits from the joint and ended up so wasted that they passed out on Patrino's front lawn.

The next day, Peter Patrino made a rare trip to the house and found Boi still riding Grover while Joe laid flat on his back with a steaming pile of horse shit on his chest. It was the first time Boi met Patrino, a quiet, bug-eyed forty-something with balding Elvis Presley hair. He looked more tired, older, and a lot smaller than he did in his movies, and Boi was stunned that the actor was a nice, shy man. Was this the same guy who, infused with animal DNA, ran around trying to rape a chicken in his last movie?

When a sheepish Patrino shook Joe awake, Joe looked as if he was going to have a heart attack. The actor put his head down and offered to buy them lunch. When an embarrassed Joe politely refused, Patrino went to his tool shed and came back with reins. He put them on the horse and handed them over to Boi. "I'm never here," said Patrino. "Poor President Cleveland. You can have him."

Stunned, Boi looked at Joe.

"No, no braddah. We cannot take um," said Joe, still brushing horse shit off his chest.

"Please, you'd be doing me a favor," said Patrino. "I have to pay a vet to come over and check up on him. You'd be saving me money."

Joe grinned. "Not afraid you gonna lose your ag status?"

Patrino smiled. "My lawyer tells me some crazy stands outside city council meetings holding protest signs. A one-man million-man march. My production company is thinking about making a screwball comedy based on all this. Loosely. Of course, in my movie, the dolt wins."

"You saying he no can win in real life?" asked Joe.

"In real life, a guy like that could lose his poi contract with the supermarket and have his ag status re-examined. That's what my lawyer tells me, anyway."

Boi rode the horse in slow circles around them while Joe stewed. Now he was the one looking old, tired, and small. He turned and faced Patrino's house, the second story twice as big as the first, half of it held up by ten-foot tall pillars. Joe glared at Boi. "Get off the goddamn horse." He took the reins and handed them to Patrino. "Thanks, but no can."

Patrino shrugged. Joe and Boi started to walk back home. Joe stopped and turned his head. "By the way," he said. "I like your movies."

Boi looked at his father, shocked, wondering why he said it.

5.

It was around that time that Joe started neglecting his farm and drinking more and more, telling Patricia the alcohol helped him with his now-flaring chronic back pain. Patricia had gained thirty pounds since Boi's arrival. Hell-bent on looking good dancing hula at the Polynesian Cultural Center, she started diets every few months. Come home hungry and pissed and grab envelopes filled with pink paper from the mailbox. Then shake Joe awake and scream at him. Their property taxes were skyrocketing, and they couldn't afford to pay. Joe would wink at Boi then stagger on his hands to his bedroom.

"I had it with him," she'd say. "I had it."

And it got predictable. Joe cracking open his first green bottle at two, trashed by the time Patricia got home at nine, and despite the yelling, cracking open a beer at two the next day, Patricia yelling at nine, saying she had it. This is when Boi started to think about his real father, trying to remember who he had been. But all he could come up with was a hazy recollection of flowers placed on a roadside oil stain.

By the time Boi was in high school, he made sure he didn't come home until ten when Joe was already passed out in the spare bedroom. Patricia would sit in front of the TV watching Korean soaps munching on fat-free microwave popcorn, shaking her head whenever a rat bolted past her doorway.

Trying to find something to do from two to ten every weekday was hard for Boi. After all, Kahuku was just a couple of miles of beach and small rural acreage shadowed by mountains and sandwiched between the Turtle Bay Resort and the Polynesian Cultural Center, a little Hawaiian town choked out by tourism. Boi enjoyed the ocean, but he could only surf, fish, and dive so much. Sometimes his friends would fight each other, record the fights on their cell phones, post them on YouTube. Or they'd hike up the mountains with their dogs and their fathers' AR-15s, and hunt pig. One day, Boi and his friends formed a five-man gang: the Kahuku Point Mafia. They spent an afternoon tattooing KPM on their ankles. Boi's tat turned green, faded, then eventually disappeared.

When the sky grew dark, even more boredom. Then the boys and girls would emerge from their TV-lit dwellings like ghost crabs and look for beer, pot, or crystal meth. The last was the easiest to get. So they'd hit the pipe and go to school wired the next day, giggling on zero sleep.

Boi passed when his friends got into drinking and smoking ice. He remembered his biological mother, Makana, how she'd pawned her mother's bracelets, got high, burned him with her lighter whenever he smiled at her because she thought he was getting wise. His siblings had learned fast to not even look at her, but Boi, it just made him smile more.

He'd spent enough time watching Joe get drunk to know he didn't want any of that either. Instead, he stole cars and motorcycles, searching for a keeper. When he finally found what he was looking for, a full-sized Chevy 4x4 that rode high on 38.5-inch MadDog radials and a Tuff Country lift kit, he drove it to an isolated corner of Peter Patrino's lot, took it apart, and spent nights figuring out how to put it together again.

From working on cars, Boi's hands became thick, cracked, grimy mitts that came in handy during his after-school YouTube fights. Friends called him Boi Vise Grip and watched in awe as he bent nails and ripped phone books in half. Girls started to notice, too. Chastity Fu, famous for giving boys head in the bathroom in the sixth grade, said to just about everyone, "I like jump his bones."

Boi's friends set it up. They told Boi they wanted to go hunting. When they arrived at a clearing a mile up the trail, there was Skank Fu sitting on a boulder with a boom box and an old pink blanket. She had a bandaid on her neck. "Let her suck your dingding, but no put inside," said Small John, one of Boi's friends. "Look the bandaid on her neck. Pilau. No like get AIDS."

Boi's friends left him with her. Chastity pressed play on her boom box. It was an old-school tune about a chick who would rather go blind. Chastity grabbed Boi's hand and led him to the blanket. She was tearing up. "No believe what they all say," she said. "It's not true."

Boi must've looked dubious, because then she peeled the bandaid off her neck. Thin lines of scabs traced the black letters. Kahuku Point Mafia. "My mom going kill me when she sees this," said Chastity. "But fuck her. She get how many tats."

They did it three times before they walked down the mountain. On their way down, Boi offered to carry her boom-box for her, but Chastity shook her head. She was quiet the whole mile down.

The next day at school, everyone knew. It was his friends, not Chastity, who spread the news. They had been hiding in the bushes, watching, and filmed it with their cell phones. They were laughing and laughing. Boi didn't like that, so Small John was the first one he fought. The security guard had to pull Boi off him. Boi was suspended for one week. When he came back, everyone was still talking shit. Kamuela Peters, a junior, was next. Boi grabbed Kamuela by the neck, pinned him to a cafeteria table, and hammered his face. Suspended again.

The teachers all decided Boi was on ice. Probably had been smoking it for years. And once they pegged him as an addict, they decided that Boi was no good, he just was no good. So another name stuck. No longer Just Boi or Boi Vise Grip, he was Boi No Good. Pleased with how it rang out, he found his calling: living up to it. A month-and-a-half later, Boi No Good was kicked out of school for good. Chastity Fu was pregnant.

Boi had been ducking Chastity ever since they had walked down the mountain and everyone started teasing him. Right before Spring Break, she grabbed him by the arm before second period and told him in front of his friends, "Listen, asshole! I hapai!"

Boi looked around. His friends acted like they were getting stuff out of their lockers. Small John put in his ear buds, blasted his iPod, and shook his head.

"Well?" Chastity demanded.

Students streamed past them. Some of the seniors laughed as they walked by. Boi wished he had books or sunglasses, something to adjust, put on, or hold onto, but there was nothing he could put between him and this pissed-off girl whom everyone called Skank Fu. He wanted to say something nice and mean it, but he couldn't think of anything . The anger started to bubble. He wanted to hit something. But before he could find something to hit, Chastity pulled her arm way back and launched a fist at him. Not like one girl, but like one man. Twisting and clenching her fist, last second, everything. She hit him on the left side of his jaw and walked away.

As Boi made his way to ag class, which met in a double-wide with a broken, rusty air conditioner window unit that constantly dripped water, his friends followed quietly, but he could hear what they were thinking anyway.

Ho, so what? You and Skank Fu gotta get married now she hapai, right?

Watch, if the kid come out haole or popolo or with borinki hair, maybe then you off the hook.

We told you no put inside. You stupid or what?

They laughed and laughed in Boi's head. He tried his best to ignore them as he entered the trailer. The teacher, Mr. Chun, was a balding Chinese ex-hippie and considered cool because he admitted he'd grown weed at his house before Green Harvest. But he smiled at Boi. "What's got you so blue today, Mr. Rapun?" asked Mr. Chun.

Boi spit in Mr. Chun's face. Expelled that day. But when the school called his parents to come and get him, it was Patricia's cop cousins who picked him up instead. A couple of days ago, Peter Patrino had gone for a walk and found the stolen half-built Chevy truck sitting under a blue tarp in a corner of his twenty-five acres. It was the first time Peter set foot on that side of his property.

On his way to the police station, Boi No Good stared at Peter Patrino's house as the cop car rolled past. He eyed the stilts under the second story. The sky was the color of smudged ink as it began to rain.

6.
___

On the day of Boi's court date, Patricia insisted that Boi dress nice. The only problem was that Boi didn't have nice clothes, so Boi and Patricia had to find some of Joe's old stuff, stuff he used to wear back when he actually attended weddings, baby luaus, and funerals. Patricia mumbled to herself as she rummaged through boxes: it was her fault that Boi was like this, maybe if she just dressed him nice once, he wouldn't have all these problems. After a couple of hours, they settled on khaki pants, an aloha shirt that was faded and looked turned inside out, and a belt with a brass "B" buckle. Patricia thought the belt was cute since it was the first letter of Boi's name, but Boi thought it looked lame, especially since green oxidation was speckled all over it. But Boi put it on and even tucked in his shirt for her.

On their way to court, Patricia reassured Boi that he was not going to get sent away. She talked about a newspaper story she'd read, how all these Japanese PTA moms were caught embezzling school money for their facials and BMWs and got off with no time served. In fact, they weren't even forced to pay back the money. "You young yet," she said. "The judge going understand."

Joe just shook his head and blamed the politicians.

The first thing Boi noticed when he stepped into the small family courtroom was how many people showed up. There were teachers and other adults, Kahuku parents he guessed, most of whom he didn't even know. An old Chinese judge entered the courtroom and took his seat behind the bench. He read off the facts of the case. Then he eyed the Japanese prosecutor. "I understand we have people who want to testify to the character of the defendant," he said.

The prosecutor nodded.

"What the fuck?" Joe said.

Patricia ignored him, but for the first time that day, she looked scared. She whispered into the haole public defender's ear. Looking irritated, he waved her off. "Don't worry," he said. "I know what I'm doing." Sucka must've been like twenty five years old.

One by one, they approached the bench. The first to testify was Carl Santos, Boi's old math teacher. He told the court how Boi had once mixed lemon jello in the teacher toilet bowls. He also told the judge that Boi had called the Marines recruitment office last year, said his name was Carl Santos, and that he was interested in enlisting and fighting for his country in Afghanistan. Mr. Santos had to change his phone number.

Boi looked at the public defender, who rifled through filed papers and said nothing. Boi stood up and called Mr. Santos a liar.

"You didn't do those things?" asked the judge.

"I did, but he no more proof." Patricia tugged on Boi's sleeve. "The school never even bust me."

Patricia pulled harder on his sleeve. Boi sat down.

More adults came up to testify. Mrs. Nagata, who taught health, told the court how Boi once broke into school at night and hung amputee porn in her classroom. Others came up, like Small John's and Kamuela Peters's mothers, and said how Boi sent both their sons to the hospital. Boi stood up again and called bullshit.

Boi had been winning against Small John (who was actually the one who'd hung amputee porn in Mrs. Nagata's classroom), but the guard pulled him off before he could do any real damage, and Kamuela was a two-hundred-fifty pound junior who ate Boi's punches, no problem. In fact, if that one hadn't been broken up, Kamuela would have probably recovered and lit Boi up.

The judge banged the gavel until Boi sat back down. Boi looked around the courtroom. There were zero kids there, no one who could back up his story. The public defender wasn't saying shit. It was just adult after adult approaching the bench and talking about how Boi was a menace to the community, that he was no good. The one that killed Boi the most was Chastity Fu's mother. The inked-up chronic skank told the court that Boi raped and impregnated her daughter. Half the courtroom gasped. Boi closed his eyes. He hadn't told his parents about Chastity.

Patricia put her hands over her face and wept while the bailiff had to escort a screaming Mrs. Fu out of the courtroom.

After it was all over, the judge spoke. He explained that the problem with the justice system was hoodlum juvies getting off easy then thinking that they'd get off easy again when they grew into villainous adults. Kids like Boi needed to be taught that judges, at least this judge, wasn't a bleeding heart social worker.

Some of the "community leaders" applauded. Joe had talked about them before. Haole parents who sent their kids to public school because homeschooling interfered with their recently discovered love affair with the ocean, and the early morning, two-hour drive to a private school in town was too harsh.

"Six months," the judge said.

This time it was Joe who stood up. "Bullshit!" he said. "This all fucking political!"

"Sit down!" the judge said.

Joe stepped on the table and raised both arms. "He neva do shit!"

People in the courtroom looked down or shook their heads. Red Roof Joe. Patricia was looking down, too, as Joe and the judge went back and forth—sit down, bullshit, sit down, bullshit. The judge banged his gavel again and again. Boi's hands shook and his ears started to buzz. He opened and closed his eyes and fists then stuck a finger in each ear. The buzzing just got louder.

"One year!" screamed the judge.

"Fuck you, braddah!" Joe screamed right back.

The bailiff, who was twice the size of Boi, grabbed Joe. Boi went after the judge, who shrank in his chair as Boi approached. Boi snatched the gavel from him. "Stop already!" said Boi.

The bailiff let go of Joe and slammed Boi to the ground. "Stop!"

The judge was breathing heavy from all the yelling and gavel-banging. "Two years," he whispered. "Two years."

Boi's ears buzzed louder and louder as the bailiff led him out of the courtroom. Patricia burst into tears.

7. _____

According to the history and geology teacher at the boys' home, Mr. Melvin, an educated man could explain the things around him. When Boi was released twenty-five months later, he felt like an educated man. Now, when Boi looked at the Kualoa mountains, he did not just see mounds of jagged rock rising to the clouds. He saw the western wall of the volcano that made Oahu. He saw a tree line that legend said was the back of a giant sea monster.

And when he looked to the ocean, Boi imagined the original location of Kahuku, once an island floating in the sea until the ancient Hawaiians used whale bone hooks and olapa ropes to pull it in and connect it to Oahu. He imagined the squid god, Kanaloa, fishing with his father Kane at Kewala Bay, the last un-developed bay on the North Shore.

But most of all, wherever he looked, he pictured tens of thousands of Hawaiians who once lived there, fishing, farming, war-ring, and fucking. Now most were gone. And what was left? "You know what school get the highest percentage of Hawaiians in the state?" Mr. Melvin asked Boi during his very first class.

Boi shrugged.

"This one," Mr. Melvin said.

Boi was thinking about his two-year education as he dug a ditch in the Bolosan backyard. The day he had returned to the Kahuku farm, there was no welcome home party with streamers, balloons, and squid luau—there was just Patricia telling him how useless his father was. How it was Boi who needed to work the farm, or they'd lose everything. She'd told him this every time she had visited him at the boys' home, too.

Boi tried to visit Joe that first day. Joe, who'd never visited Boi at the home, stayed in a room with an old computer and a mini-refrigerator stocked with beer. "He blames himself," Patricia told Boi. "He shame. He cannot look at you yet."

"Wasn't his fault," said Boi.

"Leave um. He drinking mornings now, too," she said as she shook her head. "Useless. And you know what? Was his fault. Let him rot."

So every morning that first week, Boi would wake up to crowing roosters, stand by Joe's closed door for a minute and listen to him pecking away at a keyboard. When it became obvious Joe would not step out of the room, Boi would head outside, grab a shovel, and dig. Patricia would go to work a few hours later, still as angry as the night before.

After she left, Boi would look at mauka and makai and think about all the things he now knew. He'd think about his time at the boys' home, and he'd think about the one-year-old daughter he'd only seen once.

When he'd first arrived at the boys' home, he spent the first night listening to other kids whimper for their mommies for hours in the dark. The next day was better. The kids spent their downtime from classes and lectures teaching each other crippling arm bars, leg locks, and chokeholds. Boi quickly made friends and joined in. The baby gladiator academy stuff didn't scare him. He could always fight and the other boys somehow knew it. What scared him was that the days were so easy for him because he probably belonged here, which meant that chances were one day he would end up in the adult prison, too.

Classes had been boring, just like on the outside. Kids were supposed to read books they didn't understand. One time, they were assigned to read Queen Liliuokalani's book, but no one finished it. Then they were told to draw a picture of what they'd learned from the book, like Boi remembered doing in the first grade. All the boys drew the same thing: the picture of the queen on the book's cover.

That's when Mr. Melvin came. He looked Japanese but said he was Hawaiian, just like most of them. His hair was dyed an orangey blond and the fucka was yoked. Even his neck had bulging muscles with a bunch of triangle tats all over it. He was a substitute teacher and replaced the old haole history teacher who had a stroke or something.

They never had to read a book in Mr. Melvin's history class. He would just tell them what the book was about. After he told them the story of Queen Liliuokalani's book, they drew their pictures again. One boy drew tanks surrounding Iolani Palace. Another had stealth bombers laying waste to straw hut villages. Boi sketched a flyin' Hawaiian firing at American infantry with an AK-47. "I like this one," Mr. Melvin said. "It's the only one where the Hawaiians stay fighting back. Defend Hawaii!" He often used "defend Hawaii" like a period to end his sentences.

Big-word rants against everything wrong with Hawaii, those classes with Mr. Melvin, whom everyone had to call "kumu" to his face, left Boi angry. When he and the boys would practice their arm bars and leg locks, Boi found himself torquing the holds harder and harder. When other teachers (not Mr. Melvin) scolded him, he imagined ripping their white and Asian faces off. And the guards. Over those two years, Boi grew. He wanted to take all those bossy wannabe gansta mother-fuckers.

After Boi finished the ditch digging his first week out of the detention center, he moved onto the sawing. He sawed and sawed. He thought about his daughter.

Boi had thought about her a lot when he'd been at the detention center. At first, he'd been embarrassed. A kid with Skank Fu: he'd never live that down. But then it occurred to him that he wasn't the one who should be embarrassed. It was the kid who'd have to live with having two fucked up parents like it did who should be shame. He made a promise to himself that he'd stay away from it. Even Patricia had thought that was a good idea.

As Boi sawed and sawed, he thought of the one time Chastity visited. It was the worst day of his two-year incarceration.

The kid was a year old at the time, pudgy faced and thick in the thighs like just about every one-year-old. She'd waddled more than walked, she sucked her thumb, and she tried to stick things in her mouth—pens, cobwebs, and paper clips—that would make her sick or even kill her. Boi had been watching this little girl in the visiting room while Chastity babbled about what everyone was up to in school. He watched the little girl dressed in pink and it seemed to him, as she grabbed a power cord, she must spend all her waking moments trying to get herself killed.

"She looks like you," Chastity said, not even looking at the kid.

"Ho," said Boi as he stood up and grabbed the little girl before she could chomp into a power cord.

"Yeah, she's a rascal."

The little girl took one look at Boi and wailed. Boi handed her off to Chastity, who put her on the floor and started talking about people from school again. The kid went straight for the power cord. Boi grabbed her again. She cried and cried so Chastity just talked louder as Boi, for the first time in ages, thought about Makana, the bus, his grandmother's bracelets, Glorya, and Chayne-Marcos.

"I want to name her Nina," Boi said as he tried to comfort the screaming kid.

"I don't care. You're the one standing in line to change the name when you get out, though."

Boi looked at the kid's face. She had big pores on the tip of her nose, just like him.

That night, in his room, hours after Chastity and the baby had left, Boi was filled with rage, and he didn't know why. He grabbed anything he could find and hurled it at the wall. He threw his roommate's stuff, too, and when his roommate tried to stop him, Boi whipped him against the wall as well. Then the guards came. Boi dropped the first one. When the others came and piled on top of him, he screamed and struggled. He wouldn't stop. Finally, they brought in the gurney and strapped him down. They sent him to the state mental hospital where they fed him a lot of applesauce.

Awake or sleeping, Boi dreamed all the time at the hospital. He imagined broken-down buses stuffed with little kids, some of them spilling out of the windows. He saw brain-eating zombies chasing his daughter, gold bracelets clanging against her wrist as she ran. Giant tentacles and squid beaks smashed and ripped the zombies apart. Sometimes the little girl would escape. Sometimes she wouldn't.

He'd spent a month in that hospital. And the only thing that kept him calm enough to pass for sane by the end of his stay was the thought of what he was going to do once he was released from the boys' home.

And now, back at the farm, during the middle of week two of his release, the rain started. Boi was nearly finished sawing. It rained the next day and the day after that. Boi checked the news. Flash flood warnings. Rain for the whole next week. Boi couldn't believe his luck.

While Patricia went to the store and stood in line to buy gas, bottled water, batteries, canned goods, and .223 caliber bullets (despite the fact that she already had a storm kit that could sustain them for twenty years of caveman living), Boi put the finishing touches on his ditches. He looked up at the pig pen and smiled. This was going to be his masterpiece.

Boi walked in the house. He knocked on Joe's door. No answer. He knocked harder.

"I just going bust it down if you no open um," said Boi.

He heard a sigh behind the door. "What?"

"I got something I want you to watch."

Joe opened the door. He'd grown his hair out while Boi was away. He wore a beard, too, or as much of a beard as his Filipino genes would allow. It was a spare, craggily thing that looked more itchy than distinguished.

Boi looked around. The room wasn't as messy as Boi thought it would be. Sure, there were a ton of empty beer bottles, but they were all stored in their boxes and stacked head high against the wall. The computer was a pathetic mess of naked wires cooled by a plastic oscillating fan, but each power cord was coiled neatly next to a power strip. Joe sat in front of the computer with his back turned to Boi and pecked at the keyboard. Apparently, he'd replaced early afternoon farming with spouting anti-government rhetoric on the Honolulu newspaper's online comments page. Boi read his user name: KaNaKaInSuRgEnT.

"What you reading?" Boi asked.

"This fricking haole probably going run for governor."

"Dad..."

Joe turned around, avoiding eye contact. "What?"

"Fricking haoles are the ones who post on that shit. Anyway..."

"What?"

"They all dumb."

"How you know?"

"My teacher told me. Plus, you think smart people write for free?"

Joe thought for a second then turned back to the computer and deleted his reply.

"You going hate whoever wins anyway," said Boi. "What's the difference?"

Joe looked up. "I take one corrupt Jap, Flip, or Hawaiian over one corrupt haole any day."

"Why?"

Joe didn't have an answer.

Boi inched closer to Joe and looked over his shoulder. A giant haole man, his arm around a stunning hapa-Japanese woman wearing weird-looking silver jewelry, was smiling at the camera. A tall kid with dark eyes and wavy hair stood next to them, a world-by-the-balls grin on his face. He was the summer-job-swimming-pool-lifeguard type, this kid. Boi blinked. Then he bent closer to the screen. "Holy..."

"What?" asked Joe.

"Chayne-Marcos."

"Who?"

"He..."

"What?"

"That's my brother."

Joe stood and Boi slid onto his chair. His whole body was shaking as he sat in front of the computer screen. Leaving the computer, Joe stepped out of the room. Boi clicked and clicked, searching for more. He pulled up an article on the high school water polo state champs. "Shane Knotting," he said. "Fucka even got one new, cooler name."

Joe came back to the computer and took a long swig of beer then burped. "Probably one rich, spoiled haole now."

Boi nodded. "Look at him" is all he could say. "Look at him." Shane in speedos and a rubber cap strapped under his chin holding up a yellow rubber ball away from outstretched arms.

"Must be one mahu. Look what he wearing," said Joe.

Boi ignored Joe. That could be me, he thought. Pictured in the newspaper like an Olympic statue instead of a two-line blurb in the police beat. Joe wiped beer dribbling from his chin. "You like one cold one?" he asked.

Boi looked up. "You never let me drink before."

Joe shrugged.

"No thanks," said Boi. "I no drink."

Boi closed the page as the rain picked up and began pelting the corrugated metal roof above him.

8.

The rain washed loose shingles off roofs, flooded oceanside roads, and took country electricity out. Boi looked out the picture window, which was marked with an electrical tape "x," and waited. Joe drank beers while he fried hot dogs in ketchup on his portable gas burner. Soaked, Patricia walked in with groceries. "Ho, this fricking rain," she said as she took canned goods out of wet plastic bags. She looked at Joe. "What you doing out of your room?" she asked, irritated.

Joe ignored her and flipped a hot dog.

Patricia shook her head. "And you," she said. "Why you just sitting there like one lolo, looking out the window?"

Boi shrugged. "You never think that one giant rain like this going flood the loi?"

Patricia glared at Joe. "Useless."

"No worry," said Boi. "I took care of it."

Patricia left the groceries on the table and went to her room. Boi watched through the window as clumps of mud slid down the mountain and the pig pen filled with water. The pigs snorted then squealed as muddy water pooled in the concrete foundation. It was morning, but it was so dark that Joe lit up a gas lantern.

The rain kept coming. The water from the pig pen overflowed into the duck pond. First slowly, then, in raging rapids. The duck pond flooded and sent a waterfall toward the taro patch.

Joe handed Boi a plate of hot dogs. "So what you wanted me to watch?" he asked.

Boi put the hot dogs down on the table. "Just watch."

"We going lose that crop, Boi."

Boi nodded. "I know."

"What they did to you in there?"

They educated me, Boi thought.

"I sorry..." said Joe.

"No worry," said Boi, still looking out the window. "It's all good."

The taro patch funneled water downhill through the ditch that Boi had dug. The water headed to Peter Patrino's house. The water pooled under the white stilts holding up half the second story. More mud eroded and the water level rose as the rain continued to fall.

Soon, even Joe's house sprung a leak. Water collected in a ceiling corner under the blue acrylic paint. The bubble grew into a plump sack of liquid overhead. Joe grabbed a bucket and popped the bubble. That's when Boi heard Patrino's house creak. He turned back to the window. The water under the stilts was no longer a still pool. Brown waves crashed against them. It was working.

Patricia came out to the living room, looked around, then screamed. She pointed at the front door. Roaches, big ones, B-52s, slipped into the house under the door. Six or seven of them raised their tiny heads and waved their antennae like windshield wipers. Boi ignored the roaches trying to escape the flood outside as Patrino's house creaked even louder.

While Patricia ran around stomping roaches and Joe planted pots under leaks springing from the ceiling, Boi grabbed a chair, stood on it, and ripped off the tape from the window. He kept his eyes glued on Patrino's house. When the water rose to the point where half the stilts were underwater, he called out to Joe. "Watch!" he said.

Joe left his pots and joined Boi. "You hear that?" Boi asked.

"What, the rain?"

"No," said Boi, pointing at Peter's house. "The buggah loosening."

The house let out a loud creak then half the second story tilted and crashed off its stilts. It splashed against the ground so hard, a wall cracked open and oozed furniture. First a bookshelf, then a TV stand and mattress spilled out. Boi felt like taking off his shirt and running in circles around the room waving it above his head, but he just grinned. Patricia, who must've heard the crash, was standing next to him now and slapped the back of his head. "What you did?" she asked.

The house let out another creak and the second story began to rip in half. Wide-eyed, Joe turned to Patricia. "He sending that fucking house down to Kanaloa."

It took hours. Electricity was restored, the rain slowed, but eventually Peter Patrino's house was pushed over a cliff and into the Pacific Ocean.

"I can't believe it," said Patricia, sitting on the sofa, hands over her face. "No good."

Joe wiped tears from his eyes. "My son."

Patricia glared at Joe. "Now for sure he going back the boys' home."

Joe pointed at the window. "How they going know?! Everything getting sent down to the bottom of the fricking ocean!"

Patricia stood up and faced Boi. "I got no feeling for you right now," she said. She stomped off to her bedroom.

Boi looked down at his big toe. "She's going to leave," he said. Joe nodded.

Boi looked up at his father. "I never even seen my kid since I've been out."

Joe dismissed the confession with a wave of his hand. "I had one dream. I dreamt you was meant for something big. The squid god, Kanaloa, told me you was meant for something... massive."

Boi took out the gold Nina bracelet from his pocket. He had grabbed it from the dresser after he'd seen the picture of Shane. It was the same bracelet he'd snagged before being shipped off to foster care. It was the only thing he had taken with him from the broken-down circle island bus. He rubbed the bracelet with his thumb. "Like what?" Boi asked.

"Dunno," said Joe. He pointed out the window. "But Kanaloa stay on your side."

"Mom's right," Boi said. "I going jail. They all right. I no good."

Joe grabbed Boi by the shoulders and shook him. "No listen

to them. You going do something massive, and when you do that kind, not everyone understand."

"What you like me do?" Boi asked.

Joe looked out at the severed stilts on Peter Patrino's plot. He picked up the streams of tape Boi left on the floor and crumpled them. "I was thinking," said Joe. "All I know is us people in country, we always play defense. Need to play offense, too, if you like win. Like you did tonight. First time I seen us play offense since we ate Captain Cooke."

Boi looked at Joe. "Win what?"

Just as Joe was about to answer, Patricia walked out of her bedroom with two packed suitcases. Boi couldn't look at her and faced the window. "We gonna lose the farm," said Joe.

As the rain drops pinging above him slowed, and he watched the ducks flap their wings and squeeze out of their busted, upended cages, Boi thought about his family, the first one, the lighter-burning mother, the petrified grandmother, the sister, the brother, and the father he knew he'd met once or twice but couldn't remember. Then Boi thought about something he'd learned from Mr. Melvin. It was called plate tectonics. When he watched mud slide down the mountain and into the ocean, he realized that tonight Oahu was getting smaller. He knew that the island did in fact get smaller every day as the Pacific Plate pushed the islands northwest, while in the southeast an underwater volcano was producing a new Hawaiian island. Hawaii was just a natural 1,500 mile conveyor belt that produced lava rock that went from assembly to destruction, and billions of years from now, Oahu would be pushed to its final underwater resting place in the middle of the Pacific Ocean. Normally the thought chilled Boi, but tonight he was thinking billions of years is too long—he wished it would happen much faster. Like now.

When Patricia opened the door, a soaked Grover Cleveland stared at her with big, angry eyes. Shocked, she couldn't move away fast enough. Peter's horse chomped, taking a chunk of flesh off her forearm as she screamed.

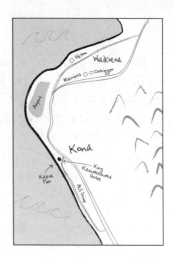

III. Knotting for Governor

1.

After the Dems took over in 1962 and a haole ex-cop became the second governor of the State of Hawaii, the party set up an informal rotation for the office. First, it would be the Japanese turn. Then the Hawaiians turn. Then the Filipinos turn. Then they got stuck when it was the female Japanese turn. But they're sticking to the plan, and Charles Knotting couldn't be happier. It's early May, and according to polls, he is twenty points ahead of Maxine Honda, a fellow state senator, and the Democratic candidate for governor.

Everyone in Hawaii went to school with Japanese girls. Nice hair. Unassuming, good grades. Lithe, daikon-legged bodies. Too short to sport, too polite to provoke, too schooled in the samurai art of keeping their mouths shut in public, they were the stuff of middle school crushes, prissy school spirit, and winter dance courts. Even the bad ones were ninja sluts, girls who everyone knew gave it up, but did so in stealth mode, not in their boyfriends' cars in the school parking lot, but in the comfort of their Hello Kitty pink-painted bedrooms when their parents weren't home.

So when a pure-blooded Japanese woman ran for governor, it just didn't look right. They grew up to be pediatricians, civil attorneys, elementary school teachers, admin assistants, and bridesmaids who gave sappy, squeaky-voiced speeches at wedding receptions. Japanese men could get away with an utter lack of warmth, wit, charisma, and charm because it passed for strength. But Japanese women? No.

It's during the summer campaign, two months before Shane is off to college, that Boi pops up about once or twice a week, finding Shane no matter where he is. He can be on a date about to see the latest superhero movie, feel a tap on his back while standing in line, and Boi will be standing behind him, grinning. Shane can be on the phone at campaign headquarters, pitching his dad's intelligence and ethics to a stranger complaining about a neighbor's tree that is growing over the wall in his backyard, and Boi will knock on the plate glass window and wave Shane outside. Even when Shane is out surfing, trying to get in sets of six-footers before heading to the East Coast, a head will poke out of the water, spit out a snorkel, and Boi will raise a speared moray eel over his head, as if to show Shane he has no idea what lurks beneath him, but not to worry, Boi has his back. Sometimes, Boi is even at Shane's destination before he arrives—the last time it was the private canoe club where Shane pulled up and saw his brother cuffed face down on pavement, a cop's knee digging into his back. Boi had tried to walk into the beachfront private club to find Shane and ended up arguing with the ancient front desk clerk who fondly remembered a time when darkies had not been allowed in the club, when famous writers married to Jap broads were forbidden to buy houses in the area.

At first, Shane sees his brother's ability to find him uncanny, but after the third time Boi finds him at Black Point, lounging poolside with a bikini-clad Lucy Cho, sipping Red Bull and vodka while they watch waves crash against jagged rocks and feed the salt water pool, Shane realizes that his world is a lot smaller than he thought. Nine times out of ten, Shane can be found in a five mile radius from Ala Moana to Kahala, on the third largest island in one of the most isolated parcels of land on the face of the earth. He's a tourist anywhere else.

But Shane doesn't mind that Boi always finds him. With Charles and Helen campaigning sixteen hours a day and no summer school or sports summer leagues for the first time he can remember, boredom, what his parents often refer to as the "achievement assassin," belly creeps upon Shane whenever Boi isn't around. It's not that there's nothing to do; it's that he's not interested in doing the easy stuff (mall, TV, first-person shooters, two a.m. tequila swigs with friends on the beach) and feels too lazy to do the hard stuff (learn the guitar to play Hawaiian songs for all the blond East Coast co-eds he will meet, take out Charles's thirty-foot boat for deep-sea fishing, planting "Knotting for Governor" signs in front yards across the island). When Boi is around, Shane peps up like a trishaw-riding puka-shell tour guide, showing Boi how the wealthy, southeast side lives. This is where we surf this side. This is where we dive this side. This is where we drink this side. This is where we screw girls this side. He introduces Boi to one of his friends, the son of a movie star, a large, mustached haole who's pretty good at beach volleyball, only to find that Boi has an irrational hatred toward big screen heavyweights.

No matter where they go, Shane feels tougher when he's with his brother. When they crash Hawaii Loa Ridge gated community grad parties, Shane tilts up his chin and holds his arms a bit further from his body, Boi's own swag inflating him. At the last party, a sushi bar catered kegger, Shane called out a house full of private school boys when he couldn't find his green lighter. "One of them probably stole it," said Boi. "You gonna let them get away with punking you like that?"

Shane went ape shit, tossing hand-stitched sofa cushions out an open window, threatening lives over a ninety-nine cent lighter while Boi watched grinning. No one called Shane on it. No one ever did.

2. _____

It's the end of June the first time Boi has dinner at the Knottings' home. Somehow Shane expects his brother to be a well-behaved museum patron, but when seventeen-year-old Boi walks in toting a wine box and a two-year-old girl capped with highlights and wearing diamond earrings, the first thing he does is plop her down on the koa dining room table and change her dirty diaper. When Charles and Helen step in, followed by their campaign manager, Monte Clifford, whose business hocks suntan lotion, Hawaiiana cookbooks, and palaka-printed shopping cart covers for babies, they take one look at the baby's blond streaks and glimmering earlobes and gasp. Shane knows what they're thinking: her pierced ears and highlighted locks are portents to future years spent in family court and welfare lines. Boi stands and wipes his hand on his shorts. "Boi," he says.

Charles and Monte shake his hand. Helen pecks his cheek. "Helen," she says.

"Helen? That's someone famous, right?"

Helen nods. "A Trojan princess from long ago."

"Oh," says Boi. "I was thinking about the bird chick at Chuck E. Cheese. Her name Helen, too."

Boi glances at Charles's framed surf pictures. His eyes lock on a *Surfer* magazine cover, a lip of whitewater curled thirty feet over a young Charles's head. "Ho," says Boi. "You used to be the man."

Charles grins, towering over Boi. He flexes his arm. "I still am the man."

Boi points a thumb at Charles and smiles at Helen. "How's him."

Helen laughs. "Are you hungry?" she asks, watching the little girl put handprints on her cherry wood coffee table, her bracelet clanging against the sheet of glass protecting the mother-of-pearl engravings.

"Hell yes," says Boi, as he scoops up Nina and blows hard on her stomach. The baby laughs and laughs.

"May I?" Helen asks.

Boi hands the kid over to her.

The kid's eyes narrow. "Juice," she says.

Helen looks over at Charles, who grimaces. He steps forward and takes the child. He inspects her ankles and lower back while Helen heads to the kitchen. "She isn't tattooed or anything, right?" Charles asks.

"Knowing her mom," says Boi, "tat next year."

Charles puts the girl down. She runs to the piano and bangs keys. Helen returns from the kitchen with a cup of guava juice. She squats in front of the little girl and hands it to her. Helen closes her eyes, wincing as the little girl raises the cup to her lips and drinks. "Whew," says Charles.

Monte clears his throat. "I'll pick you up in an hour," he says.

"Say goodbye to the kid," says Charles, grinning.

Monte steps to Nina, his shaking hands out with the same measure of caution as someone approaching a chained pit bull. "Jesus, Monte," says Helen. "She's twenty pounds, tops."

Monte picks Nina up. She pokes at his shirt, pineapples set over a black canvas, like fruit floating in outer space. "She's cute," says Monte.

Nina bares her teeth and bites a pineapple. Monte howls as he peels the girl off him, almost dropping her. Charles and Helen laugh. Nina runs into Boi's arms. "I trained her to bite haoles," he says. Charles and Helen laugh harder. Monte marches to the front door, slamming it behind him.

Shane watches Nina wrap her arms around Boi as he stands. She flashes her grill at Shane. "Hey man," says Shane. "I was meaning to ask you. How come you were the only one with silver teeth as a kid?"

Boi turns around, puzzled. "What?"

"What?"

Boi frowns. "We all had um," he says.

"Bullshit."

Boi shrugs. "I guess I was the only one who smiled."

Shane looks at Helen and Charles for confirmation. They both nod their heads.

3. _____

By the time Boi comes over for dinner for the second time just a few nights later, Charles and Helen are sold. In fact, they seem to prefer Boi over any of Shane's friends. And Boi doesn't even put on an act. He isn't even polite. He treats Shane's parents as if they're a couple of crazy haoles who go about being wealthy all wrong. How you gonna run for governor, pull sixteen-hour-days kissing people's asses, when you rich enough to just kick back for the rest of your life? How you gonna drive one station wagon when you can buy one mean car, no problem? How come you cook at home? You get money, hire one maid, one chef, and the kind guy answer the door in one tuxedo or something. If you like the water so much, why you no build one giant swimming pool outside, the kind that make waves you can surf like at the water park?

The second time he's over for dinner, this time without the kid, he's saying stuff like this while digging into a plateful of boneless, skinless chicken breast stewed in Indian curry, Helen glowing the entire time. When she offers Boi food, he eats till he's stuffed while Charles tells him he's wise beyond his years. "Why you get all this old furniture?" Boi asks, pouring soy sauce on his basmati rice. "Should get new kind. Cheap at Walmart."

Charles gets a kick out of that. "Let me ask you something, Boi. Let me tap into that rustic wisdom of yours. After I become governor, what should I try to fix? What's the biggest thing wrong with this state?"

Boi chews. "The people."

"Like who?" Helen asks.

"All of them," says Boi.

"Give me an example," says Charles.

Boi swallows. "Rich haoles from the mainland buy up land then think they instant kamaaina; people act like their names gonna ring out after they die when even their kids gonna forget them; locals that just like money job selling nothing you can touch, send their kids private schools, and no think at all."

"I hate people who stand in doorways," says Shane. "It's rude." No one's paying attention.

"Hawaiians proud that they still run the prisons from the inside," says Boi. "Babooze that think they can save the world by recycling bottles and not using plastic bags and get piss off when you no waste your time like them. Crazies that treat their dogs and cats better than they treat people. Lolos that live on one island and can hardly swim. People that call themselves street smart because reading hurts their manini brains. Book smart people that don't know anything else because when they step outside, the hot sand burn their haole feet."

Charles winks at Helen as Boi takes a breath and continues. "People like one train in Hawaii; people that no like one train. People that spend all their money on firecrackers New Year's Eve; people that like force them to spend all their money on fricking car recons and cigarette tax instead. People.... get rid of all the people and Hawaii would be cherry."

Charles smiles. "Don't think I can run on that. So what's the second biggest thing wrong with this state?"

"Not enough fish."

Helen laughs. "What?"

Boi shrugs. "My dad told me used to be you could go anywhere, catch fish. Would be nice if could still do that, yeah?"

Charles and Helen both nod, smiling. Helen spoons more curry on Boi's shoyu-soaked jasmine rice. Charles punches Boi's shoulder. Shane rolls his eyes. He's had enough. They're acting like he isn't even in the room.

"What?" asks Boi.

"More fish?" says Shane. "C'mon."

"He has a point," says Charles.

"I agree," says Helen.

As Shane watches his parents bask in Boi's presence, he thinks he gets it. He'd heard the term "haole" all his life and just accepted that it meant Caucasian, white. But it's more than that. His mother isn't even white, or all white anyway, but he's looking at her now and thinking, *haole*. And it's not because she collects museum furniture, wears fashionable Third World jewelry, or calls herself a foodie and cooks exotic cuisine. And his father isn't haole just because he's rich, has membership on exclusive boards and clubs, and is white. They're haole because they believe they have the power to change things. They believe they have something to say. They believe that they're right. They believe they matter.

What his parents fancy, above all else, are people who voice strong opinions, opinions that they can either embrace and expand on or feel superior to—it doesn't matter. They love having opinions on opinions and telling other people about them. In fact, in that regard, Boi, who is now shaking his head at Helen as she stuffs saffron-spiced rice in her mouth with her fingers, is more haole than Shane ever was.

Shane wonders why he doesn't have an opinion on anything. He never has. When his psychotherapist, Dr. Kim, told him he had Narcissistic personality disorder, he didn't even have an opinion on that. All he did was gaze at the framed diplomas on the wall and one picture of the doc holding a spear gun next to a fifty-pound ulua. And now, watching his parents and Boi form an imaginary triangle that Shane somehow finds himself banished from, he can't help but wonder, do Charles and Helen think they adopted the wrong kid?

Later that night, after Boi invited himself to sleep over, Boi and Shane argue over who is going to turn the light off. Boi, in the top bunk, tells Shane he's closer to the switch. Shane, shaded by the top bunk and scared of the dark anyway laughs and says, "Doesn't bother me."

Boi swears under his breath, hops out of bed, and turns out the light. He kicks Shane on his way up. "Frickin' air conditioning," says Boi. "I could sleep twelve hours straight in this room, no problem."

"Your senior year starts soon. Stoked?"

Boi laughs. "I not going back school. I not going back Kahuku."

"What?"

"I just going live here, no problem."

Shane wants to change the subject. "Hey, that girl. Chastity or whatever. She's your girlfriend?"

"Nah."

"But you guys have, like a kid together?"

"Yeah."

"So why you got so pissed when I was checking her out?"

"I wasn't pissed."

"What?"

Boi yawns. "Who you think put her skank ass up to it?"

"Why?"

"I wanted to see what kind of guy my brother is."

"And what'd you find out?"

Boi's already asleep.

Shane always imagined it'd be cool to have a brother in the top bunk. They'd talk about their parents. They'd debate who's the most doable out of a group of top-tier, cat-eyed, anorexic celebs. They'd cover each other's asses when one snuck out of the window at eleven p.m. on a school night to go screw a girlfriend.

But now, as Boi grinds his teeth, sawing through enamel with pendulum rhythm, Shane's not so sure. What does Boi want from him? What does Boi want from his parents? And how come his parents like him so much? Why does Shane Knotting, son of a soon-to-be Governor, off to the Ivy League in the fall, want to be this ghetto kid so badly? Twenty years from now, Boi will either be limping around on bad knees, collecting workman's comp, or in jail. Why does neither fate sound so bad to Shane?

Because going to jail and collecting disability, that's what real men do. That's what real men in Hawaii do. Everyone else is just a haole or a scrub. With that, Shane realizes he just had his first real opinion.

4. _____

The next morning, as Boi shovels a spoonful of some granola crap in his mouth, he looks around the table and can't help but think, these mother-fuckers have no clue who he is. Charles has already been up a few hours, playing a yet-to-be-released campaign video on loop while talking to his campaign manager on the phone; he hurries through a half-cut papaya. Helen, face already painted with make-up, cuts the tags off new aloha shirts while sipping some green sludge for breakfast. Shane grinds granola, and scrolls through messages on his phone—Boi had heard about this sort of thing before. Families that eat dinner at the same table every night. But breakfast, too? This shit is whack.

At first, Boi felt guilty about hooking up with the Knottings. Mr. Melvin would say that what people like Charles needed was terrorism, Al Qaeda style.

But what surprises Boi now is that he never feels like blowing up Charles's stuff. Maybe because Charles doesn't even seem to care about stuff. He doesn't wash his car. He doesn't even look at his giant house or perfect lawn when he steps out. According to Shane, his boat just sits there in an Ala Wai slip, attracting barnacles. If it was Boi with all that money, he'd be all about cruising in a dope, two-coats-of-polish ride, with a swimming pool and hot tub out back, and a yacht hooked up with gold Penn International reels. But Charles? The big haole just wants to be governor. Boi can respect that.

And seeing how hard Charles works, pretty much all day, every day, Boi actually wouldn't mind if the big man won. This family has its shit together. It has a water purifier attached to the kitchen sink. It exercises regularly. It even has silverware that matches. This family is cool. This family, eating breakfast together every morning, he wishes it was his family. "So Boi," says Charles as he dumps his papaya in the trash. "A first class ticket to the Big Island with us next week says I can beat you in arm-wrestling."

"Jesus Christ," says Shane as he tosses his spoon on the counter.

Boi smiles. The two of them square off at the marble topped island in the middle of the kitchen. "I was two-time frat champ at Yale," says Charles, flexing and pointing at his bicep. "You don't know who you're dealing with."

Boi grabs his hand. "You no like stretch or something first? You not too young."

Helen and Shane watch. Boi has to inch forward because Charles's forearm is longer than his. Fricking big and veiny his forearm, too. And his hands, not too soft. Not as rough as Boi's, but can sand wood with those hands. Charles looks at Shane. He squeezes Boi's hand hard. "Call it," he says.

Shane, looking bored, cups his hands over theirs and sighs. "Go."

The big old man is strong. But like Boi told himself before, these mother-fuckers have no clue who he is. He's Just Boi. Boi Vise Grip. Boi No Good. He bends nails and rips phonebooks in half. He's got the hardest hands in Kahuku. He's a boys' home vet where all they did was share choke holds and arm wrestle. He's the knocker-upper of Kahuku skanks. He's the destroyer of movie star houses. He knows about leverage. Using all of his stringy one-hundred eighty pounds, he strains and pulls toward himself. He curls his wrist and uses his body weight to push down with everything he's got. Lactic acid fills his muscles. He feels like every fiber in his arm is stretched to the limit and it'll all soon rip then coil like burning hair. The pain just makes him try harder. He pumps with bloodshot effort. He arm shakes as he imagines that if he doesn't put this big haole's hand down on the marble slab, he'll die.

Charles, wide-eyed, loses.

He looks at Shane. "Jesus, this kid's strong."

Boi, panting, flexes his bicep and points at it. "Olomana Boys' Home. Two-time champ."

Charles and Helen laugh. Shane's the only one not laughing. He's just eyeing Boi suspiciously, like Boi's a crackhead walking by an open car window.

Boi hates when people look at him like that.

5.

When Shane said "hotel party," Boi figured he knew what to expect. Fifty kids crammed into a $100-a-night room, bathroom tub full of beer and ice. Boys showing off to girls, climbing over the rails of the twentieth floor balcony. Look, no hands. Security busts it up a several hours later, a select few maybe sticking around over night for some cards, probably pepito.

But Shane's friend's hotel party is ten beachfront cabanas near Boi's house in Kahuku. It's the same resort where his father Joe fell three stories into a pit of money. An outdoor catered buffet with fresh poke, fruit and salads made of weird, jagged leaves, lomi salmon, kalua pig, and brown beer kegs. Servers dressed in white swat at flies with ti leaves. The kids, some blond, some Asian, a few Hawaiian, and a few even Samoan, pile food on their plates and go off to the cabanas—one with a DJ spinning in a make-shift rave, one with a poker table for high stakes hold 'em, and another where barefoot boys and girls pop haole drugs—shrooms, ecstasy, and acid. The kind of drugs that make you see a strange reality. Not the kind that make you feel powerful enough to break it. Boi follows Shane to this cabana.

Shane plops down on a bed and pops a pill. He sits, throws up a little on his shirt, and laughs. He takes off his shirt and tosses it in a corner. A skinny hapa wearing a bikini top barely covering her big, fake tits, sits on Shane's lap. They brush each other's skin lightly with the tips of their fingers. Shane just laughs as he pops tent. The girl pokes at his hard-on, leans down, and baby talks to it. Shane, grinning, talks to it, too. Crazy haoles. Boi gets up and walks outside for some air.

Shirtless, barefoot haoles and Asians toss footballs and old-school frisbees as they fry on acid. One kicks a soccer ball into the surf and yells, "Goal!" A few of them, like Shane's good friend Don, toke weed and wave to security as they pass by on their golf carts. There's one kid, he's dark, but not Filipino or Polynesian. He's not black or Micro. He's got dark, thick eyebrows and is singing karaoke out on the patio like a champ.

Shane steps next to Boi and puts his arm around his shoulder. "Bharat. He can sing."

"Bharat? What kind name is that?"

"Indian. Like from India. On the other side of the world. Should see him play the alto sax. He's awesome."

Boi frowns and nods. Shane grins. "What?" Shane asks. "Don't know where India is?"

Boi shrugs. "I went immersion school small kid time."

"Someone gotta learn to grow taro."

"Security no bother?"

"Shit," says Shane. "Mark's dad is a major stockholder in this resort."

"Turtle Bay?"

"No. Hilton."

"And what? No parents, either?"

"Mark got his own money."

Boi looks around. This spread must've cost five figures and some eighteen-year-old kid fronted that kind of cash like water. And Boi knows: these kids, acting silly on the kind fuck drugs that don't hook you like batu, drinking their bitter beers from glass mugs they brought home from trips to places like England and Germany, they are the future alii of Hawaii. Even the Indian dude, wherever the fuck that is. Boi doesn't even know what an alto sax is. "Sometimes," says Boi, "I wish I was you."

"I am the man." Shane giggles.

"Shit. While all you guys college, I going be home digging my ass."

"What do you want?" asks Shane.

"At first, I look at something like this, I like blow um up."

"And now?"

"I dunno," says Boi. "You ever think about your dad?"

"The big man? All the time."

"No, your real dad."

A haole kid tosses Shane a can of beer. Shane catches it, pokes a hole in the can, and shotguns it, one crack, then drops the empty on the grass. The kid and his friends cheer. These guys already prepping to be frat boy assholes.

"I was thinking of looking for Glorya-Maree," says Boi.

"Who's Glorya-Maree?" says Shane, wiping his mouth.

"Our sister, numnuts."

"Why?"

Boi wonders if Shane remembers anything. The bus. The full-on paralyzed grandma who used to tell them old Hawaiian stories and take care of them before she got frozen in her own body. The juice bottles their mother filled with straight corn syrup when she was too fucking high or lazy to mix it with water. Which was often. The days without food. Boi trying to open canned goods with wrenches, knives, and finally by smashing them against the floorboard. The screaming. The slaps upside the head. The lighter burns. The time Makana garroted Boi with her purse strap and left a ring of black-and-blue around his neck. The bracelets their mom used to steal from their grandmother. Boi never forgot. He just didn't think about it all very much. But then he saw the picture of water polo captain Shane in the paper, and he instantly missed his brother and sister. All he had was Joe, Nina, and Patricia. The picture moved something caveman in him. He wanted blood. He wanted family.

But Shane doesn't want that. He doesn't even remember. Even though, by now, his dad is probably dead like Boi's, Shane doesn't think about where he came from. And if Boi was Shane, he probably wouldn't remember or think about it either. He'd just chill at these parties and wait for the money to pass down to him. Wait for his turn at bat. These guys, they get softballs pitched to them underhand. Guys like Boi, they get Cy Young motherfuckers throwing heat. Even their girls are more hot, confident, bikini-waxed, all tanned and toned up, veterinarians or whatever you call people who only eat vegetables. He turns. Shane's grinning all goofy. "What? Why you looking at me like that for?"

"I dunno, I wish I was you, sometimes," says Shane.

"You teasing me?"

"No. I..."

Boi shoves Shane. Shane shoves him back. Both smiling, they fall to the ground in each other's arms. It reminds Boi of how they used to sleep as kids, him, Shane, and Glorya-Maree all tangled together because it was so damn cold. They never even had blankets back then.

A crowd of kids gather and cheer. At first the brothers are playing, big-pawed puppies trying to pin the other. But as the haole boys howl, Shane's grip tightens. As the Asian girls giggle, Shane digs his elbows into Boi's side. Hard. He raises an elbow and smashes it against Boi's rib. The crowd, voices high-pitched and scratchy, ooh and ah. Oh no he didn't.

Boi digs one foot into the gritty dirt and spins. He grabs Shane's ankle. He squeezes, twists, and pulls. Shane screams. "Tell everyone you like sucking cock," says Boi.

"Fuck you!"

Boi yanks harder. "Tell um!"

"No!"

Boi pulls harder. Shane's in tears. Boi knows what he's thinking. His pride or his ankle. Boi would let someone rip off his ankle before he'd say it. He wonders if his brother is made out of the same stuff.

"I love sucking cock!" yells Shane.

The kids laugh. Boi lets go. He gets up and dusts himself off. A haole kid with light brown dreadlocks and bad skin puts his arm around Boi like they're bros or something. Boi glares at him. The haole kid removes his arm and steps back. "Shit," Boi says, brushing freshly cut grass from his hair. "I just said say you like sucking cock. Never need say 'love.'"

The kids laugh harder. Boi tries to help Shane up, but he pushes Boi away. "What? Was just joking," says Boi.

Shane gets up and limps off toward the beach. Boi watches as his brother plants ass alone in the sand, his feet in the surf as he stares at the whitewash rolling in. The soccer ball that was punted out there earlier floats to Shane. Shane grabs it, stands, and hurls it past the breakers. The ball bobs over the channel. Shane sits back down. The rising tide thrusts water on sand and soaks Shane. Shane doesn't move.

Boi turns away. That's right, motherfucker. All you motherfuckers. I might be cleaning fucking toilets in a resort like this ten years from now, but you give me lip, I take any of you motherfuckers down.

But it rings empty. He'd rather be one of them. He'd rather be Knotting. He heads to the drug cabana to check if there's a chick there high enough to fuck some low-class, country-ass scrapper like him.

6. _____

A week-and-a-half later, the day Boi is scheduled to fly to the Big Island with the Knottings for a campaign tour, he turns the corner and approaches the house, straddling seven-hundred pounds of smoking chrome. He pulls up to Shane and Charles, twists the screwdriver impaling the dash, and kills the engine. Charles frowns at the screwdriver. "Lose your keys?"

"I would lose my head if wasn't connected," says Boi as he gets off the bike.

"Attached," says Charles.

"What?" asks Boi.

"I'd lose my head if it wasn't attached."

The two of them have been doing this for the last week, Boi at the house every night, misquoting a cliche in front of Charles and Charles correcting him. Boi never does this when it's just him and Shane, so Shane wonders if Boi comes armed with a botched cliche or two for Charles on purpose. "Well," says Charles. "You can't leave that stolen bike here. Park it a few blocks over or something."

Boi looks at Shane, acting hurt. "Why everyone think I burg?"

Because you're a thief.

Two shirtless Hawaiian boys step out of the neighboring house. One with a huge head, bitch tits, and a plume of boxer shorts spilling over a denim waistband. The other, capped with a bushy topknot, wearing slippers three sizes too big, and hair-gel handsome. They walk onto the street, throwing a neon green foam football to each other. Charles frowns.

Two years ago a kooky Japanese billionaire who owned over thirty properties in the area was catching Kahala community hell because he'd spent most of his time in Japan and left his houses in various forms of disrepair. The Japanese guy, maybe out of retribution, maybe not, decided to rent some of the houses out to homeless people dirt cheap. One of the families moved in next door to the Knottings. Charles installed a new alarm system and ranted at the city council the next day.

The mother, a skinny woman who reminds Shane of a calabash aunty who'd gotten so drunk she kissed him on the lips at a wedding reception once, yells at her sons. The two boys ignore her as the top-knotted one fakes out an imaginary defensive back and runs a crisp crossing route. The mother picks a river rock off the ground and whips it, missing them by at least ten feet. The rock skips off the pavement, bounces, and rings a stop sign. "I going get the chili pepper water!" she shouts.

"No hope in drugs," says Boi.

"In dope," says Charles. "In dope." Boi smiles and winks at Shane.

Charles lights a cigar, waves to the kids, and smiles. "I actually got the mom to wave signs for me."

Shane grabs the cigar from him. He takes a puff then hands it back. "I should give them my sports stuff. I'm not shipping it with me. What about you, Boi, you need stuff to take home?"

"I don't play for fun," says Boi. "I play forreal."

Shane rolls his eyes. Charles nods. "The big-headed one has a good arm."

Charles rolls his neck, spits in his palm, and puts out the cigar as the mom yells at her sons with profanity-laced threats. "For months I thought the older one was named 'faka,'" says Charles. He smiles and waves at the mother who stoops her shoulders, grins, and waves back. "Ready for Kona?" he asks Boi. "Flight leaves in a few hours."

Boi shrugs. "I guess."

"I don't feel like going," says Shane.

Charles frowns. "You're off to college in a month. C'mon, son. Quality time."

Shane shrugs. "You'll be fine. After I'm gone, you'll have Boi to keep you company."

Shane heads inside. A misfired football spirals and hits him on the back of the head. Shane turns as the two neighboring kids run into their house. The mom grimaces and waves apologetically. Charles has his arm around Boi as they both laugh and laugh. Shane's eyes well as he enters the house and slams the door.

7.

The ballroom at the Hilton Waikoloa on the Big Island is filled with more white people than Boi has seen in his entire life. Bolo-head white men with steel-rimmed glasses, small beer guts hanging over their gold-buckled belts. Papaya-shaped white women in muumuus capped with permed, dyed, thinning hair. Silver and turquoise earrings hang from their ears. Younger white dudes in striped shirts with their sleeves rolled up. Veiny, curly-haired forearms clasped with waterproof watches. Tanned wives and girlfriends wearing florescent bikinis under their thin dresses. Man, they all talk a lot.

Shane, who is wearing an aloha shirt and purple and white flower leis, steps to the podium. He testifies a bit about growing up in a busted-up bus in Wahiawa, raised by an addict mother. He says how grateful he is that Charles and Helen adopted him. He talks about how he's going to an Ivy League school, thanks to Knotting life lessons about ladder-climbing, boot straps, and Our Lord God. The speech is stiff, robot tiki style. But Shane's been this way for a week now, a pouty little bitch. If Shane were Boi's kid, he'd slap him across the back of the head and tell him to get over it. Not like Boi actually kicked his ass.

After Shane finishes introducing him, Charles, looking all tangled with leis, steps to the podium, holding a pink pastry box. He waves as the applause get softer. Boi, standing in the back of the ballroom by a sweating silver punchbowl, ladles juice into a glass and drinks sweetened passion-orange as Charles thanks Shane and tells the audience how proud he is of his son.

"Thank you, thank you," says Charles as he adjusts the mic on his flower-printed collar. "Many towns across the state claim that theirs is God's Country, but we know that God's hand is in Kona, building still, far beyond the sixth day. It's a pleasure to be home." Applause. The Knottings have a house on every island except Niihau, so to them just about everywhere in Hawaii is home.

"Now, as you can see, I brought props with me today." Charles lifts the pink pastry box so that everyone can see it. He opens the box and pulls out a white, dome-shaped barbeque pork bun. The crowd is silent, curious.

"This," says Charles, "is a manapua. It seems harmless enough, right? A Cantonese pastry filled with chewed-up pork, brought over by migrant Chinese workers from plantation days. Back then, field workers would bring home a pink box identical to this one for Sunday breakfast before getting the kids ready for church..."

His voice booms and Boi wonders if he even needs the mic clipped to his collar. "A couple of generations later," says Charles, "the arrival of the Manapua Man. A guy in an ice cream truck driving up your block, carnival music ringing, barefoot kids chasing the truck, loose change clanging in their pockets..."

Charles reaches a hand in his pocket and shakes imaginary change. He clears his throat and continues. "But now, there are no more plantations, no more Manapua Man. Let me tell you folks something. Today, the manapua is being used to duplicitous purpose. Today, the manapua greases more wheels in Hawaii than Castrol, my friends."

A handful in the crowd laugh. Others frown, curious. The clanging of dishes dies down. Even the waiters and waitresses, holding wicker baskets of purple taro bread and stainless steel coffee pots, are listening. "Every time you need something from some state office, you better bring a box of manapua. You need an environmental pass for a construction project? You better bring manapua. You need re-zoning for a baby strip mall you saved for years and want to develop? You better bring manapua. You need to put up a new sign in front of your auto body shop? You better bring manapua to each of the dozen or so state offices approval must move through."

The crowd nods. "And what happens if you don't bring this succulent, leavened mix of yeast and baking powder? Well, your perfectly reasonable requests can get lost in the shuffle by incompetent state workers who are either lazy or inept because they were appointed on the lone qualification of being a cousin of so-and-so. If you do not bring the manapua and bow down to these bureaucrats, your requests will get stuck in the system, passed by giant corporations with giant pockets who give these fat cats the best manapuas of all."

Charles rips the manapua he's holding in half and pulls a hundred dollar bill from it with the hand flair of a magician. He holds up the bill so all can see. The crowd cheers. The waiters and waitresses put their baskets and pots on oval trays stationed by each table and give Charles their full attention. Charles waits for them, nods at one in particular, a Japanese woman with glasses probably ten years past retirement age, probably a die-hard supporter of Maxine Honda. He smiles at her then goes on.

"It's disgraceful if you think about it. A half century ago, maybe you'd bring a box of manapua to uncle for helping you fix your truck. Maybe you'd bring a box over to aunty because she helped you prepare for a luau for your child's first birthday. Maybe you'd bring a box over to tutu, thanking her for watching the kids after school. The giving of the manapua used to be a tradition of gratitude. But my opponents, they somehow corrupted this pure custom. The manapua is now just cold, hard currency. It's a key to the backroom door. It's a mafia c-note, passed from a friend of ours to another. But not anymore. Not on my watch. My friends, when I become governor, the reign of the manapua will be over!"

A standing ovation. Boi puts down his punch and claps, too. A Hawaiian waiter wearing a black bow tie and vest, the only one not applauding, pushes a plastic cart, stops by Boi, and re-stocks ice with a shovel. "Pretty good speech so far, yeah?" says Boi.

The waiter shrugs as he shovels ice into a silver bowl. "I no even like manapua. But I guess if had the kind with money inside, would be mean."

The waiter pushes the cart away to the next table. Boi takes a seat in the back corner of the ballroom, at an empty round of ten. All the cloth napkins are still folded, and there's a fishbowl center piece. Boi picks up chopsticks and tries to catch the lumpy-headed orange fish. Shane walks up to Boi and sits next to him. "So where we going after this?" asks Boi.

Shane sighs. "My dad has a party on a catamaran. Open to the public."

"Catamaran? What is that?"

"You don't have to act dumb with me," says Shane.

Boi puts down the chopsticks. "What?"

"The dumb act works on my dad but not me."

"You calling me dumb?"

"I'm not scared of you," says Shane. He picks up a glass of water and drinks. Water dribbles down his chin. Boi stands up.

With his fists balled, Shane sticks out his chest, his eyes all watery.

Boi sticks his hand in Shane's glass, pulls out a few cubes, chews, and smiles. "Relax."

Shane looks away. "When we get home, you should go back home. For good."

"Shit, you going be off to college or whatever. Why you care?"

Boi turns and faces the stage. Charles describes a coming golden age in Hawaii, when the state will finally be released from the stranglehold of labor unions and calabash uncle cronyism. "If you could have anything in the world, what would it be?" Shane asks.

"What kind of faggot question is that?"

"I'm serious."

"I dunno. Maybe I want to find Glorya," says Boi. "My *other* sister."

Shane nods, ignoring the insult. "What else?"

Boi wonders if he should tell him what he really wants. What will give him the sway to find Glorya, to save Joe's farm, to help his moms find one easy diet so she not so grouchy all the time. And to get custody of his kid because her moms is a welfare ho. To find his real father's and grandmother's grave to make sure they got a good burial. To find his fucking lighter-burning, tweaked-out biological mother to make sure she's dead and buried (if not, he'll do it). He wants to send more 6,000 square foot haole houses off cliffs into the Pacific Ocean. He wants to make sure he doesn't become some blue-shirt workingman who comes home and drinks canned light beer every night after work, telling his kids with drunk, red eyes how everything in Hawaii is politics, that everything in Hawaii is *political*. He wants to make sure he doesn't turn into one of his Kahuku Point Mafia friends who steal cars and smoke ice, sometimes for three days straight, no sleep, talking large, living small. He doesn't want to be just another motherfucker with a hard luck story dreaming big. He wants to help Charles rub out all these manapuas infesting the islands.

Lately Joe's been sending visions of his future: drunk, two a.m., wall-of-text ramblings sent via email. And really all Boi wants is to be the squid god. Kanaloa, the water finder, the magic teacher, creator and destroyer of worlds. To live and smash forever. As Joe has told him time and time again, to the point of driving him out of the being-foreclosed-upon house and farm, Boi needs help from the gods to do something *massive*.

Before he can stop himself, Boi says it. "I want your last name. I want to be Knotting."

Shane frowns then laughs. He's cracking up now, bent over, hands on his knees.

"Nah, just kidding," Boi says, doing his best to spray ink all over his confession. "I no like shit. Fuck haoles."

Shane nods, still cracking up.

"I just like to squeeze and watch you fuckers squirm," says Boi. "Like this."

He stands up and sticks his hand in the fish bowl. He pulls out the orange fish and pops it in his mouth. The fish wriggles on his tongue. Boi opens his mouth to show Shane. Then he bites down and chews as Charles talks about sensible cuts and balanced budgets and how the eradication of a Chinese pastry will resurrect these cherished American ideals.

8. _____

After a couple of hours of what Charles calls pressing flesh in the ballroom, Boi and the Knottings get on a resort boat that taxis tourists from tower to tower. Under the water's oily surface, papio, stingray, and yellow reef fish dart away from the boat. As the pilot, a local chick with bushy black hair and sumo thighs, pulls to a dock to pick up more passengers, Boi spots a dead unicorn fish floating on the surface. Charles sees it too and signals for Boi to keep quiet as he scoops his hand in the water and pulls the fish out. He tosses it on Helen's lap. She jumps out of her seat and screams.

When they arrive at the dockside lobby, Charles steps off, followed by Helen, Shane, and Boi. Two brown men on their hands and knees scrub grout as a maid empties gold waste baskets. A bellman pushing a cart full of luggage follows a young Japanese woman with super-white skin scribbled with blue veins that run up her calves.

Once in the car, Charles unyokes himself from two pounds of flower leis. Helen takes off her rings, rubs her fingers, and checks her make-up. Shane leans against a window and falls asleep.

The twenty-five mile stretch of Kohala Coast lava fields, running from the resort to Kona Town under blue sky, is what hell must look like on a sunny day. Sparse dry weeds sprout from the jagged, sun-blasted black rocks, and bleached coral spells out names and declarations of love, eco-friendly graffiti. Men in spandex ride bicycles along the side of the highway, training to be iron men. Wilted tropical flowers mark memorials on the side of the road: victims of head-on collisions remembered then soon forgotten. There's a bunch of these by Joe's house, too. Every few miles, they pass a beachfront resort packed with timeshares. The ocean, even at the shoreline, is special-effects blue.

When they arrive at Kailua-Kona, they turn onto Alii Drive and drive down the coast—shops, bars, hotels, galleries, and landmarks crammed across the street from the sea wall, a mini-Waikiki. King Kamehameha's personal heiau next to the King Kamehameha Hotel. They pull into Kailua Pier, home of the Atlantis Adventure Submarine. Charles's charted catamaran, a 170-foot motorized canoe, is docked. A group of older haoles, the campaign manager Monte Clifford among them, wait for the Knottings holding leis cased in clear ballooned plastic. The flowers sweat in their bags. "After this is all over," says Charles. "I'd like to see the final tally on flower costs."

"I'll set everything up," says Helen. "Put the flowers on ice. You boys should maybe walk around, take in the town?"

"You're the tourist," says Charles to Boi. "Want to check it out?"

Boi glances at Shane, who ignores him. He shrugs.

9.

The three of them end up at an American smoothie franchise sucking fruit slush and amino acid powder through their straws. Charles talks about the history of the west side of the Big Island,

how King Kamehameha the Great's mother was a Kohala princess and how the Hawaiians were always warring over control
of the territory. "Listen to revisionists," says Charles, "and they'd
have you believe Hawaiians fished, grew taro, and sang 'Kumbaya'
all day. They were just as violent and mean-spirited as any other
people. It's just that they used wood sticks instead of gunpowder.
Well, until Kamehameha got his hands on guns, that is."

"My dad says he's descended from Kamehameha," says Boi.

Charles smiles. "Half the Hawaiians I know think they are,
too. Kamehameha must've been the Wilt Chamberlain of his
time."

"My ag teacher used to..."

"Wait, you had an agriculture class in high school?" asks
Charles.

Boi nods. Charles laughs. "What a goddamn waste of time.
The United States is slipping fast in math and science and our
public schools are teaching our kids how to plant fruit. Go figure."

"Well," says Boi. "Ag is science."

Charles nods. "The science of the third world."

"They still got you on the plantation, Boi," says Shane.

Charles, excited, sits up. "Exactly." He points at his cup. "See
this here? The scientists engineer the powder. The businessmen
sell the product."

"The workers?" says Shane, glowing under Charles's sudden
attention, smiles at Boi. "They just pick the fruit."

Charles and Shane grin at each other, as if they are letting Boi
in on a well-kept secret. Boi glances to his left and spots two local men in slippers, one skinny, one fat, like an old school comedy
team. Both wear beat-up jeans and faded tee shirts, rags hardly
good enough for wiping polish off cars. They eye Charles with
looks of almost recognition. They catch Boi looking at them. Boi
rolls his eyes. The skinnier one nods punchy.

"Must be nice being you guys, ah? So smart," says Boi. "After
numnuts here goes to his fancy college, we should take out your
boat. I can show you the spots."

Charles laughs. "I've spent more time in the water at North Shore than you've been alive. But seriously, when Shane leaves, that's when the real work starts."

"What you mean?" asks Boi.

Shane grins. "He means, he won't have time. His campaign schedule gets ramped up the closer and closer he gets to November. In other words, go back home, Boi."

Charles glares at Shane but doesn't say anything.

Boi slouches and shrugs. "That's cool."

"My door is always open," Charles says to Boi. "You know that. I just won't have time to horse around is all."

Boi takes the straw out of his drink and twists it.

"He wants to be one of us," says Shane. "He told me earlier. Then he ate a fish."

Charles perks up, curious. "What do you mean?"

Boi throws the straw at Shane, leans toward him, and clenches his fists. Shane smiles. The pussy thinks his old man will save him. "He wants our last name," says Shane. "He wants you to adopt him. Like he's a baby or something."

Boi looks at Charles. He's hopeful, and doesn't know why. He knows it's crazy and will never happen, but he wants the old man to say, sure why not? He wants the old man to say, hell, I'd rather have you as a son than this pussy loudmouth sitting with us. Boi wants Charles to say, hey, welcome to the family. Charles clears his throat and sips his drink. Shane shakes his head.

"Well..." says Charles. He sits there searching for the right thing to say, but can't grip words, like a man trying to rip a slippery fish in half. He doesn't have to say it. Boi gets it. He's too old. He's not good enough. His name is Boi, and even spelled correctly, no one in the history of Hawaii amounted to anything with a name like Boi. Things you'll never hear in Hawaii: Boi Avenue, Boi High School, The Mandarin Boi Hotel, The Boi Rapun School of Medicine. Boi for mayor. Uncle Boi's Limo. And when he daydreams up his biological, road-kill father, which he is doing now, he never pictures a rich or successful guy, or a chief cloaked in red and yellow feathers. Instead, the best version he can come up with is a tough guy who once fought hard for pride because pride was all he had.

Even if his last name was Knotting, he'd still just be Boi No Good. It's in his blood. Destined to do something massive? Joe was blowing smoke up his ass. Boi can't believe he was buying into the ramblings of a man people called Red Roof Joe. He can't believe he thought that this big haole man was going to help him be something else, be something bigger, be something Knotting. He feels like crying, but he won't. He learned long time ago, even back when his mother used to burn him, crying is weaksauce. Crying doesn't protect your ass. Take that feeling and turn it into rage. Then motherfuckers will know no matter what they do, they can't hurt you.

Boi stands up and glares at the two locals one table over. They're still trying to place a name with Charles's face. "What the fuck you looking at?" says Boi.

The two men look at each other, puzzled, then stand. They step toward Boi, puffed up, eyes full of bad intentions. Boi shifts his right foot behind him. Charles, wearing a politician smile, steps in front of the two men. "Don't mind the kid," he says, towering over them.

Shane is sitting in his chair, frozen, looking down. They both eye Charles. The skinnier man slaps the fatter one's back. "Ho, The Gov," he says.

"Not quite yet," says Charles. "But with your votes, maybe. Listen, I'm having a campaign party tonight. The catamaran at Kailua Pier. You guys are welcome to join us."

"What? Free drinks?"

"Tell you what. First round on me."

"Au-right!"

The two men look at each other and nod. Boi sits back down, rips the cover off his cup, and gulps his drink as the men walk away. He's still wound tight, and his hand shakes a little as he crumples the cup into a ball. Shane stands up, stretches, and lets out a fake yawn. Charles turns around. "If you ever..."

"What?" says Boi, squeezing the cup so hard he wonders if it's possible to turn styrofoam into a diamond. "Tough guy over here had my back." He nods at Shane.

"It's not about that," says Charles. "You ignorant local kids think that's what life is all about. Who can lick who. Who's got whose back. The world is bigger than that."

Boi tries to casually shrug, but his RPM's are running so high his lip quivers instead. He bites it. "Yours maybe. But you one man, right? You not afraid you raised one pussy? All show, no go?"

Charles looks at Shane. "Pussy? That's just being smart. It keeps you out of trouble. Gated communities are filled with pussies procreating with beauty queens. Prison is filled with tough guys boning each other. Where'd you rather reside?"

"I'm going to the boat," says Shane. He turns to Boi. "We're done." He walks away.

Boi looks around. He wants a nail to bend, a phonebook to rip in half, something to get this rage out of him. "Man, look at this place. Haoleville."

"King Kamehameha built this place."

"What place? Jamba Juice?"

Charles tosses his cup in the trash, shakes his head, and leaves Boi, who stares out at the horizon wondering who really built this place, this shorefront lava rock housing, what Mr. Melvin would call tiki commerce. God? Pele? Geology? Physics? His eyes turn south toward the Royal Kona Resort, which from this distance looks like an ocean liner beached upside down. A part of him wants to rent a room there, maybe hang under the blue hut-looking thing and watch white girls in bikinis sip pina coladas poolside. The other part wants to see a raging rapid river of lava burn it to the ground.

All the while he still feels the adrenaline rush. Maybe there will never be a Boi Street, Boi Beach, or the Boi Medical Center. But maybe, just maybe, there can be a Tropical Storm Boi, a Boi Wilkes Booth, or a fucking Category 5 Hurricane Rapun.

People like Charles, they don't get rage. They don't understand how a person can go from tap warm to boiling while standing in a slug ATM or grocery line, getting cut off in traffic, or just getting a sassy look from a wannabe tough guy's face. They don't get that dizzy, shaky feeling that often wakes Boi up in the middle of the night, an electric vibe that Boi has to fight by sprinting, doing push-ups, or putting his hand through walls or sedan windows. They don't get how a person can feel like killing every day of his life. Boi looks around at tourists standing in the different food stand lines—Korean, Chinese, and Japanese food kiosks.

He inhales the sweet smell of burning teriyaki. He drops his crumpled cup, sticks out his shaking index finger, and starts firing. Bang, bang, bang. He'd kill them all, no problem. They, none of them, understand the rage, how it floods from his feet to his head. And when it rises to his throat and fills his mouth, at that point, for Boi, it's either spew or drown.

10.

A black and white of King Kalakaua and Robert Louis Stevenson sitting in front of a card table hangs over the catamaran toilet. Normally, Shane would take note of the picture and like it, the last king of Hawaii and his favorite writer fronting three hanging mirrors and two manservants dressed in white.

But he can't enjoy anything now that he knows his dad thinks he's a pussy. "That's just being smart," Charles said. Charles who had thrown blows for respect as a kid. Charles who had surfed giant waves. Shane knew Charles respected toughness. That's why he liked Boi so much. When Charles equated "pussy" with "smart," he was lying.

Shane glances at the Stevenson picture again. What would Long John Silver do if he were Shane? Have Boi walk the plank? No, real pirates either marooned their victims or chopped them to bits and threw them overboard like chum. Both ideas are agreeable to Shane right now. Boi probably doesn't even know who Long John Silver is, the ignorant fucktard.

When Shane exits the bathroom, the sunlight blinds him. He squints and joins the rest of the crowd, a mix of waterfront business owners and their brown and slant-eyed minimum wage workers small-talking in a cloud of body odor. He sneaks another drink. Sixth of the night. Thankfully, Boi isn't aboard. Probably picking fights in Kona Town. Shane hopes Boi finds a guy with arms big enough to fill lava tubes. All show, no go. If the Knottings didn't adopt him, Shane would be tougher than Boi. They didn't know what he was capable of.

A bearded Hawaiian capped with a blue bandana strums the acoustic guitar strapped over his shoulder and calls Helen onstage. The musician plays "Hiilawe," and Helen, barefoot in a slinky red dress, dances to it, her hands vibrating as they mimic a gentle pour off Hawaii's highest waterfall. Helen started taking hula several years back because it's good for strengthening and toning the core. Shane even took it with her for a few months but quit. It made him feel like a homo.

Shane gulps down the last of his drink, some rum and pineapple concoction that warms his chest. He burps up a speck of vomit that shoots out of his mouth and lands in the silver hair of an old woman standing in front of him. Sneaking away starboard, he leans against a rail. Plumes of lava ash rise from the now distant, smoldering island. He doesn't like being this far away from shore. He spits overboard. He now envies Boi for not coming along.

When he turns around to grab another drink, he spots them. The two local guys Boi had called out earlier, one thin, buzz-cut, and yellow-eyed, the other bushy haired and wide around the middle with loose skin. Both chins cocked above patches of ill-kept neck beards. Shane waves to them. They nod back. They're the real deal, country boys who probably grew up fighting shirt-less and barefoot. Men stuck in a middle-of-nowhere, Neighbor Island time-warp who probably still used words such as "beef," "scrap," and "throw" pronounced "trow." Shane decides they're the most real people onboard and staggers toward them as more and more guests with sweat stains under their arms crowd the center of the main deck, hooting and whistling as they watch Helen dance.

The skinny one drapes an arm over Shane's shoulder, his breath a mix of rum and gum disease. "You was with The Gov," he says.

"I'm his son."

The two men look at each other and smile, the fat one missing teeth. "Adopted?"

Shane nods. That's right. He's not really a rich man's son. He's not really a haole. You won't catch him giving advice, constantly rambling "do it like I say." If he hadn't been adopted, he'd be one of them. An older lady, wide-waisted, dimple-legged, maybe forty, walks by toting an red-faced, screaming infant. Shane marvels that someone had the courage to mount and knock that up.

"Must've been like hitting the lottery," says the wide one.

"That's his wife, the one dancing, yeah?" says the skinny one. The crowd cheers in front of the stage—more old ladies with permed hair helmets, puffy up top, short in the back, hairstyles their husbands probably wore in their prime. "I would tap that."

"You went tap um, yeah?" says the fat one, grinning.

"What?" says Shane. Helen finishes her dance, and he can't hear over the now roaring crowd.

"You went poke squid, yeah?!" says the fat one as he sticks an index finger in a closed fist and slide its in and out.

Shane pushes the skinny one's arm off his shoulder. "That's my mom," he says.

"But not really," says the skinny one, who Shane must outweigh by at least thirty pounds. The fat one spits a glob of tobacco juice over the rail. It splatters on a lower deck window. He's heavier than Shane, soft with an Obese Class 3 body mass index, and Shane's thinking diabetes, gout, or both. The liquid courage is kicking in. "Fuck you guys," says Shane. They frown then turn to each other. They're about to say something to him, so Shane steps toward the stage, lats flexed, arms sticking out.

Shane passes men with unfinished tattoo sleeves that run down to their wrists. He passes a group of mentally challenged kids wearing red "Got Aloha?" tee shirts. Aloha—Shane isn't even sure what it means—more slogan than word, more tee shirt catch phrase than anything else. He's never felt it whatever it was. He's pretty sure the two guys, looking pissed, now following, never felt it either.

Shane pushes past a man carrying a bushel of green bananas over a shoulder. He pushes past a group of Tahitian dancers who dab at their beading foundation and cracking eye shadow. Their grass skirts ride so low he can see hip bones. They smile at him. He approaches a biker haole as tall as Charles. He's so big, if the catamaran stalls, he can probably paddle it in. Shane gives him a wide berth and passes, wishing he was as big. World's strongest man big, big enough to roll cars on their roofs. Kamehameha the Great big. No one would mess with him then.

Shane approaches more tough-looking guys, probably prison guards or cops, and he tells himself to stop pushing through. In New York, Tokyo, Hong Kong, pushing through is fine. Pushing through in Hawaii can get a guy punched in the face.

Shane glances back. The guys are still following. He squeezes past more guests. He's Shane Knotting. He's supposed to be untouchable. These guys didn't seem to know how the world works. Like Boi. Shane heads for the middle of the crowd.

Charles mounts the stage, flashing shakas and tossing gold coin candy to extended hands. "A symbolic gesture," says a mic'd-up Charles. "All the tax money that will be returned to your small business coffers."

Shane raises his hand, trying to get Charles to look his way, but his father doesn't see him in the sea of raised, candy-catching hands. He looks around for someone who will help and spots a uniformed cop wearing sunglasses, looking bored. About to shout to get his attention, Shane notices a pretty haole girl. A few years older than him, she's one of those from-the-mainland, retro-pin up wannabes, dark red lipstick, big black belt, polka-dot dress, red hair just released from twenty hot rollers—except for the koi sleeve tattoo running down her left arm, she looks as if she should be painted on a B-52. Shane eyes the red and gold fish inked on her shoulder. One million people in Hawaii, 250,000 koi tattoos. But he can't cry out for help, not when standing next to this girl.

The two guys catch up to Shane. The fat one puts an arm around him. "You smoke?" he whispers, out of breath, pointing down at his fanny pack hanging under his belly roll.

"Shit," says the skinny one, hiking up his jeans and re-stuffing his parachute boxers under the denim waistband. "He too good for us, too haole."

"Smoke what?" asks Shane, trying hard to keep his voice under falsetto.

"I smoke," says the pin up girl. Just like that, not even scared.

The two men look at each other and smile. "Come with us," the fat one says. "Too fucking hot up here anyway." He puts Shane in a loose headlock while Charles, up on stage, pulls out another manapua with a hundred dollar bill in it. Shane looks up at Charles, but the skinny one grabs his arm. The fat one tightens his grip around Shane's neck and leads him to a spiral stairwell going down. The girl follows.

His shame is almost as unbearable as his fear, especially now that they have this girl coming, too. And the worst thing is, he knows Boi would feel zero shame, zero fear. He'd throw these mokes overboard or die trying.

Shane, the pin-up, and the two men are alone now in a quiet lower deck cabin. Skinny Kona boy locks the door. The fat one rolls a joint on a wooden table inlaid with an eighteenth-century world map. The girl, sipping a drink, plays with a brass spyglass mounted on a tripod. She points it at Shane. "You're cute," she says. Probably drunk, she's got that brash haole way about her as if nothing in the world can touch her.

The skinny one eyes Shane. "What about us? What, we not cute, too?"

She just laughs. The fat one hands her a joint. She fires it up and takes a deep breath. Shane looks away. He can take these guys. They look like Micros; they might be Micros, Shane isn't sure. He never could tell the difference between Micros and dark Filipinos, Igorots, the ones that his friend Don claims to this day have tails. Shane tightens his fists. He wants a drink. A refill of liquid courage. "You guys Micronesian?" Shane asks.

The fat one glares. "What the fuck you called us?"

Shane takes a step back and shrugs. "I was just wondering. Filipino then?"

"We not Micros or Flips, you dumb ass," he says.

"Hey, we were all Micros once," says Shane. "I mean, Hawaiian, Samoan, Filipino, whatever. We were all low man on the totem pole at one time or another."

The skinny one takes his knife out from its holster. He unfolds it and points the blade at Shane. The man is a good five feet away, but Shane backpeddles until his shoulders touch the door. "You call me one Micro or one totem pole one more time," the skinny one says. "That's it."

"Oh, stop it," says the girl, coughing out smoke.

"Yeah, stop it," says the fat one. "Look, he's about to cry."

Shane can't stay here. He can't breathe. It's like those dreams that wake him up at night, the savages holding him over lava, the housing project thugs breaking into his house. If they attacked Charles, if they attacked Helen, would he have the balls to stop them? In his dream, he always fails. He steps over Charles's beaten body on the floor of the hardwood hallway, hears the thugs raping Helen behind her closed bedroom door. Weeping, he reaches out for the knob, pulls his hand back, and runs away.

He feels the knob behind him now. "I gotta go," he says. "I gotta piss."

"Hold up," says the fat one, smiling. The girl slumps on the couch between the two men. She nudges them with both elbows to make room for herself. The fat one takes the joint from her. He tokes it, then the girl reaches over and takes it back. The fat one looks at the skinny one. "Gov's son, first," he says.

"Fuck that," says the fat one. "I no like his sloppy seconds."

"Gov's son first. He do um, we do um, we all above the law together."

Shane and the pin-up girl look at each other. The fat one shoves Shane away from the door. He drapes his arm over Shane's shoulder.

Grinning, the skinny one leans over and squeezes the girl's throat. "Fuck this haole cunt," he says. "Bend her over and fuck her so hard she go back mainland and never come back."

Shane pushes the fat one's arm off his shoulder and takes a step forward. He pauses. What would Charles Knotting do? He would rescue the girl. Maybe Boi would, too. Shane wants to, but he'd like a weapon, a magic pill, something.

He takes another step forward, this one smaller. This is his chance to be the son that Charles wants, to actually help someone in real trouble for the first time in his life. The girl, the two guys, they are all waiting, watching, wondering what Shane will do.

"I..." says Shane. He feels his eyes welling.

The fat one shoves Shane against the door. "You what?" he says.

"I..."

"You going first, right?" the fat one asks.

Shane takes a step back, looks down. Shrugs.

The girl screams. Ripping the skinny one's hand from her throat, she shoves Shane out of the way and rushes the door. When the fat one tries to stop her, Shane sees another potential moment of grace, to hit or grab hold of the fat one, delay him for just a second, so the girl can escape. But he doesn't. Instead, the girl swings an arm at the approaching fat one and somehow manages to karate chop his throat and stun him. She bolts.

Shane just stands there frozen. The two guys, one holding his throat and the other pointing at Shane, laugh and laugh. Tears are streaming down Shane's face now. They're laughing so hard, their eyes are half-closed.

Shane turns the knob, opens the door, and darts out. He looks both ways. He runs further down the bowels of the cruise ship. He glances behind him. The two men, smiling, follow. Shane checks knobs for unlocked doors. He finds one on his third try, steps in, then closes and locks it. The two men pound the door from the other side, drowning out the party-goer laughter from the upper deck. "C'mon, we just playing!" says one. "We wasn't going do anything!"

"Better beat it!" says Shane. "Before I come out there and kick your asses!"

The two men pause then pound the door some more. Shane turns around and surveys the room—storage for pots, pans, fishing gear, and ladles. He rummages through the stocked shelves, looking to arm himself. There's a tackle box filled with wire leader, lead sinkers, and tiny hooks. Rubber squid lures, heads stuffed with bullet-shaped steel weights line the walls. The only half-ass weapon he can find is a fold-out corkscrew. He clenches his knuckles around it, the coiled metal protruding below his middle knuckle. He prays someone on the other side of that door will stumble onto this mess and clean all this up.

The door-pounding stops. Shane waits. Why is he like this? Why is he so scared? He fought before. He fought Boi. And even though he lost, he feels he held his own. He hit Boi and bled him. But was Boi holding back? Was Boi toying with him? He will lift weights when he gets back home. He will take Brazilian jujitsu. He will lift and grapple and lift until he gets so big that no one will even think about messing with him. He will shave his head. He will grow facial hair. He will wear tank tops so no one mistakes his muscles for fatness. He has to piss big time.

Shane unlocks the door and peeks out. The two guys are gone. No one saw. No need to be shame, he tells himself, but it rings empty. Shane closes his eyes and takes a breath. He sneaks toward the stairs and peeks around the corner. The guys aren't there. They probably went back up top.

It's here, for an instant, Shane wishes they were here. The two of them, climbing the stairs, laughing with arms around each other's shoulders. He'd kill them. He wants to kill them. He has to piss bad. Shane walks downstairs to look for a bathroom as the boat rocks over a large swell.

Feeling queasy, he steadies himself as he swings a door open to a lower deck. The sound of cheers fades the lower and lower he gets. The cheers for Charles. Charles for governor. Charles the famous. Charles who has a son who can't even stand up to a couple of chronics and save a girl, a kid with no sand, no heart.

He finally finds a restroom and rushes inside.

The two men, limp dicks hanging over the same toilet, have their backs to him. Shane freezes. The two men laugh with each other. They have a good story to tell their friends when they're back on dry land. How they bullied the soon-to-be gov's son, how just as they thought, all rich kids are pussies. Full of shit, no guts. Shane takes a deep breath. They don't hear him. He clears his throat and they don't hear that either. To them, he's nothing. To them, even if Shane wasn't adopted by the Knottings and left in that bus in Wahiawa with his tweaker mom, he'd still be a muff, still be all show, no go.

The boat hits another swell, pushing Shane toward the two men. Momentum rocks him forward. Locked onto the back of the skinny one's neck, he jumps and throws a superman punch. But he closes his eyes at the last second. He misses the neck, and hits the guy right above the shoulder blade.

The man lifts an arm and bends his elbow, hand thrashing at his back like he's got an unbearable out-of-reach itch. He falls to his knees, squealing.

There's a corkscrew now buried in his shoulder.

"What the fuck you did?!" the fat one screams over and over again. He's on his hands and knees flinching every time he touches the corkscrew as he pulls it from his shoulder. The skinny one yelps and falls back into the fat one's arms. The fat one cradles him. He's tearing up. For the first time, Shane notices how truly out of shape the couple are. Zero muscle tone, not much muscle for that matter. And they're kind of old, too. Neither could lift two-hundred pounds nor run a mile. It occurs to Shane that just because someone is brown and poor, it doesn't make him tough. These guys are the ones who are all show, no go. The pussies.

Shane feels hard now. He wishes the girl were here so he could get a second chance at rescuing her. He'd do it this time. He also wishes Charles and Boi were watching him now. He steps forward to hit the skinny one again. The fat one helps the skinny one up and barricades himself between Shane and his friend. "Enough already!"

"Help!" screams the skinny one.

"What?" he asks.

"Help! Security!"

Shane takes a step back. The skinny one screams again. The fat one starts screaming for security, too. The only thing Shane can think of doing is run. He bursts through the doors at the end of the hall as his head swivels back and forth, looking for some kind of escape. He needs to get to Charles. He needs to explain. As he heads for the upper deck, the plucking of guitar, ukulele, and stand-up bass gets louder and louder. When he reaches the last set of stairs, he sees the pin-up girl at the top of the stairwell. She's talking to a man with a thick neck and gelled salt-and-pepper hair. She stomps her feet, points to the bowels of the boat, and bursts into tears. The man turns, sticks two fingers in his mouth, and whistles. The back of his blue windbreaker reads "security" in yellow letters. Shane's as brown as those guys. But he didn't stand up for her. He shrugged. Now she thinks he's one of them. Shane turns around and head back down.

Shane starts to run, trips and spills, breaking his fall with his hands. A sharp pain in both wrists instantly forgotten. He reaches up for a wall-mounted ring buoys and pulls himself up. Runs faster. He bursts through a stairwell door and hurries down as far as the stairs will take him. He pops out into the lowest deck. No portholes or windows. He feels cornered.

There's only one door. The engine room. Keep out, the signs says. What is he doing? Maybe he doesn't have to run. His mom and dad will understand. He was just trying to be a man.

Shane turns, thinking about grabbing one of those ring buoys and launching himself overboard. Maybe he can swim back to Kona. Pretend he never got aboard the ship. Regardless, he needs to get big. He needs to get so big that pussies like those two guys never even think of messing with him. He blames his thinness, his big eyes, his lean face, his clear skin, and his shaggy hair—a lack of intimidating features—for all his present problems.

Just as he's about to go back up the stairs, he hears something from behind the engine room door. Someone's swearing. He pauses. He *knows* those curses.

A sound of steady pings gets louder and louder over the sound of spinning metal as Shane gets closer to the door. Shane opens it.

The entire room is wall-to-wall steel with control panels, box-shaped machines that hum, and pipes bending from a giant, screeching cylinder that must be the engine. *Ping!* Shane sneaks around a metal tower with lit buttons. Two blue torpedo-shaped tanks mounted to the walls probably hold some kind of compressed gas.

Whang! And a shirtless Boi covered in sweat chops away at them with a fireman's axe, the handle wrapped with a tee shirt.

Boi kicks off his slippers, inhales deeply, and swings. The ring hurts Shane's ears. The axe doesn't even put a scratch on blue tubes.

Boi holds up his arms like a prophet. "Help me you fuckas!" He shouts it three more times over the shrieking engine before he turns around. He looks at Shane, then the axe head, then back at Shane. Shane holds his hands out and steps back. Boi looks back at the tanks. "I can't sink it," Boi says. "I can't figure it out. I can't sink it."

Boi swings at the cylinder one more time with so much force he knocks the axe head off. It clanks off the steel grate floor. Shane laughs. He laughs so hard, he cries. A panting Boi tosses the axe handle and sits next to Shane. "I rushed," says Boi, panting. "I didn't think enough. I can't sink it. I need help. I can't fucking sink it."

Shane thinks of the skinny man in the bathroom, blood oozing from his shoulder. He thinks of the pin-up girl and imagines being lumped together with the other two to face attempted rape charges even though he didn't lay a hand on her. He looks down at his clean hands then glances at Boi's—callused, oil-stained, palms covered with blisters. He'd kill to have those hands. Those thick-knuckled, flat-fingernailed, vise-grip hands that everyone takes seriously. If he had hands like that, he could've told those two guys to fuck off, and they would have listened. If he had hands like that, he could've told those two guys to lay off the girl, and they would have obeyed. But maybe hands aren't enough. Shane needs a neckless mountain body to match. He needs arms as big as those two blue tubes Boi was chopping away at. Shane turns to Boi. He reaches out to touch him then changes his mind.

"I can't sink it," Boi says again.

Shane rubs his wrists and looks around the metal box, thinking he better get used to being locked up in one of these. The boat rocks over another swell, a ten ton, one-story roll of water that may or may not become a wave.

Don't worry," Shane says. "I think I just did."

PART TWO: SIX YEARS LATER

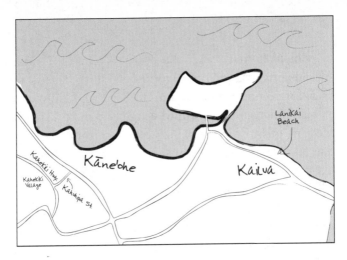

I. Kry-lua

1. _____

First Watch. Still-dark morning. The crumbs are everywhere. It's September, Kona weather, and homeless mutter to themselves while they push bum-wheeled shopping carts to their beach tents. Yellow-fingered chronics behind steel barred windows pass around lab flasks souped-up to smoke meth. Pyro bums hide behind dumpsters, ready to set today's trash on fire. It's District 4, Sector 2. Kailua. Or as the cops call it, Kry-lua. A now twenty-three-year-old Boi doesn't know who he hates more: the crumbs or the haoles who call 911 every time they catch a whiff of dog shit from the neighbor's yard. Kry-lua. Lani-Kry. Hawaii-Kry. All filled with haole crybabies. Most didn't even grow up in Hawaii.

Boi is two years in and doesn't have his own beat. He's not a motorman yet either—the cops who patrol in their privately owned cars, free gas, $600 a month for expenses. He's a swingman in a blue-and-white, a slave to sergeants chasing rank, company men who hunt for DUI's, pull over a drunk driver, then call Boi to do the arrest and paperwork. More DUI's, more court, more overtime. One speeding ticket a night, one DUI a month, and guys like Sergeant Nakasone are set. Lieutenant in no time.

Boi likes first watch the best. 10 p.m. to 7 a.m., O.T. and special-duty friendly, the workhorse shift. There's not enough O.T. for second watch (6 a.m. to 3 p.m.), family watch as they call it. And even though third watch (2 p.m. to 11p.m.) is best for meeting girls, Boi gets to pick Nina up from second grade every day, takes her to ballet, helps her with homework before dropping her off at her mother's. Chastity Fu, forever rotating community college F's and N's with shit pay, part-time work, welfare the only thing preventing her from becoming a crumb herself. He'd like to scream some sense into the bitch, but he'd get ROPA'd (Restriction of Police Authority) and lose his job. He's seen cops get ROPA'd when crazy girlfriends and wives threw around abuse claim lies—and these cops had to give up everything—their houses, their children, half their paychecks just to settle. Being accused of domestic abuse is no joke in the HPD. Immediate suspension without pay. Likely termination unless they bend to their angry women, and the charges didn't even have to be true. When Chastity took Nina in to get matching mother and daughter navel piercings, Boi had to eat it.

Sergeant Nakasone is calling him on the radio. The sun's about to rise, and it's time to dustbust some crumbs at Krylua Beach. When he gets there, Motorman Fukuda, a short, skinny Japanee who likes his toys, his boot knives and tactical grappling hooks, adding to what's already near twenty pounds in gear, is shooting down a bum with pepper spray while Beatman King, a sandbox vet, grips his extendable NB—Nigger Beater—backing Fukuda up. Fukuda's wife just filed for divorce. The crumb must have tested him. Nothing the magic typewriter can't fix.

Boi steps out of his car. A woman wearing a wicker sun hat covers her daughter's eyes then leads her to a car. To Boi's right, Na Mokulua, the Twin Islands, barely visible. Sunup Kry-lua kayakers paddle to the islets three-quarters of a mile offshore. Boi turns back to the crumb, who is holding his palms up to his eyes, screaming. King cuffs him. "What he did?" asks Boi.

Fukuda wipes sweat off his veiny forehead as King tosses the crumb in the backseat of his squad car. "Making trouble with the early morning haoles. Says his name is Jakey Perez. You know him?"

Boi takes out his brown notebook and looks through the pages, names of crumbs. No Jakey Perez. Another chronic probably tossed out of his parent's house. Or jail. "Must be new."

"These fuckers," says Fukuda, looking out at the kayakers. "Fuck, I grew up Kailua. No even look the same anymore."

"President coming next month," says Boi.

"Fuck me."

A Presidential Kry-lua vacation meant Secret Service, undercover, SWAT, concrete squad car barricades with check stops, cops putting seven miles on their odometers, moving their cars ten feet back and forth to let people in and out. "I tell you, Rapun," says Fukuda. "Sometimes I sit in my car fifteen minutes before my shift starts. Just mentally gearing up, you know?"

Swingman Rapun. He is Boi No More. "Fuck!" yells King from his squad car, stepping out, slamming the door.

Boi and Fukuda turn around.

"He took a dump in the car!"

The crumb leans forward, grinning at Boi through the windshield, flat-nosed, raccoon-eyed, toothless, like he got punched in the face daily all his life. Take a shit while cuffed in the back of a squad car—that was the problem with these crumbs, every damn one of them—the purse snatchers, the woman beaters, the chronics, the home invaders, the cop car defecators—they were pathetic. They didn't know how to be no good. Boi could show them. But not Swingman Rapun. Rapun's a family man. Rapun has responsibilities. Rapun has uncles in the department he can't shame. Rapun knows the Governor.

2.

After his shift, his sweat-soaked bulletproof vest stinking up the passenger side, Boi heads out to Chastity's. Kahekili Village, public housing, two-story walk-ups furnished with broken-down stoves and refrigerators, a laundry room that's been condemned. He passes shirtless boys on bicycles and teens installing car stereos they burged the night before. They stiffen when they see him then act like they're getting ready for school, despite the fact school started over an hour before. Boi pulls up to Malu, a kid so fat he's got stretch marks scribbled across his belly like he recently gave birth to twins. Boi rolls down the window. "You burning again, Malu?"

"No, not me, officer," says Malu. His bulbous flesh stained black at the joints. A spliff rests on his ear.

"Put on a shirt for Christ's sake," says Boi before he pulls away.

They're all on notice. Anything happens to Nina, his daughter, anyone fucks with her, Swingman Rapun will burn this whole motherfucker down.

Broken-down toys and mushy piles of light-brown dogshit front Chastity's ground-floor unit. Boi steps over a three-hundred-dollar rocking bear he'd bought Nina two years ago, its fur spotted with cigarette burns, and knocks on the door. Chastity answers in panty and bra, a towel wrapped around her head. One of those teen moms who easily shrank down to their pre-preggo weight. Chastity leans forward and kisses Boi on the cheek. "You stink like hell," she says.

Welfare queens tend to be pack rats, and Chastity is no different. Piles of discount store clothes sit folded on the couch. Glossy magazines with peeling subscription labels, none addressed to her, spread out on every table. Her new hobby is cooking up Hawaiian salt blends, some with garlic, some with lemongrass, some with rosemary, some with chili pepper, bottling them in glass vials and selling them for a buck-fifty each. She always liked her crafts, which explains the scissors, construction paper, paint brushes, fake flowers, and origami paper crammed in stacked pink and purple plastic cabinet boxes.

Boi sits at the table and samples a guava rock salt blend. "Guess who I seen yesterday at the farmer's market?" says Chastity as she puts on a robe.

"Who?"

"Your brother. Shane."

"At the farmer's market?"

"Yeah. Didn't even recognize him."

It's true. Shane looks nothing like he did in high school. After hitting his second Hawaiian puberty at twenty, he ballooned to three-hundred-pounds. He's all blala'd out now, buzzed hair, goatee, like a dock worker or a musician picking ukulele with sausage fingers at a Waikiki tourist trap. He was nowhere to be seen when Charles Knotting won his second term. "You gonna get big like that, too?" Chastity asks.

"A fat fuck?" says Boi. He can still take that motherfucker.

Chastity picks up a folder from under a pile of magazines. "Shit," she says.

"What?"

"Nina forgot to put her homework in her bag."

That's your job, dummy. "I can take it to the school."

Chastity turns on the TV, pushes a pile of laundry to the side, and plops on the couch. "That'd be good."

California haole aunties with fake tits and too much Bondo spackled on their cracked faces yell at each other on TV. Reality TV, they call it, their voices natural cock softener. "Listen, I got my three days..."

"Take her."

Boi nods and walks to the door. "Hey Boi," says Chastity as he opens the door. "It's good yeah? Good we get along."

"Yeah. It's good."

Boi heads out. He doesn't know how much longer Nina and Chastity will be here. Kahekili Housing is losing its funding while a government-funded dog park, a gift from Charles Knotting to his supporters, is being built in Kry-lua. Boi wishes he and Shane had managed to sink that giant canoe in Kona six years ago. But that shit was the Titanic forreal, and even with a son facing assault with a deadly weapon and attempted rape charges, Charles Knotting, with an ice-cream truck filled with manapua, went ring-a-ding-ding straight to the Governor's mansion and got Shane off all at the same time. Uncle Charles was still The Man. And when he got Boi, a GED Olomana juvie, into HPD, Boi buried Boi No Good for good.

As much as he wanted to believe Joe was right and he was destined to do something massive, that he was the second coming of a squid god, that the gods would help him destroy the world, he grew up. He walked off that campaign catamaran, flew back to Oahu alone, and went to his daughter and cried. He told Nina and Chastity he'd be more of a dad. He told them he'd be more of a man. And a month later, when the Knottings came to him with a deal, a trade that included community college enrollment and a future job at the HPD, he decided that the best thing he could be for his little girl was Swingman Rapun, not some half-ass motherfucker with hard hands, a man with belief in the magic land prophetic, a sad, one-man terror cell.

3.

Walking into a classroom filled with twenty second-graders, it's easy to see who will become branch managers, teachers, longshoremen, teen mothers, hotel employees, government workers, and crumbs. Three boys with mohawks: future elevator repairmen, police, or crumbs. Chubby Japanese twins with perfectly cut school girl hair: suburban housewives, possibly dental assistants. Short kid with gelled hair, already muscular, can't sit still: firefighter probably. Little Filipino girl with cute pigtails? Hotel concierge in the kind of twenty-floor monster that has giant aquariums filled with colorful reef fish for tourists to admire. Boi'd put money on it. Doctors, politicians, major league prospects, and CEO's? They go private school. None of this two-classes-to-a-room-split-with-aluminum bookshelves for them, twenty kids on one side, another twenty on the other. Boi had toiled in classrooms like this one, sketching blueprints for pranks of mass destruction while the teacher's voice crackled like a rickety window-mounted AC unit.

Nina spots Boi and sprints, her arms pumping faster than her platform slippered feet. She hugs him. The teacher, Mrs. Ikeda, a one-time college cheerleader who has epilepsy (she had to send a letter to all the parents, notifying them of her condition) eyes Boi. "Sorry," says Boi. "She forgot her homework."

Mrs. Ikeda nods. "Well, since you're here, can you please tell the children safety tips? How to be good?"

Boi nods as he guides Nina back to her seat. He tells them not to talk to strangers. He tells them not to take things that don't belong to them. He tells them not to put anything in their growing bodies that's unhealthy. He glances at Nina while he lectures, her pierced ears and frosted highlights. Teen mom. God help him.

"Hi uncle," says the little Filipino future concierge. "Hope you're having a good day. Will you send us to jail if we don't listen?"

"Pfft," says one of the mohawk boys. His name's Camden. Held back one year. Lives with his grandparents. Never gets his homework book stamped with a smiley face. Nina says he eats a beatdown from his grandpa whenever he doesn't get one, which means he's beat every week day. Nina says he can't add ten plus ten and he's on reading level D. "You cannot go jail till you're an adult," says Camden. "So might as well have fun now!"

Crumb. Definitely. Or cop. Boi likes the kid. Reminds him of someone he used to know. Camden asks if he can see Boi's gun. He wants to know if Boi ever killed a man.

Boi glances up at a collage of crayon drawings, trying to spot Nina's. Two stick figures holding hands framed with crooked hearts. One's named Nina. The other one's named Camden. Looks like they're on a date.

4.

Boi's next stop is one he'd been dreading all day. Face time with the Governor's wife. Former Miss Hawaii, Helen Knotting. Three-time Insurance Salesperson of the Year, Helen Knotting.

First Lady of the State of Hawaii, Helen Knotting. Stage Four Metastasis of the Lymph Nodes, Helen Knotting. Helen Knotting, age fifty-six, dying of cancer.

Boi's always dug Mrs. Knotting, but there's only two things she talks about nowadays: death and Shane. The poor woman's laid up in the hospital fighting for her life while Boi's father, a guy who took a three-story dive off the side of a hotel and pummels his body with alcohol and cholesterol, is as healthy as a horse. His farm now repo'd by the bank, Red Roof Joe scrapes lead paint and asbestos off houses built pre-1972 for mainland transplant yuppies. He and Grover Cleveland are living it up in a rental in Waialua while Boi's mom lives with her sister, still dancing hula and contemplating getting her stomach stapled. The woman isn't even two-hundred pounds. A fan of reality TV.

The private, $800-a-night room, with its marble kitchen counter, dining room table, spare queen-sized bed, and ocean view, is bigger and nicer than Boi's studio. Plastic tubes coming out of every orifice, some holes man-made too, Helen Knotting is flipping through pictures loaded on a touchscreen tablet. Skinny, yellow, gray roots sprouting under dyed brown hair. She looks, finally, like the woman in all those pictures hanging at the Knotting house. She looks like her mother. Helen's the kind of sick that won't get better.

Helen's not really being all samurai about it either—she doesn't whine or cry or anything like that, but she'll go on and on about getting snuffed out permanent, the pure terror of it all, in a calm way, as if she's trying to empty a crowded movie theater in flames with whispers. And she won't let up. It's all she wants to talk about, maybe thinking if she Portagee-mouths about it enough, even death will get tired of listening and go away. She never watches the sixty-inch flatscreen mounted on the wall. She's the only person who Boi has visited in a hospital who never turns on the tube.

Boi pulls up a chair, the rubber-pegged legs squeaking against mock-bamboo laminate. He'd rarely seen Mrs. Knotting without make-up before her illness, but he sees her naked face all the time now, chin forced double because of the way she has to lie in bed, black tattooed brows arched high above her eyes, always looking as if you just said something dumb. Always looking at you a little irritated, maybe because everyone who steps inside, no matter what age, will outlive her.

Mrs. Knotting points at a picture. Boi leans in. She smells funny. Moldy. Boi looks at her eyes. Probably all hopped up on morphine. He turns to the picture.

Like a tightrope walker, keiki Shane's holding a paddle and standing on a board in flat Waikiki waters. Charles, his head poking out of the ocean, is beside him. The board, probably steadied by Charles's hands under the blue surface, floats on foamy surf. "Most of the pictures are of them," says Helen. "Someone had to work the camera."

Boi nods.

Helen struggles to shut down the tablet, gives up, and hands it to Boi. He puts it on the nightstand. "I think I understand pain," she says, grimacing as she shifts her tiny body.

"What you mean?"

"I'm in pain all the time. I want it to go away, so I'm watching that clock like a hawk. The second it's time for my next dose of morphine, I'm pressing the call button like a kid playing a computer game. Then I get doped up and sleepy. Pain. Pain makes it easier to accept death."

Boi nods.

"Don't let them burn me." She tells him this every visit.

"I won't," he says.

"There's no coming back from that."

Boi nods.

Helen frowns at him. "What happened to the talker? What happened to the old Boi?"

"He grew up."

"Keep an eye out for Shane, OK?"

"He coming?"

"Every day."

"I will. Where's The Gov?"

"Still sleeps here every night," she says, hand shaking as she points to the spare queen. "Get my purse."

Boi stands and brings Helen's bag to him. It's a black bag, bumpy, the texture of charred chicken skin. She reaches in and pulls out a folded piece of paper. She thinks for a moment then, hand shaking, slips it to Boi. He unfolds it. An address. "Sorry it took so long for me to give it to you," says Helen. "Once I got sick. Well, you know..."

Boi folds the slip of paper and pockets it. "No problem."

"Will you come back later this week?"

"I will."

"I'd puke if I had the strength," Helen says as she closes her eyes. "All my life, everyone thought I was so smart. 'You're so ahead of everyone else,' they'd tell me. I was never that smart. It's just things that dawn on everyone dawned on me ten years earlier. I knew what college I wanted to go to at ten. I was a vegetarian at fifteen. I bought my first apartment when I was twenty. Went through a midlife crisis at thirty-seven. It's why I adopted Shane. Did I ever tell you that?"

"No."

"Except for having kids, I lived my life on fast-forward. I wonder if that's why I'm here now. Early for the final appointment."

"Hey aunty."

"What?"

Boi feels the slip of paper in his pocket. "Don't be scared. Hundred years from now they gonna dig you up and re-animate you. Gotta show those twenty-second-century bitches what a real Miss Hawaii looks like."

Helen fights to smile. "Now that's my Boi."

Boi winks at her, pulls his hand out of his pocket, and walks out.

Outside the hospital, a line of cars idle on Punchbowl Street. Hard hats boxed in by orange cones jackhammer asphalt. A crumb wobbles down the sidewalk, stops, and bends down in a trash can to fish out lunch. He finds a half-smoked cigarette and lies flat on the sidewalk, holds the butt up to the sun, admiring it in all its bent and black-end glory. Gossiping nurses in pink scrubs walk around the crumb, like they're avoiding broken glass. Boi soaks it all in. Life is for the living. It's just too bad not many people are doing it. Including him.

Boi takes out the slip of paper and studies the address. He thinks he knows where that is. It's in his patrol district. He thought he'd covered all the poor areas, the housing projects, the west side, Waipahu, Kalihi, Wahiawa, and patches of country with Hawaiian names, like Waikane, almost forgotten. And when he became a cop and had access to drivers license status, warrants, priors, vehicle info, NCIC (a list of wanted names locally), and NCGIS (a list of wanted names nationally), he searched her name in the database, looked up just about every variation he could think of, Glorya-Maree Ching Kehau Souza-Rapun, Glorya Rapun, Glorya Souza, Maree Ching, Kehau Souza-Rapun, cursing his tweaker mother for giving her such a long, crazy-ass name, but he didn't find anything. She had no license, no car registered in her name, no record, nothing. He was starting to think she changed her name to Sunshine and moved neighbor island or mainland or something. Maybe hooked up with a cult or a guru, some spiritual snake-oil salesman, but he knew that kind of self-absorption was a luxury only for the rich.

Each time he failed to find her, he wanted to find her more. After years, what started off as a curiosity became a mission, that unfinished thing, like a squid hole thirty feet down that he'd lost because he had to come up for air. No matter how much dirtier the water became, he'd go back down and look for it again and again because he wanted it more and more simply because it became harder and harder to get.

And there she was, Waimanalo all this time.

Two years as a cop, and he couldn't find Glorya-Maree. He wonders how long it took The Gov and Mrs. Knotting.

5.

As a huffing and puffing, three-hundred-pounds-of-muscle Shane Knotting pushes his five-hundred-pound friend up the massage parlor stairs, he wonders how he always manages to get pulled into messes like this. An hour ago, he was picking his car up from the shop when he spotted Don and the quarter-ton Patrick smoking cigarettes outside the strip bar across the street. It was 1:30 p.m. They were waiting for it to open. Shane hadn't seen Don for three years.

"Push harder!" yells Don from three steps up.

"Fuck you man. If you were back here, Patrick would squash you."

When they finally get Patrick to the second floor, Patrick is panting the hardest. "You fuckers are lucky," says Shane, hands on knees. "I'm like Johnny Appleseed."

"What you mean?" asks Don.

Shane pulls two hundred dollars out of his wallet and sticks it in Patrick's shirt pocket. "I just want everyone to be able to get apples."

Don smiles and pats Patrick's shoulder. Don took a $70,000 prep school education and ended up fixing broken fire hydrants for the Board of Water Supply. Shane knows all about wasted education.

After Shane and Don exchange numbers and promise to keep in touch, Shane walks downstairs and grins at Don's pickup, the same hooptie he had in high school. A wire hanger holds up the exhaust pipe. A garbage bag covers the passenger side window. His Korean parents must go all Madame Butterfly every time they see that eyesore.

Shane walks to the driver's side, squats down, and grabs metal. He deadlifts the pick-up. The metal bites his hands. His arms shaking, Shane jerks the driver's side to his neck then pushes with everything he's got. The truck rolls over, metal crunching against pavement. The roof slams ground with a satisfying sound. Shane catches his breath and rubs his hands, thick calluses grating together like two swaths of sandpaper. Maybe Don will get a ticket. Maybe Metermaid Boi will be the one to issue it. Either way, Shane's proud of his little joke. It's something his brother would have done back in the day, before he got all serious about life, responsibility, all that bullshit. Not that skinny Boi could lift a pick-up. Shane could snap Boi in half if he wanted to.

6.

Shane's not much of a curator, so the Knotting museum has gone to hell. Dirty laundry draped over the koa chairs, the piano now a hospice for unwatered potted plants, blueprints for a new paint-gun obstacle course tacked on the walls—Shane's latest get-rich quick scheme. Plus, when Shane brought a pit-bull puppy home, the dog, wearing a tiny spiked collar, went to town. Chairs indented with bite marks, piano legs soft and rotting from puppy piss. After two weeks Shane had to evict the dog. It's now leashed with five feet of chain in the backyard. He named the dog Boi.

Two hours until he has to visit Helen at the hospital. Time to chill. He pushes laundry off the couch, sits, and flips on the news. A breaking story. Some crazy-ass broke into Bishop Museum to steal the royal scepter of King Kalakaua. Some guy named Joe with a Filipino last name claiming to be a descendant of the great king, only he got lost in the museum and couldn't find it. Shane leans forward and smiles. Shit, he knows that guy. Boi must be losing his mind about now.

Shane remembers when *he* was on the news. Governor candidate's son charged with assault with a deadly weapon and attempted rape. Clips from the trial. All the victims' characters questioned. Real Kona punks. Ice dealers. Police records. The pin-up girl posting nude pictures of herself on the Internet. A San Francisco slut in fishnets and polka dots always looking for attention.

Boi had taken the stand, lied, told the jury that they were verbally abused by the punk and his friend earlier that day. Telling the jury that he saw them. The two punks had pushed Shane into the bathroom, wrenched both his wrists, and told Shane they were gonna light him up. "They was going assault him? Guarantee?" the defense attorney, a close family friend who only busted out the pidgin in the presence of a jury, had asked. "Yeah," said Boi. "They was going assault him bad," Boi butchering the word "assault," a kanaka trying to sound smart, like the knuckleheads— UH football this, UH football that—spouting cliches like "no more too much chinks on that defense's armor" or "ho, the braddah is really coming into his own" on local sports-talk radio. "One had knife," Boi had said. "I was scared so I never go inside."

As for the pin-up girl, Boi testified about her, too. Drunk, all over Shane the whole trip. Showing everyone naked pictures of herself on her phone. Boi just sat there straight-faced. And Boi's relationship with Shane and the Knottings was never brought up. No one even imagined someone as country as Boi could be related to Shane. He was an unbiased witness.

Passengers on the catamaran, most Friends of Charles Knotting, also testified that the Kona punks were belligerent onboard, eyeing people up. When the prosecutor asked them if maybe those were their "normal" faces, they all said the same thing. That's the problem. As for the girl, they took Boi's cue and said the same stuff, too. By the time the trial was over, it was as if the girl was stalking Shane and all he was doing was trying to run away. After the trial, the civil suit the girl filed against him went nowhere as well. Charles was elected. Shane got off. He missed college.

Instead of higher education, Shane spent four years taking Brazilian jujitsu, pumping iron, and inking his skin with tattoo sleeves that warped as his face and body ballooned. He invested some trust money in newly renovated downtown pubs, restaurants, and muay thai dojos. He can never become state senator or Governor after getting charged with assault and attempted rape even if he was innocent. But he can do whatever he wants to now.

And when night comes, Shane, all alone in the Knotting museum, passes out and sleeps like a baby.

A few hours later, a knock on the door. Shane rubs his eyes and gets up to answer. He's running late as usual. He opens the door. It's Mark Prince, Mr. Motocross, who turned pro and spends most of his time on the mainland now racing and hocking caffeine and ginseng-charged energy drinks. He's flanked by three hotties and two other guys colorfully dressed like him—skydiving goggles, kilts, and WWI German battle helmets. Shane's seen their movies before, mutilating themselves with taser guns, deliberate road rash, and live snake nipple clamps. The six of them march in, Mark towing a beer keg on a hand truck with painted flames on its black bars. "The girls wanna try acid," says Mark, winking. "You still slinging on the side, right?"

Shane is supposed to visit his mother, but they're all in the living room. The girls, two still in prep school, stare at their hands, giggling. One of Mark's friends, a pro surfer, takes the green turtle shell off the wall and straddles it as Mark's other friend bangs away at the antique piano with his forehead. Shane and Mark are the only ones who passed on the acid and drink beer instead. "Saw Don today," says Shane.

"Yobo Rastaman," says Mark, grinning at the frying girls. "What's he up to?"

"You know," says Shane. "You're the only guy from high school that turned out how I thought he would. Well, you and Do-Gi-Ho-Shar."

"Oh yeah? What's Do-Gi up to?"

"NASA. Trying to think up shit that astronauts will do once they get to Mars. They gotta wait like two years on that rock before flying back. Planets gotta align, all that shit."

Mark nods. "What's Mosi doing? Sad what happened to his knee."

Shane nods. "Cleaning grease traps at elementary school cafeterias with his old man."

"Public or private?"

"Does it matter?" Shane asks.

"This is Hawaii. It always matters."

"Stopped by the club today," says Mark. "Heard about your mom."

Shane clears his throat and nods. He leans over the coffee table and picks up a sheet of blotter paper, tiny pictures of the President lined up and squared off like a book of stamps, except the Prez is shirtless and feathered, like an African medicine man. Shane pulls off two blotters and sticks both under his tongue for quick effect. Mark grins and does the same.

"It's like Kierkegaard wrote," Mark says as his friend dry-humps the green turtle shell. "Fuck it."

Shane closes his eyes. He's already flying. The guy head-butting the piano seems to be playing Chopin. One of the girls inches her way to Shane, climbs on his lap, and curls up like a house cat. She feels small but dense. Maybe he can shot put her through a wall. That's the thing now, he spots a tiny, pretty girl, and the first thought that pops into his head is: I wonder how far I can throw this bitch?

"I'm mountain climbing," another girl says.

"I always wanted to ask you," Mark says.

"What?"

"What it'd feel like?" Mark asks, a blond now sitting on Shane's shoulders.

"Like I just grew roots and am connected to something big."

"No, dumbass. What'd it feel like?!"

"What?"

Mark grins. "Getting charged with all that shit six years ago and coming out clean."

Shane shrugs, his eyelids open and close, like they're chewing on his pupils. "Felt inevitable."

Mark laughs. "You need help."

Shane shrugs. That's what it felt like.

A knock on the door. Shane opens his eyes. He stands, the blond still riding his shoulders, smacks the side of his head.

"Giddy up," she says. Shane walks to the door and opens it. It's police. "We got a call," says a cop, short and round at the middle like a garden gnome. That's how Shane imagines him now, high as he is. White-bearded wearing a big-buckled leather belt and pointy red hat. Shane swears he sees fireworks up in the sky.

The cop looks up and frowns at the girl sitting on Shane's shoulders. "Noise complaint."

Shane looks around, his hands out. "I don't hear anything."

The girl laughs and covers Shane's ears. The cop asks, "You don't hear all that banging on the piano?"

Shane turns around. One guy is slamming his head on the piano so hard, his forehead's bleeding. The other guy is naked, fucking the turtle shell. Mark is making out with two girls at the same time.

"I gotta make some changes," says Shane to the jaw-dropped cop who's now standing next to him.

Shane lifts the girl off his shoulders and drops her on the ground, head first. The cop starts talking in his radio.

"You know a cop named Boi Rapun?" asks Shane.

The cop, checking if the girl on the floor is alright, shakes his head. Shane picks her up. She's so light. He throws her. She bounces off the wall like a plastic-tipped dart. Shane turns to the cop.

"But you know the Governor, Governor Knotting, right?"

The girl bursts with laughter, stands, then bows. The cop takes out his cuffs, and signals Shane to spin around. Shane obeys as his friends finally notice the cop and freeze. It's a funky still-life, one guy sitting at a piano with blood all over the white keys. Another guy naked on all fours, his stomach sagging on a turtle shell. Two girls and a guy, limbs tangled together. "I wanna paint you guys," says Shane as other cops march in the house.

"Don't ruin it! I wanna paint you guys!"

The cop shoves Shane outside. Shane trips over a loose brick and screams, "I wanna paint you guys!"

The cop grabs Shane by the back of the neck and pins him to the trunk of the squad car. "Call my brother!" says Shane. "He's a cop! Call my brother!"

The cop ignores him. Shane stands, his body feeling heavy. The cop on his back goes for a choke hold. Shane kicks a fender. He slams a shoulder through squad car glass. What feels better? Dropping something heavy or sticking a body part through something hard? More cops are on him now. He doesn't know how many. "Call my brother!" he screams as he falls to one knee, his shouts drowned under a pile of blue gnome bodies.

"I gotta visit my Mom! Do you know who I am?!"

7. _____

Boi rents a room in a Chinese lady's basement where her jeweler father used to plow through three packs of cigarettes a day while polishing gold with a two-wheeled, 2800 RPM buffing machine. The Chinese lady told Boi that he had his own furnace out back and melted down and purified junk jewelry he'd buy and turn them into wonderful rings, charms, and bracelets. The buffing machine still sits on the table along with a wax pump and rubber molds engraved with Japanese family mon and the Hawaiian state crest. The concrete floors slope down from all four walls and meet in the middle where there's a drain in case of flooding. If the Knottings saw where he lived, he knows they would rescue him from this place. But he doesn't want to take more from them. He doesn't want to have to give more back.

Boi's king-sized bed takes up most of the space in the room. Whenever Nina sleeps over, they play the same game. She cuddles next to him, he gets hot, moves to the cool corner, and sooner or later, she's snuggling up to him again. By the time eight hours pass, Boi's moved four times and imagines that this is what it must be like to watch a starfish chase underwater. He loves the hell out of this little girl, who, as he looks around before moving to another corner, has stuck yet another princess sticker on the microwave door, but her body is a little forty-five pound heater. And he lives in a basement in Hawaii. With no air-conditioning, it's insect weather down here. About a week after moving in, Boi had cracked open the drain in the middle of the room. He found a centipede nest and sprayed the drain with so much insecticide that the eggs bubbled and melted, and the centipedes turned yellow. Boi will still find a new centipede corpse from time to time, frozen, coiled, and golden as if they too were made into jewelry. But he knows it's from the poison he sprayed in the hole in the floor two years ago.

A day after his visit with Mrs. Knotting, Boi gets the middle-of-the-night call. Joe's been arrested for attempting to burg Bishop Museum. Boi's got Nina and Chastity is out with her friends listening to Island Souljahs or one of a dozen Jah-waiian bands that fill their songs with two-chord ukulele reggae beats and rap solos with titles like "Cool Water," "Breezie," and "Pacific Dreams." Boi can never escape the feeling that they're singing about colognes. Now he has to wake Nina up and drag her to town central booking with him. Unlike his rented room, it's cold in there, so he grabs her leopard print jacket for her.

On the way to the station, he gets another call. This one from The Gov. He sounds tired. Shane's been arrested. Again. He wants Boi to talk to the patrolmen who were on the scene, give them reason to bust out the magic typewriter. Again. He wants Boi to take care of that first, before he gets Joe out of the clink. "They're both at the same place," says Boi, but the Gov already hung up. Boi tosses his phone on the passenger seat. "Never take manapua from The Gov," Boi tells Nina, who's wide awake in the back on a pink booster.

"I don't like manapua, Daddy. My BFF says they use cat meat. It's gross."

"Good girl."

It hadn't taken much research to find Boi's price to get him to lie on the stand at Shane's trial. Shane knew what he'd wanted. So

Charles and Helen pitched their six-year plan to Boi in a board-room furnished with a koa table so big that if Boi stuck a sail on it, he could probably sail around the world.

First, in exchange for Boi's testimony, they'd pay to send him to community college for an administration of justice degree. They'd give him a stipend, too, so he wouldn't have to work and go to school. Then, they'd get him into the Honolulu Police Department so that within the six years, he could get custody of Nina—since her whore mother would probably screw up several times in the same six-year period. Then, once Boi got custody, they'd get Nina into a fancy private school. They'd pay. How could he say no? If she didn't go, she'd probably become a housing-project chronic at twelve. It's what the Knottings suggested anyway, and Boi, who grew up with some twelve-year-old chronics, believed them.

There was talk of getting Boi private club memberships, of finding Glorya-Maree. But they owned Boi for six. He needed to do what *they* wanted, and he'd see how much *better* his life would be.

Boi knows they could've done all this for him faster, but probably wanted to keep him on the hook as long as possible for times like this. But in that boardroom, with that giant table sitting between Boi and the Knottings (all these rich haoles loved their koa), Boi couldn't even bring himself to negotiate. It felt more like a sentencing than a business meeting, which was what the Knottings called it. With Charles sitting there, his sleeves rolled up and Helen telling him every thirty seconds that he looked thirsty and asking if she could get him some water, Boi imagined himself an octopus hooked to four-hundred-pound test fishing line. He could fight, but he'd just get pulled in the boat eventually. He was tired of all this shit. Let them drag him right up to the boat, yank him onboard, rip him inside-out, and put him on ice. But right before they gaffed him through the gills and heaved him over the transom, he had just one last-second request: pay for Nina's medical and dental. Get her the best dentist in the state. They agreed.

It was surprisingly easy for Boi to lie under oath, and the location had a lot to do with it. The courtroom, with its U.S. and State of Hawaii flags, its polished wood walls, its distinguished old man in a black robe holding a hammer, its overall prettiness, even though ugly shit went down there daily, it felt like a place built for lying. Plus, Boi had been in a room like this as a teen, and he'd told the truth that time and got thrown in the boys' home for it. Spinning bullshit here this time around was no problem. Everyone else was lying. The skinny Kona chronic in the neck brace talking nerve damage. His fat friend talking how scared they were of Shane, how it was his idea to bring the girl to the lower deck and get her high. The haole girl with the long-sleeve shirt to hide her tattoos, her hair in a bun, going full-on librarian mode, she wasn't even accusing those two guys of doing anything; she'd said Shane was the only one who threatened her. She was going after the money. Everyone knew she was going civil suit afterwards. Going after Shane.

The victims, the lawyers, the witnesses, the experts—they were all lying. So Boi lied, too. And the only thing that bothered him about the whole trial was that no one believed those two Kona chronics; the jury looked like they were waiting at a dentist's office whenever those parts of the case were argued, but when it came to the attempted rape charges, the attempted rape of a white girl, the jury perked up and glared at Shane. And here's the part that no one knew: Helen had been rubbing Korean cosmetics all over Shane's face for weeks pretrial. Trying to whiten him up. That shit bothered Boi as the brownest guy in the room, but now, the six years are coming to an end, soon no more court dates, no more bailouts, no more Knottings, and as Boi drives to get Shane out of jail, Boi can't wait to be free.

"Daddy," says Nina from the backseat, "my tooth fell out."

Boi glances in the rear view mirror. Nina shows him a bloody tooth. He reaches back and takes it. "How much is the Tooth Fairy gonna give me?" she asks.

Boi inspects the tooth. Unlike his teeth as a kid, white like a chip of sun-bleached coral. "Since you brush twice a day like the dentist told you, anything you want, baby."

"I want a door on my head so I can open it and look at my brain."

"Your Uncle Shane had a door like that. But he when opened it, all his brains spilled out."

Boi rolls down the window and spits. He looks again at the tooth then pockets it. He's going to be free. But what the hell is he going to do with his freedom different from what he's doing now? Is his life *better* than it would have been without the Knottings? That doesn't matter. The main thing is Nina's will be. Boi slaloms past Honolulu pot holes dug by tropical rain. It always rains in Hawaii. "Those fucking Knottings," says Boi, rolling up the window.

"What Daddy?"

"They bought me for life."

"Silly Daddy," says Nina. "You can't buy people."

8.

Fourth-floor whores. That's the way Boi sees it anyway. The top floor of the main station houses the politicos, the brass, the careermen: the chief, the assistant chiefs, the head majors for each district. He's only been up there a few times—once on a recruit class field trip, and a couple of times to deliver district reports—slipping sealed envelopes under the giant, bronze-knobbed double doors in the middle of the night. Rumor has it that the conference room up there is packed with fifty-inch TV's. A crisis center, they call it. Post 9-11. Five hundred grand. It's where the brass watch college football on Thursdays.

But Boi is not headed up there. He's parking in the sub-floor, central booking, where they keep the prisoners. "The Bodies," the cops call them. He remembers his rookie year, Waikiki, typical noob, trying to be the guy who keeps his beat safe, following rules and regulations, doing things The Academy Way. Main station is where he'd process the cruisers, the drunk military, and the pick-pocketing and purse-snatching surf rats. He prowled for crumbs back then, a new sheriff who wanted to clean up Waikiki. Some senior guys laughed at him. Some, not laughing, would pull him on the side. "Don't make us work harder!" they'd say.

It was during that first year that he learned three cardinal rules of Honolulu law enforcement: One, don't rat. Two, the magic typewriter is your friend. And three, don't sign up for special duty at UH football games. It takes the state six months to pay you.

But hard-headed Boi, he stuck to The Academy Way for a year, until one night, breaking up a fight at a back-alley gay karaoke bar, he got falsed by a long-armed, shirtless gay dude built like a 3-4 pass-rushing linebacker. Other cops stormed in. The mahu was dropping them like bowling pins, screaming with a pronounced lisp, "I take all you fakas!" It was the closest Boi had ever been to being knocked out.

But Boi got up and took a breath. He wasn't going to snap. Never again. Instead, he put the now toppled mahu in a knee bar, fighting the urge to break his leg. Two other cops scrambled forward and showered him with pepper spray. The Academy Way taught, after spraying someone, you had to make sure to rinse the perp's face with water. Two red-faced cops rinsed his face with more pepper spray instead.

By the time they got the sobbing linebacker into the squad car, his face lacerated with pepper burns, he was babbling something about getting dumped by his boyfriend. One of the senior men had a bloody nose and the other a lump on his forehead. "Want me to get him water now?" Boi asked.

"Fuck that fucker," the one with the lump said.

"We ain't saints," said the other one wiping blood off his upper lip. "Not for this paycheck."

According to the police report that Boi wrote later, the cops on the scene thoroughly rinsed the suspect's eyes with water. The two senior guys watched over his shoulder as Boi wrote it. It was the first time Boi used the magic typewriter. Like other firsts, like fighting or fucking, after throwing the first crack or pulling the panties off the legs of that first girl, it was easier to not feel dirty and to do again after that.

When Boi and Nina walk into central booking, they're greeted by Major Craig Kaulana, who Boi has not seen since academy days. Kaulana, a short, bald, doughy man with jacked-up Japanese tourist teeth, has thirty years in, and for the last two has been stuck in the sub-floor processing bodies. He'd headed up Community Affairs before that, another shit detail that involved giving speeches at schools, "No Hope in Dope," and going to neighborhood board meetings to field Hawaii-Kry complaints. One permit-less dumpster. A commercial vehicle parked on the street for more than four hours. Speeders going ten m.p.h. over the limit on Kalanianaole Highway.

"Whoa, Rapun!" says Kaulana. He spits a brown glob in a cone-shaped water cooler cup. Tiny specks of chewing tobacco stick to his crooked teeth. The major smiles at Nina and squats. He takes a mini candy bar out of his pocket. "Here you go, princess," he says.

Kaulana grimaces as he stands. Bad knees.

Despite the fact that he's the most experienced major in the department and the rank-and-file love him, Kaulana's never made the short list for chief. He and his public defender wife run a school to prep recruits for the HPD entrance exam. The brass hate it. The mayor hates it. The Gov hates it. Hard to slip all your calabash nephews into the department when other recruits are scoring high on the test. Despite his pull—Patricia's cop cousins and especially The Gov—Boi had to take the class. Charles hated that he had to take it more than Boi did. Boi was more weirded out—by meeting the Kaulanas who wanted to help him and expected nothing in return. The lumpy husband and his foxy ehu Hawaiian wife were pretty much the nicest people Boi had ever met. "So who you bailing out?" asks Kaulana.

Boi sighs. Kaulana shakes his head. "The Gov's son? Again?" Boi nods. "And the other one. The Bishop Museum guy. That's my... I know him, too."

"The fourth floor knows about it?"

Boi shrugs.

Kaulana nods and spits in his cup. He isn't going to pry. That's not Kaulana's style.

Boi posts bail for both Shane and Joe. No check or credit card. Exact change only.

Boi and Nina wait by the car. She's got her arms around his thigh. She looks up and smiles. "I love you, daddy," she says.

"I love you, too."

She tells him she loves him more. She tells him she loves him Graham's number, a number her school janitor said was the biggest in the world. This little girl, she keeps him sane.

Shane struts out of the police station looking like a guy from Local 665 walking out of a resort after a long day of toting movie-star luggage. His arm is around a third-watch patrolman who just ended her shift. He's whispering in her ear. She laughs. Nina charges her uncle, who scoops her up. Nina's telling him about some girl in her class who called her crayon drawings ugly and teased her because she runs the slowest in the class. Hard to run fast wearing platforms to school every day. As Shane approaches Boi, he carefully places the little girl on pavement. "You hear this shit?" Shane asks.

"What? About the bully girl?"

"Yeah," says Shane. "Who's her dad?"

"Fuck if I know. Why?"

"We should light that fucker up."

Boi looks over Shane's giant shoulder, wondering what the hold-up is with his dad.

9. _____

It's all politics, Joe Bolosan used to say, so often, Boi was sick of hearing it. But what he hates more, what Boi hates more than just about anything in the world is the word "auwe." It's a Hawaiian word, an expression of lament, that's used like, "Someone broke into my car. Auwe," or "Housing prices are so high. Auwe." An overused, wannabe-Hawaiian blogger word that even appears on tee shirts. Worse than "Ai-no-kea" (I-no-care). At least that ignorant shit is made up and not a real word. "The entire system is... auwe," Joe always says. Every time someone says it, including his father, Boi wants to punch that asshole through the skull.

"Politicians stuck between a choice of pitching bills that cost nothing and do even less, or voting for bills that cost a lot and never do as much as they're supposed to. Auwe."

Don't punch him.

"A few years of that, and it's not even about doing good any-more—getting names on street signs or the sides of buildings—that's the game. Just make sure that some tourist has to say your name when asking for directions a hundred years from now. Run out of streets and buildings? Construct more. Auwe."

Don't... Punch... His... Face.

Joe was right, though: even this building, the main station, pretty new, had bare walls begging for the bronzed name of a recently dead head of state. Maybe twenty years from now it'd be called the Charles Knotting Main Station even though the closest Charles got to law enforcement was probably handcuffing some rich haole co-ed in his fancy mainland college dorm room before munching on her bushy, seventies rug. Guys like Knotting, they were a hundred times worse than the Kry-lua trust-funders with vanity plates that Boi liked to pull over just for fun.

Red Roof Joe didn't know the half of it. Boi saw more as a cop. Like the public's outcry on drugs. The ice epidemic. They couldn't piece together how ice came in? Can't drive across some border to get to Hawaii. There's only the docks. Packaged crystal meth sitting side-by-side with bananas and pineapple that ripened in transit. The money later washed in illegal gambling and development projects. It wasn't rocket physics. Right before Boi went into the academy, he asked a cop uncle messed up by vertigo and panic attacks if he was doing the right thing by becoming HPD. His uncle told him he should be a stevedore instead.

The import of drugs was federal jurisdiction. Agents from places like Maine or Minnesota who'd never been to Hawaii before were called to do two-year tours in the islands. Once they almost figured it out, almost found a source, they were re-assigned and shipped out for the next group of noobies. The couple of times that the Feds did catch a shipment? Dog luck.

Boi made the mistake of telling Joe all this last week in Waialua. Joe was bitching and moaning about all the kanaka maoli (he never called Hawaiians Hawaiians anymore) hooked on batu while sharing a cold pack with Grover Cleveland. "Shit," Boi said. "You don't know how it comes in? We no more border. It comes from the boats. And who you think works the docks?"

Joe took it bad. He cut Grover Cleveland off and went inside to mass Facebook message his sovereignty buddies.

Now he'd tried to steal the royal scepter of King Kalakaua. What the fuck was Joe thinking? That possession of a two-foot gold rod, the Ensign of Kingly Power entwined with a red velvet middle, was a magic wand that would make all the bad guys disappear? That's how Joe was, though. Full of prophecy. Full of soothsaying. Full of stories about gods like Kanaloa who taught people magic. Still telling Boi the gods would arm him with fiery holy fury in his right hand and typhoon thunderbolts in his left. Still full of shit. Auwe. King Kalakaua's scepter? Boi No Good could do much, much better than that.

While they wait for Joe to be processed, Shane sits in the back with Nina. She's telling Shane how she's disappointed in him for getting arrested again. Shane claims innocence. Always innocent, that guy. "Your mom gave me an address," says Boi.

"I heard," says Shane, now grim.

"I'm going tomorrow."

"Where?" asks Nina.

Shane tickles Nina. "Why you want to find her so bad?"

"Our sister? Family."

"Who, Daddy?" asks Nina.

"Is that supposed to be some kind of explanation?" asks Shane.

"It's the only explanation I got," says Boi. "Maybe she isn't a fuck-up like you. Sorry, Nina."

"It's okay Daddy. He is kind of a fuck up, isn't he."

Shane leans up to the front seat. "You realize she's the one who stayed with the crackhead."

"In Waimanalo?"

Shane leans back and shrugs. "Maybe her homestead finally came in after waiting a couple hundred years."

Hawaiian homestead. Land parcels for Native Hawaiians. One-dollar rent a year. Ninety-nine-year lease. Decades-long wait lists. Boi wouldn't apply even if he qualified. He'd probably be eighty when his turn came up.

"Need fifty-percent Hawaiian blood for that."

"Still got Hawaiians with fifty-percent blood?"

"Is Mom still alive?"

"No idea," says Shane.

"You're a fat fuck, you know that?"

Nina, sucking on her thumb, passes out. Shane kisses her forehead then leans up to Boi's ear. "I don't know where the fuck she is, and I don't give a shit. And you call me 'fat fuck' again, I'll rip your fucking spine out of your fucking throat."

The steering wheel of the parked car shakes even though they're still parked and waiting for Joe. It's not the usual Honolulu slalom course of potholes causing the vibrations, it's Boi's hands.

A barefoot Joe Bolosan walks out of the station screaming something about lawsuits, his threats echoing off thick under-ground concrete walls. Boi and Shane step out of the car. Joe's older now, but doesn't look it. He's bald, even his eyebrows sparse, but his brown, now-tattooed skin is still taut. Joe takes off his shirt like he's about to beef the whole building. He doesn't wear shirts too often anymore.

"Three Hawaiians standing outside a police station at two in the morning, a little welfare girl sleeping in the back seat," says

Shane. "One cop. Two perps, one shoeless and shirtless. Welcome to Hawaii."

Boi ignores him and opens the back door for Joe. "I need one new computer," says Joe. "Fuckers probably went hack mine before it broke. How else they caught me?"

Boi shakes his head. "I told you, get a phone. Same thing."

"Fuck that. They can tap that shit."

Shane holds in a laugh. Just as Boi is about to explain, a flash. More flashes and clicking.

Someone is hiding behind the bushes snapping away with a camera. Ronnie Bijarani, the last real newsman for the *Island Voice*, a free weekly whose one-time political reporting has dwindled to puff pieces on Hawaii's art, music, and nightlife scene—Shakespeare in pidgin, yoga studio reviews, foodie write-ups on Kry-lua joints that require diners to eat their food blindfolded, and blurbs on street artists with names like Coolie-Z, Mystik Guerilla, and Kanaka Prime. Only Bijarani keeps the political stuff alive, a guy from half way around the globe, who after spending a year in Hawaii figured he knew everything that was wrong with the place, bailed out the *Voice* with family money, and started writing about the problems as he saw them. He is, of course, one of Charles Knotting's sworn enemies, which is how Boi recognizes him.

Shane lumbers after Bijarani, but the reporter is gone. Shane gives up the chase and walks back, breathing hard, his hands on his hips.

"Who was that?" asks Joe.

Boi slams the door. "Another haole trying to save the world."

10.

It's a pokane night—black, no moon or stars—the kind of night where the spirits roam. After dropping off Shane, Boi is driving Joe out to Waialua, Nina still passed out in back, Joe sitting next to her. They pass the Mililani suburbs and drive through Wahiawa, one of the last old plantation towns on Oahu—liquor stores, gas stations, fast food restaurants, hole-in-the-wall strip joints, pawn shops, used car dealerships, a laundromat, and even a Southern BBQ rib joint. Most of the businesses now cater to the local chronics and the mainland grunts stationed at nearby Schofield Barracks. They pass one of the strip joints, an old-school titty bar with a red velvet drape hanging over the entrance. Boi wonders: did his mom once work there? His sister? Hell, maybe Nina, married to a junkie jarhead drunk with a retro V8, twelve years from now. He hopes not. "What kind of girls get at these clubs?" asks Boi.

"I seen um," says Joe.

"Oh yeah?"

"Mostly haoles and popolos. But get one local one I like. I call her Beef Curtains."

Please God, don't let Nina to grow up and become Beef Curtains.

Boi and Joe stop at Seven-Eleven to get gas. Mug shots of crumbs taped to the window. Boi scans the pictures as usual. No Glorya-Maree, if he could even recognize her by now. They drive on, cross a bridge, and roll toward Whitmore Village, sixty-year-old houses roofed with rusty corrugated sheet metal. It's where Boi spent the first years of his life with his brother, sister, mother, and grandmother, on the bus parked on the red-dirt lot. He'd gone back when he was in high school, before he got sent to the boys' home. The bus was gone.

He'll find his sister tomorrow. The sun will come up tomorrow. It's like that song Nina's ballet crew performed on Ala Moana Center Stage. He revs past two skinny crumbs holding will-work-for-food signs but about to throw curb-turf blows. Toothless, long-haired, white-bearded men. Kahunas once upon a time. Two poi dogs wearing cheap sunglasses fuck at their feet.

Between Wahiawa and Waialua sits acres and acres of fallow, red-dirt farmland sprouting blond, dried-out weeds. Telephone poles line Kaukonahua Road, one of the most dangerous roads on the island, especially on a black night like this. Boi glances into the rear view mirror. A sleeping Nina is leaning against the door, little hands in the booster-seat cup holder. "Pull her up," says Boi.

"What? She's fine."

"I don't like her leaning on the door like that."

Joe sighs and props her up as they bounce over an old railroad track and wind down to Waialua, whizzing by "Do Not Pass" signs sprayed with blue graffiti. "You talk to your mother?" Joe asks.

"No, but she probably seen it on the news."

"That's not why I was asking. She family. Family is everything."

Boi'd heard this before. It's almost a state motto, repeated by guys up top like Charles Knotting down to the chronic who beats her kids with a clean sock stuffed with a bar of soap. Boi hasn't talked to Patricia in ages. Besides dropping off a ham every Christmas Eve and occasional babysitting for Nina, he hardly sees her at all. When he does, she asks about the Knottings. She was happy when he took the Knotting deal. She was happy he became a cop like her cousins. She wants the best for him, she said. "Stay away from this side of the island," she'd told him. "Long time ago, I wanted to move town, and my life would've turned out different if I did."

"So what the fuck were you thinking?" Boi asks Joe. "You steal the scepter, you become king of Hawaii or something?"

"Someone gotta do something. This nation is going to shit. Think about the world your kid is gonna grow up in. Somebody gotta make noise."

Boi knows what he's saying. When he says "nation," he means the Hawaiian nation, not the United States. He's also saying it should be Boi fighting the good fight, not Joe. "Hard to make noise from prison," says Boi. "We keep The Bodies quiet there."

"We?"

"Don't start," says Boi. "You made a fool out of yourself."

There's something on the road up ahead. Boi jerks the wheel, grazing a piece of plywood. Maybe a plank from a bookcase or a cabinet door.

"Fuck them fuckers. They took everything from me. My farm. I cannot pay tax on my farm while get millionaires in Manoa and Black Point pay practically nothing cause their house used to belong to some luna fricking hundred years ago. Historical places. Fuck them. Auwe."

Boi feels his blood pressure rising.

Nina's leaning against the car door again. Boi eyes the door lock, unable to shake the image of the door opening, Nina sliding out. "Who? Who is 'them?'"

"All of them."

Boi sighs. "Get her off the door."

"Ho, fricking paranoid, ah?"

"It wasn't the real scepter."

Of course Joe didn't catch the ten 'o clock news. A couple of patrolmen had called Boi to tease him about it.

"What?"

"It's a replica. My friends seen it on the news."

"Auwe. Where's the real one?"

Boi's about had it. "How the fuck should I know?"

Boi rolls down the window, hoping the wind will drown out some of this back-seat noise. Instead, all he hears is quick-beat ticking. It's a nail stuck in his tire. Must've ran it over when he grazed the piece of plywood back there.

Boi tries to ignore it and rolls his window back up. He still hears it though, faint, irritating like the constant whine of a puppy left alone at home, locked in the bathroom. A typical Kry-lua 911 complaint call.

Tack, tack, tack. That fucking nail. Boi's sweating as they near the coast. He looks into the mirror. Joe's eyes go wide. "Pull on the side."

"What?"

"Pull over!"

What the hell, he can use a break, stretch the legs, take a deep breath. Then find that nail. Boi downshifts and pulls over. Joe's out of the car before it comes to a complete stop. Boi grabs a flashlight and steps out. He shines the light on the front driver's side wheel well, squats, and rubs the tire with his hand. Joe's looking into the stale, windless night. "What?" Boi asks, his attention more on the tire.

"Ho, fricking chicken skin," says Joe. "You didn't see um?"

"I got a fricking nail in my tire."

Joe looks up at the black sky. "They out tonight."

"I don't see shit."

"Yeah. I know you don't."

Joe pulls a fistful of rock salt from his pocket, spreads it over the dirt like he's feeding pigeons, mutters a prayer in Hawaiian, then spits.

"What? You carry rock salt with you now?"

Joe shrugs. "You never know."

Boi's thumb brushes against a flat piece of circular metal. He doesn't even know why he looked for it. Pull it out, the tire will go flat. Leave it in, his tire will go flat, just more slowly. He stands and brushes his hands on his jeans. "You could've at least researched," says Boi, now looking for obake in the bushes despite the fact that he knows they don't exist. Not any more. But then again, he didn't think nosy reporters existed anymore either.

"Like I said, my computer broke," says Joe. "And look, she sees um," says Joe, pointing to the car.

Boi faces the car. A wide-eyed Nina is pointing down the dark road. Boi follows her finger. He's blinded by the hightlights of an on-coming, jacked-up SUV tricked out with dubs and surf racks. It's barreling straight for Boi's car. Boi opens the back door, dives on Nina, and wraps his arms around her. He understands how stupid and futile the act is, as if the five-thousand pounds of haul-ass metal will hit him and split in half.

The SUV swerves right before impact. Two blonds scream and wave as they pass. He sees tits. Empty beer cans clank on pavement in their wake.

Boi, his heart beating fast and his ears now buzzing, pulls Nina out. She feels long, her feet dangling and kicking his knees.

When did she get so tall? His ears buzz as his blood pressure rises. "You dumb ass, ghost-hunting motherfucker," says Boi to Joe. "Get in the motherfucking car. I had it with you."

"Daddy!" says Nina.

"You no talk to me like..." says Joe.

Boi puts Nina back inside, straps her in, and gets in.

"She could have..."

"Then what? What would you do?"

Boi looks in the rear view. Nina's staring outside into the dark. He wonders what she's seeing, what she daydreams about. Good stuff, he hopes. Stuff with rainbow colors. Stuff he never dreamed about when he was her age. He glares at Joe. What would he have done if something happened to his daughter? Get his murder on, is what.

Joe sighs, looking disappointed as Boi pulls out onto the road. "That's fine," Joe says. "But if you would've killed me and let those fucking haoles live, then I would haunt you for the rest of your life."

Boi drives. The nail, the buzzing in his ears—Boi's sweating and dizzy. He tries to grip the steering wheel for balance and almost swerves. He sticks a finger in his ear then yanks it out, using the tip like a plunger. Gooey wax lodges under his fingernail. "I don't got time for this shit."

Joe looks out the window and sniffs the air. "Storm coming," he says. "You know what? I had another vision while I was locked up."

"I don't wanna hear it."

"Kanaloa is coming," Joe says.

"What did you see, Papa?" asks Nina.

"Your Dad," says Joe, "your makuakane, is going to do something great. He just gotta wake up first. He gotta start his second life. Believe."

"I believe," says Nina.

"He gotta believe," says Joe. "Or..."

The car drags to the left. The tire's leaking air. Joe's about to say something. Boi feels the word coming and sticks a finger in Joe's face. "Don't you say it," says Boi.

Joe shrugs. "Hey braddah, I just saying, when you start your second life, pick the right targets. Pick the right targets."

Afraid to stop, afraid to go on, ears buzzing like bees, Boi drives on three good tires. The fourth flops on pavement. If he keeps driving, the rubber will rip.

"Don't you say it," says Boi.

Joe smiles. "Auwe," he says.

If Nina weren't in the car, Boi would plow into the nearest telephone pole.

11. _____

The next day, Boi and Shane are summoned to the governor's official residence, Washington Place. With its red-brick walkway, white pillars, and broad porch, just throw some slaves out on the lawn and it'd resemble a place where rednecks go to heaven. Boi learned about this place from Mr. Melvin back in the day and in his community college Hawaiian history class. Built by a nineteenth-century sea captain, the mansion has housed big names since then, including thirteen governors, Hawaii's last queen, and the guy who wrote the Great Mahele.

Even though it's still the official residence of the Governor, it's more scene-of-the-crime museum now, the place where the last monarch of Hawaii was dethroned and arrested. It's only used for state dinners and fund-raisers, like when the biggest contractor in Hawaii had his son's wedding here a few years back. There's another party tonight, this one an engagement party for a distant cousin of the emperor of Japan and her New York investment banker boyfriend.

Shane and Boi wait on the porch while the outsourced staff scrambles in and out with boxes of booze and silver chafing dishes. "Mah, such swelterin' heat," says Shane, acting like he's fanning himself. "Might I trouble you for a tall glass of lemonade?"

Boi shakes his head. "You're retarded."

"Why Colonel, such language is not befitting of an individual of your station."

Boi feels like laughing, but doesn't.

A black town car pulls up and idles. The driver and another man step out, both wearing aloha shirts, sunglasses, ear pieces, and gunfighter mustaches. The Gov's Royal Guard. They wave Boi and Shane over. Boi yawns. He's as tired as hell from the bailout adventures the night before.

The boys sit in the car, the kind Boi imagines Sicilian mob bosses prefer, bulletproof glass and all. The two bodyguards stand next to each other outside, arms crossed. Shane's in the back with Charles while Boi sits in the front—the garrotte seat. Charles has started to wear baseball caps since he began losing his hair; he takes off this hat and bends the bill with his clawed, now-arthritic meathooks. A wooden box the size of a baby coffin sits on his lap. "I wish your mother..." says Charles. "Seems impossible to do the job without her. Hell, it seems impossible to breathe without her."

His voice is gravelly. He sounds about as tired as Boi. And though his body is still Olympic-fit from daily dawn patrols, mile-long, choppy water swims, his face is beginning to crack and sag, a face that looks like art when photographed in black-and-white. That the sixty-something old man can probably still out-swim him pisses Boi off.

"She'll get better," says Shane.

Boi looks out the window. A Filipino kid trips over his own feet on the red brick walkway and drops a set of a hundred-year-old steak knives. An older Filipino, probably the kid's father, picks up a knife and throws it at the kid. The kid charges his father. The other staff swarm to break up the fight.

"What the hell were you boys thinking?" asks Charles.

Boi turns around. "What the fuck did I do?"

"Are you kidding?" says Charles. "You get caught walking out of main station with the Governor's son on one side and the numnuts who broke into Bishop Museum on the other? Looks like a goddamn conspiracy."

"What kind conspiracy?" says Boi, looking into the big man's yellow, sleep-deprived, drinker's eyes that turned bloodshot after a couple of beers, liver working overtime. Boi's seen those eyes in crumbs dozens of times. The Gov's probably been putting them away since his wife's gotten worse. Old school guys like him don't believe in pharma. The bottle does fine.

Charles turns to Shane. "And you. I stopped by the house this morning. The place is a wreck."

Shane, looking real sad, says, "Sorry I not smart like you. You know where I come from. Must be genetics."

Charles sighs rubs his eyes with his palms. Fricking Shane. Boi wants to laugh. Charles drums the wood box with his fingers then puts a hand on Boi's shoulder and squeezes. "Well, how's our little girl doing?"

"Tired as fuck at school because of this bullshit."

"Okay," says Charles. "Okay."

"You," says Charles, pointing at Shane. "You need to go visit your mother. How you can put her through this?"

Shane nods. Charles glares, waiting. "What, now?" asks Shane. "Yes."

Shane sighs and steps out. The car lifts slightly, the shocks relieved after screaming for mercy under the fat fuck. Shane leans down and takes one last look at Boi through the window. Boi flips him off. Shane clenches his jaw. Boi rolls down the window. "Eh, I need one ride to Waialua after! Gotta pick up my car!"

Shane, still walking away, raises an arm, and sticks middle finger. Boi rolls the window back up. Charles sighs. "Take care of him," he says.

"The fucker needs one shrink, not one cop."

"No. Right now he needs family."

Family. What the fuck. And here's him looking for another one, his sister, probably all fucked up just like the rest of them. He's like that old haole fucker who poked his eyes out after oofing his mother. What was his name, Rex Caesar or some shit? His ears start buzzing.

"What about the reporter? The towel head one?" asks Boi.

"He's not a towel head, he's Pakistani."

"OK. So what about that Arab son-of-a-bitch?"

"Don't worry about it."

Boi shrugs. "He probably digging shit up right now. Probably even gonna throw in some of that boat shit."

Charles goes quiet. The big haole likes to run his mouth on just about anything, but when it comes to the boat, how Shane nearly sank his campaign, The Gov shuts his mouth like the cata-maran thing is some kind of ugly war memory full of guts and gangrene. That's why Boi likes mentioning it now and then, to remind Charles that his once golden boy, King Bull Nuts Junior, is a fat, three-hundred-pound, failed project. Boi figures The Gov hasn't had enough fail in his life and needs to be reminded that it's possible, even for him. "It's what I'd be doing if I was after your ass," says Boi.

"I'll have someone else take care of that."

Boi turns around. "What you can do?"

Charles looks down at the box on his lap and smiles. "If I were a Hawaiian gov, I could screw over the Office of Hawaiian Affairs and Kam Schools. If I were a lesbian gov, I could screw over the gays. History shows I can do whatever I want. This is Hawaii."

Boi rolls his eyes. See? Not enough fail. "I gotta go fix my tire." He reaches for the door. Charles grabs his arm and pulls. Boi swallows a face-punch instinct while Charles puts his hat on, making sure the bill is straight. "Aunty Helen and I have been talking," he says.

This should be good. That's another thing about Uncle Charles. The bullshit that pours from his golden throat, pipes like plumbing in heaven. Boi can't help but listen. He sits back down. "About what?"

"You know, it's you, not him."

"What the hell you talking about?"

"You can be whatever you want."

"I wanna be King Kamehameha then, so I can throw all you fucking haoles off the Pali." He reaches for the door.

Charles smiles, shakes his head, and puts a heavy hand on Boi's shoulder. "No haoles went over the Pali. And the guys who did, they jumped. They weren't thrown."

"Suicide is hard to walk away from."

Charles shakes his head. "I'm trying to be serious."

Boi swings the door open. "So what I can be then? Let me guess, President of the United States?"

Charles shrugs. "Go back to school like I told you, turn your associate's into some Mickey Mouse AJ or political science bachelor's degree, who knows? Hell, I know people running around with political science degrees who can't tell you the difference between the Constitution and the Declaration of Independence. They run around playing Hawaii politics, and they couldn't tell you the year of the overthrow. I'm talking state representatives. Get the paper, you can be chief. You can be mayor. Hell, when the time is ripe, you can be gov. Many a power broker started off as cop. Even dirty ones."

"And what? Don't do jack shit except build dog parks and veto tax bills like you?"

"This is trench warfare, kid. I'm holding the line, and that ain't nothing." Charles pauses. "Stop being your father's son."

Boi slams the door shut and turns around. "I not like him."

Charles puts his hands up. "Why are you so mad at me all the time?"

He's giving Boi that stoned, lazy surfer look, the one he busts out every time someone calls him on shit—Helen pissed when he lights a cigar (he'd promised to quit once he became Governor), Shane pissed when he says no to some crazy-ass pub or dojo investment, the public pissed when his name comes up in connection with some gated community development project on the Big Island or Maui. Charles just shoots that look, that, hey, I'm trying my best look. Not my fault the waves are blown out.

"Everything me and Aunty Helen did for you," says Charles. "You're like a son to us. Aunty Helen. She's so proud of you."

Charles looks down at the box and rubs the wooden lid like he's stroking a baby to sleep.

A silver sedan pulls in front. A haole guy in a tee shirt and boroboro cargo shorts with paint stains steps out. Busted up clothes. Check. Fifty K watch. Check. Super rich in Hawaii. It's how they do. Must be the New York investment banker guy scouting his Washington Place engagement party.

A bobora who looks like she should be on some poster hocking Jap brew or those used panties Boi hears they got in Tokyo vending machines, steps out beside the haole and puts her hand in his pocket. Amazingly, the giant rock on her finger doesn't shred his pants. Boi's surprised they didn't arrive in a fucking helicopter.

"Let me show you something," says Charles.

Boi turns to Charles. Charles opens the wood box, the inside lined with velvet. He pulls out a rod topped with a gold dove perched on a globe, the shaft circled with three rams' heads.

"It's the real one," says Charles.

The real royal scepter of the Merrie Monarch, Kalakaua, last king of Hawaii, not the fake one Red Roof Joe was caught trying to steal. Charles holds it up. "Kalakaua. He was only king for seven years. And everyone remembers him. I'll be governor for eight."

"How the?"

"It's been in the family for over a hundred years. My great-grandfather. Kingdom of Hawaii overthrow. Who do you think acquires all the artifacts from a beat monarchy? To the victors go the spoils. Funny, my great-grandfather played a major role, but hardly anyone remembers him."

Boi turns and looks out the window. The bobora stops a porter, pulls out a packet of baby naps, and wipes a smudge off a silver chaffing dish. "Okay, so you got the big rod. Useless unless you got the balls to match."

Charles puts the scepter back in the box and closes it. He tucks the hair on his graying temples behind his ears. He clears his throat and tells Boi about this new law he's been pushing be-

hind the scenes for the last two years. Boi shakes his head the entire time. It's Charles's Great Mahele, his Bayonet Constitution,
his overthrow, his Democratic Revolution of 1954, his statehood.
The one law he will get passed to change the face of Hawaii. All
this time, Boi thought Charles was like the rest of them, some
development cash in his pocket, free trips to China and Japan to
promote tourism, favors for family and friends, and bronze vanity
plates on a building or two, good enough. Hire a buddy who once
worked for an oil company to head up environmental impact, one
of Helen's insurance agent friends to head up insurance regula-
tion, and a condo developer friend to head up zoning, take care
of your posse and troubleshoot the term out. But Charles's plan
is way more massive than all that, more massive than just putting
his outrigger canoe racing team on the payroll. He's proposing
a bill that will change everything. And he will call the law the
Helen Knotting Bill in honor of his wife. Boi can't hear the end
of it through the buzzing in his ears.

Boi opens the box and takes the scepter. Charles tries to grab
him, but he's already out. Boi smiles at the investment banker, the
bobora princess, and the Royal Guard right before he swings the
scepter at the car window.

The scepter shatters against the bulletproof glass. He looks
down at the golden pieces, the broken treasure. The globe and
red velvet roll down the drive. The two Royal Guards go after the
fractured bits, hunched over like they're chasing chickens.

The investment banker and his fiance join in the chase after
broken pieces as Charles steps out of the car. "You can't do that
shit," says Boi, still gripping the scepter handle. "No way that shit
passes."

"What? It's no big deal," says Charles. "It's so elegant and
simple. It saddens me that I didn't think of it before."

The Royal Guard and investment banker bring Charles back
the broken pieces. One of the guards grabs Boi by the back of the
neck and pushes his head onto the hood of the car. "Let him go,"
says Charles. He grabs the scepter handle from Boi and gathers

the smashed pieces in his big hands. He looks down. "Pop the trunk," he says.

One of the guards nods and opens the trunk. Charles tosses the fragments inside and slams the door. He might as well have thrown a jack and tire iron back there, the lack of give-a-shit on his face. The guards, the investment banker, and the fiance are watching, horrified. Charles shrugs. "Anyone got crazy glue on them?"

The engaged couple turn their attention back to the workers hauling lattices and white linens. The guards turn their back on Boi and Charles, cross their arms, and watch, too. Charles leans down to Boi's buzzing ear. "It's just stuff," he says. "Just hand-held vanity that made a king think he had more power than he really did."

Boi can never win an argument against the big haole. Every time he thinks he's close, Charles busts something out that sounds a lot like truth. Boi's tired. He just wants to pick Nina up from school, help her with her homework, cook dinner, and crash.

But he knows he won't be able to sleep. Not while knowing what Charles is going to try and do. And the worst part about it is he knows Charles will win. Charles, whether it's surf contests, arguments, or political campaigns, all he does is win. Boi's starting to think that maybe he even let Boi win that arm wrestling match they'd had six years ago. What if Boi, for once, tries to stop him? What can some swingman do against the full might of one of the richest and most powerful men in the state?

"Auwe," says Boi, wanting to kill himself for saying it.

12.

Traffic, even way out in Waialua. More cars than people. That's Hawaii. As Shane and Boi head for Mokuleia, the end of the road, the last bit of pavement before Kaena Point, home of afternoon drunk four-wheelers and noob opihi pickers who get washed off the lava rocks and pulled out to sea, Shane steers with his knee while holding an ipu on his lap. He slaps it, and free-styles horrorcore rhymes. He's been doing it for the last thirty minutes, but Boi hasn't said a word. Irritating Boi often makes Shane feel better after a hospital visit with his mother, but Boi isn't biting. Helen, with her sunken cheeks and backless hospital gown, stripped of youth, humor, and dignity—recalling the image takes Shane out of the mood. He flings the ipu on the backseat. He doesn't want to be stuck in traffic in back woods country. He wants to go home.

"Why didn't you just get the car towed?" Shane asks.

Boi pulls down the passenger side sun-visor to block the glare. "What, and pay like three hundred bucks, you trust fund motherfucker? My dad found a tire for free."

At least he didn't call him fat. Shane lets the insult pass. "Why the hell I gotta take you?"

He knows the answer, but wants to hear Boi say it. Boi has no friends. Hell, the grump hasn't even had a girlfriend for the last how many years. And it's no surprise why. Look at him finger-banging his ear. He's even more grouchy than usual. Shane should take him to a massage parlor for a rub and tug when they head back to town. Johnny Appleseed, baby.

"You no like take me, pull over," says Boi. "I'll catch bus."

"Shit, we're already close," says Shane. "Should've told me that two hours ago. So what? You wanna check out our long-lost sister after, right? Might as well circle the whole island at this point."

A frowning Boi shakes his head, judging, looking severe, like a typical cop. His eyelids looking slightly swollen like they always do. "No can this week," Boi says. "Some of us get job. Some of us gotta work."

They pass Waialua High School and head for a beachside YMCA kiddie camp with rustic cabins and rope obstacle courses. It's named after some sugar plantation trust fund baron who broke his neck playing polo a hundred years ago. Shane always enjoyed history in high school. Not the heavy stuff, like the casualty-count of WWI. No, he got a kick out of listening to stories about rich and powerful men meeting their demise in situations that could be interpreted as slapstick. Like when, a thousand years ago, the canopy over some Hungarian king's throne collapsed and crushed him, or when an American sea captain in Hawaii was killed when a British ship fired a cannon to salute him. His mother loved these stories, too, an odd guilty pleasure considering it was the last thing they'd wanted to happen to another great man, Charles Knotting.

The boys turn left and pass Salvation Army. Some tourist in front of them slows and points out the window. Boi leans over and honks the horn. Shane passes the two-door rental car, and Boi glares at the tourists.

"Sheesh, relax," says Shane.

"Fucking traffic in Waialua," says Boi. "All because millions of fuckers come here every year to rubberneck the ocean."

Shane rolls his eyes. They drive over the thin stretch of road and roll over speed bumps. Houses line the shore, the beach that Shane knows sits behind them, invisible.

Shane's surprised that Joe Bolosan's house ain't half bad. It's definitely old, and has the look of an old-school Hawaiian country pad—a Hawaiian hedge (broken-down cars lining the front yard), a dirt driveway, peeling paint, screened jalousie windows, and faded asphalt shingles. But the property and house are bigger than he imagined. A crowing rooster flutters away as they pull up the driveway. Boi's car is jacked up next to the porch. A brown horse tied to a coconut tree chews grass. When they get out of the car, Boi says, "Don't go by the horse. He bites."

They step onto the patio, rotted planks held together by rusty nails. Shane tests each plank before putting his full weight on it. Boi waits for him by the screen door, which is patched with gray electrical tape. A mosquito bites Shane's ankle. He lifts his leg and slaps it, smearing specks of black and red across his skin. Boi opens the creaking screen door. Shane points at a shelf. "Is that an actual bailer cut from an empty Clorox bottle?"

Boi nods.

"Something like that belongs in the Smithsonian," says Shane as he follows Boi into the house.

The kitchen is a mess. An ant trail runs from the counter into a sink containing fried fish fins and chunks of corned beef. Empty green bottles piled in a trash can, about to avalanche. A pink-tailed rat in hieroglyph pose is stuck on a glue trap. It squeals as they pass the kitchen.

They step into the living room. A group of hunched-over, bare-foot old men wearing black tee-shirts printed with Hawaiian gibberish and an insane amount of punctuation sit in the living room, whispering secrets. As Shane and Boi approach, the men stop talking and glare. Shane gets it. A bunch of old fogies scheming for relevance one last time, scrambling to get their house in order before death comes knocking. Life, the only race you get killed for finishing.

Joe, the only shirtless one, stands and clears his throat. Shane can't believe that old fucker still has bricks. Joe grabs the boys by their arms and leads them outside as suspicious, angry eyes watch their exit.

When they get outside, Joe stops the two boys next to the horse. The horse's ears go back and its eyes get big. It swishes its tail. Shane feels like the horse is calling him out. "You guys cannot be here right now," says Joe.

"I just came for the car," says Boi. "You got the tire, right?"

Shane raises his fist and jerks his hand, trying to make Grover Cleveland flinch.

"OK," says Joe. He pauses and looks back at the house. "I get um in the back."

Flies buzz around the horse's rippled hindquarters. Shane wonders what would happen if he punched the horse in the face. Can he drop a horse? He turns back to Boi. "What's going on?" he asks. "This some sort of secret society planning the overthrow of the state and federal government?"

Joe rolls the tire to Boi's car. Shane grins. He points to a tarp covering a busted pick-up truck. "Where you guys hiding the artillery? In the back of the truck?"

"Fuck you, braddah," says Joe.

Shane points to the horse. "At least you guys have cavalry."

"After I fix the tire, get him the fuck out of here," says Joe as he drops a naked rim into the new tire. Boi walks to the house and pulls out a rusty air compressor from under the porch. Joe pours gasoline on the rim and tire. He pulls a strip-bar matchbook out of his pocket and lights one. He drops the match on the tire, which pops like a gun shot. The tire is now fit snugly around the rim. Shane's got to hand it to these ghetto Hawaiian fuckers. He's so impressed he hardly notices that the horse bolted after being spooked by the pop.

He sees it now. It leaps over the gate like an equestrian champ and gallops toward the beach. "Godfunnit!" yells Joe.

"Joe!" one of the old guys yells from inside.

Joe unties rope from the tree and tosses it to Boi. "Go get Grover," he says, looking anxious. There's a government to overthrow after all. "I gotta go back to the convention."

Convention.

"I don't..." says Boi.

"Just go get him. Please."

Boi sighs as he cleans out an ear with his finger.

Shane and Boi cut through a beach access road and walk down the beach. No sign of the horse. Shane takes off his shirt and tucks it in his jeans. He doesn't want a funky farmer's tan. The rising tide sweeps over sand and wets Shane's shoes. Boi dances off to the side.

Shane stops, already breathing hard. He's standing on a patch of rocky, slippery shoreline. An orange and black hermit crab the size of a baby's fist scurries into the surf. Shane points at it. "Wow," he says. "Did you see that?"

"It's a Halloween crab," says Boi as he squats and watches it disappear in white foam.

"Cool," says Shane.

Boi nods.

Shane scratches his back. The sun is making him itchy.

Boi looks up. "Is that cellulite, you fat, mouth-breathing fuck?"

"Fuck you. I've been carbo-loading."

"Yeah, but cellulite on your back?"

Shane ignores the question. "Fuck, where the hell did the stupid shit go?"

"It's up there," says Boi, pointing.

The horse peeks out from bushes a hundred yards away. It opens its mouth and bares its teeth. Boi runs. Shane follows, trying to keep up. The horse trots on the sand and turns around, like it's an adult torturing Boi with a game of chase master. Boi stops running and waits for Shane to catch up.

"Fuck this shit," says Boi, "If we don't get him in the next ten minutes, we'll cut back on the road at the next beach access road."

"That's not far, right?" asks Shane, panting. "We got some kind of law that makes sure people can access the beach whenever, right?"

Boi shrugs and walks on. He's looking out toward the sea as if he's some kind of oceanographer or wayfinder about to sail the *Hokulea* to Tahiti. The fucker didn't even finish high school. But he went to community college and got an associate's. He's officially more educated than Shane. Maybe that's why he turned pussy.

Boi tugs on his ear as the horse waits up ahead. Dark circles under his half-open, insomniac eyes.

"You not sleeping or something?" asks Shane.

"What is that?" asks Boi, pointing to a shiny black dome pushed up on sand by the surf. It looks like a smooth black rock polished by the wetness of bubbly, white foam. As they get closer, Shane sees not a rock, but a turtle, sunbathing. But as they near, he smells it. He kicks it to make sure it's dead. He picks it up and heaves it over the shorebreak. In mid-air, the sagging head and fins spill out of the shell like a silent bomb just detonated in its belly. "Stop fucking around," says Boi, finger still in his ear.

As Shane and Boi plod up the coast, they pass renovated, single wall-constructed houses. Carpenters bang nails into new wood cut by table saws. Blond, bikini-clad trophy brides frolic in the surf with their water-winged children. Some of them shoot

Shane and Boi dirty looks and huddle their children closer to them. Shane's panting now as each step sinks into wet sand. Every time they catch up to Grover, the horse sprints ahead. "Stupid horse," says Shane. "Let's just go back."

"Man," says Boi, not even looking at the horse. Wide-eyed, he looks awake now. "You seen one non-haole yet? This is fricking Waialua, too."

Shane looks toward the houses, most gated, property lines marked with tall wood plank fences. He turns to the ocean. Kite surfers catch air, harnessed in their $3,000-dollar rigs. Shane has one coated with dust at home. He squints up shore. "Where the hell did the horse go?"

"It took off," says Boi.

"Let's just cut across," says Shane.

"That's trespassing," says Boi, watching the kite surfers. "Private property." He looks at his watch. "It's been ten minutes. We can just head back the way we came."

It's like ninety degrees out and the fucker is hardly sweating. "Fuck walking on the sand. Let's just cut across. Walk on the road," says Shane.

Shane climbs up the sandy hill and marches toward the first non-gated backyard he sees. A tall, skinny man with long, bony legs is sitting on a porch. He's all teeth, elbows, and knees, like a once-upon-a-time third string high school center who got thrown on the basketball team just because of height. Now, he's probably some Silicon Valley inventor, the kind Charles always gets donations from, who made his fortune in tech stocks and decided he wanted to live out the rest of his life on the beach in middle-of-nowhere Hawaii. He's probably one of those guys who spent his forties and fifties re-rolling his thirties—a new wife, new location, and new set of kids for each decade. Shane can respect that. But this guy, he's not returning the respect. He seems to be glaring at Shane. Doesn't he know that Shane can throw him through a window like a javelin?

Boi puts his hand on Shane's shoulder. "Let's go," he says.

"Fuck that luna-looking mother-fucker," says Shane.

Shane walks on. Boi sighs and follows. The tall haole wearing board shorts and a surfer's tan could pass as a younger, much skinnier Charles Knotting if not for the mouth full of teeth too big for his mouth. The man picks up a driftwood stick, stands, and marches toward Shane. He steps over little orange flags that appear to mark the foundation of a soon-to-be-built backyard guest house or swimming pool. Shane puffs up, flexing his lats and traps, but the man keeps coming. "Excuse me," the man says. "You can't just cut through my property like this."

"Hey, screw..."

"Sorry," says Boi, interrupting Shane. "We just want to get back to the street. Was trying to catch my dad's horse, but that fucker is too fast."

"Well, you're going to have to go around."

Shane looks both ways down the coastline. Backyard after backyard. There is no around. "Around where?" says Shane. "Fricking Sunset Beach? We walked miles already looking for a place to cut through."

The man jabs the end of his stick in the ground. "This is private property, sir," he says. "You people need to go back from whence you came."

Boi, his eyes closed, is digging into both ears now like he's got some kind of terrible itch in each canal. If he's not going to dig into this haole instead of his ears, Shane will. He turns to the man. "And if we don't?"

The man points his stick at Shane's chest then points it down the beach. Like he's James Cook ordering his men to take the king of Hawaii hostage, pointing them in the right direction. Like he's Lono, god of, well god of whatever. Plants or rain or some other nature shit. Shane's just trying to work himself up as he balls his hands. This is how fighting is for him. He has to psyche himself up and mentally focus. He has to visualize. What the mind can conceive, the body can achieve. Shane once saw those words on a poster of a mountain climber dangling one-handed from a snowy cliff. It's his mantra before every fight. Well, the three fights he's been in anyway, two of which were broken up before he could throw a second punch.

The man, unafraid, eyes Shane. "Again, you need to go around. As you Hawaiians say, auwe."

Boi's fist smashes the man's cheek, and it's Shane who flinches. Boi's now sitting on the haole's chest. More fists pound the man's face, the sick sound of bones breaking. The man starts to scream, so Boi puts one hand over his mouth while he mallets with the other. Boi's a starving, shipwrecked sailor trying to crack open a coconut. But it's even more robotic than that, like he's one of those brainwashed Cold War wet boys trained to go off when they hear the code word. It dawns on him that Boi has always been like this since he's known him. Boi never has to psyche himself up. Boi is always ready.

When he figures the haole had enough, Shane grabs Boi and yanks him up, but Boi tosses Shane in the bushes. Boi is on the now unconscious man, swinging away again. The precision tent-stake pounding alarms Shane and he gets up. A sharp pain in his ankle: must've landed funny and sprained it.

The man's bloody profile sags in the grass, the face scaffolding that once held it up crushed. All the big teeth look cracked or gone except one that's dangling from the man's top gum. Shane limps to Boi and grabs him again. This time a panting Boi doesn't fight Shane. He picks up the stick and spits. "Your fucking dad," he says, panting, his face streaked with tears. "This is what he wants."

Boi hands Shane the stick, pulls out his cell phone, and dials 911. Shane snatches the phone from him. "Are you crazy? We gotta get the fuck out of here."

"This is what he wants," Boi says again, tears already drying under the sun, now looking more like snail slime.

Shane tugs Boi's arm. He takes a last look at the man, who is conscious now, groaning, half-rolled over, and covering his face with his hands. Shane and Boi cut through the man's property and step onto the street, Shane using the stick to limp along, one arm around his brother's shoulder. Shane checks for passing cars. The coast is clear. Boi drags Shane back to Joe's house, Shane coughing and stumbling as Boi pulls him. "If you dad had his way," says Boi, "we wouldn't have been born."

The stick finally breaks under Shane's weight and he falls on his ass. Boi pulls him up. It's way too easy for Boi to pull him up. He's three-hundred-pounds. Well, two-ninety-two, anyway. How strong is this skinny fuck? "Nina wouldn't have been born either," says Boi. He's eying each renovated house they pass. Lots of surf racks. Lots of Volvos. Lots of bumper stickers that read, "Keep the North Shore Country."

Back at the house, the old men are gone. Boi's car is off its jack, new tire in place. The old tire sits on the porch along side a gutted gas grill converted for charcoal cooking, three buckets of house-paint primer, and a stack of plastic fold-out chairs. Joe appears from the backyard. He's sitting on Grover's back. "Look who came back," says Joe.

"You gotta be shitting me," says Shane, glaring at the horse. He swears the animal is smiling at him. Boi sits Shane on the grass and rubs his face with both blood-crusted hands.

Joe eyes Boi's hands, smiles, and slides off Grover.

Joe takes Boi's hand and inspects it. "I see bone," he says. "You need stitches. Get one house I gotta scrape. Down the road. All kind lead paint. But let's take care this first."

Joe doesn't even ask how his hand got like that.

"Why you do that for them?" Boi asks as he tries to catch his breath.

"For the money. Plus..."

"What?" asks Shane, now curious.

Joe winks. "Figure all the lead dust and old fiberglass insulation I leave might poison the fuckers. Shit, sometimes get asbestos tiles under old carpet, too."

"I think I might be in trouble," says Boi as he plops down by Shane.

There's day-to-day smiles and then there's one-in-a-lifetime smiles, and Joe's, missing teeth and all, looks bright enough to be immortalized on a box of Raisin Bran.

Shane gets up and tests out his ankle. "This is what I get for skipping calves at the gym."

Shane glances at Boi's knuckles, the skin sliced pink and white. Shane's never done that to his knuckles. Joe walks inside. Boi takes off his shirt and wraps his right hand like he's either stashing a weapon or assembling a club. He looks at Shane. "How you got so big anyway?"

Shane wants to tell him he did it the real way, moke carbo-loading, post- case-beer midnight runs to the twenty-hour-hour fast food joint for half-pound burgers, plate lunches with all-mac salad instead of rice. But the truth is Shane didn't want gout. Instead he lifted heavy, sometimes two-a-days, and consumed poi-and-grape creatine shakes to the point of shitting purple. It was one of his business ideas, before the paint-gun obstacle course: a how-to-moke-out program the healthy way. He'd seen enough wannabes, most too skinny or fat, some without enough facial hair, that he figured he could make some cheddar off the idea. He wants to tell Boi about it, but Boi's focus is on Joe, who is walking out of the house with a sewing kit in his hand.

As Joe stitches Boi's knuckles, Shane watches in awe. "You're Rambo," he says.

"Gotta make do when no more medical," says Joe, smiling, as he punctures Boi's knuckle with a hook-shaped needle. "You boys need to get out of Waialua before the cops come."

"Do you even know what happened?" asks Shane.

Joe shrugs. "He cracked some rich haole, right?"

"Cracked" is not the word Shane would use. "How do you know?" says Shane.

"I feel like cracking them every day of my life."

Boi closes his eyes.

"I taught you good," says Joe. "Taught you good." He looks up at the sky. "This is only phase one."

Shane stands up and heads to Grover. The horse whinnies and takes two steps back. That's right you fucker, better be scared. "Eh, fat boy, stay the fuck away from my horse," says Joe.

Shane looks at the horse then looks at Boi. Years of lifting, years of martial arts, all this weight he has on his brother, and he's still not sure if he can take him. Shane takes a step toward the horse. Surely, if he can drop a horse, he can drop a one-hundred-and-ninety-pound man no matter who he is. Shane pulls his arm back and unloads with everything he's got.

"Eh! What the fuck?!" yells Joe.

The horse wobbles then drops on its knees. Shane rubs his fist and smiles. Ah, maybe he can make 'fat' his wet-boy code word. Before he can fully enjoy the discovery, Grover gets back up and snaps at Shane. Shane limps back. Grover steps forward and snaps again. Shane scurries to the truck and climbs on its roof. He feels it sink beneath him. But Joe doesn't care about the dent. He howls as Grover chomps at Shane. Boi, who's looking small and tired again, ignores the whole thing and looks down at his hands.

"All I want," says Boi, "all I want is to be a regular guy. Why is it so fucking hard?"

The horse rears and slams its front hooves on the truck hood. It slams its hooves down again and again shaking the truck as it tries to smash it into the ground. Shane rolls into the truck bed. The furious horse heads for him. Just as its about to sink its teeth into Shane, Joe whistles. The horse whinnies and backs off. Joe grabs the horse by its rope and leads it to Boi. He puts his hand on Boi's head. Joe's got this horse trained like a dog.

"Eh, numnuts," says Joe. "Anyone can false crack and do damage."

"That's all Boi did," Shane says, afraid to get down from the roof of the truck.

"No," says Joe. He grabs Boi's wrist and lifts his stitched hand. "He didn't just false crack. He hit again and again and again."

Boi yanks his arm from Joe and gets up. Shane's never hit anyone more than once in his entire life. That's his problem. He needs someone in his life to teach him these things, and Boi, who is now heading to the house—Shane's always been too shame to ask him. To ask would be to admit Boi can kick his ass.

"Did you teach him?" asks Shane.

"Pfft, never need teach him nothing," says Joe. "Some people, they born with it. Look at you all slow and puffy with weak ankles. Can tell you wasn't. Can smell the 'wasn't' on you."

Joe heads to the house, leaving Shane with a horse, rooster, and the realization that for him to become the guy he wants to be, he needs to get dirtied with a little bit of crazy. But he doesn't know anyone who can or will show him exactly how to ink that kind of war paint all over what Joe sees as his big fat face.

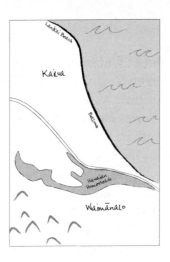

II. Morning Glory

1.

It wasn't Charles who came up with the idea for the Helen Knotting Welfare Reform Act. Instead, it was a firefighter who worked at the Waianae station. Charles, several firefighters, a few UH basketball players, and a Hawaiian slack-key guitarist were all at Waianae Intermediate to kick off the reward party for their annual Million Word campaign—the idea being that if the kids hit their quarterly goals of reading 250,000 words, they got a pizza party afterwards. This was usually the lieutenant governor's or the LG's wife's job, but Charles figured what the hell? It was back when he'd been planning for his re-election, and he hadn't campaigned in Waianae yet. Besides, it'd been years since he'd been to the west side—not since his surfing days.

Charles looked over at the firefighters, the athletes, and the musician and was pretty sure he was the only presenter who had actually read a book. He looked out at the kids, some of the lowest-scoring standardized test-takers on the island, and watched as they screamed and raised their hands as teachers tossed candy into the crowd.

Charles spoke and shook hands, promising stuff to shell-shocked teachers that he couldn't deliver as usual. When they broke for breakfast, he sat one table away and listened to the fire-fighters joke around, talking about dragging welfare moms out of their burning, one-bedroom houses and having to go in ten more times for each kid. One of the firefighters, a burly fellow with muscles tanned and toned from hours of outdoor volleyball, looked to make sure no teachers were around, turned to Charles, and said, "Hey Gov, you see some of those kids? You know what you should do? Instead of cutting welfare, you should just make it so that they have to be sterilized before they get their checks."

Before Charles could respond, his aide, a go-getter with a near photographic memory and no imagination, said, "You can't do that. It's not Constitutional."

The firefighter frowned. "Why? I not talking permanent ster-ilization. Get that stuff, right? Like one pill you can take or one sticker you can put on. I just saying, they no need take the check. We not forcing them to take the money. I just saying, you have to do this in order to qualify, you know?"

It was a crazy idea for sure, but Charles felt for this guy. He was probably a middle-classer with a couple of kids, maybe a new homeowner struggling to pay his mortgage. His wife worked long hours in some office, probably a pretty wife, a one-time firefighter groupie, who was sexually harassed by her fat, pock-faced boss who shook hands like a panty. She couldn't quit. Her husband couldn't punch the guy's lights out. No way. The money was too... adequate. So this diaper-changing firefighting Mr. Mom and his wife, they swallowed it. They probably wanted a third kid, too, but passed because the wife couldn't take time off again, and they couldn't afford it anyway.

So this guy, probably first-responder jaded, tired of resuscitat-ing drug addicts and four-hundred-pound Hawaiians who just got through mopping beef stew gravy with buttered rolls, this firefight-er, he started thinking. Look at these degenerates. Five to ten kids. Stuffing their faces with mayonnaise and processed heart-attack meats. Look at that one, look at the rims on her truck for Christ's sake. Probably paid for by welfare. Look at that other one, smoking ice while her kids fight over a plate of teriyaki hamburger patties and a pot of rice. Are my taxes supporting these people? I feel for the kids, but man, these welfare adults. They gotta go.

Charles saw where the firefighter was coming from. Besides, the firefighter was a union guy. He was a voter. Charles, a Republican, wanted to do better with the unions.

So on the ride back to downtown, after Charles had read a passage from *Tom Sawyer* to a classroom of eighth graders who went from puzzled to bored in forty-five seconds, the idea didn't sound so crazy. Who would rally against such a bill? Liberal nuts and university professors who thought everyone was racist and used Facebook to post pictures of their cats. There'd be flack from Washington, and the ACLU for sure. They all hated him anyway. But the everyday voter, the people out in the Mililani and Kapolei suburbs, a lot of them union, the people in his strongholds like Diamond Head, Hawaii Kai, Maui, and Kailua—they'd eat up a bill like this. Take any union liberal, his domicile stocked with auto repair tools and firearms, and watch the way he runs his own house, and you know he's a conservative at heart.

Charles would have to wait until his second term to introduce this bill, but what the firefighter—Charles forgot his name—what he said later was right. When was it going to stop? The crumbs, as cops like Boi called them, the crumbs are having eight kids compared to the working stiff's one or two. Extrapolate that. Soon, Hawaii would be overrun by crumbs, the government would be bankrupt trying to support them, and decent, hard-working people would have their kids enrolled in the same schools as knuckleheads who were taught by their parents that street smart is a more valuable commodity than book smart, and that's if these parents teach their kids anything besides the virtues of CZ earrings (cannot tell not diamonds! Just tell everybody they real!) and double left-hooks.

Hawaii would be a disaster. And with this bill, Charles Knotting could save it. And when he polled it a few months after he won re-election, he was not surprised that seventy-five percent of the state's population would support it. This thing had real traction. It would also gain national attention. The Fed paid for the majority of welfare after all.

So Charles wasn't scared of convincing the public.

He was a bit more trepidatious of getting his family on his side. He felt like he had to prepare them for what he was going to try and do.

Technically, his son was a could've-been-crumb, and he had to be sensitive about that, even though he had a hard time imagining Shane caring either way. Back before the cancer, before he named the bill after her, Charles wasn't sure how Helen would have felt about it, but she was always a politically loyal wife, so he assumed she'd agree publicly even if she disagreed privately. But Boi, whom he considered his number-two son; if he wasn't Boi's new father, who was? That Hawaiian-Filipino out in Waialua? Boi... well Boi might flip out and try to sink another boat.

So two years after his re-election, after he'd told Shane, who like he suspected didn't care, and told Helen, who was all for it and thought it made perfect sense, he got ready to tell Boi. Surely Boi must be as jaded as the firefighter, maybe even more so, considering the amount of crumbs he has to deal with. The chronics, the wife beaters, the home invaders, the welfare queens, the child abusers, the car thieves. Boi had to deal with them every first watch. Hell, his ex-whatever, the mother of his child, who had custody of Nina, was one of them. Wouldn't he want to tie her tubes? Besides, wasn't it Boi, years ago, who said, "The problem with Hawaii is the people."

Not all the people, just some of them.

But when Shane called a week earlier and it was Boi, not Shane, now in trouble ("Teeth in his knuckles!" said Shane, both envious and proud), Charles realizes that he should not have told Boi about it. Not the way he did. Not in the car after he just got through lecturing. Not after showing him the scepter of Kalakaua just to show him what could be his. Not when he knew Boi needed to find his long-lost sister, and like many adopted kids, tie up other personal-history loose ends before discovering his ambition. He should've let Boi find the sister first. Her very existence is Charles's strongest argument for the Helen Knotting Welfare Reform Act. Boi will find that out soon enough.

After his morning swim, Charles sips his morning acai-berry slushy in the private, "executive," hospital room while Helen sleeps. His ribs feel tight, dehydrated, one too many drinks last night. He keeps a vodka bottle in the hospital room, mixes some with grapefruit juice, to help him bed down for the night. He likes it. Makes him feel old school. His grandfather, the Knotting who taught him how to canoe and surf, used to down a few greyhounds before bed every night.

He opens the newspaper and rubs the black print with his fingers. It's the usual fluff. An interview with the star of a TV show filmed here, the story ending with a dollar amount the program brings to the grateful state. Yet another story about some poor geezer who got clipped by a car on Pali Highway. UH football. A celebrity hairstyle now sweeping the islands. Tourism's up. Housing prices are on the rebound. The overall tone optimistic, just the way Charles likes it. The paper's owner is a big-time campaign contributor. Thankfully, there's no police-beat story about some North Shore resident who nearly got beat to death at his beachfront home.

Those damn boys are blowing it, Charles thinks. Don't they know what they have access to? The Big Five plantation days are over. They are all mainland-owned huis now, companies shared by twenty different international investment groups listed on the New York, Tokyo, London, and Shanghai stock exchanges. Charles knows a lot of the board members, took them out marlin fishing as a state senator whenever they'd visit. They'd take pictures of their sun-burnt bodies standing by hoisted, half-ton bleeding billfish. Those pictures were framed and taken home, mounted on the office wall of a hundred-floor skyscraper somewhere in the world: See, I'm a real man, the pictures would whisper to visitors. Don't let the tailor-made suit and atrophied, chair-shaped ass fool you. When Charles ran for Governor, those international banker-types were standing in line to give him money. These are Friends of Charles. They can be lifelong friends of Shane and Boi if those two pull their heads out of their asses.

And despite all the union contract battles, all the gridlock of the first term, the re-election campaign went more smoothly than the first. What his opponents didn't get, what he understood, was that anger is a far more potent emotion than pity. His opponent, yet another Asian Old Boy who looked as if Charles were to sneeze on him he'd turn to dust, kept slinging anecdotes about individuals who got sick and lost their jobs and health insurance and ended up homeless on the beach, while Charles was talking about unions that made enough money to buy their own Waikiki hotels. About how Micros came by the boatload to live off free state and Federal money. About social-worker judges who let kids off easy and taught them that crime is no big deal. About how yet another lazy, incompetent state worker who got his job because he was the cousin of so-and-so, was charged with writing the environmental impact statement for an inter-island ferry and after two months came up with a five-page document Charles could have written in a few hours. About mom-and-pop kamaaina developers who spent five years going through the one-hundred step bureaucratic process to finally get their baby strip mall on the Big Island up and running, only to have their life-long dream stripped from them last minute because they didn't kiss enough ass and bring enough manapua. People got pissed. They got pissed and voted Charles Knotting. It made perfect sense. A couple of thousand die in Hurricane Katrina due to incompetence and bad luck, people feel sorry then forget. A few thousand die at the World Trade Center at the hands of a group who spits on what America is supposed to be all about, we start two decade-long wars. Most people, they don't get mad when something happens to someone else. They get mad when it happens to *them*. The Democrats were *taking* their money and spending it on Micronesian healthcare and union worker pensions. The Democrats were making it harder for *them* to do business. Charles just had to make it clear. Besides, collecting ninety-percent of the haole vote like his haole predecessor didn't hurt either. The haoles, not the Micronesians, are the largest growing demographic in Hawaii. Funny how people never point that out.

Charles finishes his acai-berry slushy and dumps it in the trash. He goes to the bathroom and washes the newspaper ink off his hands. When he steps back in the room, Helen's eyes open. She's looking more yellow than the day before. Her lips part slightly. He's waiting for her to talk, but she doesn't. She looks anxious, as if she's about to say something important. But her frozen eyes are locked on Charles, and they don't even flinch when Charles drops the newspaper on the floor and cries.

2.

As a cop, Boi was trained to notice things. Police departments call it "perceptive skills," but what it boils down to is being taught how to be suspicious. How to be suspicious at all times. It's through suspicion that Boi can spot drunk drivers, tweakers, slangers, chronics, purse snatchers, tree jumpers, car jackers, and home invaders. Hell, Boi had even taken a class on how to identify international terrorists. Be suspicious. Be suspicious 24/7. Now, whenever Boi looks at anyone, no matter how unlikely an outlaw, he sees a potential criminal. Grandma in a wheelchair rolling into a department store? Possible shoplifter. Haole girl doing a piss-poor job parallel-parking her mom's 100k European sports car? Driving without her license. Japanese man in a suit and a loosened stars-and-stripes tie feeding a parking meter and smiling at kids at the church preschool across the street? Kiddie rapist.

Boi has spent the last week working double shifts in Kry-lua being suspicious. He hasn't been sleeping much, and by the end of the week, the things he's noticing aren't meat sacks he can ticket, cuff, haul in, or beat. He's noticing things bigger than that. He sees an organic-market parking lot filled with cars that cost more than he makes in a year. He sees more single-wall constructed Kry-lua homes being renovated into McMansions. He sees a torn-down two-story walk-up being converted into a luxury old folks home. He sees Kry-lua as a pus-filled, pulsing tumor, small blobs of it breaking off and traveling through the blood stream of Hawaii. Metastasis. That's the word he's heard whispered at times when he's visited Aunty Helen. But Kry-lua is not the genesis tumor. Boi knows exactly where it all starts. Everyone does. Tiki torches, beach boys, millions of tourists a year, and man-made white sandy beaches. Eighteen miles south-west of here, where haoles first come then decide to stay. It all starts in District 6, it all starts in Waikiki.

Waikiki represents something different to everyone Boi knows. Red Roof Joe declared a life-long boycott of Waikiki. He'll never set foot in it again, he says. Mr. Melvin took it one step further and said that the only way he would go there was if he was humping a live nuclear weapon. To Patricia, it was a place with better hula gigs. And Helen, never able to let go of her insurance roots, once told Boi that Waikiki is terribly vulnerable to natural disaster, whether earthquake, tsunami, or hurricane. As for Charles Knotting, his campaign speeches cited the statistics time and time again: over four billion dollars of state revenue. Over ten percent of jobs. If Waikiki dies, the State of Hawaii dies with it.

Shane calls. On his first day off in a week, Boi's exhausted. He's been hiding out on the job, scared that he'll be pinched for beating that haole, trying to make as much money as he can to leave Nina in case he's hauled in. He's also been trying to feel normal, hoping that hard work would have that effect, but with all the noticing and suspicion, all the downtime he spends sitting in a blue-and-white, if anything, he's getting worse. He wants to go back to Waialua and destroy more rich haole faces. He wants to plop movie-star houses into the Pacific Ocean once again. He hasn't seen Nina in a week. He hasn't seen Joe, Shane, Helen, or Charles either, and when Shane calls, he's completely forgotten that they were supposed to check out Glorya, their long-lost sister. Boi just wants to sleep, but Shane pushes. "Dude, you've been on this for how many years now, and you want to sleep?"

He's right. "Pick me up in an hour."

Waimanalo, east side, just five miles south of Kry-lua. After sitting down for a lunch at one of the last old-school saimin joints, talking about Nina, why women don't have hair on their toes, and MSG, Boi and Shane head up toward the Koolau Mountains, passing chicken, horse, and flower farms. They drive by stained twin mattresses stacked on the side of the road. Shane beeps as they pass a man riding a child-sized pink bicycle while smoking a cigarette, grocery bags dangling off each plastic-streamered grip.

They hit a dead end at the gated foot of the mountain range. A State of Hawaii sign warns that the reservoir may be contaminated with leptospirosis. Boi looks up at the grooved mountain range, the result of waterfalls tens of thousands years old.

"You looks like shit," says Shane before he reverses out.

Boi hears ticking. "I think you ran over a nail," he says.

Shane shakes his head. "You're imagining things. There's no nail."

Boi listens more closely. He still hears it.

As they search for the address, Shane swerves the car at any birds that happen to be standing on pavement. He hits a cattle egret and white feathers explode in front of the windshield. Shane laughs and laughs. Boi points up ahead to a corner with no street sign. "Here," he says.

They head up the road and pass another intersection with no street sign, a metal pole sawed off at the base. They stop at a driveway with a padlocked gate. "I think it's this one," says Boi.

"No mailbox, no address, how do you know?"

Boi shrugs and gets out of the car. Shane kills the engine and steps out, too. Boi squats and rubs each of Shane's tires. Shane shakes his head. "You're losing it, man."

He's right. There's no nail. Not one Boi can see anyway. He dusts off his hands. "Let's go," Boi says.

They jump the gate and walk down a steep gravel road. Three old farmhouses sit at the bottom, one next to a toolshed, another by a porta-potty. The house in the middle, the big one, sits behind a round, tin barracks-roof and two broken-down manapua trucks squeezed together. They stop at the trucks. Boi tips over a rusty engine block with his foot. A foot-long centipede darts out. He squishes it.

Boi looks around. It's still old school in Waimanalo, at least on the mauka side of Kalanianaole Highway. Farms, Hawaiian homelands.

Someone's yodeling in the backyard. Boi and Shane head over to check it out. They pass trees ornamented with doll heads, dozens of girl-toy gallows. Wind blows and a blue-eyed one wearing a bonnet swings, lips pursed around a rubber nipple. The eyes of another flutters as her head rocks back and forth and spins around and around at the same time. Boi swears he hears sobbing. He grabs the head and holds it still. The dangling doll head stops crying. "Jesus," Shane says, still looking at all the heads. Boi grabs Shane's arm and pulls him toward the backyard.

There's at least a dozen people back there. Some wearing do-rags pick their guitars and ukuleles. Others drink from green bottles while they polish their stolen motorcycles. It's like one fricking hoolaulea block party.

The kanikapila music stops. The musicians eye the side-arm bulge under Boi's tee shirt. As a cop, he's licensed to carry a gun at all times. The guys polishing their bikes drop their rags and dart their eyes searching for an escape route. One of them tosses a greasy cloth on a screwdriver that's skewered in the motorcycle's ignition.

A girl, maybe five-three at most, a hundred pounds tops, is sitting next to a plank with the words "RIP Bones" scrawled in white. She takes something out of her pocket. It's a grenade. Shane grabs Boi's arm and takes a step back. Boi pushes Shane's hand away and steps forward.

The girl is holding the grenade, one of those old, pineapple-looking ones, in front of her face. She's inspecting it like she's one of those crazies who go through stacks of cartons looking for the perfect egg. She spots Boi and Shane and smiles. Despite the cornrows, the over-sized hoodie, and sweatpants, she's cute, a twenty-something who can pass for fourteen.

Boi heads to her. He pulls the screwdriver from the motorcycle ignition and tosses it in a banana tree patch. The girl's smile broadens, squeezing out one dimple under her right eye. She stands up. She stomps her feet.

She pulls the pin out of the grenade and tosses it to Boi. Shane runs, trips over the hibachi, and pulls it over his head for cover.

Boi catches the grenade and looks at it for a moment. Nothing happens. Then the top pops with bang and rings Boi's ears. The heat from the grenade stings his hand, but he doesn't drop it. Bitter green smoke fills the air around him. His ears are still buzzing. And under the buzz, from the front of the house, he thinks he hears the doll head crying again.

Boi tosses the grenade back to the girl. She plucks it out of the air one-handed. "How you know it wasn't live?" she asks, her little feet still pounding the dirt, marching in place.

Boi shrugs as he looks over at Shane, who's covered in ashes. The musicians and motorcycle detailers point and laugh. Boi turns to the girl. "I didn't."

The girl grins and sits back down, easing into a wide-legged gang-banger slouch. She watches Shane get to his feet and dust off his clothes. "Damn, wasn't sure who was who at first," she says. "Hi Boi. Been fricking ages."

"Where's mom?" asks Boi.

"She went moemoe."

Glorya bouquet-tosses the smoke grenade down the ravine behind them. Boi's ears won't stop ringing and all the doll heads in the front yard are crying now. "You hear that?" says Boi to all of them at once.

They all look at each other, confused. Boi puts his hand on his sidearm. One nods. The others follow suit. Shane's the only one not nodding. Fucking traitor. After six years of bullshit, of pride-swallowing school, work, Knotting errand boy, chronics, crumbs, fatherhood, of being Swingman Rapun, Boi feels sharp right now. X-ray-vision sharp. He doesn't feel like he's losing his mind. He feels like he's getting it back.

Glorya stands up and stomps her feet. She grabs a couple of green bottles from a cooler, and cracks them open with a lighter. She hands a beer to Shane then Boi. "Come inside," she says. "Let's catch up."

Weeds and mold grow from the eaves of the house. White paint scabs cover the edges and corners, and torn, dust-caked screens flap as the wind blows. Portions of the walls are slightly charred, large, lumpy designs that look like human shadows. Boi feels like he's walking into a haunted house as the crying and the ringing in his ears get louder and louder. He hands his beer to one of the motorcycle polishers on his way inside.

3. _____

Eighteen years ago, when a cleaned-up Makana Rapun was notified that she could take back one of her three children from foster care, she went to a fortune teller to help her decide which one. The psychic, a neckless, middle-aged woman with a collar of fat hanging from her chin, was unattractive enough to be credible. No crystal ball, no tarot cards, no seance with eyes rolling to the back of her head, the fortune teller told her that the decision was easy. Choose the first-born, choose the girl. When you're trying to get your shit together and change your life, never to seek help from boys. Glorya-Maree Ching Kehau Souza-Rapun was the sensible choice.

And it worked. After Makana dumped the dirt lot her mother, Cece, had left her, she found a studio apartment on the Hobron Lane outskirts of Waikiki, close to her new job as a hotel breakfast buffet waitress at a restaurant that sported an effigy of a pot-bellied Hawaiian in a hammock hovering over the bar. It was far enough from Wahiawa to avoid her exe's, chronics, every single one of them gun-owners she still owed money to. She went to the Office of Vital Statistics, stood in line behind newlyweds, frazzle-haired divorcees gripping their babies, and dark men with chalky calves and denim shorts, and changed her name to Makana Maroni, just as a final 'fuck you' to her mother. Then she went to family court and stood in line behind other ex-chronics and single mothers, some thin, others heifers with hairy armpits who didn't shave their legs or moisturize, and changed her daughter's name to Morning Glory. Then she buzz cut both their heads like hari krishnas to keep the men away.

The Maroni's had it working-class good for awhile. She would drop Glory off at school before she started her shift and pick her up after school every day. They'd go to the zoo every Wednesday when Glory got off at 12:45, and every Saturday they'd hit the beach, bringing home matching sunburned domes the first couple of trips. Sunday was clean-up day, Monday was movie rental night, and when the weather was good, which was most times, they'd hit the swimming pool on Tuesdays and Thursdays. Glory doggy-paddled so slowly that Makana was amazed she could stay afloat.

But then Makana got promoted to evening cocktail waitress at the hotel's trendy lounge that served Thai-chili kalua pig quesadillas and over a hundred brands of beer. The tips were good, sometimes three hundred bucks a night cash money. Money like that could mean private school for Glory. The girl was already having trouble with the public school boys in her class, first graders who still sucked their thumbs and touched her shaved head with their spit-slimed fingers. Hell, money could mean a college fund. Money could mean getting Boi and Chayne-Marcos back, too.

But what money really meant was babysitting costs and time spent away from her kid. After a few weeks, her socks soaked, her adrenaline still pumping at two a.m., craving something to take the edge off, Makana hit late-night to early-morning drinking sessions with the bar crew. The first couple of times, Makana brought Glory with her, the little girl asleep, curled in a ball on red upholstered vinyl chairs while karaoke blared and dart players shot for triple twenties.

Tuesdays and Thursdays were now bar nights, just twice a week, Makana keeping it under control. Besides, Glory didn't mind. The kid looked at it like an adventure, something she could do but the other kids couldn't, even though she slept through most of it. But then other patrons started shooting Makana dirty looks, childless skanks in tight jeans and low-cut halter tops, and Makana started leaving Glory home alone. She was sleeping anyway, right? Better in the comfort of her own bed.

Almost like a second birth, it took Glory nine months to go from source of hope to burden. Now, when Makana looked at her, she did not see what could be—instead she saw someone holding her back from *life*. Makana was still young, she was still better looking than most who'd popped out three kids—wasn't she entitled to some fun, some pleasure? Soon, her looks would fade, and the joy of men buying her drinks, which meant the joy of feeling good about herself in general would come to an end. When she hit twenty-five, it occurred to Makana that she would never be as good-looking again. So on her twenty-fifth birthday she left Glory home alone, went out dancing with the bar crew, and drank fourteen kamikazes. She ended the night at the foot of the bar's toilet puking herself to tears. The next morning, she made herself a bowl of ice cream and topped it with two tablespoons of grape-flavored cough syrup for breakfast.

The little girl didn't seem unhappy. Sure, Glory sort of pitched a fit the first time Makana gave her ten bucks and left her at the Children's Discovery Center by herself for three hours (so Makana could score some ice for her now under-control, every-Wednesday-afternoon crystal meth session). And the first time Glory tried to make her own microwavable pot pie while Makana was sleeping one off and refused to wake up, the little girl put it in the oven for twenty minutes instead of two, the food exploded, and Glory had to scrape the inside of the oven with a spoon for her breakfast. There were hiccups like that, but if anything Makana was teaching her self-sufficiency. Guarantee she was more independent than those private school kids who probably grew up with soccer and piano lessons shoved down their throats. Makana didn't want her daughter around those snobs. She wanted her daughter to grow up to be someone who could keep it real. Besides, with the smoking ice and clubbing, no way she could afford private school now anyway.

After two years of clubbing Tuesdays/Thursdays, batu Wednesdays, hangover Fridays, double-shift Saturdays, and straightening-up, good-enough Sundays, Benny Lee rolled in. The new bartender, Benny drove a Benz S500 (and didn't slap on custom rims because it would ruin the Euro class). Benny had his own house in Waimanalo. Looks-wise, he wasn't Makana's dream guy—in his forties, he'd battered his body with booze and looked it—gelled salt-and-pepper hair, some loose skin under the chin and over the belt, the whites of his eyes the same color as his eighteen-hole sunburned face. In fact, when Makana looked really close, it seemed as if his face was slowly melting—his right eye set a touch higher than his left, more sag on his left jowl than his right. It was as if all those open-window drives from Nalo to town allowed the sun to bake the left side of his face, and the damage was permanent. Despite that, he wasn't really ugly. He was just the kind of guy who looked uglier the closer you looked at him.

Two months after what was supposed to have been a one-night stand, Makana and Benny stood in front of a judge, Benny in a tank-top tucked into his khaki shorts, Makana in low-waisted jeans and slippers, and they said their I do's. Glory was there, too, in a pretty white dress that Benny had bought for her. Benny bought Glory several pretty white dresses and promised Makana she could try to get her sons back and would never have to work again.

Benny's Waimanalo property was deep in the boonies, down a steep driveway that led to three houses, one big with an ill-fitted, metal, hanger-shaped roof, and the other two one-bedroom cottages. One cottage was filled with old sofas covered by homemade quilts that smelled like old people (Benny's parents had recently passed away). Benny called the other cottage, which was padlocked, his office, so that was off-limits. And the big house was half tropical-themed with wicker chairs and tapas hanging on the walls, and half-meth lab—vials, plastic tubes, lithium batteries, coolers, cold medicine, coffee filters, and lantern fluid. It wasn't the sun that was melting Benny's face. It was lithium cold-burning in lantern fluid and anhydrous ammonia.

After a year in Waimanalo, Makana was a straight-up fiend—the missing teeth and skin sores type—the kind that appeared on public service ads. She smoked and scratched at the imaginary bugs crawling under her skin all day long and sometimes wouldn't see Glory for days at a time. Sometimes other chronic mothers would knock on the door, their hands around the backs of their daughters' necks, asking when Benny would be home. Makana would direct them to the office, which is where Benny and Glory spent most of their time now. He said that the big house was too dangerous for their daughter, all the chemicals, the fumes, the risk of explosion, so he'd take the little girl with him to his office while Makana burned. Once, when Makana got suspicious and followed them to the cottage, all she heard was something like pots banging behind the locked doors, so she figured they were just playing.

But they weren't playing. And every time Glory threatened Benny and said she was going to tell Makana what was really going on in the office—tweaker mothers giving their kids to Benny for an hour in exchange for just enough rocks to make it through the day, he'd lock Glory in a gutted aluminum tool locker. She was glad to be locked up as she listened to little girls weep for their mommies, Benny's hands all over them. Because when she wasn't in that locker, Benny's hands were all over her, too.

Sometimes he'd leave her in the tool locker for hours. Glory would have to stomp her feet just to keep the blood moving through her legs. Sometimes she'd be in the box so long that even when she stood outside it, like in front of the kitchen sink or the bathroom mirror, she'd be marching in place. Once in a while, when Makana was half-sober, which was rare, she'd slap Glory on the back of the head and tell her to cut it out. Glory would never even notice that she was doing it in the first place.

By the time Glory was ten, she'd spend her school-less days sitting on the couch getting high with her mother (she was only allowed to smoke weed because meth was too strong for her and might stunt her growth), dreading that knock on the door. Then when the knock came, she would squeeze Makana's hand. Makana would pull it away, scratch at her sores, and Benny would come in and lead her to the office with another little girl. And while they walked to the cottage with blacked-out windows, two kids and Benny holding hands, walking around stripped ice-cream trucks and stacks of cinder blocks, Glory tried hard to dream about castles and unicorns, but she had forgotten what they looked like.

4.

When Glory was thirteen, she waited for New Year's Eve, knowing that Benny would work a double that day, and ran away from home. She took a map with her, and using a ruler, she drew a line from Waimanalo to the opposite side of the island—Makaha. She didn't know how to catch the bus or hitchhike, so she walked. She walked along Bellows Beach as blue-bubbled jellyfish washed up on shore, their thin stingers strewn across the sand like tripwires. She walked to a dead-end rockpile fronted by a sign that read: Do not pass. Forced to double back, she walked to the Air Force base, searching for road. Hummers rolled past and jets boomed supersonic overhead.

After she found road, Glory detoured past Lanikai McMansions, old women wearing gloves and straw gardening hats watering their flowers. She felt like she was traveling through a foreign country. She walked past a steakhouse as outdoor diners sat by unlit tiki torches, looking impatient and important. One little girl was crying because she couldn't have dessert. She had a pink balloon tied to her wrist.

Glory walked past Kailua High School, the school she'd never graduate from, and as she neared Kaneohe, she passed a golf course, grown men hacking away at tiny, white-dimpled balls. She stayed far away from them. Benny liked golf. She figured they were all like him.

As the sun was setting, and the blue and green reef water of Kaneohe Bay turned muck brown, Glory entered Kahaluu, where teens stopped traffic and line-locked their souped-up cars and motorcycles on Kamehameha Highway, a sort of half-ass New Year's Eve fireworks display. As she got deeper in Kahaluu and eyed 4x4's rolling out of their gravel driveways, kids riding in the back, lighting fire crackers, and throwing them at passing tour buses and rental cars, she had to stop and look at the map again since she wasn't sure if she made a wrong turn and ended up back in Waimanalo.

By the time she hit Kaaawa, fireworks were on full display. Kamehameha Highway was now covered with a gunpowder-scented fog. PVC pipe stuck in buckets of sand launched blossoms of neon. Packs of 25,000 miniature sticks of dynamite draped over ladders or strung up on fishing poles, lit, and erupting. Glory's ears were ringing. Tiny slips of red paper stuck to her slippers and blistered feet. Illegal aerials burst yellow, blue, purple, and pink and lit up the smoky night sky. She liked the noise, pleased that there were other things to look at and wished she could blow things up, too. She made her way to Swanzy Beach Park and slept on a picnic bench carved with jagged love promises and chiseled notifications that people had been here before her.

Glory only managed a few hours of sleep before she started walking again. The firecracker popping, little aftershocks now. She looked up at the mountain range and wondered if she could hike over it. According to her map, Makaha was on the other side. But the slopes seemed impossibly steep, so Glory continued to hike on Kamehameha Highway and passed a cliff called Crouching Lion wondering why they named it that considering the only lions that could be found in Hawaii were at the zoo she loved then learned to hate.

She passed Laie, the white walls of the Mormon temple lit up like closed gates to heaven. She passed Kahuku Point, Turtle Bay, and all the big-wave North Shore beaches. The sun rose and she stopped at Waimea Bay and watched the giant winter wave-faces spew dawn patrol surfers out of frothy white foam. She went from Waimea to Haleiwa and watched tourists and locals stand in line for paper cones filled with flakes of ice soaked in corn syrup, which made her hungry. By the time she arrived at Kaena Point it was near night again. According to her map, once she rounded this island tip of unpaved, jagged, beachless shoreline filled with cratered, dusty paths imprinted with monster truck tire tracks, she'd be close to her new home. She'd seen pictures of camps of people living there, homeless, the TV said, but those tarps and tents looked like homes to her, perfect in fact, because none of them had walls. Maybe one of the people there would adopt her.

The first person Glory met at Makaha was a toothless old lady selling sea shells by the highway. The smaller, coned-shaped shells banded with brown markings sold for a quarter each. The bigger, shinier ones spotted and shaped like domes, they went for a dollar. Glory had been to the beach and never saw shells like these, and she'd certainly not seen live ones filled with slimy life in their tiny crevasses, so she wondered if the shells were real. The woman selling them, blotted with the same kind of scars her mother had, did not look trustworthy. Besides, how does a woman like this get these? Must need scuba and a powerful underwater flashlight to find stuff like this.

But the woman was nice. Gave her a shell even. Glory pocketed the shell and walked on, passing camps tucked under dry trees, clothes hanging on branches that grew sideways. The people there, all brown, but not too brown, brown like Black News Anchor Barbie, were huddled under their tarps or in their tents, eying her as she passed their barking dogs. Glory picked up a stick, just in case. But then she realized that they were hiding just like her and dropped the stick.

When she reached the first beach park clearing and stepped onto the parking lot pavement, the people seemed less tired, less scared. Two women washed their cars. A group of five sat under a tarp playing cards. The dealer wore an army jacket and sat in a wheelchair. Glory felt his crooked eyes on her as she passed. He called her over and offered her food from army-colored cans. He told her that he had these since the war, but not to worry, army food lasts forever.

Glory ate her canned chopped ham and eggs as the old man with a white beard told her how the army used to give them these with crackers, gum, and cigarettes. He asked her where she was from, and Glory lied and said Waikiki. The three women at the table, all twice the size of Glory, complained and told the man to concentrate on dealing the cards. One teased him about his crooked eyes, lazy she called them, just like him. The other man, bearded but young, looked bored and jumped on his custom built bicycle that sat low and had a long fork, it resembled a mock chopper. He rode off. The dealer asked Glory if she had a place to stay. She said she didn't. He said he had an extra tent and she could hang out here. One woman, the one who teased the dealer about his eyes, asked Glory where her parents were. She told them that her parents were dead, especially her mother. The women looked at each other and nodded like they had especially dead mothers, too.

5. _____

After a couple of weeks on the beach, Glory had enemies. She slept with men, some married, up and down the beach in exchange for food and protection from the cops, who, they all told her, were probably looking for her every time a blue-and-white motored past. Soon, the women ran Glory off whenever she came around, and few of the men, Crime Stopper suspects who littered the beach with empty plastic vials (dead soldiers they called them) didn't like the heat she was bringing down on the camp even though she was sleeping with them, too. One, a motorcycle thief who could break the steering lock on a rice burner with a single, snapping jerk, told her in his tent, as he wiped his cock with a wet cloth, that he saw her picture up at the Walmart exit, where they posted pics of dozens of girls Glory's age who went missing or ran away from home. "This world is fucked," he said. He talked smart like that. Glory wondered if he went to college. He OD'd and died a week later.

The only person who didn't want anything from Glory and didn't hate her was the card dealer, the vet with the big white beard, whose name was Simon Unabia. Every time it seemed like the Makaha homeless would get together and run her out with torches and pitchforks, Simon would just tell her to stay with him for awhile until things cooled down. Whenever she offered to sleep with him, he just laughed and said he was too crippled and too old. She didn't know whether she meant for her or in general. But they'd stay up in his tent some nights, just talk, and he'd tell her about what it was like to grow up on Maui sixty years ago, how there wasn't this or that, and how, when he got back from some really hot place called Vietnam, where he was responsible for the lives of seven other men, four of whom died, he didn't want to be responsible for anything in his life ever again.

There were other nice people, too. One man, who had been a Waikiki magician who once upon a time could turn balls of fire into doves, showed her how to cut cards with one hand. A woman who had once sold flowers to bar patrons, the kind of bars she said, with paintings of topless native ladies, tits sagging, holding a wood bowl filled with fruit, she taught Glory how to make leis. But whenever Glory ran into real trouble, like the night after she ate a spectacular beating from a two-hundred pound wife, she ended up in Simon's tent with a cold compress from his army first aid kit. "I wish I knew how to fight," she said. "I'm too small."

"That's why weapons were invented," said Simon as he rolled a cigarette like a cowboy. "Imagine back in caveman times. Those guys had to fight fucking dinosaurs. Size don't matter if you have a weapon."

"I need a weapon, then."

Simon just smiled as he lit up, shook the match out, then tossed it outside the open tent. "Violence. The international language of violence. My Dad used to say it's the only language ignorant kanakas understand. But actually, it's the only language everybody understands."

Simon reached into a knapsack and pulled out a stiff, dirty leather holster. He took out a slip of paper stashed inside and handed it to Glory. The slip was soft and felt thin, almost as thin as Simon's cigarette papers. It was a war trophy certificate for a the gun picked up somewhere in the vicinity of Khe Sanh. "I don't care who you point this at, what language they speak," said Simon, now holding the rusty pistol and pointing it at an imaginary target. "They know what you're saying."

"Does it have bullets?" Glory asked.

Simon shook his head. "Nope," he said. "Not for years."

The cops finally caught Glory two months later.

6.

The cops called her a P.S., Person in need of Supervision, when they drove her past the Chinese restaurant and pulled up to the green detention home. The place looked even bigger from the inside than the outside—a lobby with a reception desk stocked with a rusty staplers; bent, recycled paperclips; and an actual working typewriter. There was a mini-courtroom off to the side. Boys sat on mats while a man who looked and talked Football Coach tried to get them to see the light with drunk uncle words. "You gotta tink!" he said. "You gotta use your brains! No be like your faddas, uncles, braddahs, and cousins! Tink about da future!"

"Okay, sir," one boy said, a real teacher's pet.

"Call me uncle!" the man said, as if calling him anything else was an insult. Glory spotted his tats and track marks as she was led past. She wondered if he'd tried to get another job like maybe driving a delivery truck or something similar, but this job, taking care of Persons in need of Supervision, was the only one he could get.

The courtyard was tennis court green, the single-story windows covered by rusted grates. Boys walked single file on one side of the fence, girls on the other. One skinny boy was talking to an uncle, bouncing on his toes, and throwing slow-motion punches, telling a story with his body. When a line of girls walked past, he stopped jumping and said, "Woo, baby! Woo, woo! Oh, I love you, baby!"

He went back to his bouncing once they passed.

7. _____

After sleeping in a bed for the first time in months, Glory was in the mini-courtroom the next morning. The judge, an old haole, sat behind the bench while he looked through a file. Glory felt the hairs on her arms rise. She turned around. Her mother and Benny stepped inside the courtroom wearing their baby luau best—Benny in jeans, a faded golf shirt, and sunglasses perched on his forehead. Makana in a threadbare flower-printed dress, a wet bundle of curls sitting on her head. She had even showered and washed her hair.

The judge put down the file and pushed his glasses up his nose. "Look at your mother," he said in a weird accent, an accent as foreign to Glory as snow. "You're making her sick."

Glory didn't look at her. Instead she looked at another tweaker mother who walked in, coughed, and sat in the back row, picking at the sores on her arms. This one didn't shower. "You gotta understand," said the judge to Glory. "You are important. You are an important person. You have a future to think about."

Glory finally looked at Makana, whose eyes were locked on the judge, her head moving up and down as if she was in a prayer meeting or something. Benny was nodding too, then he glanced at his watch.

"We all want the best for you," said the judge.

Makana nodded in agreement.

Thirty minutes later, Makana was at the reception desk signing Glory out. While Glory marched in place and chewed on her fingernails, she could hear the judge talking to another girl. "Look at your mother," he said. "You're making her sick. You are important. You are an important person..."

8.

Benny handed Glory a bucket, called her a slut, and put her in the tool locker. She had to do two days for running away. She wasn't sure what the bucket was for. There wasn't enough room to sit or even squat. If anything, it just made things more uncomfortable because it took up more space.

Glory spent the first couple of hours trying to think a way out of the locker. When she couldn't come up with anything, she tried to kick her way out. She broke a rubber slipper, so she kicked barefoot instead. When that didn't work, she stood on the bucket and screamed, punched, and clawed at the eye-level slits until her hands swelled. After she exhausted herself, she wished she was a horse, so she could fall asleep standing up.

Glory spent that first day drifting in and out of crazy. She screamed and wept. She nodded off and smiled in her sleep as she imagined chopping Benny and her mother into little bits and feeding them to sharks. Sometimes, Simon Unabia, the homeless vet, would appear in her daydreams, holding a lance and rolling around in a wheelchair souped-up with rocket exhaust, and rescue her. "Violence is the only language everyone understands," he'd said. She planned ways to get violent with Benny and Makana. She needed a weapon, but the only thing around here was sticks, glass flasks, and cinderblocks, weapons that would only work on them if they were sleeping, and even then she wasn't so sure. Sometimes she wished for a glass of water. Sometimes she wished she was dead.

Benny came in the next afternoon with a handtruck and wheeled the tool locker outside. Glory begged Benny to let her out and promised she'd be good. He ignored her and shot water through the little slits. Glory cupped her hands trying to catch water and shovel it in her mouth. Where was her mother? Probably getting high inside, glued to the couch as usual. After Glory got all the water she needed, she stood on the bucket and peered through the slits. She tried to look through the house windows, but they were too fogged up from the years of chemical cooking inside. She looked at Benny. His face was blank, like he was just out there watering the grass or feeding dogs. One eye red, smaller than the other as usual. One look, and she knew he wasn't going to let her out early and wondered if he was going to really let her out at all. Benny carted the locker back into his office and told Glory one more day.

Later that night as Glory stomped the sleep out of her feet and rubbed the sleep out of her eyes, the door creaked open. Figuring it was Benny, Glory begged him to let her out and whispered that she would do all those things he liked without crying. But Benny didn't answer. Instead, he just sat down and leaned against the locker. Glory stopped begging and listened. The click of a lighter followed by a deep inhale and the smell of ammonia and apple rock candy. It wasn't Benny out there. It was her mother.

"I wonder how your brothers are doing," she said.

Glory hadn't thought about them in years. She looked down at her thigh. A tip of pencil lead stuck under her skin. Chayne-Marcos had stabbed her with a pencil when she was five. Glory remembered watching her mother strip him down to his underwear and burn him with her lighter five times for that one. But that was nothing compared to what Boi'd gotten. The time he'd ripped up her money. The time he'd set her weed on fire. The time he'd thought her batu was candy, ate it, and had to be rushed to emergency. Boi got lickings and then some. But then the cops showed up at the emergency room that day the doctor pumped Boi's stomach. Grandma took Glory, Chayne-Marcos, and Boi away from Makana, and they didn't see their mother for half-a-year. It was a happy six months. Their grandmother took them to the park everyday. She would tell them old Hawaiian stories. You need to know your culture, she'd say as she told them about the ogres of Kauai, the shark man of Waipio, and how Maui slowed the sun. They even got to go to school every day.

But then their grandmother got sick, locked in her own body, and Makana came back. And when she returned, she burned Boi all the time, sometimes looking at her paralyzed mother as she did it. Boi had so many lighter burns on his back that Makana had to start burning his chest and stomach. Once she even tied a rope around his neck and hung him outside the bus window for thirty minutes. And Boi, even after the hanging, would be bad again right after. It started to almost seem as if Boi liked it.

Sitting outside the tool locker, Makana started to talk nonsense, which she almost always did after her first few hits. She'd gone to community college and almost finished and liked to prove it every time she got high. "In the Middle Ages," said Makana. "In the Middle Ages, girls used to disfigure themselves so that their fathers and brothers would stop raping them. Think you could do something like that?"

Glory thought about it. "No," she said.

"I brought home the wrong child. I should've picked Boi."

"If you picked him, you would be dead by now. Benny too."

Makana laughed. "Exactly. Why can't you be more like your brother?"

"Let me out."

"No."

Makana stood up. She slipped a plastic bag though the locker slits. "What is this?" Glory asked.

"Important papers."

"Why are you giving them to me?"

Makana didn't answer. She stepped to the door and opened it. "Don't leave me with him!" Glory screamed. "Don't you fucking leave me alone with him!"

Makana stepped out and shut the door. After screaming until her throat hurt, Glory opened the plastic bag Makana had slipped her. Just birth certificates, social security cards, a checkbook, and state ID's. Shit Glory had no use for, shit regular people used. What Makana should've slipped her was a bag full of razor blades. That way, like they said in that one movie that was always on cable, she could get busy living or get busy dying.

9. _____

When Benny let her out the next day, he handed her the water hose and a bar of soap and told her she was too stink to bathe inside. Glory drank from the hose until her stomach hurt then sat down in the dirt and washed herself as Benny frowned. "You getting hairy like one monkey," he said.

Glory turned away and looked up at the mountains, an impossible wall of rock and trees that made her feel even more trapped. She glanced at the broken-down ice cream trucks. It had been how Benny's parents made their living, selling manapua, pork hash, rice cake, and candy to neighborhood kids. The three wheel-less trucks were propped on bricks, doors frozen by rust. Glory glanced at Benny. He was fat, but she wasn't sure if she could run faster. She wanted to make a break for it, but now wasn't the right time. Her legs and feet were killing her. Night was best, when Benny was working. Besides, she didn't want to end up in the locker again this soon. Is that why her mother gave her the papers? So she could run away? But she gave Glory papers for the both of them. Was she planning to run away with Glory?

She didn't want her fucking mom with her when she split. She'd just hook up with another Benny and Glory would end up in the same damn place. "Where's mom?" Glory asked.

"Inside cooking."

After she finished washing off, Glory struggled to stand then followed Benny inside the house. Her back and feet were sore and she wondered if this was what it felt like to be an old lady. Makana was standing in front of the table with all the flasks and bottles. Glory sat on the couch while Benny stepped beside Makana. Makana stripped batteries with needle-nose pliers as Benny dropped the lithium into a cooler filled with lantern fluid. They looked like a married TV couple doing dishes, one washing, one drying. The smell used to make Glory cough, but after Makana slapped her face whenever she coughed, Glory was soon cured.

Glory, glad to be sitting again, turned on the TV. It was always on the same cable news channel, the one with the fat haole who was always scribbling on his chalkboard and crying, because Benny said watching anything else would turn their brains to mush. She caught the image of a group of young men making war in the middle of some desert before she fell asleep. She envied them, their wide open spaces, their weapons. Maybe Glory would join the army if she could make it through five more years of this hell. She'd kill people she didn't know on the other side of the world to get out of this. Glory started to doze off. The cooler of lithium and lantern fluid hissed as Makana turned on the ammonia tank and sprayed the mixture. She turned it off and on, off and on, then she dropped the mud, the crushed cold medicine, into the mixture. Glory passed out.

"Gloryyyy!"

Glory opened her eyes. Her mother, still cooking at the table, was facing her, holding up glowing green hands. For a moment, she looked like a crackhead superhero standing there, sores all over her arms, her hands on fire. A wide-eyed Benny stared at her glowing hands, too. He took off his shirt and tried to smother the flames. The shirt caught on fire and Benny chucked it on the table.

"Runnn!"

Glory headed for the door. Benny stepped toward the door too, but Makana grabbed him by the belt. Benny's pants lit up. He screamed and dragged Makana halfway to the door. Glory swung the door open and slammed it behind her.

She ran on jello legs. She tripped over an engine block and tumbled in a patch of California grass. She stopped up and turned around.

An explosion rang her ears and nearly knocked her on her ass.

It was as if someone poured gasoline down a giant rat hole and lit it on fire. The pop was so big it blasted a hole through the roof. A squealing Benny burst through the door. His whole body was on fire as he ran. He screamed. He screamed just like some of those little girls did in the office when Benny put his hands all over and inside them. Screaming like Glory screamed the first time he took her there.

The flames were contagious. Everything Benny banged into lit up. The trucks, the tool locker, all lit up. He went for the water hose, but that caught on fire too. He collapsed by the faucet, now more on-smoke than on-fire. But maybe the color of the flames were just dulled by the sunlight. He smelled like food. Glory put her hand over her mouth and tried not to laugh. When Benny finally stopped screaming, stopped moving, Glory picked up a cinderblock and held it over his burnt head. Her arms shook. It was heavy. Why was it so hard to drop? She finally threw it down with everything she had. She missed the first couple of times. She kept at it until she didn't miss and Benny's smoking head popped off his body and rolled under a manapua truck.

After she was sure Benny was done, Glory dragged the cinderblock inside and looked for her mother. That woman had to be finished off, too. But when she stepped inside she saw that all that was left was a charred arm on the sofa, the spot where Glory had fallen asleep a few minutes earlier. The rest of her mother was just red paste splattered on smoldering bark cloth and blown-up wicker chairs. Glory wondered what had made her do it, but she'd been around enough to know that fucked-up people were unpredictable like that. That's why even back in the day when her mother used to burn her and her brothers, they always looked surprised right before she grabbed them. It's like Simon told her once, every crack is a false crack. People rarely expect to get hit.

Either way, Glory figured that had to be Makana's finest moment. The moment she was standing there with glowing green hands about to blow up. The way Benny had looked at her. Glory wanted people to look at her like that, too.

She walked out of the house and spotted Benny's keys shining from his melted pocket. She picked up a rake and pulled the keys away from the charcoal body. She picked up the keys then dropped them. They were still hot. She blew into her hands while she waited for them to cool. Ten minutes later, she picked up the keys and jumped in Benny's car.

Glory didn't know how to drive, but no way she was walking again, especially not after standing in a tool locker for two days straight. She turned the key. She put the car in reverse, hit the gas, and slammed into one of the broken down ice-cream trucks. She dropped the car into drive, pounded the pedal, and barreled right through the gate at the top of the hill. After taking out a few mailboxes and parked car side-mirrors, she got the hang of it. The speed, the temptation to brake, was harder to handle than the steering. She was driving good by the time she hit Kaneohe. The ride over the cratered paths of Kaena Point was rough, but that was the only way she knew how to get to Makaha.

10.

When Glory and Simon got back to Waimanalo, birds were pecking at Benny. They shooed the birds away and Simon told her to find all the dry sticks she could find and pile them by Benny's body. He wheeled himself to the big house and went inside.

The next morning, they burned everything. While they watched the giant fire turn it all from black to dust, Simon asked Glory what she was going to do. Glory shrugged and showed him the papers her mother had given her. He nodded. He told her that maybe they could fix up the place and stay here. She told him that one of the reasons she brought him here was so that he could stay with her forever. He said that he would, but that in order for this to work, she had to be his legs. She had to be his muscle. That she couldn't be one of those little girls, those victims, the kind that get kidnapped by Big Island Mexican farm hands with thirteen different names then sent to the mainland to work whorehouses up and down the Pacific coast. She couldn't be one of those little girls who think that the only way they can be safe is by fucking young men with big, strong hands and tiny, weak brains. He told her that in order for this to work, people had to take one look at her and think, no way I'm going near that crazy bitch.

"I know," Glory said.

"You show people that you aren't afraid to kill, that you aren't afraid to die."

"I'm not afraid. Not anymore."

"You sad? You miss them?"

Glory eyed the fire. "Fuck no."

"People. People treat their fucking dogs better than other people. Only way to get by in this world is to hate them all."

Simon reached into his knapsack and pulled out his old war trophy pistol and a small bottle of whiskey. "Carry both tools on you at all times."

Glory nodded. "I need something else. Something that blows up, too."

"For what?"

"So I can blow everyone up around me in case I'm about to lose."

Simon grinned. "That's my girl."

"I never going let anyone touch me again. I die before anyone touches me or locks me up again."

By the time Glory was sixteen, the name Morning Glory took on a whole new meaning. She wasn't a pretty purple flower with delicate petals, the flower that the Chinese used for a laxative or that produced psychedelic seeds. She was Morning Glory, the little firecracker, the sparkler, the little girl who would shoot fire and burn your shit down if you fucked with her. The stories spread through Waimanalo to urban myth, ghost story status. How there was this crazy drunk bitch who lived up by the mountains. She had blown up her parents. Adults would tell their kids stories about how late at night you could see the burning man running toward the mountains, screaming, as green flames flickered on every inch of his body and he left fire footprints. They would tell their kids that if anyone messed with Glory or that white-bearded old man in a wheelchair she had living up there with her, she'd light them on fire. "Morning Glory. Mess with her, she come at you like fucking dynamite," they'd say.

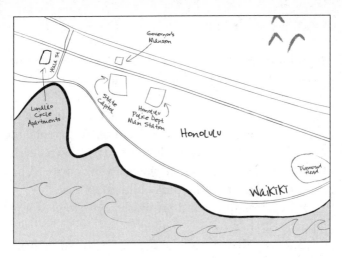

III. Loliana

1.

Helen Knotting passed away. At home, Shane took it real hard. He rampaged, ripping doors off their hinges and kicking holes through walls.

Over a week later, Boi still feels nothing. Is something wrong with him? He's heard the term "sociopath" thrown around before, but only in movies: genius serial killers who store human heads in freezers and mail Bible hints to cops. He knows he's not like that. He never read the Bible and that other stuff is pilau. But there's always that movie scene where some old man, usually that popolo one with gray hair and freckles, he'll throw out phrases like "lack of remorse and empathy" or "lack of control and inability to love." Was all full of shit, considering the smartest cop Boi knows likes to talk about the pluses and minuses of Bermuda versus Seashore Paspalum grass more than anything else.

But those movie phrases are striking a note now. Helen Knotting's dead. Nothing. Shane weeping, the most grief he'd seen pour out of anyone not the mother of a chronic. Nothing. Seeing his sister for the first time in nearly twenty years. Nothing. Even when Patricia called because she'd seen it on the news, the First Lady, dead, she cried. Boi had nothing to say. Pull out the pin and throw him a grenade. He doesn't give a shit.

As Boi drives to Chastity's to pick up Nina, he imagines all sorts of personal disasters, the death of his parents, the death of his siblings, the death of his few friends, his own death, and all of it lacks punch. Boi glances in the rear view mirror. A ballet slipper and jump rope sit on the pink child safety seat.

Except for that. He'd go mushroom cloud if anything ever happened to her.

But even then, would he *feel* it? Or would he just be using it as an excuse to go off?

As a cop, part of a brotherhood, he hears the dreams other guys have. Real ones, like a house, a wife, and sons who play quarterback in a D-I spread offense. Weird ones, like guys dreaming they're on their knees scrubbing a toilet and some fat dude comes, pushes them away, and takes the mother of all dumps. Sexual ones that almost always involve multiple girls, hot tubs, champagne, bling, and West Coast hip-hop. But Boi doesn't dream like that. Most of Boi's dreams involve breaking things as small as multi-colored Christmas tree light bulbs and as big as buildings. Boi dreams of growing six giant tentacle arms and laying waste to things around him. He also dreams of Nina standing too close to the edge on top of hotel towers as the roof tilts and teeters. Lately, he dreams of weeping doll's heads hanging from a tree. A whistling, crown-wearing Charles Knotting is the one stringing them up.

He almost doesn't make it to Chastity's. Horn-pounding drivers to wake Boi up to the fact that he's driving on the wrong side of the road. Boi jerks the wheel right. Two-and-a-half tons of tour bus blows past. He rubs his eyes and sticks a finger in his left ear. He can *hear* his hand shake. What the hell is wrong with him?

Maybe the problem is that he likes nothing and hates everything. There was a time when he'd tell people about all the things he hated, and they'd laugh and say that his brutal honesty was part of his charm. But he hadn't been trying to be charming; he was serious. And once he forced himself to stop talking about all the shit he hated so that he could become Swingman Rapun, he discovered he had very little to say otherwise. Swingman Rapun was quiet and reaper grim. Swingman Rapun didn't have friends and hardly got laid. Boi No Good, the kid who hated everything and everybody and told it to anyone who listened, had way more friends and did way better with the ladies. Granted, he attracted a certain self-destructive type—skinny, shot-swilling single Moms. Asian Catholic-girl-school graduates who wore too much make-up and posted half-naked pics of themselves on the Internet.

It's as if the gods themselves hate Swingman Rapun and love Boi No Good. But Boi does not believe in squid gods and millennial hurricanes—that's his father talking. More honking. Boi opens his eyes and hits the gas to catch up with traffic.

It's late when Boi pulls into Kahekili Village. The windows of the two-story walk-up are lit with TV flashes. Draped over the second-floor balcony: dog leashes, orange extension cords, flowered bedsheets held down by bricks and forty-ounce beer bottles. A three-year-old plugged into an iPod rides a plastic tricycle across the lane. He's wearing a dirty green collared shirt a couple sizes too big for him. Boi rolls down his window. "Where's your mom?" he asks. It's ten o' clock.

The little boy shrugs and peddles on. The turning wheels tick, plastic on plastic, like someone shuffling a new deck cards.

Boi gets out of the car and knocks on Chastity's door. No answer. Chastity and Nina aren't home. There's a party in the unit above, but Boi waits in the car for thirty minutes. He calls Chastity twice. No answer. The little boy parks his tricycle and heads up to the party.

Hard cases leaning on the second-story rail crack off beer bottles with plastic lighters. Skanks with stiff hair jangle while they walk, wrists shackled by multiple yellow gold bracelets. Boi passes the tough guys eyeing him up and heads inside.

Island Souljahs blares on cracked speakers. Something about red roses, meant to be, and kissing and hugging someone named Girl. Her name is always Girl. And things are always irie. The crowd hollers "au-rights" and "rodga dats" over the hypnotic keyboards and a rapper, plugged into Auto-Tune, who sounds like a stoned robot.

Inside, more hard cases with red eyes and puffy faces play dominos on a fold-out table. More skanks leaning on walls, one painting a green Hawaiian island on each lacquered finger. Boi squeezes past her. She yells, "Shots!" Someone behind Boi yells "Au-right!" Boi heads to the bedroom.

Chastity and three little girls sit in a circle, cross-legged on a queen mattress. Nina's on Chastity's lap, smiling, playing with her bracelet. Chastity kisses the top of Nina's head and braids her hair. The other girls wait for their turn.

Is she a good mother? Probably not. Between an EBT-purchased microwavable diet, night-with-the-girlz drinking sessions, a new "uncle" every few months, and flunking out of community college once every couple of years, Chastity is a pretty terrible role model. But she isn't a monster mother like Boi's was. She doesn't do drugs (just some weed, but nothing hard). She doesn't beat Nina (she better not, ROPA or not). She charges whatever Nina wants on her overextended credit card (she'd bought the seven-year-old a cell phone a couple of weeks ago). And she includes the little girl in her hobbies (Nina can string beads, make candles, and blend salts). But she's not Patricia Bolosan. But even more than that, she's not a Helen Knotting.

Does he want Nina doing the same shit when she's an adult?

No. He dreams big for his daughter. He wants her to do something massive.

Maybe it's time he set a real example?

Chastity finishes Nina's braid. Nina climbs off her lap and the next girl parks her butt on Chastity. Nina looks at herself in a full-length mirror covered with surf- and reggae-themed stickers.

Who does she look more like? Boi or Chastity? Boi doesn't know. He has no baby or small kid pictures of himself.

Nina makes faces in the mirror. Her mad face. Her happy face. Her tilted-head shy face. She's already practicing to be fake or, worse, practicing to be like her father. Boi leaves before they see him.

As he heads to the front door, the girl with the island-painted fingernails swigs from a tequila bottle filled with red ling hing mui seeds. She passes it to a friend. A man reaches into a big, white paper bag and tosses one-dollar fast food hamburgers to others in the crowd. Jah-waiian music booms from homemade particle-board woofer boxes set up in each corner of the room.

When Boi gets halfway through, he hears a scream up ahead. At first he's not sure if the scream is coming from the speakers or a real person. Two more screams. They're real screams coming from the balcony.

"Boi! Boi!"

He turns back. The only people who would scream his name are Chastity or Nina. But then he realizes no one is screaming his name. These are a mother's screams. He's heard enough screams on the job to know. It's a mother screaming for her son, her boy. Swingman Rapun takes over. He puts his hand on his gun, pushes through the crowd.

People are scrambling downstairs. Two rusty balcony bars jut from the second floor, ripped from the railing, bent at their concrete base. A mess of black paint chips and rust flakes litter the ground. More screaming below. Boi looks over the railing, careful not to lean against it. The three-year-old tricycle rider is flat on his back, his legs broken and twisted under him.

Boi rushes downstairs and pushes through people, half of them already dialing 911 on their cell phones. He pulls out his badge and shows it to them. He yanks the screaming mother off the child. Other mothers hold her back as she kicks and tries to break free. Boi gets down on his knees and puts his ear next the kid's pale lips. Just ticking. No breathing. Boi starts CPR, tilting the boy's head back with one hand while pushing down on his chest with the heel of the other. He pinches the kid's nose and tries to breathe life into him.

Boi leans down, ear against mouth. The ticking is faster now, like the kid's tricycle is gunning fifty m.p.h. No one's turned the music off upstairs. People behind him ask each other what happened. But through all that noise, Boi hears a weak breath.

Sirens now. A fire engine is pulling up. The crowd makes way as the firemen head for the boy toting a child-size stretcher. Boi stands and takes a step back as they work on the kid. He looks up. Kid probably leaned against those ancient bars and the rust cracked and gave. Thirty pounds of three-year-old is all it took. Fucking budget-cutting motherfuckers at the capitol. Fucking Kry-lua dog park-making mother-fuckers. Fucking, motherfucking Governor Charles Knotting.

Boi pushes through the crowd and heads for his car. The screaming mother is now weeping as the other mothers try to comfort her. The ticking in Boi's ears is still there, louder and faster now, not just sound, but popping pain. He spots the plastic tricycle at his feet, picks it up, and smashes it to bits.

Boi gets in his car. He spots Nina and Chastity along the outer rim of the crowd watching him. Nina waves. He's about to get out of his car and hug the hell out of her. Instead, he pretends he doesn't see them, starts the car, and reverses out.

Driving, the dream flashes. Charles hanging doll heads on a tree. The one he's putting up now has black, frizzy hair in a fresh braid. The wind blows and the head swings and spins. As the twirling and swaying slows, the head rocks to stillness, its dark eyes now facing Boi. Diamond earrings, white teeth, and arched, pencil-thin eye brows, a cartoon version of Nina.

It's almost midnight when Boi finds himself at a Kry-lua supermarket. Free copies of the latest issue of *Island Voice* sit by the shopping carts. He stops and does a double-take. He's on the front page with his father and Shane? He picks up a copy. No, it's definitely him. He, Shane, and Joe are in the underground main station parking lot the night Boi'd bailed them out. The caption: *Knott on the Up and Up: Corruption in the Highest Office.* Boi eyes the picture. Despite everything, his first thought is: Is Shane really that much bigger than him?

He skims the story. Like everything else in the *Voice*, restaurant, book, and movie reviews, week-old news. But Bijarani published the story a week after Helen Knotting's death. That took balls. Maybe Boi will call him and tell him about Kahekili Housing, falling three-year-olds, and Kry-lua dog parks. On his way in the store, Boi passes a woman pushing a baby in a cart. The baby grabs a copy of *Island Voice*, crumples the front page, and stuffs it in his mouth.

Boi wanders supermarket aisles, pushing a cart. He passes girls grabbing cold packs as they stumble and giggle toward the one open register. One loses her rubber slipper as she runs like Skank Cinderella trying to beat the clock. A hotel security guard soon to start his graveyard shift stands in front of the coffeemaker trying to decide between coconut mocha and vanilla macadamia nut—the hardest fucking question he'll face all day. Boi knows. He faces the same question sometimes. He rolls through the aisles. He thinks about how Charles told him he was "the one." That he could be chief. Mayor. Governor. How Charles was looking at him like his dick supposed to be getting hard considering all the possibilities.

Boi can't shake the image of the kid falling from the second floor. It's Nina he sees instead of the tricycle rider. Boi picks up a few packages of sausages. He rolls two aisles over and grabs antifreeze. He rolls past bags of dog food, one brand "pet parent perfect" at three bucks a pound. At the pesticide section he tosses a dozen boxes of rat poison into the cart.

Boi stands behind a large man with a tee shirt that reads FBI—From the Big Island—who is buying two cases of green bottles, powdered sugar, and ten pounds of ribeye. The man struggles over the credit card reader. Fucking retard. When it's finally Boi's turn, he pays cash.

Boi sits in his car at the Kailua dog park, the one Charles Knotting got built. A yellow strip cuts through the middle of a paved bicycle lane so stupid haoles avoid Segway and baby stroller head-on collisions. Haole Kry-lua moms love to jog with their babies, pushing vulcanized-rubber tire, spoke-rimmed strollers under coconut trees and past pavilions. Boi's surprised there aren't stoller traffic lights and speed limit signs either. He loads the sausages soaked in antifreeze with rat poison and smiles. It's been awhile.

He cuts up the sausage into chunks and steps out of his car. The stabbing pain in his ears has faded to a low decibel buzz. Boi looks around for crumbs. Day is breaking, so they're all gone. He places the sausage pieces at the base of the trees throughout the park. He washes his hands. Then he picks out the picnic bench with the best view and waits. The smoky sky is lit all orange as if hell is just a few miles up.

The Kry-lua blonds emerge at sunrise, their tanned faces shaded by tennis and golf-sun visors. Their ponytails bounce as their perfectly-trained, golden retrievers (even their dogs are blond) follow on slack-leashed dog harnesses (because choke chains and dog collars are inhumane, but kicking homeless people from beach to beach like cans is cool) and match them stride-for-stride. Each time one of the dogs pulls away and heads for a base of a tree, the surprised dog owner yanks the leash a little too late. The dogs don't even chew. They just swallow and continue on with their dog-park laps.

The first poisoned dog vomits mid-stride, leaving a streak of sick on its professionally-groomed fur. A minute later, the second dog sprays the two-lane asphalt with a stream of diarrhea. The third, a puppy, stops, shakes, then busts into seizure. The puppy-owner, on her knees, is trying to give her dog CPR.

Within an hour, twelve or so dogs are either laid out on the grass or in the arms of their tear-streaked, pacing owners as pissed-off husbands who were halfway to work pull up to the park and load their sick pets into their shiny cars. They look around one more time before they head to the vet. How did this happen? One with wrinkles around her blue eyes spots Boi. The wrinkles— it's as if her eyeballs are being sucked to the back of her skull. Boi stands and heads to her. "What's going on?" Boi asks.

The woman looks around at the other sick dogs. "I don't know!"

Boi shrugs. "We should call someone! Get the kind doggie ambulances or what?"

"I... I don't think so."

"Get one vet up the road. I go over there, call him. Get doggie emergency rooms, right? I tell him you guys on your way. Get the crash carts ready."

The woman nods. "What's your name, officer?"

"My name is Nalu."

"That's my dog's name!"

Boi walks to his car. Fuck Swingman Rapun. The fucking Gov, fuck his budget cuts and his new law. He probably thought maybe Boi was pissed because it meant that a law like that meant that people like Boi, Shane, Glory and half the people Boi busted would never be born. Boi didn't give a shit about that. He hated crumbs as much as the next guy. And he knew that when it came down to it, he was no good. Shane too. And Glory, with her fucked-up marching in place, was some kind of supercrumb who was probably better off dead. Fuck um. The world was better off without them. Put them all down. Realize Charles's vision of Hawaii: central island suburbs for locals who got paid salary to service the mainland haoles who paid the salaries. Who gives a fuck about the rest.

But what Uncle Charles didn't think about was that all his cuts and his new law also meant that people like that three-year-old tricycle rider, that people like Nina, his daughter, who never hurt nobody, who never even get one chance, would never be protected, or would never even be born, too. The Gov's doll head tree.

Fuck that shit.

Heading for the parking lot, Boi walks across sand blanketed with mainland grass as brown state workers in red jumpsuits pull weed eaters out of their trucks. Walking under the shade of iron-wood trees, he crushes pine cones with his black boots. A young, dreadlocked couple parks a jeep and heads for the water, the sand so soft, it kicks up like dust. Boi smiles. He feels the hole in his heart filling with every step he takes.

2.

Charles Knotting settled on Ala Moana Boulevard, even though he hated Ala Moana Beach because the water there always made him itchy. Although the procession would have to pass car deal-erships, cut through Waikiki, and cross over the stagnant brown stench of the Ala Wai Canal, at least they would be near the ocean. The cops just had to make sure to sweep Ala Moana Beach Park beforehand and boot the homeless sleeping on picnic benches. The last thing Charles wanted was to provide fodder for the liberals who saw leadership as a big room full of magic, fast-cash, money-dispensing buttons. To eliminate poverty, press here. To fix the economy, press here.

Two weeks after Helen's death, Charles had unveiled all of this to Shane as they talked over dinner. He wanted his son to say a few words at the church. Shane kept refusing until Charles pulled out a list of last wishes that Helen had written. The one-hundred-and-thirty page document was written by a woman who had thought about nothing but death for her last year of life. And there it was under the Shane section of the list, number fifty-six: I want my son to say a few words at my funeral. At least his section appeared first, before the Boi section, and even before the Charles section. He was grateful for that and agreed to speak, even though all he wanted to do was hide out at Glory's in Waimanalo and act like Helen had never died.

It's now four days later as Shane steps up to the podium, eyes the giant white walls, adjusts his belt, and resists the urge to un-tuck his shirt. It's an old church, one of the oldest in Hawaii, its congregation once made up of nineteenth century whalers and sugar barons. As he looks out at the filled pews, Shane spots The Descendants in the front row, those he's called aunty for most of his life, the granddaughters of great men with streets and buildings named after them, old white-haired women in muumuu's holding canes or seated in front of their walkers, wearing haku leis and thick-lens glasses. Shane has a hard time imagining that these liver-spotted women had once spent their time sitting on their fathers' laps in drawing rooms and playing Handel, riding horses, full gallop, on the Big Island, and losing their virginity to Ivy league leatherheads or slick men named Angelo while on Roman holiday. A few of them might have even been cum dumpsters back in the 1940s or whenever they grew up. They keep each other company now, splitting their time between mahjong to fight off Alzheimer's, lunch dates to fight off afternoon boredom, and volunteering for various preservation societies, keeping busy to fight off death itself. Their husbands are long gone. Second wives or death took them.

Shane, trying hard to not to look at the cameras or the open koa casket in front of him, looks behind the old women and eyes rows and rows of their children, grandchildren, and great-grandchildren. Young and not-so-young women with their stringy yoga bodies, the kind Shane made it a point not to have.

Charles's old surf buddies, fifty- and sixty-year-old men who still hit the gym. No more free weights, but they still devote an hour a day to rowing and elliptical machines while their wives run laps around Kapiolani Park in spandex. The Asian ones do it wearing make-up.

At first the crowd seems to get more local, mixed-race when Shane eyes Helen's old insurance colleagues and the local politicians. But really that group is dominated by balding Japanese men with paunches. The insurance guys and the political guys both sit smug with self-importance, their hands folded across their stomachs, intestines distended from years of all-you-can-eat prime rib buffet dinners.

Then there are the token Hawaiians peppered through the crowd here and there. The ones whose ancestors were in on the great land restructuring of 1850: advisers to royalty, downtown brothel owners, and husbands of princesses. But only a few of them look Hawaiian anymore, their blood diluted by generations of marriage to rich haole and Chinese. They still take advantage of the perks, though. Low-interest loans, government funds for their Big Island ranches, and Hawaiian-blood college scholarships for their children.

Hearing all these aunties and uncles yammer for years about botany, old movies, land tax, island history, canoe regattas, being vegan, the economic potential of fiber optics and ecotourism, and the "real" Hawaiians they knew or know (the famous musicians, watermen, union boys, and gangsters), he never wanted to become one of them. They always felt fake to him. Even now, with their solemn stares masking boredom, he might as well be at a masquerade ball instead of a funeral.

At Glory's, men pulled up with cinder blocks and sawdust in the back of their pick-ups. They talked about cock-fighting, new big-budget movies, and football. Women pulled up in rusting hoopties with stolen car-stereo systems worth more than their cars. They drank and they slurred "fuck this guy" or "fuck that girl" over and over again. And they all loved Shane at Glory's. They respected his size, especially the skinny tweakers who constantly asked him how much he could bench and said "ho cuz!" when he told them. He wants to be back there now soaking up the admiration and nonsense instead of up here thinking about Hawaii history and turning over the same question again and again: Why did Helen love him so much? He was a terrible son who only got worse as he got older. He knew that no one would ever love him as much as she had.

"My mom used to say, do good," Shane says into the mic. "She used to say, you are Hawaii just as much as Kahekili or Kalakaua. You are Knotting."

The Descendants nod. Finally, someone said it. Names like Knotting exerted more power on this place than any of those short-lived chiefs or kings. Whatever Hawaii was now, it was chiseled more by the hands of their ancestors than royalty.

"But today, I don't feel like Knotting. And I'm not sure that I ever did. Today, I'm just a bad son who lost a good mother."

Shane holds in tears. He should have written something, memorized something for her funeral, but he failed her even in that. "Most of you know that I was adopted. And I didn't quite realize what Helen Knotting saved me from until I reunited with my long-lost sister."

He'd spent the last two weeks at Glory's, so she is on his mind, too. But he's lying. He wishes Helen had left him in foster care. Then maybe he'd really be tough instead of trying to fake it. And he never would have known Helen Knotting and would not be all torn up now. "I have a brother, too." Shane scans the audience looking for Boi, but can't spot him.

"Anyway, sorry, I'm obviously a terrible public speaker compared to my father..."

He wants to say other things, but is too afraid they'll sound weird. For example, how all that time Helen was sick he craved foods that she loved, like Indian vegetable curry. That sometimes he'd get stoned and try to write a Wikipedia article on his mother, but couldn't really come up with anything besides Miss Hawaii, insurance, Governor's wife. That despite the fact that she got skinnier and more yellow month after month, he never thought she'd really die. Like she said, they were Knotting, and being Knotting meant being lucky like the very first Knotting in Hawaii, a shipwrecked sailor who started as a lowly clerk and became a dairy farmer and King Bull Nuts sugar plantation owner.

But his shock at her death embarrasses him now. Of course she was going to die and he feels as if he's the only dolt in the room who didn't see it coming. He looks out at the faces. Some clear their throats and text on mobile devices. Others look on the verge of passing out. A few escape for thirty-minute bathroom breaks. And it strikes Shane that they don't care. Almost none of them do. They will get in their cars after the funeral, complain about traffic, head home, and flip through television channels, perhaps commenting on how that was the longest funeral they'd ever been to, pointing out various imperfections, and maybe tell each other what they would have done differently. A dad may say to a son, "Hey, when I die, I want a short funeral. Not like that." A mother may tell a daughter, "Eww, cremate me when I die. An open casket is so morbid." Then they will head to bed, their heads filled with to-do checklists for the next day, maybe consider starting their new Korean Eight Constitution acupuncturist diets the next day, the one that they had to fly to Los Angeles to get consultation on. Helen Knotting's death, at the most, will get them to eat less red meat for a week or two. The bottom-line: they value their lives over all others to the point that all others are practically invisible. And Shane doesn't blame them. He sympathizes. He was so wrapped up in his own trivial life he didn't even see that his mother was really dying.

Helen would want Shane to go on, but he has nothing left to say. He stands there quiet, looking down. The pastor approaches. He puts an arm around Shane and nudges him. Shane's hands lock onto the podium. The pastor nudges harder, but Shane won't move. The crowd murmurs.

Charles gets up and steps on stage. He pulls Shane. Shane still won't budge. He looks out to the crowd. There's a tall, skinny guy in a suit standing by the doorway, his face bandaged like he's the Invisible Man. Shane can't see his face, but he seems familiar. Before he can identify him, a red, puffy-eyed Charles hugs Shane. "Let go," he whispers.

"I need some air," says Shane.

Charles blows his nose and nods.

Shane walks by the coffin, giving it a wide berth. He frowns as he passes the Invisible Man and steps outside.

Two mustached locals, one in a Caesar's Palace golf shirt, share a cigarette under a palm tree and swap jokes. A woman in high heels bounces a baby up and down, trying to get it to stop crying. A city bus rumbles in front of the church, stops, and lets out an old, hunched-over Asian woman wearing a blue headscarf and carrying plastic grocery bags filled with fresh leafy produce.

He should be at Glory's house. The kanikapila all-nighters. Forty-year-olds with hickies singing with jack-o-lantern grins. The girl he's been screwing for the last week or so, a hottie with the words "high class" tattooed under her belly button. People playing tour guide for Shane, telling him how the Samoans run coke, but ice is a free-for-all. Glory's stories—one about a hooker she knows who was so dumb she once called the cops on a John who wouldn't pay. Another about a crackhead who stole a delivery truck. It was filled with watermelons. Glory, always in a hoodie too big for her, hands in pockets. It was hard to guess what was under all that baggy clothes. What kind of weight she carried. She told stories about her childhood, too, her voice gruff like a teenage boy trying to sound tough. Maybe Shane tied lead sinkers to his Wahiawa Circle Island memories and dropped them in a channel, but Glory remembered everything.

He wants to go back, listen to some Waimanalo blues, and forget. He fits in and belongs there more than Boi ever could, Boi with his ballet-taking kid and middle-class cop job. Shane pulls his car keys out of his pocket and waits for traffic to pass before crossing the street. The Gov will be disappointed, but who cares. He can see his Dad up at the podium explaining to the guests. Forgive Shane. He's overcome with grief. My boy really loved his mother. Then he will get down to business and spin golden throat poetry. Probably crying the whole time. The women with their stone-faced husbands who refuse to hold hands in public will love him. The stone-faced men, on the verge of calling him a pussy, will remember that he once surfed waves they never would. Then he will quote some Auden, some North, South, East, West shit, and the audience will pause, not knowing whether to applaud or cry.

Sometimes he hates being the Big Man's son.

Just as he is about to step off the curb, Shane spots someone a block down carrying a crowbar and climbing out of a manhole. It's a cop. The officer dusts himself off and pushes the manhole cover back in place. Shane looks harder. He doesn't recognize him at first. The guy's skinny and looks as lost and batty as a homeless doomsday prophet. But then he spots the hands.

It's Boi.

Boi sees Shane, rubs his stomach and waves casual, as if he just stuffed himself at a hole-in-the-wall chop suey joint, his stomach distended with lemon chicken, kau yuk, and beef broccoli. He walks toward Shane. His eyes are blood-shot and crazy-looking, the same look that horse had in its eyes the moment it had tried to take a bite out of Shane.

"What the hell are you doing?" Shane asks.

Boi leans against a light post and tries to rub out a grease stain on his sleeve. "Just checking shit out." He looks up at Shane. "Sorry about your Mom."

"You lost weight," says Shane. He's got even more size on Boi now. Good. Shane notes the way he's leaning, not lazy, but like a person who always tries to make himself as comfortable as possible no matter where he is. Boi puts the crowbar over his shoulder and looks around, grinning. It's the old Boi. Kahuku Point Mafia Boi. Boi Vise Grip. Boi No Good, just thinner, more weathered, and dirty. Shane turns to the church and waits for it to crumble or burst into flames. But instead all he sees is that weird tall guy with the face bandages standing at the entrance, watching them.

"I wouldn't do that to her," says Boi. "I wouldn't fuck up her funeral."

Shane faces Boi and sighs. "You were supposed to be a pall-bearer. Dad's going to be pissed."

"Fuck him."

Boi takes off his cop shirt. He wipes his cracked hands, the hands Shane'd always envied, on his white undershirt, leaving charcoal smudges, like the ones on the wall at Glory's house where people put out their cigarettes. They both look back at the church's shut doors. "She was one of those people who want to see it coming," Shane says.

"What?" asks Boi.

"Death. And she watched it creep up to her for months. Was afraid to sleep every goddamn night because she thought this was the night. Was hard to watch, hard to listen to, you know?"

Boi nods.

"I don't want to see it coming," Shane says as he clears his throat. "Not me. How's Nina?" he asks.

Boi doesn't answer. He's looking at the manhole he just crawled out of, distracted.

"We've been trying to call you. Mom's last wishes. She left her a trust."

"Who?"

"Nina!"

Boi rubs the bridge of his nose, not looking so comfortable anymore. "How much?"

"Remember, she used to sell insurance for a living, so you can imagine..."

"How much?" Boi asks again.

Shane shrugs. "A couple million."

The crowbar slips out of Boi's hand, clangs against pavement once, then rattles and settles between Shane and Boi. The church doors open. People with tear-streaked faces file out. The man in the Caesar's Palace golf shirt puts out his cigarette and looks around for a trash can. "You fucking Knottings," says Boi. "Even when you dead..."

"What?"

Just as Boi's about to tell him, a squad car pulls up. Police escort? Two cops step out. An odd couple, one a white woman with giant hands, the other a Filipino with a waist so small it looks like he's wearing a corset. The cops step toward Shane and Boi. Shane takes a step back, but it's Boi they grab and cuff. The first funeral guests out of the church point and watch. A little girl takes a snapshot with her phone.

Boi's not defending himself. He's just grinning, his hands behind his back, his broad, bony shoulders flared out. Ropes of muscle pop from his smooth and hairless forearms. "What are you doing?" Shane asks the cops. "He's a cop. He's one of you."

The cops ignore Shane and stick Boi in the back of the squad car. The white lady with the big hands looks down at the crowbar, afraid to touch it, treating it like it might be murder evidence. "What is this about?" Shane asks. He bends down to pick up the crowbar, but the lady cop pushes him back.

"The haole recognized him," says the Filipino cop. He's so small, Shane could toss him on up to the gray brick church clock steeple. "Said he would be here. Said he's coming to the funeral to make sure we do our job. You know haoles."

"Who? What haole?"

The cop pulls a newspaper out of his back pocket and tosses it to Shane. It's a copy of *Island Voice*. "The one Rapun tuned up North Shore side."

Shane sees his picture on the front page. Boi's up front, so it doesn't look like Shane is that much bigger than him. "We have a funeral," says Shane, still looking down at the picture. The Filipino cop is trying to figure out how to barricade the crowbar with yellow police tape. The lady cop is on the radio, probably calling forensics.

Another squad car pulls up. A cop gets out and heads to the church entrance. He stops by the man with the bandaged face, and the two talk. Shane swears he can see a toothy smile even through all that gauze. It is him. The guy Boi beat down.

One of Helen's old insurance buddies and Charles's campaign manager, Monte Clifford, both in suits, step past the Waialua haole and wave at Shane. Time to carry mom back to the hearse. Shane bends down and picks up the crowbar. The cops tell him to put it down. He refuses. The cops are on him now, pulling out the cuffs.

They put Shane in the backseat with Boi as a crowd gathers around the squad car. "What the fuck you doing?" asks Boi.

Shane shrugs, keeping his eyes peeled for his father. "Figure I'll come with you."

"Why?"

Shane watches five men in white gloves and black suits carry the coffin out of the church. A sixth man, probably Shane's ad hoc replacement, is the pastor himself. The old guy struggles. Shane doesn't blame him. That coffin looks damn heavy. "Better than the alternative," says Shane.

"Look at all those motherfuckers," says Boi, eying the crowd through the squad car window. "They do massive kine damage and live for free. *They* should be sterilized, those trust fund motherfuckers."

Shane sees them. The grandchildren of The Descendants, investment bankers, corporate attorneys and marketers, pro golfers, heirs to shampoo and dotcom empires. Wood-chopstick using, sushi-wolfing professors who lament over-fishing and scorched earth rain-forest lumbering while they're too lazy to develop paperless classes. Others, the black sheep, forty-year-olds still living at home trying casually to become actors, writers, and filmmakers. Kids who would have to roll snake eyes on thousand-sided dice to lose.

Shane laughs. "I can always count on you to cheer me up."

"What?" says Boi.

"You and Nina are one of us now."

"What you mean, 'you?'"

"Mom left you money, too."

Boi blinks and turns his head. He tries to raise a hand, maybe to stick a finger in his ear, but he's cuffed. He leans back, shoots his head forward, and head butts the window. Glass splashes on pavement.

"What the fuck?!" says Shane.

"Better than taking a dump in the car," says Boi, blood dripping from his forehead. "I not one crumb. Fuck that."

And Boi reminds Shane once again that he's the real deal. That when it comes to being a man, Shane's on a much steeper learning curve, an arc that seems to be increasing without bound. When he gets out this yet-another-mess, he'll head back to Glory's. She's got enough broken cars out there for Shane to practice window-head-butting on.

The cops, the funeral guests, the pallbearers, they're all looking at the cop car. Then their eyes move to the backseat and look past Shane and focus on Boi. Some seem shocked while others shake their heads. Charles, standing behind the hearse, is looking at Boi, too. Shane remembers what Joe told him weeks before in Waialua. "Can smell the 'wasn't' on you."

Shane's shoulders already ache from having his wrists cuffed behind him. He glances at the hearse once more. The pallbearers have slid the coffin inside. After fifty-six years of life, all that's left of Helen is in a box filled with skin, bone, and embalming fluid. Shane turns his head. Static crackles from the cop radio up front. Boi, frowning, leans forward and listens. He nods as if the white noise is talking to him.

3.

Here's how it works. A bill is introduced by the fifty-one member House. It's read then kicked to committee. The committee reports. It's read again. It goes back to committee. The committee reports again. It's read for a third time. If it passes, the bill gets kicked up to the Senate.

The bill goes through the same amount of readings, committees, and reports in the twenty-five member Senate. The Senate adds changes. The Senate votes. If the House agrees with the changes, the bill is kicked up to the Governor. If the House disagrees, the House and Senate meet in committee to hammer out a compromise. If the Senate makes no changes to the bill, it's sent to the Governor. The Governor either signs the bill into law or vetoes it. The Legislature can override a veto if two-thirds of the members vote for the law.

That's the version for the kiddies, anyway. It's the version Charles Knotting learned in the fourth grade when he went on a field trip to the then-new state capitol building, wondering why it lacked prestigious white Greek pillars and instead looked like an upside down chocolate wedding cake fronted by mossy, knee-deep brackish ponds that were supposed to symbolize the Pacific Ocean.

Decades later, as a state senator and Governor, he learned how government really works:

First, you gather statistics, hopefully with big and/or offensive numbers. Jot down anecdotal evidence, too. In Charles's case:

Stats: Nearly half of all pregnancies in Hawaii are unintended. One out of five mothers binge-drink before pregnancy. One out of ten smoke during pregnancy. Sixteen percent of pregnant women are obese pre-conception. Seven percent report violence from their intimate partners.

Of every twelve dollars of state taxpayer money, one dollar goes to welfare. About one billion dollars a year. Bill Gates could only cover welfare for the one-hundred-forty thousand people collecting in Hawaii for, like, fifty years. And who knows how much of that money is being spent on stuff like Vegas vacations. Twelve million of California's welfare dollars were spent in Sin City the last few years.

Anecdotes: One woman in Puna (let's call her "Luana") collected $20,000 welfare dollars while the employed, biological father of her children lived with her. Another woman (let's call her "Destiny") collected $10,000 and her child was not even living with her. And another woman (let's call her "Sierra"), the worst, an already mother of four, was on fertility drugs paid for by Medicaid.

Take all this to your buddy at the newspaper. He'll publish it. Let it soak in. Then poll:

Seventy-six percent, more than three out of four people in Hawaii, believe that limiting welfare to those who volunteer to be temporarily sterilized is a good idea. Some people added that all Micronesians should be shipped back home. Others wondered when the pothole in front of their house would be fixed.

Convincing the people was easy. The campaign financers wouldn't care. It was a social issue. Convincing the Speaker and the Senate President was the next, more difficult step.

Knotting knew getting a big bill passed Nationally was as monotonous as watching two kings chase each other at the end of a chess match. But in Hawaii, the Dems had a near-full set of pieces. In fact, they had enough to override his vetoes. Laws Charles Knotting vetoed in his first six years as governor but became law anyway: a bill that created a task force to study medical marijuana (privately, Charles had no problem with marijuana as he'd smoked a ton of it during his surfing days, but government funded research? C'mon), a bill that enabled the Department of Hawaiian Homelands to begin construction projects even if it did not have enough money on hand to pay full costs (build only what you can pay for. Is that so wrong?); a bill that placed a cap on itemized tax deductions (deductions the life-blood of any small business); a bill that mandated further training and continuing education for prison guards (Charles had yet to see any "further training" program actually change the way people conduct business in the public or private sector); a bill that allowed the grandchildren of elderly project housing residents to live with their grandparents under extenuating circumstances (he figured he was doing grandparents across the islands a favor)—there were thirty other bills that Charles vetoed but became law anyway.

Ethan Chang, the Speaker of the House from District 22, was a kumu hula from Kaimuki who was openly gay and spammed the legislature with lessee-friendly condo bills. But beyond sticking it to condo associations (Chang owned half-a-dozen apartments in town), the Speaker had one chief political ambition: to get a gay marriage bill passed in Hawaii, a bill that had always been vetoed and always lacked the votes of a legislature override. Charles reached out to him and cut a deal. Charles had nothing against gay marriage. His false opposition to medical marijuana and his proclaimed love of The Lord Jesus Christ was throwing The Party a bone. But this time, to get the Helen Knotting Bill passed, he would sign the gay marriage bill into law.

Dealing with District 17's Senate President Maxine Honda from Mililani was tougher. He'd beaten her up pretty badly during his first run for Governor, and she hated him for it. She was supposed to be Governor. It had been her turn, after all. And for the last six years, she sat quietly in the Senate like a Hello Kitty ninja assassin, killing any bill that had the support of the Governor's office. Even a bill that would have protected sharks from shark-fin fishermen. Not that there were any sharks in her central Oahu district, but still.

She was gettable, too. Thank God for porta potties.

Maxine's husband, a bit of a character named Regis Holmes, was the Porta Potty King of Oahu. Pass a high school carnival, and blue and yellow Holmes porta potties sat next to lighted-up cotton candy trailers and amusement park rides. Pass a construction site and there sat Holmes porta potties under the shadows of tower cranes. Pass through the parking lot at Aloha Stadium, Holmes porta potties for hibachi tailgaters and their forced-to-play-flag football little boys. Yes, Regis Holmes was the Porta Potty King of Oahu, or, as the Hawaiians would say, the Porta Potty Alii Kane O Oahu. He'd achieved his lofty status by muscling out the competition. Ten years back, Nakashima Porta Potties had the University of Hawaii football contract, until all sixty units were fire-bombed after a homecoming game. The police eventually chalked it up to excited tailgaters getting carried away when UH beat bitter rival Boise State. Drunk tailgaters wearing "Buck Foise" tee shirts, Hawaii both the Aloha and Insipid Tee Shirt Slogan State. But everyone knew that Holmes was behind it. To be the Porta Potty King of Hawaii you must be ruthless.

What Charles Knotting lacked in legislative political sway, he made up for in other ways. He was connected with mainland and local finance and construction. He was connected with most of the big private schools in Hawaii—his alma mater hosted the most celebrated high school, porta-potty-filled carnival every year—and as Governor, he appointed state justices. He appointed the University of Hawaii Board of Regents members. The ones, who, among other things, decided who got the University of Hawaii football porta potty contract, a contract that was about to expire. Charles offered Maxine every porta potty contract he could get his hands on, including the granddaddy of them all, the twenty-six-mile long contract for the Honolulu Marathon.

At first, Honda resisted. She declined, flashing that grand-motherly smile of hers, the same one she used when a Democratic splinter group tried to unseat her as Senate President. The same one she used when the same group of dissidents refused to vote for a near $100-million tax break for a developer who was building a resort on Maui—three baby-poop-colored forty-floor towers shaped like giant tikis. The developer was her sister's boy-friend's brother. It was the same smile she flashed when Charles vetoed the tax break and she filed a lawsuit against him the next day. That smile of hers, tight-lipped, as if she were hiding sharp teeth—it was like a declaration of war.

But a week later, she arrived at the capitol with a black eye. And her aide called Charles's aide and made the deal.

So here Charles is at the ground floor of the Honolulu Police Department Main Station one night, just two days after his wife's funeral, about to create a landmark law and solidify his place in Hawaiian history books. But he just feels gassed and disinterest-ed. His wife is gone, his boys are still in trouble, and as he walks up the four flights of stairs to the top floor of the main station to meet the head luna of all the cops on Oahu, his stomach feels bloated and his legs feel tight and heavy with blood—if he trips and falls, he might splash instead of tumble.

At the top someone unlocks the door. It's the chief, short legs, barrel-chested, a caveman put through a manly make-over. He's white like Charles, but a different kind of white, darker, wire-haired with thick eyebrows. Like all cops, his cop cap is too big for his head.

"Hey Gov," the man says, extending his hand.

"Chief Holmes," says Charles, shaking it. The Chief of Police and the Porta Potty King of Oahu are brothers.

"Sorry about the first lady."

Charles nods. It's the first time he's seen the chief since their June, beginning-of-hurricane-season confab with the Hurricane

Advisory Committee. The meeting was a real hoot. The scientists clamoring like a bunch of Incan prophets predicting the rapture. The architectural experts chiming in with their own apocalyptic visions of what a hurricane would do to the island, especially the high-rise urban sprawls of Waikiki. A developer's number three son, Kato, head of the Waikiki Safety Board, sweaty and anxious at having a resume-padding gig suddenly make him responsible for over forty-thousand tourists in over seventy hotels owned by conglomerates across the globe. It takes a month of email correspondence just to get in touch with one part-owner.

Since Katrina, everyone's neurotic. Of course it will be worse here if a hurricane ever comes ashore. We live on an island. Nowhere to run. We get it, say the same Dems who had fought to raid the Hurricane Relief Fund to balance the budget. During his first term, Charles had to hang onto that fund for dear life. Maybe it was the surfer in him. He knew the ocean was a fickle monster that could turn on you at any time. Charles sided with the scientists and architects on this one, but once again this year, the end of October now nearing and only a month of hurricane season left, not even a tropical storm had approached the islands.

Chief Holmes leads Charles through the main station top floor. Vacant desks jockeyed by brass cleared out for the night. Framed pictures of families pushed precariously at the edge by stacks of manila-foldered paperwork. Five-wheeled ergonomic chairs that cost the city and county twenty grand. The chief steers Charles past the half-a-million-dollar crisis center. All of the flat-screen televisions on, the doors shut, Boi inside, leaning forward, eyes darting from screen to screen, looking starved and shaky like he's the subject of some sophisticated Cold War brainwash.

The chief ushers Charles to his office and shuts the door. Charles wonders if their ancestors had met like this once, maybe the first Knotting and the first Holmes in a plantation office, owner and luna talking about the next shipment of Asian sugar-cane field-hands due to arrive at Honolulu Harbor the following week. This time around it's a Holmes behind the desk. The chief answers to the mayor, not the Governor of Hawaii.

"We released Shane," says Holmes as he picks up a Las Vegas snow globe off his desk and shakes it.

Charles nods. "Thanks."

The chief shrugs. "Misunderstanding."

The chief watches the snow fall, maybe remembering the last time he hit a five-grand jackpot on a downtown Vegas slot. "But Rapun in there, he's in big trouble," he says. "A haole like the one down North Shore. No way we can shut him up. You know the type."

Charles gets it. Holmes is saying he, the governor, is the type. "How's your brother doing?" Charles asks.

"If he wasn't so hot-headed, it would be him sitting here, not me."

Porta Potty King Regis Holmes had been a cop like his brother, but was thrown off the force after he'd shot and killed a fleeing, unarmed teenage car thief at a fast food drive-thru.

The chief puts down the snow globe, laces his fingers behind his head, and leans back. He stares at Charles's stomach, maybe imagining that a giant pink box sits on his lap. He's waiting for Charles to hand it over. The box of manapua. Despite Charles's campaign promises, it's how Hawaii still works, how it will probably always work, it's how people as high up and Charles and Chief Holmes got their jobs, it's how people as low as the convicted felon who runs the Waikiki street-sweeper fleet got his, too.

"Saw the Senator's shiner the other day," Charles says.

"My sister-in-law. Clumsy Japanee."

This pisses Charles off. He stands up and flexes muscles he hasn't flexed in ages. A tweak, a near cramp in his lower latissimus dorsi. Charles turns around so the chief doesn't see him wince.

"I'm thinking about retirement," says Charles.

"You got two years left."

"I don't mean literally. I mean just taking it easy for the rest of my term." The cramp fades and Charles turns around, facing the chief. "You know, do the appointments and contracts and ribbon-cutting and all of that, but stay out of the legislation process. It's been a really tough year."

The chief nods. "Might be a good idea."

Charles sits back down. He would like to retire, forget about his law, and maybe, after the grief over Helen dulls a bit, spend the next two years crushing Holmes Porta Potty into a contract-less fine powder. Not too many people knew it, but Charles Knotting could buy out every single porta potty business in the state and his inheritance would hardly break a sweat. He was not a politician who depended on his salary and backroom deals for golden parachutes, estate-trust positions that paid six figures for doing nothing. He took them, but he didn't need them. He was like those guys that pop up in American politics from time-to-time, governor of Massachusetts, mayor of New York City, the super long-shots for President of the United States, the kind that can finance their own campaigns private jet and all.

But Maxine Honda, she needs her parachute doesn't she? How else are the Holmes brothers going to spend their golden years on Alaskan fishing trips, Las Vegas gambling safaris, and Cialis-charged Thailand whoring? The chief wants manapua, and knows that Charles has a few Guinness Book of World Record-sized pastries left.

"Your sister-in-law. She's part Hawaiian, isn't she?"

Chief Holmes nods and scratches at his landscaped unibrow that's in need of plucking. "Yeah, but she's a pinky-toe Hawaiian."

Single-digit blood quantum. Not that it mattered nowadays anyway.

"There will be a trust position opening next year."

The chief sits up and leans forward. "Which trust?"

"The big one."

The chief sighs and leans back. "Thought they turned the spigot off on that one."

Charles shrugs. "That was twenty years ago. Fourteen years of Republican-appointed state justices who in turn appoint trustees. People forget fast here. It's Hawaii."

The chief laughs. "Man, we old."

Charles nods. He feels it.

"What about the North Shore haole?" asks the chief.

"I know him," says Charles. "Well, I know someone who knows him. Just one of those social-network guys. Probably started out as a natural recluse and is a downright hermit now. Just wants his privacy, you know? I'll reach out."

"Man, you haoles stick together."

"What are you? Hmong?"

The chief picks up the snow globe. He shakes it again, his eyes transfixed, as the gold foil flakes swirl in clear, light oil.

"Does it even snow in Vegas?" Charles asks.

"Hardly," says the chief. "But figure climate change will take care of that. Man, remember that Hurricane Advisory Committee meeting? Science guys."

"Me too," says Charles. "They had me going for awhile, too."

The chief puts down the snow globe. "Ever feel like us old guys, we're lucky? We'll be dead and gone before people finish off the world."

Charles watches the gold flakes float down. He's thinking about loss. He's thinking about Helen. "Tell your brother, if he ever hits his wife again, I will make it my life's mission to make sure he never even sniffs another porta potty contract again."

The chief smiles and nods.

As Charles steps out of the chief's office with Holmes's arm around his shoulder, his legs feel like water sacks again. They head to the crisis center. Charles looks through the window. Boi's eyes are still darting from TV to TV.

"Why you care about him so much?" the chief asks.

Charles doesn't answer. None of his business.

The chief opens the door, steps in, and uncuffs Boi, who still looks like a boy. A few slivers of hair jut out of his chin like charred wood splinters, his dark skin is taut around smooth forearms and broad, sunken cheekbones. But those heavy-lidded octopus eyes? Windows with some crazy white and yellow fire behind them.

The video images stream on the TV screens. Breaking news. Yet another oil spill, yet another natural disaster. A contest to see who can eat the most chicken wings, contestants' lips wet with spicy orange sauce. A United States congresswoman with crazy, doped-up-looking blue eyes rails against tax hikes and gun control after a shooting that took out fifteen kids at a school. An ex-governor speaks while teleprompter images reflect off her glasses. Models turned journalists predict the end of the world. A monster truck rolls over station wagons and sedans. A motorcycle launches over a school bus lit on fire. All together, it looks like an excess party, an excess celebration, hosted by a trio of brunette sisters who make their living hocking sweatshop swank and catered by a chef grilling fifteen-pound hamburgers.

The chief pats Charles on the back and leaves him with Boi. Charles walks up to the televisions and turns them off one-by-one. "I saw a kid fall off a second floor balcony the other night," says Boi.

"Where?" says Charles.

"I looking at all these TV's and no more even one story on it," says Boi. "What you trying to do is whack."

"What?"

Boi points at the now blank television screens. "It ain't fair. You should sterilize the whole world."

Charles sighs. "Let's go."

Boi doesn't get up. "You know what I saying, right?"

Charles nods even though he's not sure. Is it the hypocrisy that's driving Boi crazy? People who cry out against overpopulation but have two kids of their own. Politicians who rally for war yet ensure their own children never have to serve. Baby-kissers who pontificate on the importance of education yet cut school budgets while their children attend private school.

Heads of state who want to sweep all the crumbs off the table except for the ones on his plate. Charles reaches in his pants to check on his keys even though he knows exactly where they are. He feels the bulge of metal in his pocket. The thing is, these two boys. Right now, they're all he's got left.

"They cheat the system," says Charles. "People are tired of it."

"Everyone cheats the system," says Boi. "No one cheats it more than people with a shitload of money."

He's right. For every Luana, Destiny, and Sierra welfare scam artist, there's a Margaret who will write off her newly purchased pomeranian as a small business guard dog, a Richard who will deduct a first class family vacation package to Disneyland as a business trip, and a Bernard who is hoarding his money in a bank in the Cayman Islands.

"Why her?" Boi asks.

"Why who?"

"Why come after kids like Nina? What she did?"

Charles frowns. "Is this what all this is about?"

Boi glares at him. His big hands are shaking, recent scars piled on his knuckles like barnacles. Charles sits next to him. "Listen. You do realize that Nina is a first-born, right?"

"Yeah."

Charles puts his arm around Boi. He wonders what this kid could have been if he and Helen had gotten to him earlier. A doctor, an engineer, a Governor. Hell, he could've been one of those hurricane scientists. He thinks about what this kid can still be. Item one on Helen's list to Charles: take care of her boys. "Well, it's the violence that offends people, you know?" says Charles. "The beefs, the boozing, the drugs, the thieving, the abuse—children in adult-sized bodies. The ignorance. People take that personally."

"So burging and beating the shit out of someone is worse than taking people's houses or feeding them poison on a massive scale?" says Boi. "And people believe that shit. You guys are good."

"My idea doesn't affect first-borns. It's all the children after that."

Boi gets up and walks out. Charles stands and follows. A speaker mounted on a hallway wall spits out police radio static. Boi stops, looks up, and for a moment, seems transfixed. Eyes still locked on the speaker, Boi slowly nods his head.

"What?" asks Charles, feeling tired and beat-up.

"First-borns," says Boi. "Almost Biblical the way you said it."

"I suppose it sounds Biblical."

Boi's turns his head from the wall speaker. He grabs at the side of his belt. There's nothing there. He looks down and frowns as his fist clenches air. "Guess what?" he says.

"What?"

He turns his head up and glances at the speaker and smiles. Then he looks Charles in the eye. "I can be Biblical, too."

He can be Biblical, too. What does that even mean? He can unleash locusts, cure the blind, and turn people into pillars of salt? The kid is losing it. Charles can't save him. Not anymore. It's time to let him find his own way. Sorry, Helen. Our little social experiment has failed.

We taught, we nurtured, and we loved, and we still could not take damaged boys and make giants out of them. Charles hates to admit it, but maybe Boi and Shane are the best examples of why something like the Helen Knotting Bill needs to be passed. Look at Boi now as he walks away, still grabbing at his belt, like he's reaching for a holstered gun or a portable radio that isn't even there.

4.

A lunch wagon that serves vegetarian live-forever basmati rice and eternal-life eggplant parmesan fronts the Lunalilo Circle Apartments retirement home. Old women, mostly Asian, stand in line as a soccer mom van rolls into visitor parking, rims gouged from curb collisions. The man steps out of the car and walks to the entrance. He stares at the listing of apartment numbers and puts his fingers on glass as if touching it will help him remember what floor his mother or father lives on.

It's a week after Helen's funeral, and Shane and Glory stand in the grub line with the old ladies. It's their turn next. "Sure you don't want something?" asks Glory. She's marching in place.

"I can't eat that shit," says Shane. "I might turn fag."

Glory shakes her head and orders baklava and a mini eggplant parmesan plate.

They head to the entrance of the human junk yard and wait outside the lobby. Glory chews, then burps. A Handi Van pulls up and the doors hiss open. An old man covered in wrinkles and liver spots steps down like he's negotiating the descent from atop a Himalayan mountain. His hand shakes as he grips the railing. "Damn, boy, you rude," Glory says as she puts her plate down then helps the old man off the bus.

They sit there for a half-an-hour before Glory's connect shows up. He's a dark kid in scrubs, yet another Filipino grandfathered into the health care industry. His hair is spiky and gelled, a hairstyle right out of the twentieth century, and a tip of ponytail slips out of the back of his shirt. He steps to Glory and shakes her hand like she's a guy. "We go up," he says.

Glory dumps her plate and puts a cinnamon stick in her mouth. She's trying to quit smoking. Shane and Glory follow the nurse's aide in.

The three of them pass one-bedroom apartments decorated with welcome mats and potted plants. Shane walks behind Glory, who pimp-rolls past redwood doors. One woman, the first fat one Shane's seen here, crouches down in front of her welcome mat and makes sure her sandals sit in the middle, perfectly straight. Another, one door over, sits on a lawn chair while a younger woman, maybe her daughter or granddaughter, cuts her chalky, yellow-marbled toenails. Other than that girl, Shane hasn't seen anyone under the age of fifty yet.

When they get to the apartment, the Filipino, whose name is Gary, stops and grins, like he's got a surprise for them. He unlocks the door and they walk in.

The apartment looks like something between a storage unit and a garage sale and smells vinegary, like stink feet. Boxes piled against one wall. Plates, at least twenty, stacked in the sink. Something cracks under Shane's foot. It's a pile of sunflower seeds. A green bird with gray wings swoops down from the ceiling fan and lands on Shane's shoulder. It climbs to his ear and chirps then takes a dump on his shirt.

"Is that you, Crisanto?"

A voice from the bedroom.

"It's me, papa," says Gary as he fiddles with the little home stereo.

The bald old man, wearing boxers and a wife-beater backwards and turned inside-out, steps out of the bedroom. He's got big arms for his age, especially around the wrists and elbows. Probably has that old-man vise grip, the kind one gets from grabbing things hard for seven decades. Gary winks at Glory. "He thinks I'm his Filipino man-servant from back in the day. Crazier than fuck."

Gary turns up the volume on some 1990s club hip-hop tune about the usual—semi-automatic weapons and plump, round asses. He steps to the old man and leads him to the couch. The old man points at the green parakeet. "I have ten dollars on the blue, Crisanto," he says.

Gary ignores him. "Well, look around. Take whatever you want. He won't notice."

When Glory told Shane she burged for a living, he imagined her wearing a catsuit and cutting glass outside a third story window. But this isn't subterfuge, car chases, and laser-motion detectors. Shane sighs. "This is lame."

Glory ignores him, takes a box-cutter out of her pocket, and slices through taped-up cardboard. She pulls out a few paperbacks and tosses them on the floor. She moves on to the next box, which is filled with newspaper clippings and pictures the old man probably took when he was younger—backpackers on the Great Wall, a blond sunning herself on some radioactive atoll, a little black girl filling a bucket with water in some village. The old man's not in any of the pictures, a lone traveler it seems. Glory reads one of the clippings. "Looks like he was somebody back in the day."

Glory hands Shane one of the clippings. It's an article about the man, an accomplished travel writer. Africa, Asia, the Pacific. Twenty books in all. Shane picks up one of the paperbacks. "He wrote these," he says.

Glory shrugs and moves on to the next box. "Good for him."

"Why the hell did you bring me here?"

"You the one said you wanted to see what I do."

"Really? Is this it?" Shane asks. "I'm outta here."

"Wait," says Glory. "Need you in case get anything big to carry."

What is he, a forklift? He actually wouldn't mind being a forklift. Would be cool. Looking at the senile old man with more hair above his eyes than on his head, grinning at nothing, he starts thinking about Helen. Maybe his mom got off easy. He wonders if she'd have rather been deranged or dead. Personally, he'd rather be dead than like the vacant wrinkled husk on the couch.

Glory opens the next box. It's filled with notebooks. Gary steps into the kitchen and opens the fridge. The man, still sitting on the couch, rocks back and forth wringing his hands as Glory tosses the notebooks against the wall. Gary steps out of the kitchen holding a carton of orange juice. He takes a swig then wipes his mouth.

"There ain't shit here," says Glory. "Where the fuck are his credit cards?"

Gary points at a man-purse on a table. The bird sits on it, pecking at the zipper like it's trying to get to sunflower seeds hidden inside.

"Well get it, motherfucker," says Glory. "We don't got all day."

The man gazes at his fallen notebooks and rubs his bald head. He looks as if he's about to scream. Shane's feeling about as far from tough as he can imagine. Ripping off a senile old man? He didn't sign up for this. And if he gets caught, it'll be straight up embarrassing.

"Listen," Shane says, taking a step to the door. "I'm gonna take off."

Glory picks up a box, turns it upside down, and shakes it. "Don't be a little bitch," she says as she throws the now-empty box across the room.

"This is about as 'little bitch' as I ever felt," Shane says.

Gary puts the carton of juice down on the table and grabs the man purse. He opens it. Bird feed, loose change, a pen, and Kama Sutra scribblings on wrinkled supermarket receipts. "Whoa, think he's a perv," says Gary as he takes out a wallet. He holds up one of the receipts. "Damn, what position is this? He's got her by the legs like a wheelbarrow."

Shane laughs. Glory doesn't. The bird squawks, swoops up, then kamikaze dives.

Gary backpeddles and swats at the bird. The bird, flapping its wings so hard that it looks like a pillow exploded, screams and jabs at his hands.

Shane remembers his prep school badminton days. He steps up and slaps the bird. It crashes head-first against the wall and drops to the floor. Wings twitching and talons spread, it resembles a toy on its side, something Helen would've bought him when he was a kid. Something he would've beheaded with his German pocket knife. Shane bends down to pick it up.

The man on the couch stands and starts screaming. Glory steps to him and puts her hand on the his mouth. The loose skin on the old man's arms swells and tightens as he grabs Glory's neck and pins her against the wall. Even though the man's old, Glory's giving up at least eight inches and sixty pounds. The man's still screaming, foamy spit running down his chin. Glory struggles but can't move. Her eyes get big and watery, her feet pumping up and down. Her feet pump faster and faster, pistons firing in neutral.

Gary steps to the stereo and pumps up the volume. The old man crams four fingers in Glory's mouth. Now he's dry humping her. Glory gags and digs her fingernails into the man's arms, but he's got her locked up against the wall. He's really pumping away, this old guy, and Shane feels like laughing for that look on Glory's face, those big wild eyes. Shane grabs the old man and pulls him off her. He's so light, Shane can toss him if he wants. But he doesn't. He sits the old man on the couch. "Shhh," he says. "Relax."

The man stops screaming and nods. "Shhh," says Shane again. He hands the old guy the dead bird. The old man holds it in his lap and strokes it. Shane glances at Glory. She's still against the wall, quiet, looking shell-shocked. Maybe she needs to be comforted, too. It's okay, Big Shane will take care of all of them.

"We gotta go," says Gary.

Looking at the old guy's white eyebrows, Shane wonders what color his hair was. Dark, maybe? He glances at the pictures scattered on the ground. No luck. He wants to grab one of those paperbacks or articles, maybe catch a glimpse of the old man when he was young. He turns back to the old man. He's got brown eyes, but with a face like that, a face spidered with so many wrinkles it looks like someone took a bat to shatterproof glass, white's the only color that looks natural. Shane imagines him anyway with a head full of brown, blond, and black hair, like he's creating a computer game character.

That's when the box-cutter slices through the old man's throat and sprays blood all over Shane's face.

"You fucking perv!" screams Glory. "You fucking old fucking perv!"

Gary puts his hands over his mouth like he's already trying to keep all this a secret. The man, holding his neck, thrashes on the floor. Shane tries to pull Glory off the man, but she ducks under his arms. Glory's on the old man again. She stabs his ribs with the box-cutter. She hits a sweet spot. The man stops moving. Blood flows on the floor. The newspaper clippings soak up blood. The paperbacks, too.

Glory stands up, panting. She retracts the box cutter blade as she looks down at the old man.

"What the fuck!" yells Gary. "You crazy fucking bitch!"

Shane turns away. He thinks he's going to be sick.

"What the fuck!" Gary says again. "We all going jail! What the fuck!"

Glory turns away from the old man and glares at Gary. She takes a step toward him. Gary sticks his chest out. "What..."

She extends the box cutter razor. Glory slices him across the chest. When she draws her arm back to take another swing, Gary pivots, turns around, and runs. The blade catches a bit of ponytail and by the time the hair falls to the floor, Gary's gone.

Shane looks back at the man. He wants to throw up, but would vomit be evidence? "Should we pick..."

Glory's coming at him. Shane catches her arm and tosses her across the room. Pure reflex. She smashes into a wall, knocking over a halogen lamp and an end-table filled with prescription bottles. She hops back on her feet and heads right back toward him. Shane's ready to throw her again, but something tells him that she'll just get up and keep coming. He turns and runs.

"Pervvvs!" yells Glory. "I kill all of you!"

Shane runs down the hall. He almost crashes into a blind old woman tapping the ground with a collapsible white cane. After fifteen feet he's already breathing hard.

At the door, he looks back once more just as Glory steps out, fist clenched around the box-cutter, like one of those horror movie dolls possessed by the soul of a serial killer, glaring with plastic eyes. She sees him.

Shane bursts through the fire door. He's in the stairwell, panting, leaping. His big knees buckle as he echo-lands a half-story at a time.

Shane lets out a final, throat-bursting cough. He wipes his mouth and starts running again.

5. _____

Town versus country. Since back in high school. Townies: don't know how to fish, cannot clean fish, get lost in the mountains when they hike (And who the fuck walks in the mountains for fun anyway? Hunt something, shitheads.), get swept off the rocks by waves when they go look at tide pools, take two years to parallel park their lifted trucks, cannot throw net, cannot sharpen knife (just buy new ones when they get dull), cannot back one trailer in the water. Banana stumps, imu rocks, keawe—wood, then rocks—cannot imu a pig. Can't even make hibachi without self-lighting charcoal and a hairdryer. Cannot do shit except shop, play computer games, throw hotel parties, and surf small-ass townie waves.

Country: Burn trash. Fight chickens. Lots of mayonnaise and Bondo. Zero exercise. Teen moms and GED's galore. Get lost when trying to find Waikiki (And who the fuck goes to Waikiki for fun anyway? Get a job there, shitheads). Can't afford to fix their cars. Can barely read. Can't speak English. So can't get a job. No air-conditioning, mosquito bite-retardant, caveman mother-fuckers. Jalopy pick-ups, rifles, dogs that hunt, country music, hot tempers—paint their faces white and their necks red and you get the picture. Toothless, ignorant, inbred Klansmen if they didn't have such dark complexions.

When Boi first became a cop, he figured he wouldn't have to listen to this kind of shit anymore. But even in the HPD, town versus country. For town cops, town meant more action, more bodies to process. They worked harder. For country cops, country meant a much larger territory to patrol, crumbs more widespread, hiding in the bushes, and harder to dustbust. They worked harder. A swingman could start out as a town cop, fresh out of the academy, and feel superior to the guys in country. Then he could get re-assigned to District 4 and tell his buddies fuck those District 6 cops, country is where it's at. It was as if opinion was not rational but geographic.

Boi never engaged in these arguments. He'd been a swingman in both District 4 (country) and District 6 (town) and saw stuff tough to look at in both places. The townie chronic was just like the country chronic. A bloated, dead body floating in the ocean smelled the same on the southside as it did on the northside. Heads mashed by hiking trail rockslides or jealous boyfriend baseball bats looked the same. He hated it all pretty equally except when it came to his first beat: Waikiki. And now, so tired his eyes burn, he's back.

Quiz: Where is the worst traffic on the island? Waikiki. What is the foulest body of water in Hawaii? Ala Wai Canal, Waikiki. Where can you find the most tourists? Haoles try to learn to scuba and tandem surf, boboras on brand-name shopping junkets, tourist ladies in spas with hot black rocks perched on their naked backs. Tourist men peek through hula dancer grass skirts, then maybe pay for some street slag later to relieve themselves. All of them thinking while they sit by palm trees wrapped with Christmas lights and watch the nightly fireworks, maybe we should stay. Maybe we should buy a house or timeshare here. Maybe we can be kamaaina. The original tumor. Metastasis. As Mr. Melvin used to say when he'd give the boys' home kids this very Waikiki quiz, his veiny neck muscles bulging: fucking Waikiki. Then he'd sing a song he wrote about it.

Where can you find the most criminals? The blinged-out black pimps hang out at the old Kuhio theater, the hookers streetwalk behind boutique hotels with no-ocean views, the chronics and surf rats toke in shoe-box apartments on Hobron side, the homeless teens purse-snatch blue-haired, varicose-veined grandmas, the westside Samoans come on weekends to get drunk then lick haoles. All of them like big-eyed aweoweo, coming out from under their rocks to feed at night. Waikiki.

All of this going on next to global fashionista chain-stores that sell purses for a thousand bucks. Next to celebrity chef restaurants with trendy one-word names like they're pop stars. Next to hotel towers that house enough tourists to field a North Korean army. Next to eroding white sand imported from Manhattan Beach, California. Next to fallen uke players busking on Kalakaua. Next to private clubs that trademark the Hawaiian names of champion surfers, then name bars and foundations after them, and sue when the champ's family tries to use the name to turn a dime. Next to a shopping center that was once the biggest in the nation.

Boi hates Waikiki, and here he is, in front of one of these boutique rich-Japanee-owned hotels three blocks away from the beach. Standing in uniform by a "sidewalk closed" sign while construction workers in neon green longsleeve shirts jackhammer asphalt behind him. After a week of suspension without pay and reassignment back to Waikiki, he's been demoted from Swingman Rapun to Orange Traffic Cone Boi. He's the only millionaire Orange Traffic Cone in the state. After finding out that Helen Knotting had left him a couple million, too he's been thinking about quitting. After he finally calmed down and figured only an idiot would be pissed about inheriting seven-figure scratch. Helen the Great. Saint Helen. The Face That Launched Four Million Mahalos. What is he doing here? Fuck this job. Taxis honk at lost tourists driving with maps in their laps. Pasty newlywed boboras still in tux and wedding dress step out of a white limo across the street. Shirtless middle-aged haoles dart by, flaunting their peeling, sunburned fat, looking like shedding albino lizards. Boi feels bad. He should've been a pallbearer for Aunty Helen instead of sneaking around in the gutters, trying to figure out a way to undermine, sabotage The Gov's and Shane's alma mater across the street. Put an end to the stream of shitheads that graduate from that prep school. All it did was prep kids for a life of being rich assholes. Someone needs to turn that valve off.

But now Boi's rich, too. He's a trust fund baby, too. Patricia is the only one he talked to about the money, and when he told her over the phone, she said, "See? Wasn't it worth the sacrifice?" She said that she was tired of watching people lose their asses, like Joe blowing all his money on a farm he eventually stopped working. Told him to invest it safe and long-term just like the Knottings would. When he asked if she'd invest it for him, she refused. "Just because your name is Boi," she said, "doesn't mean you never have to grow up."

What should he do with his new money? Nina's college, her first house, all covered, no problem, by her trust. He can move out of his crummy studio—the Chinese lady's basement—no sink, no stove, just a microwave, a toilet, golden centipedes, and a shower. He can buy a house. He can buy a car. He can flip out like that local actor who'd played Bruce Lee, build a house in the middle of nowhere on the Big Island and live off the land. Away from people. He can farm. He can bring Red Roof Joe on the condition he never says the word "auwe." Definitely bring Nina and maybe send her to that fancy private school in Kamuela. Try to stay away from all the billionaire haoles in Waimea, with their private hospital and their private planes on standby at their private airport in case one of them steps on wana or something.

The hotel manager, one of those haole-looking Hawaiians, asks Boi if he wants something to drink. "No thanks," Boi says.

"You really look like you should drink or eat something," the manager says.

People keep telling him stuff like that. He hasn't been hungry or thirsty for days, maybe even weeks now. He can't remember.

Boi and the manager turn around and watch the hard hats shovel dirt. Buzzing, crumpling, and static fill Boi's airwaves.

She doesn't ask them if they're thirsty.

Boi looks down at his Jaguar 700 P portable and adjusts the volume.

"You sure you okay?" the hotel manager asks. Boi's been getting that question a lot lately, too. He ignores it and looks down. There's an exposed pipe in the now six-foot-deep crater. One of the hard hats climbs down the hole. The hotel manager drones on, about her daughter, about a new townhouse in Mililani Mauka, heritage hickory laminate flooring, and the benefits of feeding babies poi. A smiling local hotel guest holds the front door open for a pair of silver-haired tourists. Probably worked Waikiki so long he can't help but play doorman.

Just as the manager starts asking Boi if he knows any cops stationed in Mililani—there's a creepy homeless man who hangs out at one of the seven jungle-gymed parks—the jackhammering stops. The hard hats gather around the hole and look down. The crater's flooding.

It's filling fast. The hard hat inside scrambles. The hole geysers and spits the hard hat out. A tree-trunk sized gusher blasts up fifteen feet up in the air. Boi helps the hard hat up. He's already soaked. The manager steps back.

The hard hats look at each other and shrug.

Some water gets in Boi's mouth. It's salty. It's ocean water, hopefully beachside, and not Ala Wai Canal side. The manager asks if he needs a towel. "No," Boi says.

"They broke the pipe, didn't they."

Boi licks his lips to make sure. "No. It's salt water."

"But the hole is only six feet."

Boi looks toward the ocean, the view blocked by shopping centers and hotel towers, the biggest one owned by a private-school trust. He calculates the distance. Not even a quarter mile. He turns and faces the Ala Wai, the polluted, brackish water moat that separates Waikiki from Kapiolani Boulevard condos and walk-ups. Even closer, maybe a couple hundred yards. Waikiki—tens of thousands of tourists, thousands of $8-an-hour jobs, a square mile of hotels built on swampland, the Pacific Ocean seeping underneath.

Boi thinks about all the Waikiki landmarks; the war memorial natatorium; the Queen's beach; King Kalakaua's old pad now a shopping center called King's Village; the white Moana Surfrider, Waikiki's first hotel; The Pink Palace of the Pacific, where the Shirley Temple was invented. The Duke statue, his hands held out like he's asking, "What the fuck happened here?" draped in leis. All next to Diamond Head, a volcano turned off for the last 150,000 years.

What if someone turned on the volcano?

Boi frowns down at his radio and turns it off.

More hard hats come. Some try to shovel dirt in the hole, but the gusher just spits the dirt back and splatters the hotel walls with mud. Others grab buckets and bail, racing the rising water. A hard hat with a giant wrench jumps in the pool. But there's nothing to turn off, no pipe to shut down. More water blasts and explodes in the air. The ocean, warm, probably heated by the dungeon hotel basements with their generators, employee break rooms, and punch clocks, will not be denied.

A hard hat screams into a hand-held radio as the hotel manager flips frantically through the yellow pages. Who needs a farm on the Big Island? Boi steps under the gushing sea water, tilts his head up, and holds out his arms. He bathes in the salt water. Fuck a new house. Fuck long-term investment. Fuck a new car. He needs to do something big, not a new car. He needs to do something massive, not a job. Then Nina will watch what he does and be proud. The Gov will watch what he does and know he's not messing around. He will have a crisis on his hands and will not be able to concentrate on the bill he's trying to push through the open-to-the-highest-bidder legislature. And the local people will watch. They will watch and maybe finally wake up and see what's happening to their home. To Hawaii. How men like Charles Knotting are trying to get rid of them, not just through the usual means of skyrocketing property prices, low wages, pay cuts, and layoffs, but by fucking sterilization.

Soon, it'll just be summer job or slack-ass rich kids from the mainland who love to surf who will work menial Waikiki. There will be nothing left for us. Those from here will be pushed off the rocks.

Boi opens his eyes and looks around. The trolleys, the vendor trucks, the state-of-the-art street lights. Across the street, tourists step off airport shuttles and wait for scrambling bellmen wearing sashes and kukui nuts to take their luggage. The same shuttles fill with tourists on their way back home. A white van pulls up to the boutique hotel with the sprung leak. The manager reassures the driver and the tourists seated behind him that everything is fine. This will not effect your vacation whatsoever. When the tourists step off, the employees line up to kiss ass. Even the hard hats walk up to the tourists and apologize. Boi imagines newspaper want ads, all of them listing the same thing: looking for a kiss-ass. Minimum wage. Must speak two languages. He understands now. He's gotta take it all down.

Boi looks up at the sky. An airplane probably packed with tourists jets far above Diamond Head. Clouds, not puffy, but in streams like ghost hair, streak across the blue. Boi utters a genuine prayer for the first time in his life. He wants the eight-tentacled power of a squid god so that he can rip a hole through to the Waikiki water table under his feet. Hurricane Power.

Fuck you, Uncle Charles. I can be Biblical, too.

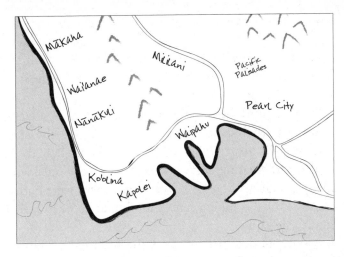

IV. Boi No Good: Part Two

1.

Glory had been in a foster home that looked sort of like this one: chest-high white stucco wall, iron spear fencing. Cleared out, well-swept carport with a fridge, television, and deflated blue kiddy pool. A single-story house with barred windows and a steel-framed security door with black grating. She had been there with four other foster kids—identical twins she could tell apart because one was smaller and had bad asthma, and a seven-year-old girl who weighed over a hundred pounds and hated Glory for being small. Every time the big girl sat on Glory's chest and pinned her legs, screaming for Glory to say uncle, her skin-tight pink shirt rose up, her kidney fat spilled over her waistband making Glory think of the way beef grease and mayonnaise drips over the side of a burger when bitten.

Her foster parents had been nice enough, but frugal motherfuckers—five-hundred twenty-nine CPS dollars per kid, not counting the money for clothes and school supplies. Glory and the other kids lived on rice, vienna sausages, and canned green beans. Most of the money went toward car payments, menthol cigarettes, and cell phone minutes. But Glory didn't complain. The couple didn't like to touch the kids and at least she wasn't with her Mom.

The house she's standing outside of now, Gary's parents' house, has that same, quick-clean-up-in-case-the-state-inspectors-drop-by foster vibe, and when a short-haired, dumpy retarded girl wearing coke-bottle glasses steps outside, Glory remembers Gary did once say that his parents were both registered nurses. Probably taking care of invalids at home for a living. Good money, he said.

The retarded girl turns on the hose and waters the plants. She's gentle at first, softly pressing the nozzle trigger so that the garden is showered with mist. But when she reaches the aloe, she blasts it, and mud splatters on the white walls. She won't stop, either. She's got a vendetta against prickly plants with healing properties. It's not till an older man, probably Gary's dad, steps out, and tug-of-wars her for the hose, does she stop. The dad, skinny except for an old-man double chin and a third-trimester belly, lectures her back inside. If you shiv that belly, will it bleed faster than a normal stomach, or maybe even pop? When Gary's dad looks her way, she flips her hood on her head, sticks her hand in her pockets, and walks away. She steps over a roach stomped flat and entwined with hair, like a cat had shit it out before it got stepped on. Glory rounds the corner.

The kid's in there. Hunting local people in Hawaii, easy. The heat's on them to leave all their lives, cannot afford house, gas, kids, even food sometimes, and Glory can imagine the dozens of conversations Gary probably had with his parents. Go mainland. More opportunity. But he didn't leave and he never will. So where is Gary gonna go when it gets real hot? Hide out at home like a dumb fuck. Even that haole, that extra-chromosome bounty hunter mother-fucker on TV, the one who looks something between a cowboy, a hair-band front man, and an elderly male stripper, he can hunt people in Hawaii. Gary's in there somewhere.

And he's got to be got. He's a witness, a witness with zero backbone. The cops get to him, he'll spill his guts. There's no way Glory's going jail. All those people touching her like Benny used to. The male guards. She'd heard about all that shit. She ain't down for that. She heard that if you complain they ship you to the mainland, to places like Arizona. The mainland. White gangs, black gangs, Mexican gangs. No Hawaiian gangs. She wouldn't last two seconds. Besides, the sky must be so big in the mainland that Glory would have to grip the ground with her toes or she'd fall right into it. No way she's going to prison in the fucking mainland. No way will she be locked up and touched again. Like Gary, she'll live and die in Hawaii. Gary first, then Shane.

2.

After two days of staking out Gary's, Glory learns a couple of things. One, these caretaker people, they never leave the fucking house. And two, after watching these neighbors who aren't caretaker people, these Japanese and Filipino Pearl City-ites, leave the house and come home at the exact same time every day, she's tripping on their tight schedules. One-by-one, the houses light up in the morning. Underground pipes rattle as hot showers turn on. Microwaves beep and processed meats sizzle. Cars start up, blowing out start-up exhaust as the backseats fill with kids. Then the neighborhood goes mute except for dogs occasionally barking, some not house-broken, trapped inside bathrooms, standing on wet newspaper while they scrape at door cracks, crying. Then, as the sun sets, it all happens again in reverse. The cars return. The microwaves beep. Food sizzles. The pipes rattle and the houses light up. Same shit every day. And for some reason it feels like all they're doing with the second halves of their lives—the work, the kids, the monthly life insurance payments Glory sees in their mailboxes while she rummages for fresh credit cards—is prepping for death. These people even put all their Halloween decorations up on the same day.

After the neighborhood clears, Glory stakes out Gary's from the house across the street. Jalousie windows, easy to break into. The dining room is deco'd 1950s drive-in style—a booth upholstered with striped red and white vinyl. A mini-jukebox on the table. It's all set up in front of a picture window, so Glory has a clear view. The caretakers, they come out once in awhile to sweep up and water plants, but the one who steps out of the house the most is a hunched-over grandma. She's dirt old, and walks slow and careful, bones held together by frayed rubberbands. She don't do anything but look around like she forgot or lost something then goes back inside.

The old man she'd cut the week before, she didn't want to kill him. But when he started humping away, it was like what Simon used to tell her about his buddies who came back from war all fucked in the head. Flashbacks. Next thing she knew she was on the guy.

Glory presses A-5 on the jukebox, puts her head on the table, and tries to take a quick nap. She likes the song. Some guy's singing about getting kicked in the head. Sleep don't come, just a waking-dream whisper. She stands up and paces. She stomps her feet on the floor. After Gary and Shane, she might have to go back to the old folks home and unplug all of those senile motherfuckers, just to be sure.

3.

It's the end of day four, Friday, and amazingly enough, Gary's caretaker parents are leaving the house. The dad's yelling for someone, saying "ma'am" or "mom." With his thick Pinoy accent, Glory can't tell the difference. The grandma steps out and the dad ushers her to the van. Glory tries to gauge how long they'll be gone by the way they're dressed—the mom in a black sequined blouse and high heels, the dad in slacks and with enough pomade in his hair to grease an axel, and the grandma in a muumuu, the back of the dress caught in the waistband of her diaper. The dad gets the grandma correct before helping her in the van. They obviously aren't going out dancing. Dinner, maybe? Special occasion? Glory tries to think if it's a holiday, but realizes she only knows the exact date of one: New Year's.

The dad takes cash out of his wallet and slips it in an envelope. He licks the glue, seals the envelope, then hands it to the mom before getting in the van. Wedding. Glory had heard tales of crystal-chandeliered hotel-banquet halls, three hundred guests lined up out front holding envelopes stuffed with cash waiting to drop them in a slitted box on a reception table. She'd thought about maybe robbing weddings, but Simon'd told her too many witnesses.

After the van leaves, Glory slouches in her car and waits for dark. Other neighborhood cars start up. Teens off to malls. Or to hang out in front of convenience stores to try to get someone to buy them beer. Young parents off for date night. Maybe they gonna go booze cruise and dad gonna get laid. But most of the cars stay parked in their carports, resting up for the Monday morning traffic grind. For them, it's same as any other night, except their televisions might stay on an hour or two later. Glory waits until the lights shut off at Gary's.

The lights go off at about nine. Glory puts on her hood, steps out of her car, looks both ways, then crosses the street. It's quiet except for sitcom laugh-tracks muffled by single wall construction. Glory opens the gate and steps to the security door. She counts them. Four locks in all. She goes around back. A rusty washing machine. A limp laundry line with whites with brown stains held up by wood clothespins. A toolshed, not one of those plastic home store sheds, but one handmade out of cherry wood that would only look natural next to a log cabin, creaks as the wind blows at the open door. Glory wishes Benny'd had one of these, locked her up in something like that instead of a cramped metal tool locker. She closes the door.

Glory walks up the patio stairs. Like a lot of these old houses, no bolt on the back door. She takes a lock pick out of her pocket and sticks it in the keyhole. Two seconds and she's inside, gun in one hand, lock pick in the other.

It's like stepping into a hospital room. White sheets, beeping machines, three beds lined up next to each other holding gowned sacks of blood and bone. Each patient, drooling, mouth open, stares at the popcorn ceiling. Two are old, but one, a girl, is about Glory's age. Glory steps to her bed and slowly waves the gun in front of the vegetable kid's face like she's giving her a DUI test. The girl's eyes don't move. Satisfied, Glory looks down the hall. Flickering blue light slips through the frame of the last door. Must be Gary's room.

Glory walks down the hall, trying to keep the floor groans to a minimum. She passes an open door. Another invalid rigged to a beeping machine and staring at the ceiling. Glory closes the door and walks on.

When she gets outside Gary's room, Glory checks the safety on her gun, making sure it's off. One shot then she'll walk out. With all the Flips in the neighborhood, the shot can pass as an exploding cherry bomb—troublemaking Pinoy kids at it again. More than one shot, and she'll have to run. It'll sound like gunfire. Glory opens the door.

The retarded girl Glory had seen watering the plants four days earlier is splayed out naked on Gary's stained, sheet-less queen mattress. Gary, also naked, his long slip of ponytail draped over his shoulder, has got a shotgun barrel up inside the girl while he's flipping through TV channels. Glory doesn't even raise her gun. "What the fuck?" It's a question that needs to be asked.

Gary drops the remote, pulls the shotgun out of the girl, and aims it at Glory. Glory dives out of the room.

The shotgun roars and puts a hole in the wall big enough for a man to crawl through. Ears ringing, Glory stands and smiles. She didn't know Gary had it in him. The retarded girl, she's screaming, palm-cracking the side of her own head, and Glory gets super pissed. Gary pumps another slug in the chamber. She stands like she's bulletproof and starts blasting.

Gary goes down after the first shot. The other three bullet holes are kind of pointless. Amazingly, he's still alive. Glory kicks the shotgun away from his reaching hand.

"Crazy bitch," Gary whispers.

Glory leans down. "You mad at something, you sick fucker?"

"You the sick... Chick..."

A chick. Skinny, weak arms, small feet anchoring broad hips and ass, flaps of fat drooping off chests. All the things Glory tries to hide under her baggy hoodie.

Glory nods and puts a bullet in his head.

The retarded girl is screaming louder now, pulling her hair, and all the beeping machines in the other rooms start going off like smoke detectors. Glory aims the gun at the girl. What would Simon tell her to do? She looks closely at the naked girl bathed in flickering television light. She's not a girl. She's got to be at least thirty, maybe forty. Glory leaves her and heads for the living room. She's not gonna start blasting retards, but the beeping is driving her crazy.

Just as she's about to step outside, Glory pauses. She spins around. The young girl, the vegetable one she DUI-tested earlier, she's looking right at Glory. Her eyes aren't accusing eyes or witness eyes. It's more like the girl is asking her to do something before she leaves. Glory knows she should walk right out of there, run in fact, but she's remembering her grandmother now, how her grandmother used to give her the same look back in the day when they all lived in that bus—the memory tugs Glory to the girl's bed. Glory stands over her. "What?" she says over all the beeping and screaming.

The girl's eyes go right back to the ceiling and will probably be locked there for another twenty years. Glory inspects the breathing machine by the girl's bed, nods, and kisses her forehead. She leaves the girl there and gets the hell out of Pearl City.

Down the hill from Palisades she passes a church. Cop cars whiz past. It's a breezy night. The wind picks up as Glory's car climbs out of the gulch. It's blowing so hard, Glory has to steady the wheel to keep the three thousand pounds of steel in its lane.

It makes her nervous, but she likes nervous. She feels like she's being tickled. Glory puts up her hoodie, downshifts into third, and punches the gas. Too bad about Shane. She'd hoped that as a smart private school boy he could tell her who was dangerous and who wasn't, take Wheelchair Simon's place. Too bad.

4.

"Let's be real," says Charles Knotting. All cameras are on the governor as the Senate President and Speaker of the House, arms crossed, stand like bodyguards behind him. "Taxes are necessary. Let me say that again for those who imagine me as an irrational fiscal conservative: Taxes are necessary."

Charles pauses. There are others behind him as well—officials—the police and fire chiefs and the head of the teacher's union. They resemble tired housewives with thirty years worth of frying-pan-burned, dish pan hands. "Yes, I said it. Now you all know I have no political ambitions beyond this office."

The crowd, which includes reporters from all the network and cable news outlets, laughs. Charles looks tired, as if he'd spent the last six years digging ditches instead of sitting in a fifth floor air-conditioned room signing papers. He takes a sip of water then puts the plastic bottle down on the podium. "I will not go down as the Governor who shreds education. I will not go down as the Governor who shreds transportation. And I will not go down as the Governor who shreds healthcare. We need our schools. We need our roads. And make no mistake, people, as good as you are feeling now, as eternal as you may imagine your life to be, one day it will be your turn, whether it be sudden chest pain, a wooziness in the morning, or an unfortunate automobile accident. Make no mistake: Chances are you will end up in an emergency room. A hospital room. And truly understand what a twenty-percent co-pay really is. No one, and I mean no one, should go bankrupt because they get sick. And like I said, most of us will get sick at one point or another. When my wife..."

Charles pauses to compose himself. "When my wife fell ill. We were so fortunate to be surrounded by excellent medical staff..." The president of the largest medical center in Hawaii is standing behind Charles, too. "I think everyone deserves to be as fortunate." The Democrats behind him nod. Maxine Honda reaches up and puts a hand on his shoulder.

"Now, do not misunderstand me. I am not saying certain things cannot be trimmed and made more efficient. They can. And everyone standing behind me agrees with that. But it occurred to me, maybe we can do more than just trim. Maybe, it's times like these, times of fear and uncertainty, when real, long-lasting changes can be made, changes that better the state, changes that better this aina, this land of aloha, in meaningful ways."

"Now, I am going to throw out terms that some of you will be familiar with and some of you won't." Charles looks down at a piece of paper.

"Section 8. Funding for housing for those less fortunate..."

"SSI, or Supplemental Security Income, for those suffering with debilitating illness..."

"Medicaid. Health care for those who cannot afford it..."

"SNAP. Supplemental Nutrition Assistance Program. A program designed because no American child should go hungry."

"Now at the risk of sounding like a liberal, I will say this." More laughs. "Even though Hawaii, like every state, must pay a rather significant percentage of each of these Federal programs, I do not want to cut them. I will not tell a mother who falls sick and cannot work through no fault of her own that only those with money have the right to medical care. I will not tell a hungry child living in the wealthiest nation in the world that we cannot afford to house or feed her.

"I know what you're all thinking, is he, the conservative Governor of the fiftieth state, going to hug a tree next?" The audience laughs.

"No, I will not. But I will add this. I will add, that, like all of you, I am rather upset about the entitlement-program abuses that occur. And I think that if we end these abuses, we will not only be doing the right thing, but we will also dramatically cut budget deficits. And these are not one-time cuts. These are long, sustained cuts that will last for generations."

"What kind of abuses am I talking about? I'm talking about people who sell their children's Social Security card numbers to other people looking for a tax break at tax time."

"I'm talking about people who coach their children to act crazy, so they can collect SSI checks."

"I'm talking about people who sell their food stamps fifty cents to the dollar, so they can purchase drugs."

"I'm talking about the worst kind of people, the kind of people who use their children to get a free ride. I am, in fact, talking about people who do not and will not stop having children, because for them, each child is not a miracle, but instead, a government-funded paycheck. Let me show you something..."

Two young female interns, fresh out of college, step up to the podium. Both roll up their left sleeves. Both wearing plastic, Band-Aid colored patches on their shoulders.

"This is Jenna and Lani. One is trying to quit smoking. One is wearing a birth control patch. Can you tell which is which?"

Charles waits as the girls roll down their sleeves and step back. Charles shrugs. "I sure can't tell the difference."

"What I'm proposing is this. We do not cut entitlement programs. We don't take a cent away from them. What we do, instead, is create a law that requires young women to wear a patch, like the girls here, before they collect."

Murmurs in the crowd. "Let me be clear. What I am proposing is not a law that requires invasive surgery, not a law that is infringing on individual rights. I am not saying you cannot have children. Have all the kids you want. But what I am saying is that if you want government support, you need to be responsible. We have similar laws when it comes to driving, to gun ownership, to food production, and construction. We have these laws to ensure that the public will not be harmed by irresponsibility."

Charles pauses. He points to the cameras. "As you can see, I invited national news outlets out here to introduce this proposal. Some of you watching out there, you will think this is crazy, that a law like this cannot and will not be passed. How, you will ask, can a Republican Governor and Democratic state legislature work together to create such a landmark bill? In this age of gridlock and partisan politics, how can an old Caucasian surfer, an openly gay Speaker of the House, a liberal Japanese-American Senate President, and union leaders across the state join forces, when it's these very forces we see battling each other across the nation? Maybe something like this can only happen in a place where words like 'kokua,' 'malama,' 'ohana,' and 'aloha aina' hold almost mythical meaning, words that fill our hearts with remembrance of what this land used to be..."

Charles wipes a tear from his eye. "A land where kapuna were respected and embraced keiki they passed on the road instead of fearing them. A land where neighbors shared their bounties instead of worrying that someone was trying to steal them. All of us, the Speaker, the esteemed Senate President, the Chief of Police... We remember these times and want to work together to bring them back."

"With the support of Senate President Maxine Honda and House Speaker Ethan Chang, I present to you Bill 636, which will be introduced in the next legislative session. My last significant act as Governor. My last significant act as a politician. I present you the Helen Knotting Bill, in memory of my wife..."

It's the night before Halloween and Shane, two guns on his lap and a lit joint between his lips, is watching all this at home. He's got the house alarm on and the pit bull tied up out front as he curses Boi's name. If it wasn't for his brother, they never would've dug up this crazy sister of theirs who, Shane is convinced, is coming after him. He's supposed to be at the press conference with Charles, standing behind his father, but when he started imagining Glory in a crowd of reporters waiting to do him in, he decided to stay home. He wants to see her coming.

The pit bull barks. Shane swivels the chair toward the door. The lit joint drops from his lips and falls on his lap. The guns fall to the floor as he pats his jeans, trying to snuff out the sparks. He picks up both guns, walks to the door, and peeks through the window. It's just a guy passing the house on a fold-out bicycle.

Maybe he should have called someone for back up. But what could he say? That there might be a girl from Waimanalo who weighs about as much as a bag of rice coming to take you out? He'd rather die than make ass.

But maybe he's going about this all wrong. He turns the TV off and heads upstairs. Since his parents moved to the governor's mansion, Shane's taken over the master bedroom. Polished wood floors, Hawaiian bark cloth rug, gold-framed black and white portraits of Hawaiian royalty, a California king mattress plopped on a wood frame a big as a parking space—the only thing missing is a couple of naked Hawaiians waving feathered fans and a sign outside that says summer palace.

Shane puts the guns on the bed and opens the window. There's a picture of Helen on the dresser beside him. He tries not to look at it as he goes back to get his guns and climbs out onto the second story eave. A strong breeze blows the window shut behind him.

It's better up here. He can see everything. The Kahala Mandarin, Kahala Mall, Kahala Elementary, Kahala Avenue—everything around here named Kahala something. Shane can't remember what Kahala is. A mythical Hawaiian woman or a fish? He's not sure. Waves that sound like the muted splash of broken glass wash sand behind him. It's nice up here. Maybe his parents in their younger years shared joints and laughs while perched up here.

Maybe, he thinks, he should do something with his life. Something his Mom would've been proud of. Maybe make movies? He's always liked movies, especially movies about inner-city life in places like New York, Los Angeles, and Boston. True Gangs-tas. Maybe he can make movies about hard-scrabble Honolulu, maybe show people on the mainland the *real* Honolulu, not the picture postcard, but the—Shane stops himself. He's starting to sound like a book blurb or movie poster. But maybe. Hell, maybe he can call a truce with Glory and bring her on board. She has stories to tell. Maybe Boi will be willing to invest in the project with his new money? Between them, they got millions. Maybe he needs to go to film school since he's not even good at taking pictures with his smart phone.

Yes, he will make movies. How hard can it be? He creates a frame with his thumbs and pointers and scans the area. He swiv-els slowly taking a second-story panoramic of everything Kahala. He'll have to go country to make his Hawaii gangsta movie. Or maybe Downtown or Waikiki. Definitely Waianae. Need to show the homeless in all their blue tarp, busted rides, tent-city glory.

Still holding out his finger frame, he scans Kahala from Dia-mond Head to the Mandarin. He shifts back to the cars parked, lined up on the street. A possible swooping helicopter shot. Then he sees her in the frame. Glory across the street. Hood on, she's pointing a gun at him. She fires.

Shane grabs his guns and stands up. He holds them sideways, gangsta style. He mashes both triggers. The bullets miss her by a good twenty feet, and the recoil from the gun in Shane's left hand kicks so hard he drops it. The gun slides down the eave and hits the red brick walkway. Another round goes off. The bullet hits a car windshield. A car alarm chain reaction blares up Kahala Avenue.

Glory, who is not holding her gun sideways, but using the sights on the top of the barrel, walks toward the house and fires again. Wood behind Shane shatters, launching splinters into his neck. Shane turns around, opens the window, and jumps through it. The house alarm goes off.

The pit bull outside barks. A gunshot. The dog stops barking. Shane slides open a mirror closet door and crams himself inside.

He touches his neck. Blood. He points the gun at the doorway. All he wants to do is make movies. Why is this happening to him?

He reaches back with one arm and touches the hanging clothes behind him. His hand brushes against a soft coat, probably the mink one that as an animal rights advocate Helen would never wear but could never bring herself to get rid of. He touches other slips of hanging fabric, silks and sheer dresses. No one even thought to pack up her stuff or get rid of it. Who's responsibility was that? His? He needs to get out of the closet. He shoves the closet door, and its wheels skip off its tracks. The mirrored door falls to the floor and shatters. Shane steps out and catches his breath. Shit, now Glory probably knows where he is, where he's hiding.

All his life, all he wanted to be was a real Hawaiian—not just a real Hawaiian, but a ghetto Hawaiian. The kind of guy who drives around in a monster truck, State of Hawaii flag sticker on the rear window, the bed splattered with rusty tools and empty beer bottles. The kind of guy who barbeques with kiawe and a blowtorch. The kind of guy who pronounces "kids" "keeds" and spends unemployed afternoons throwing around guys in Gracie jujitsu dojos. The kind of guy who people give a wide berth when they walk by him on the street. The kind of guy who drops Samoan bouncers at clubs, two at a time.

He'd spent years lifting weights, avoiding the dishonor of doing cardio, and drank gallons of protein shakes to become that guy.

But he's not the real deal. The real deal, all hoodied, one-hundred-pounds of her, she's walking up the stairs right now. No truck. No fear. All crazy. She's coming for him, and all he can do is wait.

Sirens. A quick response. Thank God he's in Kahala, that the Gov's house gets its own team. He hear the footsteps, the size sixes, pitter-pattering down the wood followed by a rushed slam of the door.

Shane sits on the bed and looks at Helen's closet and remembers times when she wore each outfit. The yellow sun-dress at his high school graduation. The beige slacks and white blouse during the last day of his trial. The strapless green gown at Charles's inaugural ball. He grabs a magazine, bends down, and sweeps broken glass on it with his hand.

The door opens. For a moment Shane's stomach sinks as he expects to see Glory standing there pointing a gun at him. But it's a cop. The same one busted him when one of his boys had been fucking a turtle shell and he threw that girl against the wall like she was a rubber dart. The cop holsters his gun and looks around. He shakes his head.

"I thought you were gonna make changes," says the cop.

Shane puts down the magazine. He's breathing hard. He brushes tiny slivers of glass off his hands. "This time," he says. "This time, I will."

The cop picks up the gun off the floor. "You need help."

Shane nods. He looks around the room. "I do need help. And there's only one guy I know who can help me."

Shane turns around and puts his hands behind his back. The cop slaps on the cuffs. "The Gov?"

"No. My brother."

5.

It's Halloween and Chastity Fu opens the door wearing a slinky black cat-suit so tight that Boi can see nipple rings and camel toe. Her two friends, Nikki and Cheyenne, stand behind her, one dressed as Little Bo Peep in thong and white stockings, and the other dressed as a mermaid, aqua-sequined, skin-tight bottom with fin flairs by the ankles. No visible panty lines. Starfish bra.

"Wow Boi," says Cheyenne, flapping her fins. "You look like shit."

"I thought I smelled tuna," Boi says as he enters the apartment. Cheyenne, the mermaid wearing hooker make-up who lives in a welfare Waikiki walk-up, slaps his shoulder.

Maybe we should blow up her building, too.

But Boi has been in a good mood all week, inspecting sub-ocean-level parking garages and main sewage lines big enough to crawl through. He spent last night at an Internet cafe wearing a *Lord of the Rings* tee shirt, read *The Anarchist's Cookbook* online. Today, he skulked underground in the sewers capped with a lighted hard hat like a Waikiki moleman. He's in the Halloween spirit, and he's going to need explosives. Lots of explosives. He could also use help from the weather, like he got when he sent Peter Patrino's house off a cliff and into the Pacific. If his father's right, he'll get help from the gods. But even if he doesn't, there's water all over the place in Waikiki. Ocean water. Brackish water. Sewage water. Golf course water. Fresh water that feeds into all 30,000 hotel rooms, spewed forth from water-saving shower heads that wash California sand out of tourist butt-cracks. There's so much water. Trick is how to bring it all to the surface.

When Nina steps out of the bathroom, Boi's relieved she isn't dressed as a sexy nurse or an Oktoberfest beer wench. Instead, she's in a video game princess costume that's too big for her. She charges Boi who scoops her up.

"You look tired, Daddy."

He feels tired, but in a good way.

"I'm working overtime tonight," says Boi.

"Every night this week," says Chastity, adjusting her cat ears. "And Nina's right. You look like shit."

"She said I looked tired. Tuna said I look like shit."

Chastity shrugs. "Rev is going to be okay."

"What the hell is Rev?"

"Hello," says Chastity, "Rev is the boy that fell of the balcony. The one you saved."

His name is Rev, as in "Ho, fricking rev the car full throttle!" Jesus Christ. Boi hasn't thought of Rev for awhile now. He wonders why.

"I just came to drop this off." Boi hands Chastity a jewelry box. He'd spent so much time in Waikiki over the last week, it just felt weird not buying a two-hundred-percent marked-up piece of jewelry. "It's for Nina. But I can't take her."

"I want to go with you, Daddy," says Nina.

"Fine," says Chastity. "We'll take her with us."

Yes. Take her with us. Boi imagines the itinerary. Convenience store slushy mixed with rum for the drive over. Drinks at the tourist bar that serves beers in glasses shaped like giant cock and balls. After pretending to blow the beer mugs, they'll do a couple laps around Kalakaua and Kuhio, make sure their skeeve is on full exhibition. Then maybe a drunken trip to the four a.m. strip bar. Make out with each other and flash titty at all the horny guys. Grab stripper ass. Girls like these, they were worse than frat boys at strip bars. Cheering each other stage-side, dollar bills in their mouths, more than ready to lean into a pubic patch of two coats of mix-berry body-sprayed skank.

"Hell no," says Boi.

Nikki and Cheyenne roll their eyes and step outside. Nina's tugging on the sleeve of her costume. "I think one of my arms is longer than the other one."

Boi puts Nina down and adjusts it. Chastity opens the jewelry box. "You need to return this," she says.

"Why?"

"Wrong birthstone. They changed the astrology signs. She's not a Pisces anymore. She's an Aries. Needs to be a diamond, not aquamarine."

"I thought it goes by month."

"You thought wrong."

Boi holds out his hand. "Fine, I'll take it back."

Chastity puts it in her purse, which is mocked up as a giant cat toy wrapped in pink yarn. It hangs by her stomach, a small pooch under the black lycra. She's getting older, gaining weight. The other two girls look as if they're picking up a bit of weight, too. "I'll do it," says Chastity. "Give me the receipt."

"I don't have it."

Chastity sighs. "Well, where'd you get it?"

She's fishing.

"10-4," says Boi.

"What?" says Chastity.

"Nothing."

Chastity's frowning at him. Boi didn't tell Chastity about his inheritance, and he doesn't plan to. When she'd learned about Nina's trust, she scooped Nina up like she'd just brought home a report card full of ME's (Meets Proficiency with Excellence), hugged her and said, "Wanna buy mommy a house?"

A house. The Church of Property. It seems as if every middle- and working-class ass hat searches for salvation in an over half-a-million-dollar, fifty-year-old asphalt shingled house and thirty-year mortgage. Most of the cops Boi works with attend that church. Monthly payments that they can't cover with their salaries. Graduates of all-boy parochial-school cop farms, climbing over each other for overtime like a bucket full of crabs. Wife out of work. Wife left. Wife ROPA'd me. Fuck the wife. One sniff of Nina's trust and Chastity was instantly ready to receive an ash cross on her forehead and convert. She was disappointed when she'd learned that except for any possible private school and college tuition costs, Nina can't touch the money until she turns twenty-five.

"Don't worry where I got it from," says Boi. "I'll take it back."

"So the old haole lady didn't leave you anything? After all the time you spent with that family?"

"Not one dime."

Nina grabs the aqua pendant from Chastity. "It matches my costume," she says.

She hands it to Boi and turns around. Boi fastens it around her neck. Chastity's eying them, her nipples like crab eyes under the black lycra. Boi picks Nina up.

"Don't carry her," says Chastity. "She's not a baby anymore."

Boi and Nina step out of the apartment, Nina holding a big bag of Halloween candy she scored from trick-or-treating earlier. Nikki and Cheyenne are outside, chewing gum and sharing a cigarette. Shirtless neighborhood boys on bicycles ride by and hoot and holler. "Pervs," says Nikki as she winks, bends over, and jacks off her Bo Peep cane, which if rubbed long and hard enough ejaculates a white slime mix of corn syrup and water out of its curved tip.

6.

Boi needs to pick up some old blasting caps and water gel from Joe that his father had stolen from various construction sites he'd worked as a kid. Boi and Joe used to use the stuff to clear out banana trees.

As far as babysitting options go, Boi only trusts one person. His mother. Patricia Bolosan lives with her sister in Laie, in an eyesore squeezed between two houses with gazebos and skylights. The house, fronted by a rusty washer and lawnmower and a Buick LeSabre with banana trees growing through its floorboard and sunroof, has been in the family for years. In fact, the two adjacent properties used to belong to the Kahele family as well, years ago, before Patricia had been born, but those houses went to fund hospital bills and college educations and now there were Kaheles buried as far as Alice Springs, Australia and Greenville, Maine, uncles and aunties Patricia had never met, family who long forgot the sound the ocean makes at high tide.

Boi wonders if he needs to think up an excuse for not bringing Nina over for the last six months. But unlike Joe, or even the Knottings, Patricia never demands to see the little girl, never guilt-trips him into holiday weekend visits. Boi figured it was because after raising Boi, she'd had enough of kids, enough of that heartbreaking disappointment that fills a parent when a child does not meet expectations, the kind Charles has written all over his face whenever he looks at Shane. And the bitch of it was, unlike Charles, Patricia's expectations weren't that high. Be good. Just be good. And Boi couldn't even do that.

"You should visit grandma more," says Nina.

"I know."

"I have a test tomorrow. About Squanto."

"What the hell is Squanto?"

"Daddy. Squanto is the Native American who helped the Pilgrims."

Squanto. That dumb motherfucker.

Nina plugs herself into her portable game console and plays a game about a plumber rescuing a princess, the thirtieth version of that story. It was her birthday present from him last year. He'd figured playing that crap was better than her watching what her mom watches, flipping through what her mom reads, and like most kids, she spent so much goddamn time in cars with nothing to do, he felt bad. Little did he know he'd spend the last-half year completing hard levels for her, the plumber jumping over pipes and turtles and shooting fireballs at Venus flytraps, while Nina cheered him on. He'd have taken her fishing instead if there were any goddamn fish left.

"Daddy, this level is too hard."

"Dammit, sweetie, that's what you said when I taught you to swim! And to ride bike, and read. You gotta learn to do things on your own."

"Why? You can just do it."

"I'm not always gonna be around."

"Yes you are. Grandpa said he can tell the future, and he said that the squid god Kanaloa is on your side, and people will make statues of you one day."

Red Roof Joe.

When they pull up the driveway, Patricia steps out of the house wearing gym clothes. She's dropped at least fifty pounds since he's last seen her, and to show off this new energy, this new body, she leaps down all three steps in front of her. She jogs to the car and opens the back door. She pulls Nina out of her booster seat and hugs her. Boi gets out.

"Jesus, what the hell happened to you?"

Patricia looks bug-eyed. "I should ask you the same thing."

"I'm fine," Boi says. "Just working a lot."

"I had the operation," says Patricia, holding Nina while doing calf raises. Her eyes are all over Boi, making him feel guilty before he's even done his deed.

"When?" he asks.

"Three months ago. I not going let fricking Mormons cut me from the 'Pele: Goddess of Fire' show without one fight. I fricking choreographed it."

"Why didn't you call?"

Patricia shrugs. Make-up, snug sweat pants, and fingernail polish the color of sin. Hair coarse and out-of-control, like a tumble of volcanic glass threads spun by wind. "You going trick-or-treating or something?" Boi asks.

Patricia walks to the house carrying Nina. "Don't be stupid. Come inside. Eat something. You look like one fricking prisoner of war."

Boi follows. He passes a guava tree. Dead leaves and feral cat shit covered in white fuzz sit by the trunk, which looks wrapped in ancient paper. "Where's aunty?" Boi asks.

"She went gym."

"There's a gym in Kahuku?"

"Yeah, just opened. We both go now."

When conquering lands, America doesn't plant flags any-more. It plants fast food joints, cable TV, and gyms—straps people in self-defeating mouse wheels that make you fat, has you watching television shows that make you feel guilty for being fat, then sends you to the gym to get skinny. Where the TV-show sexy people eating french fries, like the one currently blaring in front of Patricia's all-in-one home gym.

There's a lot of pictures in the house. Black and whites that go back to when the camera was first invented. Hawaiians tug-ging rope out of the ocean, nets made from olona pregnant with fish. The old Kahele property when it was measured in acres instead of square feet. Then the changes. The hukilau nets not as full, the property not as big. As the pictures turn from black and white to color, pictures of luaus become pictures of protest. The last black-and-white, a shot of Patricia's grandmother carrying a wicker basket full of plumeria, looks partially rubbed out by an eraser.

All this time, Boi figured his rage had been lit by a lighter-burned childhood that left him assassin cold, or a dad who egged him on to play offense instead of defense and blow up the world, or a hypocrite uncle Governor who with one hand wanted him to become somebody and with the other wanted to make sure the likes of Nina would never be. Or maybe the rage was to hear his name, Boi No Good, ring out across the islands. Maybe he just wanted people to make statues of him. All that, maybe it played a role. The way a hurricane builds, layer after layer of warm air rising off the ocean's surface feeding and feeding swirling clouds above until it takes off toward land like a top, maybe that was it.

But these pictures egg him on even more. These pictures, they're not like the Knotting pictures, a prosperous family becoming more prosperous. They're not like the pictures that japs, pakes, flips, yobos, and borinkis had in their houses, either. Snap shots of ancestors cutting sugar cane, boys in army uniforms, first cars, first votes, then prep school and university graduations and four generations of family lined up for portrait, in the middle, an Asian great-great grandmother still alive because these fucking Asians, they live forever. Patricia's pictures are all wrong.

They're going in reverse.

Give it another generation, and all of Patricia's little nieces and nephews will be living in busted city buses in red dirt lots, too. Or Alice Springs or Greenville, Maine. Their line, Boi's line, too, will die out, especially if Charles Knotting gets his way.

Enough is enough, already.

Nina's pulling on Boi's arm. "Daddy are you listening to me?"

"Sorry. What is it?"

"Is Grandma going to help me study for my test?"

Patricia nods, chewing on a low-carb cracker covered with black seeds.

"She will, sweetie. Say goodbye now. Daddy has to go to work."

"What you really up to?" asks Patricia, one eyebrow raised.

"No good," says Boi. "No good."

Patricia shakes her head and hands him a tofurky sandwich.

Boi kisses Nina then turns to Patricia. Turquoise chandelier earrings. Jangly bracelets made of silver charms and leather. Ankle weights. *She's one of them now.* Like something out of a bad zombie movie except the zombies in this one get more pretty after feasting on brains. He left her for the Knottings, and she ended up like them.

Nina takes off one of Patricia's ankle weights and puts it on. She walks to the living room, dragging one heavy foot behind her, as she laughs at a television commercial with a singing octopus hocking renters insurance. She turns around. "I love you, daddy," she says.

"I love you, too."

"Sometimes I want to say something else, like 'have a nice day,' but 'I love you' comes out instead."

Boi feels like crying. He clears his throat. "It's okay. I never get tired of hearing it."

Nina turns back to the TV. Boi remembers that first day he saw her. She was running around in a diaper, twin antennae pigtails on top of her head, trying to eat electricity at the boys' home visiting room. He'd picked her up and looked at her. She had his eyes. She had his chin. She had big pores on the tip of her nose like him.

Later he'd learn that her first word was "ball" but her favorite word was "up." That she liked egg whites but hated yolks. That she could make a strange clicking sound when she bent her left middle finger. That she called birds "fftt, fftt, fftt" because that's the sound their wings made when they flew away. He'd learn that to this day, she called breasts "babas," which as far as he knew, was a word she made up on her own.

But back then, the first time he'd hugged her, all he knew was that it was the first time in his life he'd hugged another human being and meant it. It was the first time in his life where he wanted to squeeze the other person even harder. Even now, she's the only person he can hug and feel something other than uncomfortable extreme.

Boi reaches for the door and has a hard time opening it. He has to convince himself he's doing it for her. He's doing it for her, for Joe, for Patricia, all of them. *This thing you got going on will make her life better.* He almost believes it as he walks out. *It'll make everything better.* Boi looks down. He didn't bring his Jaguar radio.

It'll make everything better. His thoughts or someone else's? As if someone planted tiny receivers in his ears while he was sleeping, only he can't figure out who, or even when, since he doesn't remember the last time he slept. Maybe it was those state hospital workers who force fed him applesauce when he was a kid? No. No way they could strap him down now. He almost wishes they'd try. Maybe it was one of Joe's revolutionary buddies or Joe himself? Maybe the CIA? No, that seems far-fetched. It has to be something with more mana than that. Something so stealthy and secret that it can move through this world and not be detected.

You know who I am.

Boi sticks a finger in his ear, plunges out some of the buzzing, ticking static. His phone rings. He answers. It's Shane. "Can we talk?" he asks.

"I busy," Boi says.

"It's about Glory," Shane says. "What the hell did you unleash on me?"

Boi sighs. "Fine. I'm going to Waianae District Park."

"For what?"

"To watch a football game."

7. _____

The Beef Bowl, the annual game between the Kahaluu Broncos and the Waianae Tigers, goes back some thirty years when the first full-scale brawl between the two teams and their parents broke out on Waianae's home field. The field, up a narrow country street and next to a District Park tennis court, is notoriously anti-visiting team. Guests sit on bleachers squeezed between tennis court fence and football sideline, and when the game is over, they need to cross the field in order to get to the parking lot. When the Broncos lose, it's a long walk across the field to the cars, twelve-to-fifteen year-old boys from the Midget Division jeering, their fathers, with their mountain boar-necks collared with thick gold chains, mocking the losers as well. But it's an even longer walk when the Broncos win. Glares, threats, and shoulder brushes—if it weren't for the ten or so Kahaluu chronic fathers who just don't give a fuck, who take off their shirts after the game, just to show they're ready to throw, the Broncos would be humiliated after every game even if they won.

They don't fight every year, and there have been moments of solidarity, like the time both the Broncos and Tigers flew up to Disney World to play in the national playoffs and the Broncos got into a one a.m. brawl with a Baltimore team and the Tigers jumped in to back their Hawaiian brethren (all three teams were suspended for a year), but ask the refs, the poor guys who volunteer their weekends for nothing, and they'll tell you, it's the worst game to officiate. Accusations of blindness, impotence, and maternal fornicating accompany every flag thrown or not thrown, and the refs dream of ejecting parents from the field, but that would get their asses kicked, too. Many a ref has quit the league after officiating a single Beef Bowl.

Boi spots Joe, an avid Pop Warner fan, sitting top row, visitors' bleachers. Shane, wearing a working man's florescent green, long-sleeve shirt, is sitting next to him with an extra-large bag of movie popcorn on his lap.

That fucker never work one construction job a day in his life.

Boi rubs his ears then climbs the bleachers and sits next to Joe. He doesn't want to get too close to Shane, who's wearing some kind of stank ass body spray that makes Boi sneeze. Or maybe it's the lack of sleep making Boi sneeze. He's not sure. Joe looks at Boi. "You look good," he says.

"Everyone else tells me I look like shit."

"No listen to them." Joe looks up at the sky. "Weather funny kine. I bet hurricane coming soon."

"Every November you say that. Season's over already."

"Something different this year. I feel it. *You* feel it."

Boi ignores the comment and looks at Shane. "So what you like?" says Boi.

Shane shrugs. "I'm in trouble," he says as he grabs a fistful of popcorn, shoves it in his mouth and chews.

"What? You went movies?" Boi asks.

Shane shakes his head. "I was just craving popcorn, you know?" he says over his loud chewing.

"Well, what kind of trouble?" Boi asks as Joe spits boiled peanut shells into a plastic bag at his feet.

Shane tells Boi and Joe about Glory. Boi shakes his head while Joe laughs. A pass interference call sends half the Bronco fans to the sidelines. A crackhead dad's already got his shirt off while a mom's got a finger in the ref's face.

"And what," asks Boi, "you scared?"

Shane pulls an unpopped kernel out of the bag and cracks it with his teeth.

"Fuck," says Boi. "My balls weigh more than her."

"She got guns!" says Shane.

"Call the cops."

"That's what I'm doing!"

"Shut up," says Joe. He stands. "This the good part."

The shirtless crackhead runs on the field and grabs the ball. The refs blow their whistles as the Tiger players chase the man. But he's fast. It's the end of the third quarter, and the Broncos are getting blown out 35 - 7. The man cuts behind the goalpost and punts the ball over the tennis court fence before getting gang-tackled by the Waianae defensive backs. The linebackers then defensive linemen pile on, too. The man under the pile screams. The Waianae parents head to the end zone to pull their kids off the crackhead. The players on the Bronco bench have their faces in their hands, disgusted, like they're losing by 100 instead of 28.

Joe sits back down. The Tiger's defense gets off the crackhead and heads to their bench. A ref jogs to the tennis court to get the ball. "Can stay with me if you like," says Joe. "She try come my house, Grover Cleveland take care."

"I don't got time for this," says Boi. "I need my stuff."

Joe nods. "Bring big boy over here. Get choke to carry."

Boi shakes his head. "Shane. Go tell your dad or something. Frick, he's the one who found her the first time. Two years, and I couldn't find her. That guy, two days and guarantee he get SWAT all over her."

"You don't care about her anymore?" Joe asks.

Boi spits and shakes his head.

"That's my Boi," says Joe. "That's my Boi."

A Waianae defensive back intercepts the ball and takes it into the endzone for a pick six. The Waianae fans cheer. Now the Ka-haluu chronics have had enough. They take off their shirts and charge the Waianae side of the field. Ten or so separate skirmishes break out. Men circle each other, hands up, chins tucked to their chests as their wives and girlfriends scream at them to stop.

"You played football?" Joe asks Shane.

Shane doesn't answer.

"Didn't think so," says Joe. He stands and watches the fights. The kids, their helmets off, are squaring off against each other, too. The refs head for the parking lot, and the coaches catch cracks trying to break things up. "Fuck," says Joe. "This one beautiful game."

8. _____

They wind down Kamehameha Highway, headed for Kahuku. Joe, head out of the window, passenger side, cracks open beer cans before launching them at Shane's car. Boi downshifts and passes the car in front of him. God, his eyes are burning. Grover Cleveland's horse trailer is hitched to Boi's new truck, the only thing he's splurged on with the money Helen had left him. As much as he hated tapping into the cash, he needs a truck for what he's got planned. A ten-year-old, four-cylinder sedan won't cut it.

Boi feels the weight of the truck, like he's dragging a battleship anchor across the circle island highway.

They race past big-wave beaches like Sunset and Banzai Pipeline. Haole-owned houses across the street—*surfboard address signs and plastic hieroglyph turtles nailed to wood plank fences, haoles for sure.* The waves are getting bigger. A sure sign that winter is approaching.

"I want in," says Joe, who is out of beer grenades.

"No," says Boi.

"What you gonna do?"

Boi doesn't answer.

Joe points back. "What you going do about him? He's The Gov's son. He going rat, guarantee."

They approach the giant white windmills and pass a broken down convalescent home—a stone and rusted rebar hull. Down the road, seventy-year-old hippies sell glass floaters and bikinis from their tourist trap shacks. Three Kahuku shrimp trucks are parked on the side of the road, one with a Hawaiian sunset airbrushed on its side.

Shane's still following as they pass more surfboard address signs, A-framed fighting cock houses, and a cardboard sign that reads "smoke meat and pit bull pups for sale." They pass the old Kahuku sugar mill, nothing left of it except for giant blue and yellow gears displayed as monuments. It's a strip mall now, a sub sandwich franchise and a store hocking Turtle Bay timeshares.

After passing their tenth church, Boi hangs a left heading toward the shore on an unpaved road cratered with muddy, bathtub-sized puddles. They pass actor Peter Patrino's new house, a castle built with heiau rocks. Next to it, the old Bolosan property. There's a No Trespassing sign stapled to a post. Boi runs it over. *Fuck the damage. That's what trucks are for.*

The loi, the duck pond, the pig pen, the house, all gone. Even the hill itself flattened. In its place stand three two-story house frames, fronted by jawed, yellow construction vehicles and a cement mixer. It's Saturday, so the crew has the day off. Boi parks next to a crawler excavator.

"Why did you leave the stuff here?" asks Boi.

"So I don't gotta carry it all back here to blow this shit up," says Joe. He gets out of the car. He raises his hands to the sky. "I'm still here!"

Shane pulls up next to him. Eyeing the yet-to-be-built Mc-Mansions, Boi imagines what they will contain in another year or so—stationary bikes, pool tables, electric pianos—shit that will get used for a week then will serve as places to hang beach laundry. Maybe a bikini top hanging off stationary bike handlebars and wet towels tossed across the piano bench as they undress and bone on green pool-table felt. They'll throw parties, drink Europe beer set on surfer hieroglyph wood coasters, and smoke a lot of weed because haoles love their weed. Maybe they'll pass around a hand-blown glass egg with a jellyfish inside and giggle trip on it. Or they'll race their koa six-man canoe models across their wood floors like toys. Then they'll wake up hungover in the morning, the neighbor's fighting chickens crowing before the sun even comes up. After two weeks, they'll call a cop like Boi, file a noise complaint, a trash complaint, an animal complaint, and two weeks after that, they'll start calling City and County and try to get their roads paved and sidewalked. All the while, they'll have "Keep the Country Country" stickers on their back bumpers, giving the other haole drivers something to think about while heading to town to watch an aerial burlesque show.

It's not just Kry-lua, Lani-kry, and Hawaii-Kry anymore. All of it, the circle island, the beaches from north, south, east, west. It's the whole fucking place. They're everywhere. It's all Kry-waii.

Boi eyes Shane. He parked too close to Boi and is trying to squeeze his fat ass out of his car. Shane slams his driver's side door into Boi's new truck. Joe rolls down the window. "Just reverse out and park again!" he yells.

Shane slams his door into Boi's truck once more before he gets back in his car and re-parks.

He's such a waste of space. As usual. Carried. Carried by Charles, carried by Helen, carried by inheritance, carried by Boi. And at three bills, he's not so easy to carry.

"This island needs a fresh start," says Boi.

Joe nods.

What Oahu needs is a good old-fashioned natural disaster. It needs a Katrina, a Haitian earthquake, a Japanese tsunami. And not the kind Charles Knotting is planning, not laser-guided strikes that bend over and donkey-punch mostly brown people, so maybe not a Katrina or a Haitian disaster, but a bang that turns the lights out. People think better in the dark. Rich haoles with their pantries filled with Haleiwa Heat and Pele fire macadamia nut oil, mango chutney, and purple pikake-scented candles. Middle-management Asians and Hawaiians with their polished SUV's, wholesale warehouse swingsets, kids-to-private-school commutes, and their underground termite-repellent systems, no-talent shitheads who act like having clean, no-talent shithead kids, a clean house, annual Vegas and Disneyland trips, and bills paid on time make them somehow superior to everyone despite the fact they are not-great-at-anything motherfuckers. And half-assed intellectuals with their half-assed links to the islands—that time they got their hands dirty digging taro or waved protest signs with "the people"— the ones who always take the unpopular position, because if everyone else is dumb it makes them smart, and they write their minority reports in untranslatable bullshit that no one else but smug assholes like themselves can read. The working class meathead, all hopped up on Bushido, forty-five-pound barbell plates, and cock enhancement drugs, who thinks how many beers he can drink or the size of his truck tires measure his manhood. The Micros, the latest immigrants, irritating, something you wanna pluck out like ear hair. The crumbs. All these people, every single one of them, think they're saving the island by changing it for the better, that or sustaining it, maintaining it, or keeping it real. When actually they're destroying it. They all need a moment in the dark. And Boi is going to pull the plug and wake them up black.

Shane knocks on Boi's window. Boi rolls it down.

"So   what   are   we   doing   here?"   Shane   asks.

"We going dig," says Boi.

"Mister construction worker," looking at his florescent green shirt. Movie popcorn bag shoved in his pocket—*he's the worst one.* If a crumb is a person who soaks up free money, who keeps his parents awake at night in fear, who does whatever he wants, then Shane is a crumb. Only no one gives him shit about it because his dad is somebody, because he don't live homeless on a beach, because he knows what's going on in "the world" and can name more than five different African countries or some shit like that. Boi remembers wanting to be Shane, to be Knotting, but now, all he sees standing before him is a sucking machine, a giant hospital-grade breast pump. *That's why he's so big.* That fat fuck feeds and feeds and feeds. *No good. No more.*

"What are we digging up?" asks Shane. "Our ancestral bones? Dibs on great-great Grandpa's femur."

Joe pulls four, smooth, black ili ili stones out of his pocket and places them in a row in front of him. He starts to chant:

> *E iho ana o luna*
> *E pii ana o lalo*
> *E huli ana na moku*
> *E ku ana ka paia*

Unlike the way Boi's seen the chant done, by kahunas, Joe's not facing the ocean, the mountain, or the sun. Joe's glaring at Shane now as his low, rumbling voice, full of hair-raising sorcery, almost cracks on certain words.

PART THREE: ONE YEAR LATER

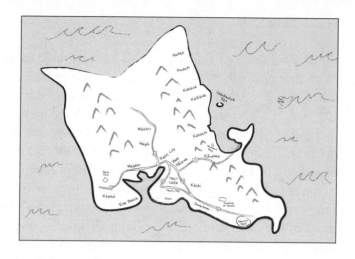

1. The Magic Typewriter

1.

Waipahu. By the old sugar mill smoke stack converted to a YMCA. Across the street, the old No. 12 fire station, now a Filipino fast food joint. Then it's bar, liquor store, rickety physician office. Hair salon. Church. Get wasted, find out you're knocked up, do your hair, get married. Ads for Democratic candidates and light beer. As Charles Knotting rounds the block and passes a bus-stop bathroom fronted by a security guard and eight-bedroom houses sheltering families of thirty, some without screens backing the jalousie windows, he tells his driver to round the block once more before they stop at the Filipino Community Center. He spots an empty birdcage through a cracked second-story window. They probably cooked and ate the bird.

Shane's been missing for a year now. He's disappeared before, but only for a week or two, once to Rio Carnival and another time to Black Rock Desert for Burning Man—twenty-first century wannabe hippies with fake breasts painted gold praying to a three-story man lit on fire. For the first few months, Charles had the cops and an army of private investigators scouring the island and beyond for Shane. They turned up nothing. Charles himself has dragged Boi around this island at least twenty times in an attempt to retrace Shane's last steps. But they only knew a few places to start: the old folks' home where Glory killed the old man; the Knotting house, where cops turned up broken glass and bullet holes; and Glory's house. They never knew where to go from there. The cops turned Glory's house inside out and found one intact body and parts of two others. Forensics identified a crippled Vietnam vet, a bartender who went missing over ten years ago, and Makana Rapun—Shane and Boi's biological mother. The cops were excited, talking serial killer, but Boi didn't buy it. Charles offered to pay for a proper burial for his mother. Boi responded by saying, "Fuck her. Let her rot."

The sister. Glory. Her sentencing is a week away, and even though she was convicted for the murders of the old man and the male nurse, she claims that she has no idea where Shane is. The chief, the lead detective, Boi—they all think she's lying. Charles thinks she's lying, too.

This girl firing off rounds at Charles's Kahala home. Kahala! The fact that his family is vulnerable to these people is unacceptable. As Charles pulls into the community center, he wonders how many others out there are like her in a little west Oahu town like this, with its own Salvation Army and dialysis facility. There was a story in the paper a few weeks ago about a young man who cat-called a group of titas hanging out in front of a Waipahu project. They jumped in their car and ran him over. These people need to be stopped. There's now more MMA schools than tutoring centers on this island. You know it's bad when the girls are as violent as the boys.

A gaggle of Filipino Catholic protesters wave signs. Protest all you want. Last year, Charles was bombarded by personal tragedy and lost in the legislature. But this year, he will get the votes. It's his last year, his last chance. He just needs to man up for one more year, then he can grieve for the rest of his life. The Helen Knotting Bill will become law during the next legislative session. And after it does, Charles will retire from public service. He's blaming the job for a lot of this. Helen dead. Shane missing. The job made him less vigilant. He could've told Helen to go to the doctor sooner, stage four was too late. He could've made a stronger argument for Shane to come live with him at the Governor's residence. And he's the one who turned up this crazy sister for Boi in the first place. All those years spent prepared him for facing danger when it was right in front of him, but perhaps it made him too instinctive, too in the now.

After the law passes, Charles will quit everything.

He takes a deep breath, steps out of the town-car, and waves to the protesters. At first, fringe anger used to hurt Charles, but now it's just amusing. These dozen or so sign-wavers are mostly women wearing pink tee-shirts and black visors. The captions read: Freedom from Tyranny! Cue Class War! Reproductive Rights Held Hostage! One gray-hair, a grandma far beyond her reproductive years, has the audacity to hold up a "Don't Tread On Me" flag. They just don't get it. Welfare, like driving, is a privilege, not a right. It's what he'll explain to them at the podium once he's inside. He's not taking anything away. He's just adding a rule of the road. Have all the babies you want. Just not on the government's dime.

The reception in the auditorium is warmer. The gentrifying middle-classers have gathered. Unlike last year, there are no TV cameras, no standing-room-only crowds. Charles has to start from scratch. But the few who are there applaud. One man stands and gives a standing ovation. Others join in. Charles is moved. To answer Boi's question of long ago, this is why he ran for Governor. This is why he pulls sixteen-hour days. It's not just about legacy, making something meaningful with his life that people will remember, it's about making Hawaii better. All his life, people looked at him like he was an outsider, an invader, a haole, but his family goes back five generations in Hawaii, more generations than the Chinese, more generations than the Japanese, and definitely more generations than the Filipino protesters outside. Charles Knotting was born and raised in Hawaii.

He loves Hawaii. Did his money make him love it any less than these people? Absolutely not. In fact, it made him love it even more because he owns more of it. He pays taxes on conserved, undeveloped family land across five islands. He spent his youth surfing Hawaii waters, for Christ's sake. He, along with Helen, donated to the Hawaii Wildlife Fund, the Daughters of Hawaii, the Aloha United Way, Pacific Historic Parks, the Surfrider Foundation, and dozens of others. If it weren't for people like him and Helen, the sugar mill smoke-stack next door would just be a hulking, rusting metal tube instead of a state-of-the-art YMCA for community kids. If it weren't for his ancestors, who brought all these Chinese, Japanese, and Filipinos to Hawaii, they'd have starved to death in their homelands, their own ancestral lines cut like twine.

In fact, Charles has done more for Hawaii than most Hawaiians. He's done more for Hawaii than just about every Hawaiian. And as he heads for the stage, he thinks, he'd just like to say it once, to say the hell with PC, and tell everyone the truth. I have done more for Hawaii than most who have Kamehameha attached to their name. And when this law passes, and the effects come to fruition in the next ten, twenty, thirty years, normal, Hawaii-loving people won't have to fear that a wrong look will get them punched in the face, and won't have to fear that that some addict will shoot up their Kahala home. Kahala! Who does this little girl think she is!

Charles steps to the podium and clears his throat. It's happening again. He's dizzy and can't speak. Charles Knotting can't speak! The sparse crowd murmurs.

"It's cause his son," someone says.

Charles gathers himself. He will pull these people to his side, one-by-one if he has to. When the number of third-generation chronics and welfare queens is cut in half, they will all know Charles Knotting did more for Hawaii than a Kamehameha. They will know that he loves Hawaii more than just about any person who has uttered the word "aina" in island history.

2.

There was a story about a celestial woman, a moo, who lived on the Koolau mountains, back in the days when dreams meant something. She had a dog. One day, a group of villagers spotted the dog and thought it'd make a good feast for their chief, so they caught it and roasted it. On their way back down the mountain, they ran into the woman sitting by a pool. She asked the dog where it was going. The dog, a broiled carcass, told her he was going to go meet the chief. The woman called the dog to her. Instantly restored to his former glory, the dog leaped from the net and into the woman's arms. Both splashed into the pool and disappeared. Scared shitless, the villagers hauled ass down the mountain.

It was November, cold and rainy, and Glory was thinking about that story that her grandmother had told her as she hid out in the only place one can on Oahu—the mountains. She'd been up there for three months, and after she got used to the initial shock of cold, filth, boredom, loneliness, and sleeping on hard places, she often imagined herself like that moo of the mountains, a magic woman who lived out in the boonies who people feared.

After the news had broke, the murder of an old man travel-writer (a picture of him helping African children learn to read, not of him fondling young girls in their tents), the murder of a Filipino nurse named Gary (a picture of him volunteering for a hospice, not of him raping a retarded girl), the disappearance of the Governor's son (a picture of him standing over his mother's casket, not of him punching a guy with a corkscrew), and Glory's photograph appeared on every television station and Hawaii's Most Wanted (Glory's picture has her smoking a cigarette, drinking whiskey, and flashing a shaka like a gang sign), she packed a sleeping bag and canned goods and headed up the mountains. At first, she was thinking she was not like the moo. She was more like the dog. And sooner or later, she'd be caught, roasted, netted, and lugged back down the mountains. There would be no magic woman to save her. But that was ages ago. They still hadn't found her. And now that Glory was used to this mountain living, they never would.

She spent the day hiking down the mountain to scout houses to burg. She needed to restock. She carefully avoided trails and clearings and walked past gnarled trees and mossy rocks slick with life. She stopped at a stream to take a drink. The water tasted clean. She looked up. Helicopters couldn't spot her under koa and ohia canopy. Sometimes, when a chopper did buzz above, Glory would say a prayer and pick a red ohia flower. Legend said every time you picked one, it rained. It hadn't worked yet. And when a chopper doubled back and Glory thought she'd be spotted, she remembered that many hikers went missing up here, bodies never recovered, and the fear washed away. She was just afraid that one day she'd trip over tourist bones and fall off a two-thousand-foot cliff.

After breaking into a Mililani house perched at the edge of the mountains, she took her bag full of stolen canned goods up to her camp. It was evening by the time she got there, and she could hear rats cracking seeds. She spotted mongoose feasting on native bird eggs, their sleek, short-legged bodies built more for slithering than running. Their gorging made her hungry, so she turned on her flashlight and opened a can of chili. She thought of Boi as she ate. Back when they'd lived on the bus, and their mother had left them alone for days with their invalid grandmother, Boi could spend hours banging cans against the floorboard. Can Opener Boi.

Glory wondered if Boi remembered. She knew Shane didn't. Maybe was all PTSD'd out or was pulled so far away from the Wahiawa Circle Island, that all of it, the lighter burns, the rocks, the days they were hopped up on fruit punch, the foodless nights, even the time Boi stabbed their grandmother in the leg with Makana's cosmetic scissors to test if she could feel it, maybe Shane could not remember because it was now as foreign to him as a high-school history textbook. White-bearded guys in togas warring and philosophizing. Guys in bronze and red feathers taking over the world. Guys in metal suits and armed with swords getting their Jesus on. Guys wearing red coats marching in snow. It pissed her off that Shane didn't remember. That might be why she'd wanted to kill him, too. Fuck um all. She didn't need people. She could do this time on the mountain standing on her head. It was solitary, yes, but it was not confinement. But as she polished off the can of chili, she had to admit, she missed the food. She'd kill for a fast-food meal deal.

Glory opened a can of creamy corn soup, stuck a straw in it, and pretended it was a milk shake. She fed as it began to rain. At first, she'd missed the world. She longed for mattresses, refrigeration, light switches, and machine white noise—none of this insect buzzing shit. She'd thought she could build a log cabin or something up here, maybe those A-framed tents the Hawaiians used to live in. There'd be pig to hunt. An endless supply of fruit to pick. But the only thing she knew how to tie were shoe laces, so building the tent was out. And she had a lighter to make a fire and maybe cook, but everything up here was too wet to burn. She hated to admit it, but her camp looked pretty much like it did on day one: a dish rack, a bucket, a toolbox, and sleeping bag. A trash bag full of magazines and things to huff—permanent markers and whipped cream—when she was super bored and lonely. Off to the side, a rusty lantern she hardly used.

It started to rain. Glory pulled out a magic marker and took a big sniff with each nostril. The rain was falling hard, rattling the leaves above. She was bored. She checked her gun and decided she'd give it a try for the hundredth time. She'd hunt a pig. She knew where all the tunnels were by now and could find them even in the dark. She headed for the closest one, the small one.

Glory spotted the small tunnel cut through a thicket of thorns and branches. She'd crawled through these before and come up empty each time. She flipped up her hood, got down on her hands and knees, and crawled inside. It was deep, this tunnel, and Glory fantasized that it led to a dry clearing, maybe a grandma prepping an ahaaina spread, a pig on a spit, not a dog, because eating dog was straight up foul. She moved deeper inside. At least it was more dry in here. Maybe all she needed was a nap. Then she'd be able to figure out her next move. She'd been up here a few months now freezing her ass off, and despite how hard she tried to fight the idea, some prison three squares was sounding pretty good right about now. As long as it wasn't mainland prison. Glory looked back. She couldn't even see the entrance anymore.

As she got deeper, the tunnel got smaller. Thorns snagged her hoodie. She yanked her sleeves out of the brush but stopped when she heard snorting up ahead. It was dark so she took her lighter out of her pocket, wiped it with a dry slip of sweater, and spun the wheel with her thumb, hoping it would light. It took a few tries, and Glory cursed because she wanted to conserve fluid and flint, but flame eventually popped up. She extended her arm and held out the flame like she was saluting an old school rock ballad.

There was a big, neckless thing looking right back at her.

"Fuck."

"Eeeewwwwweee!"

"Fuck, fuck, fuck."

"Eeewwwwweee!"

Glory reached for her gun in her backpack, but there was not enough room in the tunnel to take off her bag. The wild boar charged. Glory had nowhere to go. She covered her head and the pig stampeded her. Dizzy, she put her palms on moist dirt, trying to steady herself, despite the fact she was on her belly and couldn't fall. It was only after a few moments that she felt the pain in her neck. Broken collarbone maybe. Snapped ribs. She tried to back out, move in reverse. But the pain was too sharp. She rolled on her back and used her legs to try to inch her way out of the tunnel. She moved two feet and was already out of breath. She tried to scream. It was like being stuck in Benny Lee's tool locker all over again.

3.

Glory spent two days flat on her back inching her way out of the tunnel. She'd pass out now and then and dream deals with a god she knew didn't exist. She repented. She was sorry for the old man. She was sorry for Gary.

Death was coming for Glory and she was straight up scared. It wasn't that she felt like she'd missed out on anything, like she'd always wanted to see the world—she'd seen about enough of the world as she could stand. And it wasn't that she had responsibilities to tend to—no real family, friends, or children—no one would miss her. It was that she imagined death like being in Benny's tool locker permanent. If death was just nothing, just a black void, she could deal with that. She could use the rest. But to be trapped in that locker for all eternity—maybe she should be praying to the devil instead of the god she knew didn't exist. The devil. That pointy red-eared motherfucker with the pencil mustache was forreal. She'd seen enough to know that.

Besides, it was easy to see how she was going to go, all alone in the mountains. That asshole pig. The ants. The rats. They'd all eat her alive while she watched. No one was coming for her. Not up here, they weren't. She was a good seven to ten miles away from road. She had one choice. Take the gun out of her backpack and make some noise. Maybe someone would hear and check it out. Though not too many people she knew head toward gunfire. Most ran the opposite way.

That or she could turn the muzzle on herself and put her own lights out.

But the tool locker. She wasn't ready for that.

So when Glory finally got out, she struggled to pull the gun out of her bag. She could barely hold it. She wondered if she should squeeze off a round each day around noon, or if she should just unload. Fireworks. Make it so if there was anyone one around, guarantee they'd hear. She held the gun with both hands below her stomach hesitant, like she was a man about to take a stank-ass, drippy dick, clap-infected piss. She winced as she pulled the trigger.

She dropped the gun. She was too sore to empty the clip. She'd have to fire off one shot a day. Glory passed out.

When Glory woke up, a haole man and a woman were standing above her. The man, brown-bearded and pony-tailed, had a mesh sack full of little metal cages draped over his shoulder. The woman, small like Glory, poked Glory's leg with the stick-end of a butterfly net. "Are you okay?" she asked. Both of their eyes were red. Glory wondered if they were stoned.

Glory strained to pull herself back-first against a tree trunk. The man bent down to help her, but Glory slapped his hands away. The woman spotted the gun under Glory's leg, the gun she'd forgotten about, and grabbed it before Glory could. "Hunting, I presume?" the woman asked.

Glory nodded.

The man pulled a cellphone out of his pocket and stepped away as if he was making a private call. The woman slipped the gun in her backpack and sat next to Glory. She told Glory that they were hunting, too. That they were looking for the Oahu Elepaio, a small brown forest bird endangered and indigenous to Hawaii. That they wanted to help save it. She told Glory of other endangered Hawaiian species, like the duck, the bat, the turtle, the hawk, and the monk seal. Glory doubted that Hawaii has ducks, bats, and hawks. She'd never seen them. The woman told her that when they'd heard the gun shot, they headed right to it. These two haoles, they must've been stoned.

The man put his cellphone in his pocket and headed back. He and the woman nodded. Glory liked these two haoles, but then she thought, maybe she was being tricked. "Who did you call?" Glory asked. Her voice was hoarse. She hasn't spoken in days.

"911," the man said. "You need medical attention."

Glory cursed. She should've grabbed the gun as soon as she'd waken up. She wished she was one of those endangered birds these two haoles were trying to catch. If she were, maybe they would try to save her, too.

But they didn't save her. They ratted her out. And now she's sitting in an O-Triple-C jail cell, waiting for her sentencing. She has one more chance to convince everyone she didn't kill Shane. Fuck them. She refuses to go down for that. But she's been telling them she has no idea where Shane is for over seven months now. They don't believe her. Seven months of waking up at six AM and spending the day being herded from one cage to another, each door opening with a buzz then closing with the sound of bolts slamming into locks.

All three of her cellmates so far, same story. Parents on drugs. Parents get busted. Kids sent to live with grandma. Parents finish recovery program, then kids snatched from grandmas. Sooner or later, the parents start doing drugs again, get busted again, and kids are sent back to grandma's house, again. Years of this shit, seven different schools by the time they're seniors, if they make it that far. Most don't. Grandma's dead, and now they have kids, too.

But these other girls, at least sometimes they get phone calls, visitors, and some cash dumped in their commissary accounts. No phone calls, visitors, or cash for Glory. The other inmates, and even some of the guards, seem to sense her isolation and look at her with hungry eyes. That's when her feet start moving. And every time she's told to hold still, which happens at least three times a day, her feet start moving again. When the guards get pissed and fed up, they throw her into TLD—Therapeutic Lockdown. And when she's all alone in another cell, receiving her mental medicine, which consists of her being left alone 24/7 in the dark, all she can think is that back up in those mountains, she should have turned the gun on herself.

The girl in the next cell over must be thinking kind of the same thing too, because right now she's screaming and kicking her feet black-and-blue against the steel.

At least Glory's home and not in some mainland prison.

4.

Like every other morning for the past several months, Boi is standing in his master bathroom a few hours before his shift starts wondering where he went wrong. Pan and wall liner. Check. Backer board. Check. Mortar and ceramic tiles. Check. This is the third time he's renovating the tile shower. The first two times, the shower leaked, once through a wall corner, once through the base. Boi steps out of the bathroom, sits in front of his computer, and watches the step-by-step YouTube video for what feels like the thousandth time. The bearded haole man makes it look so easy. It only took Boi a few hours to demo the bathroom. It's now four months later, and the only thing operational in the shower are the roach glue traps he has set up because ever since he ripped out the pan and part of the drywall, revealing thin copper and thicker PVC pipes, the B-52s flood in at night. Boi can't help but think he would've been able to do a better job on this when he was a kid. Something happened to him. He can't build or fix things properly anymore.

Boi checks the time. It's Sunday, and he has to wake Nina and drop her off at Chastity's before work. He keeps her Wednesday nights, Thursdays, Fridays, and Saturdays. Two more nights than he used to. When Chastity agreed to this new arrangement because she saw Rev roll past her everyday in his wheelchair, blowing a plastic tube to make the thing go, and she'd wanted to go back to school, her fourth try, Boi rented this two-bedroom cottage—kitchen, living room, two bedrooms, and now just one working bathroom. Mostly for Nina, but he must admit, he likes the place. It makes him feel more normal, more human. Besides, it is close to the private school Nina will be attending next year. She didn't have the academic skills to get her into one of the good ones; fortunately, those super-religious ones always have a spot or two open.

Boi steps over a pile a Nina's homemade toys—paper dolls with big eyes, long eyelashes, and red hair. He scoops them up and puts them in her nightstand drawer along with the rest. The drawer is packed with these confetti-like dolls, along with other tiny pictures of diamonds, stars, and mermaids, all of which he saves. Boi closes the drawer and wakes Nina up. He carries her to the couch in the living room.

Breakfast is already waiting. Three microwavable chocolate-chip pancakes and half a banana diced next to a dollop of whipped cream. Nina rubs her eyes and digs in. Boi worries that he feeds her too much sugar, but she refuses to eat anything not sweet. He also worries that she's not growing enough. During her last check-up, the doctor told Boi that she was behind her projected growth rate, so she should exercise for an hour and drink three cups of milk a day. Nina doesn't like sports, so an hour a day of exercise feels impossible, and Boi is lucky if he can get her to drink one cup of milk with dinner.

After breakfast, Nina gets dressed, brushes her teeth, then plants herself on Boi's lap so he can brush her hair. Like every other morning, she complains through the whole process. It hurts, she says. He's amazed at what a wimp she is. He wonders if he ever even had the chance to be a wimp. She's seven and he has no idea whether he should even be brushing her hair at this age. At moments likes this, she reminds Boi of Shane.

"Daddy, when I go to my new school, I have to wake up earlier, right?"

"Yep."

"And I have to catch the bus?"

"Yeah."

"Why don't buses have seat beats? That's dangerous."

It's dangerous. Everything is dangerous to this little girl. And it's Boi's fault, too. From the time she could talk, suspicious Boi pointed at cars, roads, lighters, knives, strange dogs, and even the ocean, and explained how all these things could be dangerous. The baby who once tried to eat electricity is gone.

"Are you finished fixing your bathroom yet?" Nina asks.

"No."

"Maybe you can call Uncle Shane to help you."

"I told you, sweetie, Uncle Shane is gone. No one knows where he went."

"I hope he's being careful, Daddy. It's dangerous out there."

Boi's hands sweat as he tries to put her hair in a half-decent ponytail.

5.

It's eight a.m. and Boi, who's now on Second Watch, is staking out a residential stop-sign intersection for some asshole city councilman who lives on the corner. The councilman complained that he sees drivers Hollywood stop all day long through his second-story picture window, and he used his sway with the HPD to get round-the-clock surveillance. Boi has been ordered to ticket these outlaws and collect data so that the rep can present these stats in the next legislative session and get a traffic light installed at the intersection next year.

It's been a slow morning so far. Only a dozen or so cars have passed through the quiet street. Boi hears one before he sees it. A dropped rice burner, sub-woofers blasting reggae. Its rickety body is practically dragging on the ground, and the tinted windows are so dark that Boi can't even make out the silhouette of the driver. This guy is going to rack up some tickets. Probably a kid driving home from a strip bar all-nighter where he made it rain one-dollar bills, and pretended he was a big-time dealer or gangster. His evening capped with a stop at a twenty-four-hour Korean yakiniku that serves after-hours beer in stainless steel rice bowls. Dipshits like this, with their spinning rims and bazooka speakers, beg to get pulled over.

Of course, the driver doesn't come to a complete stop. Boi flickers his lights. The car in front of him pulls to the side and the hazards start blinking.

Boi steps out of the squad car and approaches the driver—

a Hawaiian about his age, shirtless, wearing sunglasses, neck scribbled with tattoos. The driver asks Boi what he was doing wrong. Boi ignores the question he's heard a thousand times and asks for license and registration. The man opens the glove compartment and pulls out a wad of papers and fast-food napkins. As he shuffles through expired documents, Boi spots his drunk driver kit in the glove—eye drops and a tin of breath mints. Among the documents the driver hands Boi is the business card of the major who runs Kapolei to Waianae. But that doesn't catch Boi's eye as much as the name on the driver's license. Johnnethan Makuakane.

"Small John?" Boi asks.

"Who dat?"

Small John's tone changes from scared and apologetic to cocky. It's probably not the first time he's been pulled over by an old friend, and it's certainly not the first time Boi's pulled over a former anything. At this point, Boi's pulled former teachers, cousins, and cousins of cousins.

"It's Boi Rapun."

"Boi!" Small John slurs.

"Where you going?"

"I going church!"

Boi shakes his head. Figures.

"I cannot let you drive like this," says Boi.

"Give me ride then."

Boi looks around and shrugs. Why not? Screw the city councilman. Besides, Boi should probably check out this church thing before he sends Nina off and blows over fifteen grand a year.

"Heard you dropped out of school end of ninth grade. What happened?" asks Boi.

Small John shrugs. "I had to wear the same clothes to school four days in a row."

Hence the car with the neon-lit undercarriage. I don't have to wear the same clothes four days in a row anymore, motherfuckers.

6.

The place is more theater than church—the Sunday session starts with fifteen minutes of electric guitar Jesus songs. Big-screen testimonials on how Jesus came to save this crumb who stole his grandma's jewelry or that crumb who used to smoke cock for rocks. Half the audience looks like they are on furlough from the Oahu Community Correctional Center. They raise their tattooed arms whenever they hear something particularly righteous, which is every thirty seconds.

The head pastor takes the stage after the videos. Boi recognizes him immediately. Brody Soares, ex-professional big-wave surfer. He was in all the papers ten years back. Busted for shipping his drug-packed car from California to Hawaii. Out early because of good behavior, which meant the prison was too crowded already. Brody is bigger now, still in shape, probably still surfs, but his shortsleeves and tie, the uniform of many an ex-crumb, covers what was once one of *People* magazine's sexiest bodies. Mic'd up wireless, hair slicked back with industrial strength gel, Brody walks to the middle of the stage and praises the Lord. Goes on for an hour-and-a-half.

Though Boi nods off through most of it, the stories of talking snakes, rivers of blood, and dead guys coming back to life, one bit catches his ear. Brody says he had a hole in his heart. He says the women, the fame, the drugs, even the waves eventually could not fill it. Boi sits up for that bit. For some reason, he thinks of Shane. Boi nudges Small John, who is snoring beside him.

"Eh, wake up."

Small John rubs his eyes. "Sorry, sorry."

"I taking off. Still on duty."

"Okay, okay. Thanks for the ride, braddah. Keep in touch, ah?"

Boi nods. As Brody talks about how Jesus now fills his heart, Boi makes his way to the back of the church. The congregation's singing some song with no pain, therefore, no heart. The kids to the right are wearing team jump-rope tee-shirts. They close their eyes and clap. They probably jump rope for God. The muscleheads off to the left, they probably break cinder blocks over each others' heads. For God. And the back row church hotties, the ones with their hands up, hands with tats running from their fake bejeweled fingernails to their shoulders, who knows what they do with those hands for Marriage AKA God. He recognizes a couple of them from high school. Boi can't help it. He envies them all. It's like they're on drugs without all the life-ruining side effects.

Before he gets to the door, Boi spots another familiar face. Boi didn't recognize him at first because the once-yoked boys' home geology and Hawaiian history teacher is now a graying, crinkle-faced, middle-aged man. Boi never had Mr. Melvin pegged for one of those buff guys who shrink super-fast when they stop pounding weights, but it makes sense, especially now, his eyes closed as he claps away, bouncing away in his aisle seat. Weak. Boi bends down. "Ho, what happened? Off the roids?"

Mr. Melvin opens his eyes and frowns, not recognizing him.

"It's Boi," Boi says.

Mr. Melvin's still trying to place the name with a face. How many boys with the name "Boi" passed through the boy's home, Boi wonders. Probably at least fifty. "The flyin' Hawaiian with the AK-47," Boi says.

"Boi!"

Mr. Melvin invites Boi to sit next to him. Boi slides into the seat.

"Ho, you one cop now?" Mr. Melvin asks.

"Yeah," Boi says. "Better watch out. I bust old fut revolutionaries like you."

"Haha, you fricka. Still one wise ass, ah. Nah, nah. What, I get wife and kids now. Cannot be one revolutionary anymore, you know?"

Boi looks to the left of Mr. Melvin. No wife and kids. He's about to get up and leave.

"Stay, stay," Mr. Melvin says.

Boi remains seated. Brody's still on stage talking about how him and a couple of his other church surf-buddies have formed a surf team called the Hui O Jesus, and how they need to collect donations so they can go to Mexico and surf in a contest and save Juarez drug war orphans all at the same time.

"You get wife and kid?" Mr. Melvin asks.

"Kid. No wife."

"The kid live with you?"

"Yeah. But just recently."

Mr. Melvin's voice turns bitter. "And where you live now? One house, I bet. You get rent, you get car payment, you shop for the kind all-in-one cracker, meat, cheese, juice, and snack lunch, but you only buy um on sale, and you send um with your kid to school."

Boi shrugs. "And what?"

"Shit," Mr. Melvin looks around, hoping no one heard him say it. It's church after all. "You no remember what I taught you? How even though no more armies, guns, and battlefields, we at war?"

Boi nods.

"Well, we lost. Me and you, we lost. We casualties, braddah. Casualties. Look at me because this what you going look like in ten years."

Instead of looking at Mr. Melvin, Boi eyes the muscle heads several rows up. They all stand. From the back, one looks like Shane.

"All is forgiven!" Brody says.

Boi doesn't want forgiveness. And no, he didn't lose.

Boi gaining joint custody of Nina, then Boi finding out the Helen Knotting Bill died at the state leg—he won. Shane was the casualty, not him. And even though he feels super bad about Shane, like Joe told Boi as they watched The Gov's bill bite the dust, he had to go. Charles could hardly function after that. Shane, not the state legislature, killed the Helen Knotting Bill. With only a year left as Gov, Charles is done. And if by some miracle the next Gov tries to pass that messed-up bill, Boi still has barrels of ammonium nitrate, water gel, and blasting caps stored at Joe's house. He still has the truck and wagon to transport all of it. He still has the job that gives him cover to plant it all, too. It's not his season anymore. But if the season comes, he's not glass-jawed like Mr. Melvin or even Joe, who, since Shane's disappearance, thinks the cops are after him and never leaves the house because of it. Boi's not like that. He knows himself. He knows that he'll throw down even if losing is certain. It's his best quality. He has heart.

A collection bowl goes around the room. Brody and his surf buddies are on the big screen now, sliding down waves on boards decorated with crosses and blood-covered crowns of thorn.

"Look at that," Mr. Melvin says. "They soul surfing forreal."

Boi's phone vibrates. It's the chief texting him, sending him a reminder: Glory's sentencing is in a week. We have one more chance to get her to cop to disappearance and possible death of Shane Knotting. We need you there tomorrow.

Boi puts away his phone and looks on stage. The surf video is over and there's a giant wooden crucifix on-screen with a thin, ripped Jesus dangling from it. Boi tries to hold it in, but can't. He chokes on laughter. Mr. Melvin elbows him and frowns.

Boi can't stop. Others turn around, face him, see that he's a cop, then quickly turn back around. A few of them probably on probation. Boi laughs even more. He gets up and heads for the door, both hands covering his mouth. He's laughing because he's imagining Shane up there on the cross, an unwilling martyr, and he can't help but picture the cross tipping over with all that weight on it. It's horrible, he knows, but it's better than crying. He knows he won't sleep tonight again. He'll dream of that damn cross creaking then falling over and over again.

7. _____

The meeting is being held at the University of Hawaii. Every year during hurricane season, June to November, there are about four or five storms that show up in the Central Pacific. Every time one is detected, the scientists call for a pow-wow. Only five hurricanes have made landfall in Hawaii since 1950. Some say that vertical windshear above the state breaks down storms before they can arrive. Others say it's because the islands, with the exception of Kauai, are protected by Big Island volcano peaks that slow storms down. Translation: Pele herself is protecting Hawaii.

Charles and Boi sit in the backseat of the Governor's car as the driver/bodyguard turns left into East-West Road and pulls up to a guard shack. The driver flashes a parking permit at the Samoan security guard. The guard nods, and the driver turns left on Correa Road and passes board short and rubber slippered students whizzing by on mopeds.

"I don't know why I need to come to this," Boi says.

"Just keep me company," says Charles.

He watches Boi shift into a slouch, tilt his head, and narrow his eyelids. It's Boi's young punk look. It's the look more and more young men in Hawaii have co-opted, even the ones with nothing to be mad about. In fact, the car passes two such kids now. Two boys riding skateboards, their parents probably flight attendants or bank branch managers, glaring ahead, trying to look sullen and tough despite their comfortable middle class childhoods.

Years back, when Shane was applying to colleges, Charles told him that the University of Hawaii would never be an option. That UH was nothing but a state-run middle-management farm packed with public school kids with lackluster SAT scores. It was filled with future civil servants and assistant hotel managers. Now Charles just wishes Shane was around.

"Thinking about college yet?"

"I not going any more college."

"Not for you, for Nina."

Boi eyes Charles suspiciously.

The driver parks in front of the Institute of Geophysics building, next to the Sustainability Courtyard, and gets out of the car. Charles asks the driver to wait with there. He winks and says, "Officer Rapun will guard me."

Students stand in line in front of vendors serving an assortment of vegetarian plate lunches. Charles marvels at these skinny

eighteen-to-twenty-three-year-olds who are already preemptive-
ly battling cholesterol and free radicals. Kids coast by on bicycles
and the whole scene, the girls wearing tiny shorts to show off
their tanned, taut legs, and the boys humping giant backpacks
while texting makes Charles feel unbearably old. As he and Boi
enter the geophysics building, one girl, a pretty hapa with kitty,
slipper, and monkey charms dangling from her purse, who smells
sweet as Japanese erasers, jingles past him. Charles wonders if she
even knows who he is. Probably not.

Boi doesn't even look at her. If Shane was here, he would
have nudged Charles and said something like "look at the shoyu
bunny."

When Charles and Boi step into the Central Pacific Hurricane Center, they're the last ones to arrive. The professors, balding
white men who look laughably like caricatures of physicists, and
representatives from the first responders and Mayor's office stand
in front of televisions glowing with Pacific Ocean maps that look
splashed with swirling tie-dye. There are a few reporters and two
TV cameras. The head professor, a seventy-one-year-old, wild-
haired, wild-eyed haole with an actual pocket protector attached
to his vertical-striped button-down shirt, shakes his head as he
points to one of the television screens. "This one here," he says to
a local Japanese man standing next to him. "Off the coast of Baja."

Charles knows the middle-aged guy standing next to the
head professor. It's Rich Kato, number-three son of Dean Kato,
proprietor of Kato Construction, the largest local construction
company in the state. Rich serves on the liquor commission
board, the Honolulu Country Club board, and heads the Waikiki
safety board. As a number-three son, he won't take his father's
place as the head of Kato Construction. His older brother, Dean
Kato, Jr., DJ for short, is the heir apparent.

Rich shrugs and sits at a student desk. "What? Is it going to
hit us?"

Charles and Boi take back row seats as the professor shakes
his head.

"Then why are you even pointing at it?" asks Rich. "You call me every single time a hurricane is anywhere near the Central Pacific. What, four times a year? And none of them ever pose a threat."

The professor holds a finger to his lips, nods at the TV cameras, and rubs a charm hanging from his neck, some trinket he got in Indonesia or some place like that. "You ready?" he asks. The lights go up as the cameras move in. He explains why Oahu is such an unlikely hurricane target. Talks about unfavorable westerly winds and cool water surface temperatures. Points at a big red swirl that looks like an angry owl's eye. "And that's why this one will die before it gets here."

He seems almost disappointed. All these old professors, they *want* a hurricane to come. Charles knows one of them is a storm chaser, willing to risk his life to get inside these monster storms and maybe get something named after him. As for the others, the police and fire department reps tap away at their phones while the mayor's rep digs grime from under his fingernails with a bent paper clip.

"What the hell am I doing here?" asks Boi.

"The press finds out there's a storm system a couple thousand miles away, so they come to get answers. I show up to reassure the public. It's a game. It's about getting funding, grants, TV ratings."

"No, I mean what am *I* doing here," Boi says.

In lecture mode, the head professor is talking Category 5, the highest classification of hurricane on the Saffir-Simpson Scale. It means a tropical storm with winds of over 155 miles per hour. It means anything within three miles of the shoreline without concrete or steel-framed construction is washed and crushed by storm surge.

"About the girl," Charles says. "Are you ready to get her to talk? Last chance before she's sentenced."

"Whatever," Boi says.

"Listen, I miss him, too," says Charles. "A part of me thinks he's still out there somewhere, playing the ultimate practical joke on me." Charles turns to face Boi. "What about you? Do you think it's possible?"

Boi stands up. "Let's go."

Charles grabs his wrist and pulls him back down to his seat. "Not yet."

Once the prof is done with his lecture, Charles heads for the front of the room. The TV cameras turn to him. The professors make room. Charles takes a seat next to Rich Kato. A yawning journalist asks Charles if the state is hurricane prepared. He says it is. The journalist then turns to Rich Kato and asks whether as chair of the Waikiki safety board he can guarantee that Waikiki is prepared. Rich says it is. Satisfied, the reporters pack their cameras up and head out. Boi walks down to Charles and studies the giant TV directly behind him. Rich Kato leans over to Charles. "Terrible evac routes, one-hundred-and-twenty-thousand tourists packed in glass ocean-front towers on any given day. Sure, Waikiki is ready."

Charles shrugs. He watches Boi staring at the big red swirl off the coast of Baja. "Don't worry," Charles says. "Neither is the state."

Kato shakes his head and laughs. "I got all these hotels, dozens of different landowners, Japanese billionaires, East Coast investment conglomerates, local families whose ownerships are split between thirty descendants, and now Mainland Chinese ownership. How am I supposed to get them on the phone, much less get them more prepared? I don't even speak Japanese or Mandarin."

Charles nods. Honestly, he doesn't even care. He's thinking about Glory, hoping that they'll be able to get some information out of her. Some closure.

The head professor edges past Boi. "So no way this thing can reach Hawaii?" Boi asks.

"Well," the professor replies, "1992. Iniki. 1982. Iwa. A dozen false alarms since then. But the ocean's changing, climate's changing. One of the things that has always impressed me about Hawaii since I first arrived here forty years ago is your gambling spirit. You know. Everyone does, even Mr. Kato here. But you gamble."

"What's that?" Boi asks. "Know what?"

"We are due."

Boi traces his finger over the swirl as the professor goes into lecture mode again, talking about Iniki and how it started off as a tropical wave in North Africa, whizzed east through Central America, slowed when it reached the Pacific Ocean. Charles never understood that part. How can something that slows down become more powerful and destructive?

"Well, what's the name of this one? Tiki-tiki-kaku?" Rich asks. All Central Pacific hurricanes are given Hawaiian names.

"Kikilia," the professor says. He begins to drone on again. Charles wonders if all professors love the sound of their own voices. He holds in a sob. It's been a year, but these sobs come at him as sudden as sneezes. He looks around to make sure no one noticed. Rich is on his cell, Boi's eyes are locked on the TV, and the professor is oblivious.

Rich hangs up and shakes his head. "My old man," he says.

Charles knows the old man well. In fact, he knew the old man's father, the now-dead patriarch, the first Kato, Masa Kato, the one who started Kato Construction. He was the one who helped get the first Democratic governors of Hawaii elected. He was the one who ended up building a quarter of Waikiki. Two generations later, and now there's two Kato judges, a Kato state senator, and for Katos like Rich, seats on important boards that keep the Hawaii machine going. Masa, whose portrait hangs at the Kato Construction main office—a severe-looking man on his knees, wearing a kimono, a katana and wakizashi strapped to his side—must be smiling in heaven right now. He had what Charles wanted. Children and grandchildren who would pick up the mantle and rule Hawaii. Where did it all go wrong? Shane's gone, Boi's disinterested, and maybe the only hope that Charles has left is a little girl being raised by a welfare queen in Kaneohe. He has no descendants, and he will never adopt again, not without Helen, so is his only chance little Nina Rapun?

"So my old man is out bowling with his buddies as usual," says Rich. "You know him, the only rich golf hater in the state. Anyway, I tell him about yet another hurricane that's going to whiff. He sounds disappointed, so I ask him why. He says, 'I hope one comes and knocks it all down.'

"I can't imagine I heard right. 'Dad,' I say, 'what about the destruction, all the lives and worse, the jobs lost, the economy ripped apart. I mean, two-hundred-mile-an-hour winds.' So he gives me his usual sigh, you know the kind. The one that suggests our entire generation is soft, you know, raised on microwave food and cable. As if having three TV channels and waiting for something to cook for hours promotes brain growth."

Charles is hardly listening. He's looking at Boi, wondering if he can get this kid to turn things around. There's so much he can do. He can make sergeant. He can go to school and get a degree. He can serve on committees like Rich Kato. Charles needs to get him to do it. Because as he swallows another almost-sob, the truth hits. Shane is not probably dead. He *is* dead.

"So anyway," says Rich. "I ask him, 'You *want* a hurricane to hit?' And he says, 'Yes' so I ask him why. He says, 'Who the hell do you think they'll pay to re-build it again?'"

Rich is laughing when Charles stands, grabs Boi by the shoulders, and turns him around. "He's dead, isn't he?" Charles asks Boi.

Boi's grabs Charles by the forearms and pushes his hands down. "I'm sorry," says Boi after he lets go.

"It's not your fault," says Charles.

"I'm sorry," says Boi. "If I could have saved him, I would have."

"I know," says Charles.

Boi clenches his jaw. Muscle definition, even in his cheeks: Charles has to respect the kid's strength. Boi turns away to study the hurricane again.

"We'll get her," says Charles. "You need to get her for me."

Boi nods as if mesmerized by the blue-pupil, white-iris, and red-eyeball sphere that swirls onscreen in infrared. At the border, green wisps twist counter-clockwise. Charles thinks of a screw drilling into the center of the earth.

8. _____

The next day, they're all there at central booking, hunched over. The brass, circled in chairs, are a bunch of men who made a career of not pissing anyone off. The Mayor's there, tanned and curly-haired, the first part-Hawaiian Mayor since Blaisdell. Kamehameha Schools, Harvard, Yale law. Next Governor of Hawaii after Knotting's second term is up, people say. He's talking to the Chief. He runs his hands through his frizzless curls, locked smooth like Greek statue pubic hair. The Mayor turns to Boi. They all turn to Boi now. Boi stops and looks back. No one barricading the doors behind him. He reminds himself to turn off the suspicion, turn off the paranoia. He takes a half-step forward. No one rushing him with mace and handcuffs. He doesn't take another step. Murder solve rates flash in his head. Ninety-two percent clearance this year. Ninety-five percent a year before.

Down the hall, Charles Knotting steps out of the bathroom. He's been looking jacked up for months. Eyes two broken-down fish tanks, barren except for aquarium scum and dry gravel. The brass stand and clear their throats. The Chief and Mayor step to Charles, who doesn't break stride as he heads for Boi. The Gov hugs him hard, making Boi feel squeamish. Charles's arms loosen and he's leaning on Boi. Despite his size, he feels light, The Gov. No muscle, just a sack propped with hollow bird bones. Boi nudges Charles off him, but holds him up for a moment to make sure he doesn't fall over. Charles nods. "She wants to see you," he says. "She says she'll talk. But right now, she denies everything."

Boi rubs his eyes. He turns to the Chief. "Sir, guarantee she did it?"

The Chief nods. "Guarantee."

"Where were you earlier today?" asks Charles. "I wanted to have lunch."

"Nowhere," Boi says. "Church."

Charles shoots him a suspicious look then nods.

"God is good to have on your side during times like these," says the Mayor. "Let's give this family closure." He puts his head down and shakes it.

Others in the room take the Mayor's cue, put their heads down and do the same. They all have sons. They all have brothers. "We'll get her confession," says the Chief. "We already got her for the other murders. We'll get her for this one, too."

They all look up as if the Chief said amen. All these powerful men, the Chief and his brass, back-stabbing company men. Competitors for the Chief's job once he retires. The Mayor, a Democrat and Charles's political enemy who is opposed to just about everything Charles Knotting, including the Helen Knotting Bill. And The Gov. Right here, right now, they're all on the same page. The most powerful men in Hawaii are about to run a train on Glory and they want Boi to hold her down.

Charles's eyes and cheeks bulge like he's just been seized and squeezed by a giant hand. He scrambles to a garbage can and pukes out gruel that resembles rain-soaked dog kibble. He staggers back to the bathroom. The Chief puts his arm around Boi. "He's been like this all morning. He knows it's our last chance to get a confession. Once she's sentenced to life, we got nothing to bargain with. And remember, she only agreed to this without her lawyer because we said we'd let you talk to her."

Boi nods.

"Looks like you could use some closure, too. Get the bitch to talk. Make his world right," the Chief whispers in his ear. "Make yours right, too."

"I will."

"Because, between me and you," the Chief says, pointing a thumb at the mayor. "His wife is dead, his son is probably dead, and to top it all off, he's actually trying to get his bill passed again, but it's dead for good. The Mayor and his boys are prepping to do a number on it. That's what my sister-in-law tells me anyway."

Boi perks up. "He's trying to pass it again?"

"And it will die next session again."

Boi crams a finger in his ear. "You sure?"

The Chief nods. He eyes the closed bathroom door. "It'll die there."

Boi's ears pop like grilled live oysters.

9.

Glory, half her corn-rows unraveled, is in prison orange, hand shackled to a table in Interrogation Room 1. She's sitting there, tapping her fingers on the bolted-down table, legs apart. Boi, trying hard to compose himself, half expects her to reach down with her free arm and scratch her crotch. How'd she get so tough? She hadn't been that tough when they were kids. She liked pink and horses and fast-food kiddie meal dolls with long eyelashes and glittered blue hair. She was the most scared of their Mom and burned the least. She used to be... She used to be like Nina.

Boi puts a bag and a cup of coffee on the table. He pulls out a chair and slumps in it. He waits and listens. No buzzing, ticking, static, nothing, just that one pop right before he walked in. He yawns and rubs his eyes. He knows they're all back there, the Chief, the Mayor, The Gov, behind the one-way mirror, watching, expecting. The bottom-line is this. It's either her or him and Joe. And it sure as hell isn't going to be him because if it's him, it's Nina, too. He picks up the coffee and takes a gulp. It's still piping hot, but he wants the pain to make him alert. "Policeman Boi," says Glory. "I had to see it for myself."

Boi shrugs as he eyes her. She's got a thick neck or maybe it's just that her head is too small for her body.

Glory looks around the empty room. "I feel old."

"What you mean?" he says, half-laughing. "We're in our prime."

"Shit. I don't think I ever had a prime."

Boi glances at the one-way mirror then reaches for the bag and pulls out Glory's hoodie. He hands it to her. She bunches it up and smells it, checking if it's clean. She nods and puts it on her lap. "Held up pretty good after weeks in the mountains."

"Need slippers, canned tuna, or anything like that?"

Glory shakes her head. "I'm good."

Boi takes another swig of coffee. The scratches on her face and her mess of hair are getting to him. He feels bad for her, and thinks the least he can do is help her look correct. "What about your hair?" Boi asks. "Need shit for your hair? I can get you an afro pick and gel."

Glory rubs her nose with the back of her hand. "Nah, I'm gonna chop it all off first chance I get."

Boi shakes his head. "Judge won't like that."

Glory points to the one-way mirror. "Shit, judges already made a decision. They're all right out there."

Boi shakes his head. "They aren't sure of shit yet."

Glory leans forward and tilts her head. "They as certain as death and taxes, motherfucker."

Boi leans back and laces his fingers behind his head as the caffeine in his body goes to work. If he gets her to confess, life goes on. Who is she to him, really? A little girl he once knew. A doll's head dangling from a tree. Boi can't save them all. He leans forward and whispers. He's channeling Charles Knotting now, voice slick with pretend empathy. "Why don't you cop to it then? Get it over with?"

Glory's not buying it. "Go fuck yourself."

Glory leans back, slouches, and scans the room. He knows what she's looking for. But there's nothing here, no weapon, no escape.

Boi works his face muscles and tries to make his eyes big, his lips slack, and shoots for an innocent look. He catches a cramp in his jaw. "Had to give it a shot," says Boi as he opens and closes his mouth to loosen the wound up muscles. "That's my bosses out there."

Glory tries to stand, but the cuff around her wrist is too short. She winces and sits back down. "I already got convicted for a whole bunch of shit. But one thing I ain't is a liar. So I won't cop to Shane. I didn't do that shit. I tried, but I didn't do it."

Boi leans back. What the hell is he doing in here? He's not trained for this. He's Swingman Rapun. Orange Cone Rapun. He glances at the one-way mirror. Only a matter of time before the brass pull him out of this room. "Two murders and one attempted murder versus three murders. There's no difference. Not like they take it easy on you because you tried to kill someone and failed."

Glory touches her collarbone and winces. "Still sore," she says.

"You know them," says Boi. "They gonna make shit hard for you if you don't."

Glory sits up. "How can they make shit harder than it already is? Gonna spend the rest of my life in jail."

Her feet start going. She's stomping away on the floor and she doesn't seem to know it. Boi feels like he's getting close to something. Her feet bounce pings off the walls like sonar. "Dunno, maybe they make it easier?" says Boi.

"Yeah, right."

"Might as well roll the dice. Pretend you're in Vegas or something."

The pings quicken. "Fuck Vegas."

Boi leans forward. "Never been?"

Glory looks at the ceiling. An air conditioning vent. Escape. Boi wouldn't mind crawling out of here either. "Does it look like I fucking vacation?" says Glory.

Her feet are really going now. The sound of rubber spanking concrete bounces off the walls, double-time. Glory tries to scratch her face with her cuffed hand and winces. "Me either," says Boi, leaning back. "Fuck the mainland."

Glory shrugs. She winces again. She looks down at her feet and grabs a thigh with her good hand. Her feet stop. "Never been," she says. She looks around the room. "Got some ibuprofen in this mother-fucker?"

Boi sighs. He stands up and looks at the mirrored window. Like Glory, he's feeling real old, but he knows he isn't. It's like Aunty Helen once told him. You're not old until you start thinking about death as much as you used to think about sex. He's not at that point. Not yet anyway. But maybe it's because he's got so many other things on his mind. The bill will die again next session, the Chief said. Boi's won and he didn't even have to throw a punch. But for some reason that doesn't make him happy. How can he feel good about winning by default? And if he really thinks about it, all the things he's seen over the years, chronics and lighter burns, forfeit farms and horses named Grover Cleveland, crumbs and Kry-lua, multi-million dollar dog parks and leptospirosis, auwe and manapua, fourth-floor whores and false scepters, no beach access and Waialua traffic, churches and Beef Bowls, Hawaiians on defense and dead ocean, Kry-waii has not changed. What has Boi really won?

And what about Shane?

Thinking about Shane, Nina, Waikiki, The Gov, Joe, his Mom, Chastity, and now even Rev and Mrs. Knotting, everything swims together in a gooey soup of tired. Vegas. He side-eyes Glory. She doesn't like that, does she? He turns around and faces her. His ears buzz. He's deep underwater, searching for a tako hole, spearing sand. "Back in the day, we used to send a bunch of bodies to middle-of-nowhere Kentucky, private prison," he says as he sits back down. "Was like two hundred female prisoners. Cheaper, ah?"

Glory shrugs.

"Fucking Hawaii chicks was getting raped left and right over there by all those inbred, country, eight-dollar-an-hour haoles. Even the fucking chaplain was getting some. Think couple even died in solitary. Can you imagine? Getting fucked until you die?"

Glory clenches her jaw.

"Eventually brought all the chick prisoners back," says Boi. "But you know how it is. People, they get all piss off, then they forget. It's like the beach. You know, get footprints all over. Then whoosh, high tide comes, all the footprints smoothed out by whitewash."

Glory slumps in her chair and tries to cross her arms. The chain connected to her wrist pulls tight. She bites her lip.

Boi points to the window. "That's where The Gov sending you. That's where you going if you don't cop. Only, you going be the only one from Hawaii there. Cannot keep low-profile over there."

Glory shrugs.

"I guess not a big deal then." Boi stand and steps to the door. "I tried."

The door buzzes. Boi swings it open.

"Wait," says Glory. "Where you going?" Boi glances under the table. Her feet pound against the floor again.

"We're done. You not gonna talk. I'm out." Boi takes out a pad and scribbles his phone number. "But call me if you need anything."

Glory tries to stand again, but she's yanked down by the taut slip of chain. "Wait," she says.

Boi, his hand already on the doorknob, waiting to be buzzed out again, turns. "What?"

"I dunno. Let's just talk more."

She's sitting there, hair all wanged out, looking like a rag doll chewed up by a pack of dogs then spun in a dryer for two hours. Just like Shane, that's his sister. His family. All those years searching for her, and here she is, unfamiliar to him, burnt beyond recognition by years of hell. Glory, Shane—Boi is straight-up brotherly poison. It's because of him Shane's gone, and now he's about to take out his sister. Look at her, she never stood a chance. And now he's about to bury her too. For what?

He eyes the one-way mirror. He's not gonna do it. He's not gonna get her to say it. Let them do it. They helped create her with their centuries of land-snatching, their dream machines, and the safety nets they weaved then sliced up like a failed magic trick, leaving gaping holes. Leaving Makana. They're the ones who want to see her go down for this because it's not good enough to wipe out the unborn babies. They need to get all the ones walking around, too. Unless they're proved worthy. Like Shane. Like Boi. Uncle Charles out there trying to play a blindfolded god hurling thunderbolts and frying the wrong people. Fuck him. Fuck all of them.

"I'm beat," Boi says.

Glory frowns. She slumps back down, relaxed again, tapping her fingers on the table. The fingers ring dull. There's not much nail on her fingers, chewed or ripped all the way down near each base. She sticks her index finger in her mouth and gnaws at what little nail is left. "What's keeping you up at night?" she asks.

Boi glances at the window. He takes his hand off the door-knob and turns around. He sits back down. He rubs his eyes and works up the best sad look he can muster. "Shane. My brother. Our brother."

She leans forward. She's staring at his face. "You kind of look like him," she says.

"Fuck you. No I don't."

She leans back, squints, and tilts her head. "When's the last time you seen him anyway?"

Boi tries hard to calculate an alibi lie. The Beef Bowl? Aunty Helen's funeral? No, the best answer is sometime before that. Boi feels The Gov, the mayor, and the brass all looking at him from behind the one-way mirror. Wait, what the hell is going on? He's letting himself be interrogated? He's already waited too long to answer. "The question is," Boi says. "When's the last time you seen him." Even to him, it sounds like bullshit.

"In Kahala. When I was trying to bust a cap his ass. What about you?"

Boi slams his hand on the table with everything he's got.

Glory, smiling, doesn't flinch.

"I'm out," Boi says. They both look down at the table. A wet handprint smeared like someone's slipping down a wall. Glory's eyes lock on his. Boi turns away.

He stands up, walks to the door, and reaches for the doorknob. He pounds on the door. He needs to get out of the room. The brass, The Gov, they're all watching.

Glory shrugs. "Didn't mean to piss you off," she says. "Do me a favor. Can you put my sweater around my head before you go? Cold as fuck in here." She rubs her hands together.

The door buzzes. Boi pulls it open then closes it. He sighs, rounds the table, and takes the hoodie off Glory's lap. He puts it up to his nose and smells it. It's clean. He smoothes out the sweater and leans over her. She's slouched way down. She tilts up her chin, flaunting her thick neck, and waits. It's a nice neck, unblemished except for a tiny, lightly colored skin tag, the kind old Makana used to have all over her face and dug out when she was high. Boi covers Glory's face with the sweater and yanks down. After Boi gets her head through the neckhole, Glory leans toward him. Is she going to kiss him? She chomps down on his earlobe. A quick, searing pain jolts from ear to brain.

Boi grabs her head and slams it against the table. Glory spits his bloody ear lobe at him.

"Fuck you!" she screams, clawing for a backpedaling Boi with her free hand. "Fuck you!"

Her teeth bloody, she's howling now as she yanks the chain. Skin peels off at the base of her hand. She jerks harder. Abrasions around her wrist now, curled skin clinging to handcuff steel like wet pencil shavings. Glory faces the window, and spits at the glass. "He did it! I didn't do it! He did it!"

Holding his ear, Boi yanks on the doorknob, waiting for the buzz. The door opens. Charles is on the other side, pulling Boi in.

"Fuck you!" Glory's still screaming. Her hand bones break and she slips what now looks like a three-fingered claw out of the cuff. She runs up to the glass and pounds it. "I didn't do it! I didn't do it!"

Charles holds Boi up. He, along with everyone else, watches Glory through the window. Her tiny fist smears blood on the glass.

"He did it!" she shouts. Boi goes for the door. He wants back in. To shut her up for good. But Charles and the Chief grab him.

The Chief pats him on the back. "Good job," he says. "Look at her. She's lost her mind. We got the leverage now."

Boi looks around the room, confused. They're all looking at him and nodding their heads. He turns back to the mirror. Glory's launching her entire body at the glass now, bouncing off it like a rubber ball. The other brass in the room eye Boi. "Look at her," the Chief says. "We tell her we're going to send her to Kentucky, she'll cop."

The Mayor nods. "That was a nice touch."

Charles puts his hand on Boi's shoulder. "Thank you," he says. "Now we'll get the real story. Who knows? Maybe he's even still alive."

Boi watches as two uniforms enter Interrogation 1, NB's drawn. His sister rushes one, but he cracks her with his baton. She drops. They're leaning over and hacking away, like they're working a cow in a slaughterhouse. Charles turns to the Chief. The grief on The Gov's face is gone. He looks mad. He rolls his neck and flexes his shoulders. It's the first time Boi's seen him do it since Helen dies. "We'll get her shipped to Kentucky no matter what. We're not keeping people like her in state. Not anymore."

"She won't last long there," says the Mayor.

Charles nods. His clenches his fists. He turns to Boi, teary-eyed. "You see what this is all about? My law. They're trying to stonewall it again, but I don't care if I have to spend every dime I have on it and it takes the rest of my life. Governor or not, I'll get it passed."

One pink-faced Major, his face flushed as always, slaps Boi on the back before heading to a computer terminal. Chief hands Boi a towel. Boi thanks him and presses it against his ear.

"I'm doing this for Shane," says Charles.

The Gov leaves the room. Boi knows he won't stop. He'll spend millions on a lifted, souped-up manapua truck with monster tires. He'll hand out bean bag-sized manapua to every State

Congressman, Senator, and judge that he appointed. He'll spend every dime and breath of life to get the bill passed. And Boi knows without Shane, there's no way The Gov would be this hell-bent if Shane hadn't disappeared. Charles would've just let it die in committee, stepped down as Gov, mourned his wife.

Baton cracks come over the speaker. Holding the towel to his bleeding ear, Boi watches how none of them even notice. None of them are thinking. They'll never look for Shane's body. Glory did it. The Gov is satisfied. The mayor is satisfied. Another murder solved. 95 percent solve rate.

The Chief grabs Boi's arm and pulls him in. "Listen," he says. "Me and The Gov talked. You did a great job in there. I'm putting you on The Gov's personal detail. You stay with him until his term is up. No more swingman for you. After that, sergeant's test. The Gov said you was a smart kid. Up to you. Maybe vice or criminal investigation after."

Boi watches the pink major type away and thinks the keyboard might as well have mythical creatures shooting out of it, dragons, gnomes, Pegasus, and those three-headed monsters with lion, snake, and goat heads, it's so magic. It's the most magical typewriter of all-time. Because every word the brass is typing—all the gunshots, the gore, the fratricide—is true, even if the whole thing is a lie.

Boi stares at the magic typewriter as if the squid god is coming out, too, rolling up all eight of his sleeves.

10.

It's a warm November morning, and Clyde Sanga III would rather be in the ocean. Down, past a school of akule, thousands of the silver, big-eyed fish swirling before they contract like a closed fist. Deeper into the channel, past ulua open-water-hunting depth, where the water turns ball-shriveling cold. Down to the bottom where schools of yellow tang dart through tunnels and bridges and swim across the sandy bottom at the same speed, like traffic. But there are no yellow tangs today, just a yellow excavator manned by Clyde. And if Clyde's being honest, the akule, the ulua, the tang—he might not even see them if he were out in the ocean. They're becoming rarer and rarer.

Once he could free dive over a hundred feet. His sons laughed. He told them how their great-grandfather, Clyde I, was a professional boxer and won over a hundred-and-fifty plantation bouts. Clyde could tell they didn't believe him. He told them about a union-boss uncle who used to get comped by the mob in Vegas. A Seoul-born great-aunt who was once a famous actress and got kidnapped by the North Koreans. A Japanese cousin who ran the black market in Okinawa after the war, who'd known U.S. Senators. But the boys, they wanted proof. Because looking around the respectable, but not-even-close-to palatial home they'd grown up in, they couldn't imagine much more than a construction worker father and a diner-owner mother. They wanted pictures. But Clyde told them that there'd been a flood at the newspaper years ago, and all the old news stories got wiped out, except for one where the boxing great-grandfather was driving drunk and crashed his car into Kapalama Canal.

Clyde wonders why he's here shoveling dirt to pay for his C-student-sons' tuitions. Clyde IV, who likes to be called Junior because he hates the name Clyde, and his younger brother, Adam, both attend small, private mainland colleges, the kind with steep tuitions that anyone can get into. With a third mortgage on the house, Clyde will be happy if home prices in Hawaii stay astronomical. If they don't, no way he'll get enough equity out of the house to pay tuition. Besides, if the haoles don't keep coming and coming from the mainland to tear down old houses and raise new ones, Clyde will be out of a job. Hell, without haoles, Clyde would be scooping dirt with a shovel instead of a hundred thousand pounds of spool valves and hydraulic pumps. He's voted for the haole governor. Twice.

Clyde fires up the excavator. They need to dig deeper than they'd thought. The owner, who inherited a hospital supply company and a European league soccer team, decided that he wants to add a wine cellar. So Clyde will dig eight feet more before they pour the slab.

Clyde digs. Younger guys fresh from apprenticeship, guys with joints still greased with youth, feed the cement mixer. Older guys with bad backs and knees watch and talk about how their sons played in this year's Beef Bowl. Don Pai's son, quarterback for the Kahaluu Broncos, might get a prep school scholarship. College, then pros, Don Pai always says. Only Clyde has never seen a five-six quarterback in the pros before.

Clyde hopes his sons stay on the mainland. Hundred grand, you can buy a mansion on the mainland. Hundred grand, you live like one king. He doesn't want his sons to turn out like these guys, pushing fifty and still renting. He doesn't want them to turn out like him.

The foreman holds up a hand and whistles. Clyde jerks the excavator arm up and hoists it to the side. The foreman's still got his hand up, staring at the bottom of the hole. The others gather.

"Ho, what the fuck?" one of them asks.

Eventually, Clyde gets out of the excavator and joins them.

There's half a body down there. A big head, eye sockets and mouth stuffed with dirt. Half a body, but big. Shriveled things, sticky with dirt, black like motor oil, dangle out from the bottom half. "Ho," says Don Pai. "Where his legs and stuff?"

As he dials 911, Clyde wonders what he'll have for dinner tonight.

11.

It only takes a week for Boi to get his own leased, unmarked police car, compliments of the state. He spends his days in training, which covers things as wide-ranged as disarmament, paramedics, and Hawaiian martial arts. Upon completion, he will receive a ceremonial pololu, an ancient, feathered koa spear ridged with shark teeth.

The schedule is light enought to make it possible for him to take and pick up Nina from school every day, and when his training is done, he will be expected to simply be at The Gov's side whenever he's needed. This means brunches and buffet dinners. It means occasional trips to the Mainland, Japan, the Philippines, Korea, and China. Boi got bumped up a pay grade as well, and will receive special duty pay whenever he works a shift and overtime when he travels off-island with The Gov. Boi is expected to study for the sergeant's exam during evenings, and he has to carry around a satellite phone twenty-four-seven, a communication device as big as an old-school cell phone that allows The Gov to keep in contact with him at all times, even during blackouts. As one of the gunfighter mustached guards told him. "Could be nuclear war, braddah, and The Gov could still call us on this thing."

This time he doesn't have to false-testify in court. There's no six-year plan. He's getting this shit for free. So why does he feel like Uncle Charles has his big hand wrapped around the back of Boi's neck and is cramming his face into a rocky tidepool filled with human piss? On some days, as a sort of half-ass protest, Boi leaves the satellite phone at home and tells Charles he forgot it. Today, he left it in his locker.

During his training, Boi doesn't think about the tide pool or the sat phone very much. He's enjoyed learning how to snatch a weapon from an armed man in a blink of an eye and how to stick a tube in a person's throat to create a surgical airway. He also doesn't think about the leash around his neck when Nina's around. There's stuff to do to keep himself sane—pick her up from school, help her with her homework, take her to ballet once a week, cook dinner, maybe watch some TV—maybe beach on Saturday where he tries to get her to wear fins, a snorkel, and a mask. She refuses. It wasn't sharks she was scared of last weekend. It was box jellyfish. She'd watched a documentary on them and talked about how they can kill a man and live forever.

Nina made Boi Google it after they got home. It wasn't box jellyfish, but another species, and when its life was threatened, it aged backwards. Boi found that fascinating. When the shit hits the fan, it becomes what it once was.

On Monday, two days before Glory's sentencing, Nina isn't with him. He's at a tiki-themed Waikiki restaurant eating a teriyaki burger topped with a huge slice of pineapple. Not what he was expecting when he ordered a teri burger. Boi rubs his neck then scrapes the fruit off his meat. Normally, he wouldn't take a meal at a place like this, but it's after his shift, he's hungry, it's close to the station, and with no Nina, he doesn't have a reason to cook. His phone rings. It's Joe. He ignores him. Joe's been trying to call him all day, but Boi's not in the mood to talk. He's been ducking Charles's calls, too.

One table over, two haole men talk about the restaurant's polished driftwood railings. One, presumably the owner, says that he got all the wood from Punaluu Black Sand Beach on the Big Island. Authentic he says. Boi wants to lean over and ask where he got the authentic polyurethane-looking polish. Oil from the ancient grove outside Kaunakakai on Molokai? Shane would've gotten a kick out of the question. He'd once asked Boi why he felt the need to say this kind of stuff. Boi told him not saying it would be like seeing a camel take a dump off a hot air balloon and not point up and yell, "Ho, look!"

Shane liked that one.

Boi warned him. He told Shane that day last year at Joe's old Kahuku farm that he should leave. And what did Shane say?

"Fuck you, man. I ain't going."

And Joe wanted him to stay. After he'd finished his chant, he ask Shane if he knew how to hotwire an excavator. Shane eyed the giant, one-clawed machine and shook his head.

"Didn't think so," Joe said. He headed for the excavator, yanked wires out from under the control panel, and fired it up.

Shane, who didn't know how to operate a shovel, much less an excavator, was worthless throughout the dig. He was full of questions and wise cracks as he munched on popcorn and tossed unpopped kernels into each freshly dug hole. "Not bones? What then, the Ark of the Covenant?" he asked. He had to yell his jokes over the excavator's roar.

Joe dropped the yellow claw into the shallow pit, scraped out earth, and deposited it in a neat pile. Joe went in for another scoop.

When they got to a depth of about five feet, Boi signaled Joe to stop the excavator and climbed down into the pit with a flathead shovel. The dirt was clumpy, but soft. Loi dirt. Boi cut into ground. The shovel clanked on something. He cleared soil off an aluminum dry-box. Then another. Then a stack of boxes.

The sun was setting as they got all ten dry boxes out of the hole. Joe, his tee shirt tied around his head, a powerlifting belt wrapped around his waist, stepped to each box and unlocked it. Shane, panting, his hands on his knees, made a pirate treasure crack while Boi opened the first container.

It held fifty-pound sacks of fertilizer. "What the hell is all this?" Boi asked. He'd just come here for the blasting caps. Boi picked up a sack, the plastic pregnant with little white pellets that reminded Boi of fish eggs.

"Jesus," Shane said. "What is this stuff?"

Boi ignored Shane and turned to Joe. "We organic on the farm. You been stockpiling this shit all these years?"

Joe shrugged. "Figured might come in useful one day. Mix it with some of the diesel fuel, you know."

"Hey," Shane said, "what are you going to do with all this? Another Oklahoma City?"

"Is your burger okay?" Boi looks up to find a waitress tapping him on the shoulder. She's all tricked-out—highlights, make-up, high heels, and massive fake tits stacked under a white, skin-tight tank top. She makes Boi think of a double-blown muscle car. "Yeah," he says, and asks for the tab. As she walks away, he thinks of Nina. He hopes she never has to wait tables in a place like this. He'll have to figure out how to keep Chastity from getting her hands on her inheritance.

While he and Shane loaded each box into Grover Cleveland's horse trailer, Joe took off his powerlifter belt, draped it over his shoulder, cracked open a beer, and watched the sun set over the ocean. The sky was lit orange like a boiled lobster.

"Used to be able to catch choke spiny lobster," Joe said as if reading Boi's mind. "Could see hundreds. Just dive down and could grab them with your hands."

Like most other golden ages, before Boi's time. By the time Boi had been a kid, eight hours of trolling already netted just one, maybe two papio, if lucky. The Samoan crab, like the spiny lobster, another insect of the ocean, now an underwater phantom. Ewa Beach ogo, seaweed that resembled clumps of blood vessels, gone. Opihi, mined like rare gems and sold for about the same price. According to Joe, Boi missed clams by a hundred years. Gotta go scuba, down a hundred feet deep, for anything good, unless you wanted to eat Pearl Harbor oysters that glow in the dark.

After loading up the containers, Joe dropped a beer can in the pit and climbed back into the excavator. He fired it up then let it hum idle. Boi stepped to the edge of the pit and raised a hand. Joe waited and stepped out.

Shane stepped next to Boi, who looked down at the bottom of the hole, at soft rocks that looked like petrified sponges. "Thinking I'll go to film school or something," Shane said.

"What kind of movies?"

"I dunno. Documentaries. Maybe do some stuff on the homeless. Give back, you know?"

Boi spit in the hole and nodded. Shane could spend his whole life doing that, and he wouldn't even come close to giving as much as he took.

"But if you blow something up, let me know so I can film it, okay?" Shane said.

Boi nodded.

Joe yelled from the excavator, how it was getting dark and they needed to hurry. Hard to hear over all that smoking metal. The digger boom and surrounding trees cast faint, leg-shaped shadows that spread from the undercarriage. Boi counted them.

Eight. The smoke, the shadow legs, and the operator cab dome reminded Boi of a story he'd once heard, about a Molokai man taken by a giant hee. Its pulsing red tentacles had slithered up every orifice (ears, mouth, nostrils, and asshole), and then the octopus ripped the man apart. That's what the excavator looked like, a jumbo hee. As the sun dropped anchor on the horizon, Fat Shane, with his stupid, florescent-green, wannabe construction shirt, spat popcorn kernels into the hole.

Somewhere, under the deepest Hawaii channel, Boi hoped there was a giant octopus spit out by the gods and cast to the underworld, the squid god, Kanaloa. His grandmother had told him stories about Kanaloa. Mr. Melvin chanted to Kanaloa at the boys' home. Joe believed in Kanaloa along with the other gods like Kane and Pele. When he was sent to the mental hospital, Boi No Good had actually thought he was hearing Kanaloa. But that was the drugs they gave him. Afterwards, there was all that ocean and disbelief between them.

The waitress brings Boi the check. He eyes the burger. He didn't even take a bite out of it. He looks over at the two old haole men. They're talking politics now. They're talking about The Gov. Boi has a hard time hearing them over the buzzing and static that's lately been flooding his ears. He wants Nina here with him now.

Don't think about Glory. Don't think about Shane.

But Boi can't help himself. Even now it sounds ridiculous in his own head, but it was unmistakably a realization. Like the wife who knows her husband is cheating on her or the mother who knows her child is in trouble or the cop who knows a chronic when he sees one, Boi didn't think Kanaloa was talking to him. He *knew* it.

Joe dropped the excavator claw into the mountain of loose dirt. The giant piston hissed.

"Just tell me you aren't going to do something crazy," Shane said.

The wind picked up and blew dirt in Shane's face. Shane closed his eyes and slapped at his face. *Helpless, hopeless.* Shane wiped dirt off his tongue and smiled. He crumpled the popcorn bag and tossed it in the hole.

"You got Nina to think about. It's a responsibility," Shane said.

As if he knew anything about responsibility. Shane, the wake-up-at-noon everyday, fat, lazy fuck. Mr. Water Polo, Private School, Wannabe Kanaka, Big-for-Nothing Bitch. This fluorescent green, industrial-sized sucking machine in front of him was everything that was wrong with Kry-waii. Like a goddamn gigantic sci-fi slug. But he was also his blood. He was also little Chayne-Marcos, the silver toothed, juice-drinking addict. He was also the guy who, when it came down to it, would probably have helped Boi with anything if Boi had asked. Only Boi never asked. He made it a point never to ask for anything from a Knotting again.

He flinched as the digger claw flashed toward him. "Hey Joe!" As he dove out of the way, the claw smashed into Shane, sweeping him into the hole. Boi raced to the edge of the crater. His brother was face down, broad shoulders twitching.

Boi's whole body was ringing, vibrating, shaking. He turned to the excavator cab.

A wide-eyed Joe was looking at him through the glass. Boi slid down the hole and tried to flip Shane over. He held his head up. For a moment Shane's eyes fluttered, then searched. Finally, they locked on Boi. His lips trembled as if he were about to sob. He was trying to cry, but his body wouldn't let him. He looked so scared. Then he stopped.

Boi climbed out and marched toward Joe. The excavator claw hung over the pit. Boi walked yelling to the cockpit. Joe lifted his hand from the controls and raised his palms in front of his face yelling something back.

"He was my brother!" Boi screamed.

Joe reached for levers. Boi took out his gun and pressed the barrel up to the plexiglass door, aimed at Joe. "He was family!"

"He was one rat!" Joe said. "He was going rat you out!"

"Fuck!"

"He was! You my son!"

Boi closed his eyes. Joe started up the machine, pulling levers with shaking hands.

He slammed the claw into the side of the hole. Hands trembling even more, he tried to scoop up dirt again. This time the excavator arm jerked then swung in a circle and Boi had to duck. He wanted to scream. He wanted to jump into the ocean and swim away from all of this.

I'll take it from here.

Boi took a breath. Finally, Kanaloa had spoken. Boi yanked Joe out of the cockpit, climbed behind the controls, and started to fill the hole. The shallower the hole got, the more the tons of dirt and gravel pouring in sounded like sizzling meat.

After Boi killed the engine, he told Joe to hotwire Shane's car and follow him. But the keys were in the ignition. Boi waited until he was on the road, alone, before pulling out his cell and calling Charles Knotting. He told The Gov that Shane had called to say he was being stalked by Glory. That Glory had already of-fed an old man and maybe a Filipino nurse, too. Shane sounded terrified.

The Gov thanked him for the warning and called Boi his hanai son. *Hanai.* To adopt. To nourish. To sustain. *These fucking haoles.* Boi hung up and resisted the urge to snap his phone in half. He resisted the urge to cry. But he couldn't shut out the squid god talking to him. Because Boi would not have done these things on his own, he listened. And he and Joe drove out of Kahuku with blasting caps, tubes of water gel, and over four-thousand-pounds of fertilizer stacked in a horse trailer.

In the restaurant, even a year later, Boi wonders if he could have saved Shane. Even if he could've, should he have? Shane's death stopped the Helen Knotting Bill dead in its tracks.

Boi drops cash on the receipt, picks his keys up off the table, and gets ready to head out. Two more days until he gets Nina back, two long days. He pauses. The two old haoles, still talking politics. "They found the body," one says. "The Gov's."

Boi steps toward the two men. "A body?" he asks. He can barely hear himself talk.

"Yeah," says one of the men. "Was in the news. They found The Gov's son."

Boi stands there stunned for a moment. He digs in his ears then rubs his neck. He takes a few steps back and slumps on a stool. It's been a year. Maybe the body is too badly decomposed to find any evidence. But there at least will be bones. Broken bones. Bones that Boi let Joe break. Boi looks left and right, wondering if anyone in the restaurant can hear his thoughts. They seem so loud to him, panicked shouts that break through the static in his head.

He tells his ears to shut up as he thinks of all the evidence left behind—Joe's beer cans, Shane's popcorn bag. Will they look into the property's history and find Joe's name on a list of previous owners? Of course they will. Most cops, the swingmen, the company men, aren't too swift. But the homicide detectives, most of them are on it.

Outside on the sidewalk, Boi calls Joe. As the phone rings, Boi looks up at the hotel towers around him. The older ones are tougher, more boxy, more sumo, lower center of gravity. But some of the new ones, tall, slender, shiny, dolled up with reflective glass, they're like chicks these ones. Wait for high tide and bust their ankles, they gonna leak something underneath. To find the sweet spot, to gouge, to kneecap and watch these fuckers drop.

Two to three days, max.

"Hello? Hello?"

Boi's ears are ringing. He can't tell if Joe answered. Boi concentrates.

"I heard," Joe says.

Boi nods and thinks: eye gouge. If the three power substations flowing electrical current into Waikiki fail at the same time, lights out. Kick to the knee. Six thousand feet of main line sewer runs forty-two feet under Ala Wai Boulevard. Climb down a shaft Hobron side and bust that up. Ankle lock. Three hotels on Kalakaua Ave with underground parking garages. At the bottom of each of these parking lots, long 2x4's prop up concrete ceilings. Boi laughed when he first found them, the hotels like five-hundred-pound barbells being held up by sand-eating weaklings. Rusty water pipes clamped on cracked, rebar-exposed walls. Water pumps behind rickety chain-link. Under each water pump, a hole. Boi found a tunnel that runs under half of Waikiki. If he knocked the struts out of those three hotels—tap out. He's got his orange cones, yellow crime-scene tape, and men-at-work sign in his trunk. Give a guy a uniform, a badge, and a bunch of orange cones, and he can go wherever the hell he wants.

"Boi!" yells Joe.

"We going down for this, guarantee," Boi says.

"Was me. You never do shit."

"We done. Pau."

Joe's quiet for a moment. What will happen to Nina when Boi gets locked up for good? Back to Chastity's fulltime. Back to Kahekili Village. The near death of a kid over a year ago, and those balconies are still crumbling off their bases. A year from now, another kid will fall.

"What you going do?" Joe asks.

The wind kicks up the scent of salt water and rotten bait.

What is he going to do? Maybe he's overreacting. Everyone already thinks Glory did it. The new job, the training, they obviously don't suspect him. Maybe they won't even rake the crime scene. Now he knows why Uncle Charles has been trying to call him all day.

"Sit tight," Boi says. "I gotta find out what they know."

Boi hangs up. He eyes the laminated picture of Nina attached to his keychain and thinks about all her blood relatives on his side of the family. Cece. Gone. Makana. Gone. Shane. Gone. Glory. Soon-to-be gone. Boi's next. It's like some kind of fucking Rapun hit list. And what did Cece, Makana, and Shane leave behind? Nothing. Glory won't leave shit behind either. Will Nina? He's not sure. She's got advantages he never had growing up, namely Knotting money. But him getting thrown in jail for the rest of his life won't help her. Maybe all he's got left to give her is to show her what a Rapun, full of balls and a vision from Kanaloa, can accomplish. But what?

The Waikiki skyline, its windows, balconies, and towers tourist-trap crass, gets his rage up. That's what he's running on now, rage, and if he stops feeling it, he knows that his heart will stop pumping blood through his body. If he stops feeling it, he knows he's gonna die.

12.

Before Boi was adopted by the Bolosans, he spent a year at a foster home in Waipahu. He doesn't recall the family's name, but he remembers the dad well. The father was a Puerto Rican who never wore anything but boxers at home. When he went out, he didn't wear much more. Maybe a tee-shirt and jeans if he had to go beyond the mailbox outside. He hardly wore shoes or slippers, and his feet were padded with callouses that constantly peeled and left bits of dead skin wherever he walked. Of all things, the dad's name was Mango. Boi never found out why he was called this, and if it had been anyone else with that name, he would have laughed. But nobody laughed around Mango.

Boi wasn't sure what Mango did for a living, but whatever it was, it was during night. He'd leave at around eight p.m. and come home at five in the morning while Boi and his two foster brothers were sleeping. As far as Boi could tell, Mango didn't drink or do drugs like his real mom or his foster parents from before. Mango didn't do much of anything except eat, sleep, work, and fish. He didn't talk to Boi except for when he told him what to do.

"Take shower outside. Use the hose. Save water."

"Eat the fish bones, too. No waste."

"Hold the light like you one statue."

It was Boi's job to hold the light when they went torching on Mango's nights off. While Boi's foster brothers waded barefoot through the shallow brackish muck with Mango, Boi sat on the bow of the skiff, holding the lantern and dodging the baby needlefish that jumped at the light. Mango would spear mullets and white eels and toss them in the boat while a boy dragged the flat-bottom by a rope, scooping up crabs with a net. The other boy speared fish.

There was nothing fun about these torching trips. For Mango, fishing was work. He sold most of what they caught at the market and cooked up the rest for daily meals. Boi ate eel, sometimes grilled, sometimes stewed in a chili sauce, and sometimes wrapped and steamed in banana leaves.

Mango took torching very seriously. The first time Boi had nodded off and almost dropped the lantern, Mango grabbed Boi by the neck and dunked his head under brown water. He pressed Boi's face against the muddy bottom until Boi nearly ran out of breath. When Boi actually dropped the light because he'd seen a giant crab, leaned over the boat and tried to grab it, Mango grabbed Boi and pinned his head against the bow. He snatched a live crab from the cooler and pressed its blue pincher against Boi's ear. The crab clamped onto Boi's ear lobe. Boi screamed, grabbed the crab, and yanked it off. Only the pincher and arm dangled from his ear now, and Mango made Boi wear it like jewelry for the rest of the trip. The other two boys called him "fag" as they kicked over underwater rocks and rubber tires.

Boi wasn't sure if there ever was a foster mom. If there was, by the time he'd gotten there, she was gone. There were signs that a woman once lived in the house—the moldy shower curtain was printed with flowers, and the medicine cabinet contained a rusted device that Boi guessed was used for curling eye lashes, but other than that, nothing. Boi didn't care. He'd had his fill of mothers.

After a year, when Mango nearly beat the oldest boy to death with a socket wrench because the boy had spilled motor oil in the garage, the cops came. Mango turned to the cops and went after them with the socket wrench. They sprayed him with mace, but he still kept coming. They tased him, but he didn't drop. One of the cops, twice Mango's size, swung his baton at him. Mango snatched the baton and cracked the cop across the face. Even back then, Boi can remember thinking how beautiful it was. Mango in his boxers, hands up, had one foot forward while most of his weight rested on his back leg. Every time a cop tried to rush him, Mango slipped to the side, then shifted his weight to the front foot and unloaded. He'd get one or two hits in, then shift his weight back. Eventually, it took six cops to circle and net him. After that, Boi was off to the Bolosan's.

Right now, Boi hasn't gone in for training or slept for the last two days and is suprised he's thinking of Mango. He hadn't thought about his grim old foster father for years. But Boi's been living in his head for the last forty-eight hours, trying to figure out what the hell he's going to do. He spent the first day tracking the news. Front page and breaking. Reporters at Joe's old Kahuku farm interviewing the new owners, a couple of haoles talking about how they'd seen a wine cellar with a spiral staircase in Aspen and knew they had to have one. It was this decision that had the construction crew digging deeper, and that's why they found Shane's body. The haole couple complained that adding a wine cellar required re-submitting building plans to the city. They hoped the discovery of a body didn't delay construction even further.

As for the construction crew, an old local with bad knees talked about finding the body. The conversation quickly turned from corpses to fishing, plantation boxing, and old Korean actresses. Boi could tell that the reporters just wanted to get out of there. Boi was hoping that when the man was interviewed by the police, the cops would feel the same way.

Reporters, some even national, were staked out in front of the Knotting house. The Chief was there to take questions. No sign of The Gov. The Chief said that they were still investigating. He said that they, in fact, had a suspect. When asked if that suspect was Glory, the Chief didn't answer.

By the time the sun was coming up, Boi had enough, so he shut down his little newscenter—computer, TV, and radio—and decided to take a drive around the island to think and clear his head. He grabbed his keys, cell phone, and sat phone—both of which have been ringing off the hook—and jumped in his truck instead of his unmarked police car. They could track him in that thing.

On the road, Boi's thinking this may be his final tour, one more circle island. So as he drives through Hauula and Punaluu in his truck, he's feeling as nostalgic as Honolulu International Airport music. He passes Kahana and Kaaawa. He's in a new town every few miles. He passes a pine tree ridge above Waia-hole, the ridge of the ancient serpent's back. He'd already passed Mokolii, an islet that legend says is a sea monster's tail sticking out of the ocean.

Heading into Kahaluu, Boi gets a call on the sat phone. It's The Gov again. Boi ignores it and doesn't even know why he brought the damn thing. Before Boi left, he texted Chastity to pick Nina up, and since then, she's been calling, too. He's been ignoring her as well. He was smart enough to call in sick before dropping off the radar, but even his sergeant's been trying to call. Do they already know? He turns off both phones. It's a reflex, keeping them near him, ring volume maxed, and powered up at all times. What if there's an emergency? What if Nina needs him? It's hard, but he shuts them down anyway. He can check up on her in person.

In Kaneohe now, he pulls in and parks at Nina's school. It's recess time, kids, now uncaged, burst from Thanksgiving-deco-rated doors. The little ones head for the playground and gather, boys on one side, girls on the other. A group of older ones, prob-ably fifth-graders, lean against fences. Two make out while a third takes out a lighter and tries to light wet grass on fire.

Boi opens the door and steps out. He scans the playground— no Nina. He grabs his cell phone. He's tempted to turn it on and call Chastity. Absent? Sick? Maybe that's why Chastity was try-ing to call. He turns on the phone and dials the number. Just then, Nina charges out of her classroom. She stops, holds her arms out, and spins. Chaine, chaine, chaine—chin up, eyes focused on the jungle gym so she doesn't get dizzy, one tip-toed ballet turn after another all the way to the playground.

Boi turns off the phone. Nina joins a group of girls, wild-eyed and smiling. She leaps and bends her knees mid-air, getting only a few inches off the ground. Her vertical is terrible. But she's pleased with her jump, and arms raised, she spins, and throws her whole body into joy. A trip to the beach, to Fun Factory, to yet another animated princess matinee. Boi's always been mystified at how easy it is to make her leap and spin, to make her happy.

Boi is about to go to Nina, but he stops dead. A tall haole man wearing a cap and sunglasses knocks on Nina's classroom door. The teacher answers. At first, she's frowning, but then she seems to recognize him. Smiling, she sticks out her hand and the man shakes it. She's now bowing to him repeatedly as he puts a hand on her shoulder. He takes off his sunglasses.

What the hell is he doing here?

Boi scans the parking lot. No sign of The Gov's town car or guards with gunfighter mustaches. Did he drive himself?

Boi gets in his truck and turns the key. He reverses out. He takes one more look at Nina, who is playing hopscotch. Is The Gov checking if Nina has seen Boi? Why else would he be here? Boi's about to kill the engine, step out of the car, and ask the man himself. But then, something occurs to him. What if they know? What if they already looked into the property history of Joe's old farm. Boi knew it wouldn't take long to get that information. What if they picked up Joe? What if he confessed? What if he's already at the main station locked up with all the other bodies?

Boi picks up the phone, tempted to call Joe. He puts it down. He glares at the closed classroom door. The Gov has no right to be here, no matter who he is. The teacher shouldn't even be talking to him. Then it dawns on Boi.

He's here for Nina. He's going to take her from you.

Boi bites his lip. Helen's gone, Shane's gone, and if he knows what Boi did, Boi will be gone, too. The Gov wants another project. Another poor Hawaiian kid to save before he tries to destroy all the rest. "They try to colonize the mind," Mr. Melvin used to say. Charles had done it to Shane, and now he is going to send Boi away and colonize Nina's mind, too. People her brain with notions of take what you want and screw everyone else. Teach her that there are two types of people, those who deserve to live and those who should not. Turning her into a fat, industrial-sized tit-sucking machine like Shane.

This fucker thinks he can do whatever he wants.

Boi grabs his gun. He should march right in the classroom and put a bullet in The Gov. End all this already. He slips the truck into park and takes a breath. He opens the door and sticks one leg out before the thought of Nina stops him.

Anyway, killing the big haole won't be enough. Boi needs to do something bigger than that. Any fool can walk up to someone and shoot him. Boi needs to do something more. If he's going to wind up in prison for the rest of his life, or dead, he needs to do a thing that maybe Nina will grow to understand one day. Killing one man won't get him props. But killing a movement, an idea—that's when a man becomes history.

Boi calls Joe. He's relieved when Joe picks up. They haven't gotten to him yet.

"Bring that stuff to town," Boi says.

"How much stuff?"

"All of it."

"You sure?"

"Yeah."

Boi pulls out of the school parking lot. He refuses to look at Nina one last time. It'll weaken him. As he's driving, he looks over at Windward Mall. Two giant department stores and a ten-screen movie theater linked together by over a hundred indoor shops and franchise restaurants. Boi wonders what was there before the mall. Maybe a field. Maybe a loi. Maybe a place with its own name. There's a cemetery next to it, mauka side.

Maybe the mall is built on bones.

Boi's pissed again. Focused. All in.

Don't look back.

As he drives through Kaneohe, all he sees is targets. Blocks and blocks of single-family homes and townhouses. Supermarkets, car dealerships, and fast-food joints. Unlike earlier when he drove down the East Coast of Oahu and through a different little town every few miles, Kaneohe stretches on forever. What names were lost, names or bones buried under strip mall foundations? Like Joe always says, used to be every square mile had its own name, its own creation myth. But now places like Kaneohe are more American than anything else. So-and-so used to live here. There used to be a theater here. The scene from this movie or that TV show was shot here. The new creation myths now start with names like Castle and Cooke. The real story already forgotten.

That fucker thinks he can do whatever he wants.

When they ask him why he did what he did, he'll tell all. First, he'll tell them about Kanaloa. Then he'll tell them about The Gov at Nina's school, trying to take her away. He'll tell them that The Gov's new law will be the final nail in the coffin of this place. He'll tell them about all the things he drove past on this day. Earlier, the University of Hawaii athletic complex. Somewhere over there the head football coach's office, the fucker collecting his million a year. The downtown skyline. Glass-windowed bank buildings towering over trendy, wannabe mainland pubs, while crumbs try to catch some zzz's under banyan tree shade, resting up for the chronic night ahead. *The airport.* The fucking airport. The Salt Lake and Aiea suburbs. Piece of shit, lead-painted, termite-infested houses that sell for seven-hundred grand. Then the hulking mass of the brown and yellow steel of Aloha Stadium. More suburbs, Pearl City, Waipio, Mililani, Waikele, Ewa Beach, Kapolei. More places with new blueprint and bulldozer creation myths. The water park, with its slides and wave machines. The last time Boi went with Nina, he'd never seen more Hawaiians in one place. Wall-to-wall inked up arms and backs and jiggly mom flesh scrunched and hoisted up with gumball-colored bikinis. Then Waianae, Makaha, drugged-out and broke, barely hanging on to the old ways. A tent city near the end of the road, right before Kaena Point.

Boi takes the H-3 up the Koolaus. His hands shaking, he veers off a couple of times, almost crashing into guard rails hovering above nature under a billion-dollar-plus stretch of elevated highway that sees so little traffic it's the best place on the island to race motorcycles. He enters the Tetsuo Harano tunnel and, trying to keep his blood up, wonders for the thousandth time who the hell Tetsuo Harano is. He imagines just-another-Japanese-man, brittle and pushing one-hundred, aloha shirt, glasses, and slacks, with something big named after him. *The tunnel. It's a target, too.*

A helicopter is flying above him. He looks to his side. A cop on a motorcycle is waving him over. He checks his rear view. Four squad cars on his tail. Busted. He rubs his eyes. He stomps his feet. *Boi No Good doesn't run.* He can U-turn at the bottom of the H-3 and race back up the mountain. Kalelekaanae it, leaping mullet off the H-3, maybe blow up a par-three eighteenth hole on a golf course below.

But the cops tailing him aren't trying to run him off the road. Boi slows down. They don't pass him. More like a motorcade than hot pursuit. Boi coasts and spots Kaneohe Bay below, the barrier reef, littered at the edges with houses, its sewage camouflaged green and blue. They should have been trying to trap him by now. What the hell's going on?

Boi grips his gun and pulls to the side. He flips on his hazard lights. He eyes the rear-view mirror and waits. The motorcycle cop takes off his sunglasses. Boi knows the guy. Korean. One of those private school kids whose tuition was paid for by a mom and pop store. He's not drawing his sidearm as he approaches Boi's truck.

Boi doesn't recognize the other four cops. They're older, though. Uncles. Beer drinkers and hardcore beef-eaters by the look of their stomachs. Boi doesn't want to start blasting away at uncles. He steps out of the car and puts his left hand up. His

right arm droops at his side, fingers wrapped around gun handle.
He looks over the concrete railing. He can jump. Couple hundred
feet at least. Shut the buzzing in his ears up for good.

"Rapun!" says the Korean. "You drunk?"

"I not going in," says Boi.

The Korean frowns. He's big, this kid. Broad shoulders and
a wasp waist. Skinny legs and tiny feet, though. Not bound feet
tiny, but one big push, and he'll topple over. He looks back at the
cop and rubs his exhausted eyes so he doesn't see double. "I'm not
going in," Boi repeats.

"The Gov wants you!"

"Fuck him."

"Follow us," he says.

"For what?"

The uncle cops throw up their arms and groan. They look at
him, tired and bitter. Like he's a whiner from Kry-lua.

Boi gets it. He's *special*. He inherited. He got a sat phone, a
direct line to the most powerful man in the state. He got a cush
detail, a pay raise, and a promotion. He's hooked up.

"Just tell me what he wants, and I'll follow," Boi says.

The Korean sighs. "Hurricane watch," he says. "They an-
nouncing in an hour or so."

"All this for that?"

"Gov wants you with him."

This is how it's been. Lunch? Stay by me. Trip? Stay by me.
Speech? Stay by me.

Now, storm. Boi thinks about the red swirl of infrared at the
Hurricane Center. The haole professor said no way it would reach.

"Let's go," says the Korean.

The road, three lanes of concrete hoisted up by giant pillars
planted in canopy some two hundred feet below, feels as narrow
and thin as a plank right now. One wrong step, and he'll fall. Boi
steadies himself and waves to the uncles in apology. Hurricane
watch—he can already hear Joe chanting. The uncles flip on their
sirens, shut down traffic, and wait.

Boi pictures Joe loading up his horse trailer. The problem with the world, Boi thinks, is that it produces people with vision and produces people with balls, but rarely does it make people who have both. Mr. Melvin gave up, Joe lost his land to ranting and green beer.

Down the Koolaus, circling the mountain's belly. Nina's somewhere down there in Kaneohe. Or maybe The Gov did take her. The other kids, to Governor Charles Knotting they're just doll heads, just specks floating around, whirling windward.

Making sure his secondary firearm is secure, Boi reaches under his seat. It's there. He also feels a plastic package and pulls it out. It's a sealed jar of branch-chain amino acid powder. Shane probably left it there. Boi steers with his knee and cracks the seal. He rolls down the window and dumps the powder. Plumes of amino acid dust fill the air like ashes. Boi pisses in the jar and nearly fills it.

How did the cops find him? Boi looks over at the passenger seat. His eyes lock on the satellite phone.

Fucking Gov.

Boi waits until the H-3 splits—one lane headed toward Kahekili, the rest to Kamehameha Highway. He grabs the sat phone and tosses it out the window. Boi then pins the gas pedal to the floorboard and veers away from the other cops. Their brake lights flash as Boi races down Kahekili.

Hurricane watch. Boi shakes his head. How many times has he heard that before? But maybe he should call Patricia. He should ask her to pick Nina up. He knows Chastity won't be prepared.

Then, in a few days, he'll pick her up himself. He'll show his little girl what he has done. And they will chaine, chaine, chaine across the flooded graves of three hotels in Waikiki.

13.

When Shane was about seven, he went through a phase where he refused to eat anything that wasn't white. Helen fed him milk, bread without the crusts, cauliflower, egg whites, and steamed fish. Charles, disturbed by this trend, wanted to force him to eat something, anything, non-white, but Helen wouldn't let him. She said it was just a phase, and that it wasn't overly difficult to build a balanced diet with just white foods. Rice was white, after all, and throw in some white asparagus, peeled lychee, and cottage cheese, and he'd be meeting his nutritional needs.

Charles has been thinking about Shane's childhood since the police found his body. And what he remembers is disturbing and irrefutable. He and Helen spoiled Shane. He's not sure how this led to Shane's death because there's no direct path, but he's sure that somehow indulging Shane with psychiatrists, tutors, coaches, ski trips, trust funds, and white-only food was a complex circuit full of blinking wrong turns that somehow led to his son getting killed.

But what else was he supposed to have done? Right now, Charles is sitting in Chastity's living room, which is walled by white cinderblocks and is barely bigger than a prison cell. All the pictures, and there's a ton of pictures, both framed and placed on bookless bookshelves and pinned on corkboards that line the walls, all these pictures, and there's no sign that Chastity or Nina ever left the island. Hell, there's no sign that they ever left the Windward side. They weren't exposed to anything. Charles always made it a point to expose Shane to as much as he could. Could that have been wrong?

Chastity steps in the room and hands Charles a lukewarm juice box. "Sorry," she says, "that's all I have. Unless you want a beer?"

One cinder-blocked wall is lined with beer boxes filled with empties. The cases are stacked five across and six high. At least she recycles.

"No problem. Thanks."

He hears Nina ride by on her bicycle outside. He's nervous for her out there, a street with eroded speed bumps that runs across the entire housing project. She could be hit by a car or snatched up by a molester.

"Thanks for inviting me," Charles says. "I just stopped by Nina's school to see if she's seen Boi. I'm afraid this Shane thing has him really messed up."

"Boi messed up? What's new?"

"I guess I mean emotional," says Charles. "They were so close."

Chastity frowns. "Boi and Shane?"

"I know it didn't look it. But they were."

Chastity shrugs and smiles. Charles can tell her mind has already moved to another topic. Charles glances at the wall. A red, yellow, and green reggae flag covers the closed jalousie window, and it flutters each time the oscillating fan, dust caked on its blades, swings in its direction.

"I can't believe the Governor is in my house!" Chastity says. It's the third time she's said it.

Charles doesn't really know what he's doing here. He'd ended up staying at Nina's school for too long. Her teacher showed him Nina's work. Her spelling was bad, but her writing, full of cliches, tangents, and subjective description, at least filled the page. When Charles was about to leave, word got around that The Gov was on campus. The principal begged him to stay for cookies and punch.

The vice-principal, a Hawaiian with a smartly trimmed mustache and triangle tattoos running up his right forearm, pulled Charles to the side and complained about a lazy, tenured teacher he was having a hard time transferring to special education where she could do the least amount of damage.

Next, a fifth grade teacher, a young Filipino, who'd apparently turned down law school to teach kids, snatched Charles. She's caught a child plagiarizing. She told the student she'd give him an F if he didn't re-write it. The next day, she had to deal with a screaming single mother who threatened to sue. The teacher was sure that it was the mother who later slashed her tires in the faculty parking lot.

Admin didn't back the young Filipino teacher, even strongly suggested that she give the student a C for his copy-and-pasted Wiki article on obesity in America. The teacher will re-apply to law school next year.

As Governor, Charles has often felt like a marriage counselor for the largest multi-cultural, polygamous family in the world.

So the bell rang and Charles ran into Chastity. He agreed when she demanded that he come home with them. She made it a point to hug him several times in front of Nina's teacher and the administrators who shadowed him.

Now, he's wondering why he's here. Chastity is a single mother with zero ambition. How in the hell does someone go through life without dreams and goals? Charles sips his juice box and almost spits out the dose of warm sugar water. Enough. "It's been really nice talking to you, but I really must be going," Charles says. "Meetings."

"You look tired," Chastity says.

"I'm okay."

Chastity stands. "I'm so sorry about Shane."

"If you ever need a babysitter, or any help whatsoever, let me know. May I use your bathroom for one minute?"

"Sure," says Chastity. "Sorry, it's not clean."

The bathroom is the size of a closet. He closes the door. Toothpaste scum is smudged all over the tiny sink, and speckles of dried mucus are caked in the basin. Nina's a spitter. He'd seen her do it at school today. She'll have to stop that.

Charles pulls open the shower curtain. Five shampoo or conditioner bottles, three of them just about empty. In the shower pan brown blotches lead to the tub drain like footprints. Two shrunken soap bars mashed in a ball sit on a tray. A shower caddy stuffed with mold-spotted rags and more empty shampoo bottles bleeds rust on a shower wall.

Charles calls the Chief. They found Boi but lost him. He threw his sat phone out the window, and raced off. As for Shane's autopsy, a ton of broken bones. It's as if he was hit by a semi.

"The girl ran him over?" Charles asks.

"It appears so."

"What were they doing in Kahuku?" Charles asks.

"The girl says she doesn't remember."

Charles nods. She'll get hers when they haul her off to Kentucky.

"Please find Boi. I'm worried."

"I understand," the chief says then pauses. "He's all you got."

Charles hangs up. He takes another look around the bathroom. Tiny pellets, roach or gecko shit, litter the sill above the tub. The trash can is filled with water-stained cigarette butts and used feminine products. And when Charles lifts the toilet seat to take a leak, he see that the porcelain has been sprayed with the kind of shit that only comes out when a person consumes too much beer and cheese on a daily basis. Charles aims for these specks of feces with his piss, trying to shoot them off the sides of the of the bowl. They won't come off. They're too old and calcified.

Charles flushes and is almost afraid to wash his hands. Maybe Boi isn't all he has left. He needs to pull Nina out of this insane asylum, too.

When Charles opens the door, Chastity is standing in front of him, holding a box filled with glass jars of seasoned sea salt. Each bottle has a slip of red ribbon tied around its neck and a label that lists various ingredients—fresh rosemary, red pepper, garlic.

"I was wondering," says Chastity. "I mean, everyone loves my salts so much. I was wondering. Could you maybe have your friends try these and see if they'd be interested in buying some?"

Great, the Governor of the State of Hawaii being asked to hock rock salt.

"Do you want to taste?" Chastity asks.

"I'm sure it's delicious, but I really can't. High blood pressure."

Chastity turns her head and pouts. She's a pretty girl, and Charles can see how she'd turned Boi's head, and maybe Charles didn't give her enough credit. She has some ambition. She's trying to sell salt. Sure, she's selling each bottle for two dollars, which means that her seasoning better be as addictive as crack if she hopes to make money off this scheme, but he can appreciate her misguided entrepreneurship.

Nina opens the front door and rolls her bicycle inside. Shorts, slippers, and no helmet, of course. "Hi uncle," she says.

"Hi little girl."

Nina leans her pink bike against the wall. Both the bicycle frame and chain are rusted, and Charles imagines a pack of dogs urinating on it in the middle of the night.

If Nina stays here much longer, she won't have choices. And it's not because they aren't out there for a poor girl from Kaneohe—last Charles looked, Castle High School offered AP courses and provided college counselors. Well, he was told that it did. What would stunt her is a mother who didn't show her options, who didn't push her to work hard in school, to read everyday, and to be curious about what goes on outside this little town. Shane had every option and was on his way to Yale, he was so close, until he felt like he had to prove his manhood, until he felt like he needed to be one of these people. Island macho bullshit.

If Charles had it to do all over again, he knows he would do better with a girl.

"I'll tell you what," Charles says. "Let's make a trade."

He takes the box from Chastity. He squats in front of Nina and pulls his satellite phone out of his pocket.

"Nina, anytime you need help I want you to call Uncle Charles."

He hands Nina the phone.

"Also, it tells me where you are no matter what. Feel free to use it when you want to. Like if there's a big storm. I'm the Governor, I can send help. Of course, I won't be able to talk back right away, but I'll always answer when I can. You can call me for whatever reason—whether you need a ride, help with your homework, or feel like making a trip to town to visit."

Nina stares at the chunky phone.

"No one in my class has a phone."

"Even if they do," Charles says, "I can guarantee you none of them have a phone like this."

Charles shows Nina how it works. She picks it up quickly. Smart like Boi. He needs to help get her out of here. He needs to teach her that this local "good enough" philosophy that these people have embraced for generations is a one-way ticket to mediocrity. Math is average and reading skills are developing? Good enough. Middle school C's and B's? Good enough. Barely graduated from high school? Good enough. Fifteen dollars an hour? Good enough.

Charles steps out of the apartment, followed by Nina and Chastity. He loads the box of salts in his car and kisses Chastity on the cheek.

"Remember, if you two need anything, call me anytime."

Chastity nods and smiles. She starts to say something, but decides not to.

Charles steps into the car, turns the key, and rolls down his window. "What is it?" he asks.

"Nothing," says Chastity. "It's silly."

"No. What?"

Nina jumps. Her new phone is ringing. Charles laughs and asks her to hand it to him. "Don't worry, I'll give it right back," he says.

It's the director of civil defense director. The storm system is already turning and weakening. It will miss. "Should we call off the watch?" the director asks.

Charles thinks about it. "Not yet," he says. "Let's wait a day."

He hangs up and hands the phone back to Nina. "Don't answer any calls for about an hour. I'll get my new phone by then."

Nina nods, looking awed at her new fairy godfather.

Charles starts the engine. "Looks like no hurricane," he tells Chastity. "But there will probably still be some rough weather. By the way, what were you going to say?"

"Nevermind."

"No, what?" Charles asks.

"I dunno," Chastity smiles. "I was just going to say..." She looks at the phone Nina is holding. "I feel untouchable now."

Charles nods. He wishes them a good evening then heads off. He remembers that feeling. Untouchable. He remembers it way back from his surfing days. But after each terrible wipeout, he was reminded it wasn't true. And it seemed like every time he tricked himself and felt untouchable the most, something came up to remind him that he wasn't. Helen. Shane. No one is untouchable.

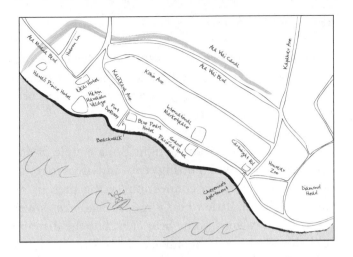

II. Hurricane Rapun

1.

Somewhere in the middle of the Pacific Ocean between Hawaii and Baja California, a hurricane is dying. Just like vast majority of the others that came before it, the storm either hit colder waters, high wind-shear, or dry air. Now Hurricane Kikilia is winding down to tropical storm status, which will mean heavy rain and flash-flood warnings across this 6,400 square mile state that sits in the middle of the five million square mile Central Pacific. Five million square miles! The chances of a hurricane hitting Hawaii feels about the same as an asteroid slamming into Earth, but the doomsayers are all out, packed in grocery stores and gas lines, talking about the last one to hit Hawaii—Hurricane Iniki. Those old enough to remember feel safe because it only directly hit one island, Kauai, while the ones too young to remember pack coolers full of beer for their hurricane parties.

Boi sits in his truck, sweating, his fists clenched, ears throbbing. He's listening to the news, all of it dedicated to Hurricane Kikilia. With Waikiki evacuations called off, the radio station is taking calls. One man says the University of Hawaii football game should never have been cancelled. He rambles on about lost revenue and a possible bid for a low-level bowl game ruined. The next caller, a woman, asks if electricity will go out because she is throwing a dinner party.

No news on Shane.

Maybe the hurricane bought Boi a couple of days. He still imagines detectives putting two-and-two together. Shane's body in Kahuku. No connection to the present owners. On the other hand, little to no physical evidence as well. No bullets or shell casings, some beer cans, but the dirt and moisture probably destroyed the fingerprints. They'll look at Shane's crushed bones and wonder how Glory did it. They'll question how Glory moved the body, then figure it out: the excavator But why would Glory bury Shane in Kahuku when she had all those others buried at her house in Waimanalo? Then, assuming, the Chief hasn't called them off, they'll find out that Shane's gravesite used to be Joe's farm. Almost half of all murders are committed by people the victim knew. They'll bring Joe in and search his property.

After what Joe did to Shane, he can't trust Joe's decision-making. He had to send him home after he brought the horse trailer. But what if he goes off boasts? Right now, the bombs are all set: at the power substations, the sewage line, and the three hotels ANFO barrels rigged with water gel boosters crowned with blasting caps—all of it covered with tarps surrounded by orange cones and yellow crime-scene tape.

Boi's parked alongside the Ala Wai Canal. He's waiting for night. And when it comes, when the buildings, streets, and palm trees light up, he looks up to the sky. It's a clear night, the wind has died, and the air feels muddy, so different from the time he'd sent Peter Patrino's house into the Pacific. There's no rain storm, and now that the hurricane's dying hundreds of miles away, no help from the weather. But he's ready, so it won't be like the "Knotting for Gov" Kona campaign catamaran flop. No hopeless caveman chopping tonight. A pile of gutted remote controls sit in the passenger seat. The controllers, box-shaped devices with triggers and wheels, they're all set to send electrical current to the blasting caps. The blasting caps will ignite the sausage-shaped boosters, and the boosters will send out supersonic shockwaves that will set off the big secondary charge. Boom. *It's easy to blow up the world.* Boi wonders why it doesn't happen more often.

Boi feels as if everything in his life has brought him to this moment. The early childhood full of lighter burns, foster parents, and corn syrup. Then later childhood with its fights, farm construction, Red Roof brainwashing, Chastity Fu, and grand theft auto. Then the boys' home, Mr. Melvin, flyin' Hawaiians waging war against the imperialist pigs of the United States. The phrase "Defend Hawaii!" fading with each spoonful of applesauce, but ringing in his ears even more loudly once he left the hospital. The Knottings: supposed to change him, they just made him worse. Dealing with chronics, suspicion, and magic typewriters—the job made him even more no-good as well. Nina's the only thing that kept him from going off.

Boi starts the engine. A man on the radio is talking about how Filipinos are hot-blooded and something's wrong with the way Okinawans think. Boi's not sure what that has to do with Hurricane Kikilia, and turns the radio off. He's across the street from the sewage line tunnel. He grabs a controller. No ceremony, no deep breath, no last second prayer. Boi presses the accelerator trigger. Kanaloa doesn't even have to tell him to do it.

The ground hiccups. Car alarms blare. Grinning, Boi heads to the first hotel, a bomb planted in the underground tunnel that runs from Duke's to the Halekulani, not fifty feet from the ocean. It's as if the very existence of this tunnel proves that the creator of worlds set all this up for Boi as well. It just makes everything easier for him. He presses another trigger. A muffled roar and a slight jolt. Tourists stop walking and look around. But nothing happens next, so they continue walking.

Grinning even more, Boi heads to the next two hotels and detonates those bombs, too.

On his way out of Waikiki, he grabs the controllers rigged to blow the power substations. They have to go off at close to the same time. He saved the fighter-jet controllers for these, controllers with one-mile range packed with gigahertz and software. He hits each trigger, one right after the other. The booms crack this time, since these barrels weren't buried. He looks at the rear view mirror and watches lights flicker then shut off behind him. He punches three dents in the roof of his truck to celebrate as he weaves through McCully Street traffic, heading mauka.

Boi crawls though gridlock Makiki, up Round Top Drive, patched into his portable police radio. He wants a topside view, watch as the now-dark Waikiki streets flood with water. He imagines the fire trucks and squad cars all lit up, racing to each site. Tourists tumbling over each other in stairwells, screaming like they're in a monster movie. He imagines torrents of water washing floating parked, convertible rental cars into the Ala Wai Canal and Waikiki Beach. He imagines the Duke Kahanamoku statue, wilted orchid leis around his neck, arms out, smiling. "That's what I'm fucking talking about," the great surfer says.

Boi shoots up the narrow, two-lane road that snakes up the mountain past cliffside houses on blocks and stilts. Trees on both sides of the road arch above as he bolts through canopy tunnels. No police radio news yet. Odd. When Boi gets high enough for a clear view, he pulls next to tagged-up concrete trash cans filled with empty beer boxes, cigarette packs, and plastic buckets of chili. Waves of wind rattle dried-out monkey pods. It almost sounds like the ocean up here.

Boi looks down and sees all of it. Kahala, Diamond Head, Waikiki, and Ala Moana.

The lights are already on.

Boi gets out of his car, steps up on a low level stone wall, and peers at the glossy scene below. No convoy of first responder vehicles head to Waikiki. No evacuation traffic lined up on Kapahulu, Kalakaua, or McCully. Maybe he's too far away to see. Boi walks back to his car, opens his glove compartment, and pulls out binoculars. He steps back on the wall and looks through them. Two joggers, knees patched with titanium tape, run in place in front of a crosswalk. Vendors squeezed between brand-label superstores hock gemstones heat-treated to bring out the color. He searches for the rigged hotels. He spots one of them. Three squad cars parked out front. Boi runs to his car to check the radio. Now the calls are coming in, but there's no urgency. Dispatch yawns as it sends units to the power substations.

"Where are you?" Boi asks.

No one answers.

Maybe the leaks he sprung are slow leaks. Not exactly what he hoped for, but slow leaks work. Boi nods his head. Sure, maybe it's better slow. Weeks of entertainment instead of days.

Boi stays in his car and watches. He's up there for an hour. Nothing from the squid god, not a word. High school kids in cars slow as they pass him. Boi takes out his flashlight and points it at pavement. Messages scrawled in chalk. Messages like My Mind is High, My Hi is Mine. Messages brought to you by the likes of the K-Town Boyz, Di-mond Tita, and the Round Top Junkies. No scenic, side-of-the-road, tweaked-out graffiti sessions for them tonight.

Pop.

Boi spins around. It's a faint, faraway explosion. Maybe one of his bombs went off late?

Boi looks out at the horizon. It's all lit up. Friday night fireworks in Waikiki. The night sky sprayed with blooming pinks, reds, blues and greens. He looks through his binoculars at twentieth-floor tourists watching from their balconies, husband arms around wife shoulders. A little water-winged boy on a tiki-torch-lit beach points up at the splash of color. A couple hundred diners at a Hale Aina Award-winning rotating restaurant look up from their plates of Chicken Cordon and Tenderloin of Beef on a Hot Rock. Nothing's different. Nothing's changed.

"Where the fuck are you?" Boi asks.

Again, no answer.

Boi starts the car and heads down Round Top, fuming. There he was, a giant, hands gripped on the edge of the Diamond Head rim, squatting above Waikiki. His stomach cramping, growling, he was there sweating, holding it in, holding it in until he couldn't stand it anymore. He was about to take a giant shit on Waikiki, spatter the entire island. But now he's thinking, maybe all he shat out was a tiny, wet brown pebble. A shit nugget that clattered down a random Waikiki storm drain.

The risk, the time, Shane, Glory. All for nothing? He has to get this shit out of his body even if it means slicing open his own belly. Is that what he should do? Maybe he can pay a visit to the state capitol tomorrow. Maybe he can take a couple of guns with him. Maybe all this time he thought he was so clever, he was wrong. Maybe he's always just been a dumb moke destined for a life of spousal abuse, crumb-sweeping, and eighty-proof rage.

Boi's on Keeaumoku now, Bolohead Row, the red light district, passing lit-up sports, strip, hostess, and dive bars with names like Champions, Cafe 10-20, 939, Club Business, 5 Star Karaoke, Imua Lounge, Winner 8 Karaoke, and Club Sandy. He pulls into a parking lot. Club Champ El...Y... See... S. He can't pronounce it. He doubts the owner can either. Boi's still on duty but he takes off his uniform top and enters the bar in a white V-neck tee shirt anyway.

It's dark. Lots of cock-rubbing and finger-banging under booth tables. Boi ignores them. He steps to the bar and hands his credit card over to an old, short-haired Korean woman who looks dressed for 1975. Two lucky cats sit on the shelf behind her, left paws up. Little Hitler Kitties. The woman is hesitant at first, eyeing his belt, his holstered gun. He orders a shot. She pours him one. He downs it and orders another. He's drinking for the first time in his life. He buys the hostesses drinks.

At ten, he tells the old woman to put on the nightly news. He can't hear. Some old drunk Filipino is mic-d up to karaoke, singing, "One in a Million You." The old woman hands Boi the remote and he turns on closed captioning. Lead story: The hurricane has turned. It's now spinning counter-clockwise south, where it will die somewhere in the middle of the Central Pacific. Second story: Police investigating explosions in Waikiki. Boi perks up.

But there's no real carnage, just ten seconds of camera shots of a burnt-up car, charcoal-colored walls, and hairline cracks in concrete.

Third story: A surfing dog. Hawaii's hundred-thousandth. Still nothing on Shane. Boi hands the remote back.

Boi, waiting for Kanaloa to speak, drinks until he pukes in the restroom toilet. A flat-chested hostess who smells like a department store asks Boi to take her home. Her name is Eun-mi.

He tried to create too many bombs—he should have made just one or two. Maybe he didn't add enough diesel to each barrel; he hurried, so maybe he didn't hit the needed ratio of fertilizer to fuel. Maybe the ammonium nitrate, buried all those years, was too weak because it absorbed moisture. Maybe he didn't have enough booster gel to blast a proper, primary shockwave. Regardless, all that frantic work—hauling the barrels out of Joe's horse trailer, pouring in the diesel, mounting each barrel with boosters, sticking blasting caps in the gel sausages, rigging the remotes—all for nothing. The risk—dodging hotel security cameras while pushing barrels in underground parking lots with a hand truck, avoiding conversations with security guards driving by in their golf carts, ducking tourists rolling in with their rental cars, and wearing his best "don't fuck with me" cop face the whole time—he may as well have thrown firecrackers at Waikiki.

He has officially become as limp as Red Roof Joe. The hostess grabs his crotch to confirm his droop. He needs to check in with Nina. He can do it tomorrow. Maybe after he checks in on her, he will turn himself in. He's tired. What a dumbass he's been. He always knew he'd never be Doctor Rapun, Chief Rapun, or Senator Rapun, but he wanted to believe he could've been Hurricane Rapun. But he's just Boi No Good, a lousy cop and half-ass terrorist.

2.

The whole world's spinning as Boi No Good tries to fuck the hostess on a fold-out futon. Even though he's trying hard to conjure up porno images in his head, all he sees when he closes his eyes are the flickering lights of Waikiki and the disappointed look on Nina's face as cops surround their house and haul him off to prison. Boi can't get it up, so he pushes the hostess off him.

He staggers to a sliding glass door, opens it. It's super warm out, and he pops sweat as he steps onto the thirtieth floor balcony. Unlike the railing at Kahekili Village, the aluminum bars up here are tightly secured. He pulls at a bar. It won't budge. This building will never rain Revs.

Boi pulls a chair to the railing and climbs on the thin metal railing. The world's spinning like crazy as he leans against a stucco wall and looks down at neon bar signs, streetlamps, and headlights that look like abyss zone, bioluminescent fish. The balcony railing shakes beneath him. Somewhere from behind, Eun-mi is screaming.

"Where the fuck are you?!" Boi yells.

Nothing.

Boi knows that fucker is down there somewhere. He climbs off the railing, grabs a metal bar, and twists and pulls with everything he's got. Nothing. He kicks at the bars so hard that he knows that if he knocks the rails loose, they might go crashing down thirty floors and his momentum will take him with them. He kicks again and budges one of the bars. He yanks the hollow aluminum off its housing, which rips skin off his palm. Boi looks over the edge. There's a giant squid hole down there. He knows it.

Boi chucks the bent bar at a circle he can barely see three-hundred feet below him. He realizes he missed when he hears the faint sound of metal rattling off hard surface. He rips off another bar, which takes more skin off his hand, and hurls it.

He fires bar after bar until all that's left is the chair, side table, a metal railing, and bloody hands. He raises the rest of the stuff over his head and flings it, too. Nothing except for the sound of metal and glass splashing against the imaginary seabed.

He turns around, and Eun-mi is dialing her phone. He passes her as he marches to the front door. The knob is instantly slippery from of the blood on his hands. He grabs harder, turns the knob, and heads out of the apartment.

Why has Kanaloa abandoned him? Boi waits for the elevator. There's only one person who might know.

Boi steps out of the condo as high-pitched civil defense sirens blast. He spots his mess of aluminum bars, a broken chair, and shattered glass surrounding a manhole cover. Boi looks up. Is he hearing things? The hurricane watch is over. Is it the first of the month? Boi realizes he doesn't even know what day it is.

Boi guns the engine and speeds out of town as the civil defense sirens fade. He's heading for country. He's heading to Waialua.

3. _____

Growing up Knotting was not as easy as everyone seems to think. Charles, the only child of a trust fund father who never held a real job for most of his life and a mother who had grown up in New York and often threw around the phrase "island fever," used to dread the inevitable and frequent periods when his father would slip into one of his moods and spend days, sometimes weeks, in bed, and his mother would fly off to the Mainland and leave Charles with him. During these times, little Charles wished school lasted forever. Because when he got home, and it was only him, his father, and a housekeeper named Maria, a plump Southeast Asian immigrant who used to peel and eat foul-smelling pickled eggs with one foot propped on the trash can rim as if she were Washington sailing over the Potomac, he didn't have anyone to talk to. Maria barely spoke English and would always find him a chore to do when Charles asked her to play. And his father, locked up in his room, blasting Hawaiian music and drinking himself into a stupor, ignored Charles's knock on the door. Thank God for The Club.

The Club, which fronted Waikiki Beach, was Charles's second home. All his friends from school were members, and they spent many of their afternoons and weekends surfing and paddling canoes. Always one of the tallest kids, he envied the short, compact ones who seemed quicker and more coordinated than him. But he worked at surfing harder than they did. He'd often be out in the ocean even after the sun went down. Part of it was for the love, but the other part was he didn't want to go home. He grew to hate people who could barely speak English and would rather scrub toilets than play with a child, and he was so sick of muffled Hawaiian music blasting behind doors, he vowed never to listen to Hawaiian music by choice. Thankfully, there was no music out in the ocean. And he began to think of waves as his playmates.

A half century later, and Charles, mounted on his longboard, still thinks of waves that way. The surf today is tiny, two foot crests of breaking water that provided little thrill when he started, and right now, less. But the waves lull Charles, and he wishes he could close his eyes and ride one forever.

Charles looks toward the shore. Rocks jut from the ocean surface. The tide is unusually low. Charles spots his security detail on the beach, arms crossed and brows sweating. They're still mad at him for taking the car by himself and driving to Kaneohe.

Both guards have been with him for the last seven years, so he knows them fairly well. The big one, who claimed powerlifting titles when he was a young man, has two daughters, both in college. The other is also big, just not as big, has four kids and manages to send all of them to private school on his and his nurse wife's salary. He says they complain about having to eat Costco chicken every night and having to wake up at four-thirty a.m. every weekday morning to catch the bus from their Kapolei suburban home to their town prep schools, but he's making it work. That's what pisses Charles off about some people. This guy, whose father was an alcoholic pig farmer who used to come home from the bar drunk and beat both his children and pigs and left his son nothing but hard feelings, this guy makes it work. He's never collected welfare. He's worked all his life. Like Charles, who was not born with the natural tools to become a professional surfer but did anyway, this guy, who is taking off a shoe and shaking sand out of it right now, this guy is willing to put in the work to succeed. Why aren't there more like him?

Even though there are obvious differences, Charles likes to think that he and this bodyguard have a lot in common. Charles is not a prince turned king; he did not inherit the governorship. He had to work for it. Charles did not get into an Ivy League college because his father built the school a library. In fact, his parents showed little interest in his grades and donated little to schools. He had to work hard for the grades to get in. And just like surfing, academics did not come naturally to him. He'd have to read books three or four times to digest their information while some of his classmates simply read the book jacket and were able to score well on essays and tests.

Granted, tuition was never a problem. He did attend private schools all his life, and his father paid for his college education, but there's no doubt in Charles's mind that even if he had been raised by an alcoholic pig farmer, he would still have become a professional surfer. He still would have gotten into Yale. He still would have become Governor.

As Charles paddles out and ducks under breaking waves, he tells himself again that Shane's failures weren't his. They were Shane's. It will be the same for Boi. Charles gave Shane more than he'd ever gotten, and even though the first five years of his life was much harder than Charles's, he was given every opportunity. As Charles waits for his next ride, he tells himself that he will continue to do the same for Boi and Nina, but at some point, if they fail, it's on them, not him.

Charles catches a wave, an itty-bitty one-footer barely big enough to ride. As he glides over the ocean surface, he thinks about the law he's still trying to pass. Right now, it's a longshot. People misunderstand it. He's not trying to get rid of anyone. There's no fetus murder, no pinning down of young women and forcing birth control upon them. They can have all the babies they want. They just won't collect government checks if they decide to do so. It's tough love. Just like Charles and his trusty bodyguards did, they will have to learn to make it work. Or they can stop having babies and collect all the welfare they want. The have *choice*. Yet, people are acting as if the law strips choice from them. Regardless, the law is dying just like this wave Charles is now riding. He needs something to happen. He needs a winter swell. He needs help.

As the wave flattens out, Charles leans over and drops in the water. While underwater, he's struck by another sudden sob that makes him shiver. He holds his breath, closes his eyes, and fights to compose himself. His son, crushed and buried. His wife poisoned with chemo again and again. Charles refuses to be like his father and lock himself in a room. He won't be like his mother either. He won't run away to the Mainland professing island fever every time things get tough. He opens his eyes and lets the salt water sting them. He then swims up to the surface for air.

His guards are waving him in. Charles climbs on his board and paddles in. The tide is so low that the bottom of his board nearly scrapes shoreline rocks. He gets off his board, unleashes himself, and walks it in.

When he gets to the beach, the guards are waiting for him, shoed feet sunk in wet sand. They're anxious. Maybe more news on Shane's autopsy, something that the docs first missed. Maybe someone found Boi. The guard with the two girls in college hands Charles a towel.

"What is it?" Charles asks.

"The Mayor, the Chief, the National Guard, they all calling."

"What's up?"

The guards shrug. The one with the four private school kids hands Charles his phone. About fifty unread texts collected in the last hour.

"How come you didn't call me in earlier?"

"We figure give you, time, sir. You know..."

They've been taking it easy on him because of Shane. Everyone has. It needs to stop.

Charles reads the texts. They're all about the same thing.

The sudden low tide—he should have known. He's been too distracted.

"Jesus," says Charles.

"What happened, sir?" asks one of the bodyguards. Charles has his head down reading, so he's not sure which one asked. He closes a text message and looks up. "Apparently, we're not completely out of the woods yet, gentlemen."

The guards look at him, anxious.

"Kikilia," Charles says.

The big guard picks up Charles's board while the other pulls keys out of his pocket and follows Charles to the car. They're in a hurry, probably to call their wives. He hands Charles his new sat phone. Charles puts the phone of the roof of the car and dries himself off. "Any news on Boi?" The bodyguard shakes his head. "Check the little girl's location."

The guard checks an app on his sat phone. "Looks like she heading from Kaneohe to town, sir."

Boi must've picked her up. For all his flaws, he's always been a paranoid parent, much like Helen.

"She'll be fine," Charles says. He dusts sand off his feet and gets in the car. They wait for the big guard to lock up the board at the club then join them.

"So you think going hit sir?" the guard asks him.

Charles shrugs. He often gets questions like these, as if being Governor has transformed him into an expert on everything. But even the scientists can't predict these things. A storm comes, it turns, it grows, or it dies. It's a moving, living thing that is shaped by a hundred different factors. He's no authority. He's just a guy who knows about North Shore breaks more than just about anything else.

"I know I'm not supposed to ask," says Charles, "but what do you think about my bill?"

The guard shrugs.

"I mean, take you for example. You grew up hard, yet you made it. And your parents didn't collect welfare, right?"

"They didn't. They proud of that, sir."

Charles spots more sand on his feet. He opens a door and dusts sand off.

"That's what I mean." Charles flicks even more sand off his shoulders and chest. "You made it work. Welfare means not having to make it work."

Make it work. Nice phrase. Maybe he'll use it if he ever runs for anything again. "You made it work," Charles said again. "And look at you, a homeowner, kids in private school. You've succeeded."

The guard shrugs. "I don't know, sir."

"What do you mean?"

"Nothing sir. Sorry. Nevermind."

"No. Please tell me."

The guard starts to say something, then pauses. He starts again. "I used to get pretty good grades, sir. Sometimes I wonder what would have happened if I even knew college existed, you know?"

Charles finishes dusting himself off and closes the door. "You didn't know college existed?" he asks.

"Nobody like us did."

Charles nods. God, more sand. He flicks a grain off his knee. "Take me home first, please," he says. "I have to appear confident and commanding for the cameras." He rolls his eyes for the bodyguard's benefit.

It's his least favorite part of the job, but Charles knows that the public needs to see a leader well put together under possible crisis. Hurricane Kikilia. What an ugly name for a storm, Charles thinks. He wonders what "kikilia" means. Probably something about the ocean or flowers or mountains.

"Do you know what 'kikilia' means?" Charles asks.

"Nothing," says the guard.

"Nothing?"

"It's just 'Cecilia' in Hawaiian."

4.

Like most kids raised by poor Depression-era parents, Joe Bolosan hardly throws anything away. The shed at his Waialua rental is filled with empty spaghetti sauce jars, plastic whipped cream containers, and even plastic TV dinner trays. Stacks of National Geographic magazines dating from 1971 are wedged in shelves next to the toilet, which constantly runs, the tank hiding a cracked, rubber flapper. Joe's shampoo, dish soap, and liquid laundry detergent are all diluted with water. Every last ounce of cleaning agent needs to be drained before he buys another. Blown-off shingles from his roof. Firewood. Rotting oyster shells crushed then sprinkled on his organic herb garden. Thanksgiving turkey bones for a rice porridge soup called jook. When Boi was a child, Joe would shake his head when Boi threw away chicken drumsticks without snapping the bones and sucking out the marrow.

The door is locked. Boi pounds on it then peeks through a screen window. No sign of Joe. Did he take off for good? Boi told him that they were going to get caught. Maybe Joe's on a flight to South America. No, not Red Roof Joe. Boi will wait on the porch.

Boi's hands need a distraction, so he rummages through a box full of grease rags and rusty fixed-spool fishing reels. The knobs and levers are frozen. Boi grabs a spray can of lubricant and greases the reels while Grover Cleveland whinnies and neighs like he's trying to strike up a conversation. The grease isn't working. Boi snaps off the bail and throws it and the rest of the reel in the yard. He grabs another and starts to work on it. To Joe, old things have value. To Joe, this rusted reel may sell on eBay for a couple hundred bucks. What Joe doesn't realize is that "classic" anything is a thing of the past. A twenty-year-old car used to be a classic. Now all a twenty-year-old car is a hooptie poverty flag. The reel Boi's working on now, an old Daiwa nicked up with boat rash and tangled in frayed twenty-pound test, he couldn't give this thing away. He cracks the drag knob off this one, and throws it in the yard, too.

By the time Joe gets home, the sun's setting, and every broken reel is scattered all over the front lawn. Joe steps out of a friend's four-cylinder pick-up, the kind they don't make anymore, but isn't classic, and the friend drives away. Joe looks around at all the reels and frowns. "I can't fix anything anymore," Boi says.

Joe nods and sits next to Boi. "What happened?" He reaches out and touches Boi's bandaged earlobe.

Boi pulls away. "Not sure. Maybe not strong enough boosters."

Joe shakes his head, closes his eyes, and sighs. "Enough already."

Boi nods and stands. "I need to crash."

"Go inside."

"My fricking ears. Buzzing."

Joe dusts asbestos off his jeans. "Let me take a look."

Boi glances at the shelves and spots a Clorox bottle bailer, the one Shane had told him belongs in the Smithsonian. Maybe they hurt The Gov enough. Maybe Joe's right. Enough already. All Boi wants to do is sleep. "If we don't go jail, maybe I should take Nina fishing one day," he says. "Teach her."

Joe shakes his head. "You gotta go way out to fish now. She going get sick."

Boi turns around. "Why you always trying to piss me off?"

Joe shrugs. "What you ever did with Captain Cook's big toe?"

"It's at my place somewhere," Boi lies. He vaguely remembers taping it to the end of a broken car antenna and converting it into a back scratcher, but now, like most of the things he'd built as a kid—like sling shots, blowguns, and car woofer boxes—he has no idea where it is.

"Let's go look at your ears," says Joe.

Boi's lying on the couch, his head on Joe's lap, as Joe holds a lamp in one hand and tweezers in another. Boi was all set to tell Joe about the squid god, but first he just wants the tiny receiver that he knows was planted there pulled from his ear. The static, the popping, the dead line, he wants it out. Boi flinches as the sharp metal probes his inner ear. "Why the hell you need tweezers?" Boi asks.

"Shut up and hold still."

Boi's too tired to fight. His ear fills with conch shell whooshes as Joe pokes around. "Jesus," says Joe, "You ever clean your ears?"

"Ear wax is good. It's acidic. Kills bacteria."

Joe pushes up Boi and searches through a scattered pile of screwdrivers, wrenches, and paint brushes in the kitchen sink. A trail of ants, drunk on the corned beef sludge pooled in the drain grate, weave to a cracked counter corner. That's what Waikiki is supposed to be like. People carrying too much scattering to exit points. But Boi failed and now Kanaloa is ignoring him. Fuck Kanaloa. He failed, too.

Joe grabs a rusty knitting needle and rinses it. He returns to the couch. The needle's long enough to stab through one ear and poke out the other. "You crazy or what?" says Boi. "You trying to give me lockjaw?"

Joe sits, grabs Boi by the back of the neck, and pushes his head down hard. It's a nice feeling, makes him feel like a kid again. Boi closes his eyes as Joe sticks the needle and tweezers in his ear. The whooshing sound returns. Metal scrapes the sides of Boi's inner ear. His arms and legs go slack as goosebump tingles flash through his body. It's like an itch is being scratched, one he never knew he had. A pop follows, then noise floods Boi's ear.

Boi shoots up and rubs the side of his head. A sawing sound echoes. He rubs the other side of his head. The sawing is more muffled and dull. Joe holds up the needle in front of Boi's face. A round ball of wax the size of a marble, a bit coned-shaped like a newborn's crown, sits on the tip. Before Boi can ask if Joe really pulled that out, Joe pushes his head down and searches the other canal. He pulls out a second marble-sized ball, quicker this time. The buzzing is gone.

Boi grabs the lamp from Joe and shines it on the balls of wax. Joe goes back to the kitchen sink and grabs an exacto-knife. For some reason, unlike the knitting needle, this he washes and thoroughly dries. He steps back to the couch and sits. He cuts into each wad.

Instead of tiny electronical receivers, each one contains a coiled, golden, fossilized juvenile centipede now cut in half.

"Ho," says Joe, "they never sting you?"

Boi shrugs, his eyes wide. "I didn't feel nothing."

Joe nods. He goes to the kitchen and comes back with an empty glass jar. Boi pokes at the centipedes with the tweezers wondering what killed them before they could sting. A dose of insecticide that drained them of color? Maybe they were too young to bite or break out of the sticky wax. Joe grabs the tweezers from Boi, drops each sticky wad in the jar, and screws on the lid. Looks like he's saving Boi's centipedes entombed in ear wax, too. A few years from now, it'll be a funny memory. Joe tosses Boi a metal rod. Boi catches it. It's a broken car antenna. Captain Cook's big toe is still taped to the tip. Boi remembers Mrs. Alani, all pissed off, clenching a fistful of tater tots. He laughs.

"I still got the arrowhead, too," Joe says.

Holding the back scratcher, Boi plops his head down on a sofa cushion. He holds Captain Cook's big toe up for a moment and eyes it. It looks sort of like a crooked white rook from a chessboard. Boi smiles. Fake or real, he'd take this over a King Kalakaua royal scepter any day. He puts the back scratcher down on his chest and closes his eyes. Ears more clear than his conscience, Boi passes out.

5. _____

When Boi finally wakes up a day later from dreamless, coma sleep, he rubs his ears. All he hears is Joe's tinkering with the broken fishing reels on his workbench. No buzzing, ticking, static, or voices. And he's hungry.

For a moment, as Boi watches Joe fix all the reels he broke, he feels worse about breaking them than Shane or Glory. He wonders why. He'd always held it against Kry-lua haoles that they seemed to care about their dogs, cars, and houses more than people, but maybe, somehow, he's become like that, too. Or maybe it's back to the same old theory. He's crazy. But psychotic or not, he wants to do something for Joe, something for this man whose wife left him, who lost his farm, and who Boi hasn't been treating very well either since he'd gotten mixed up with the Knottings and admired how rich people did their thing. What Joe did to Shane, he did it for Boi. Now Boi wants to do something for the man who just fixed him.

"The First lady left me some money," says Boi.

"So you rich now?" Joe says, not looking up.

"I was thinking. Maybe you, me, and Nina, we go move Big Island if we don't get thrown in jail for the rest of our lives. I can buy some acres."

It had been after that first trip to the Big Island, the first and last in Boi's life, that Boi'd packed up his stuff, told Joe that he and Grover Cleveland made a fine pair—a horse and a jack ass— and said he was going to move in with the Knottings for good. He'd planned on telling them some made-up sob story about how his alcoholic father kicked him out of the house, how if the Knottings didn't take him in, he'd have to go live on the beach, and he knew that the then Almost Gov wouldn't turn him down. After all, the then Almost Gov liked Boi more than Shane. Boi dreamed he'd sit at dinner with the family every night and tell them how they should spend their cash and about everything wrong with the island while eating some crazy curry.

But Shane struck first. He'd told Charles that Boi wanted the then Almost Gov and Helen to adopt him. And when the then Almost Gov looked at Boi almost sad, like he was trying to figure out a way to tell someone stuck in a hard-labor sugar camp

that there was no such thing as promotion for his kind here, Boi
snapped. He tried to sink the campaign catamaran. And when
he failed, but the Knottings needed him to have Shane's back in
court, he figured the door hadn't been shut permanent yet. That
even though he hit eighteen by that time, no matter how unlikely,
he could still be adopted and called Knotting.

And maybe he could've been. But all it took was a few tours
in the HPD, dustbusting for Kry-lua haoles, to start thinking,
maybe he didn't want to be Knotting. Maybe the Knottings and
people like them were part of the problem. So he'd spent the last
five or so years of his life figuring out what Joe told him that day
he left. "You never going be one of them," Joe said, after Boi had
called him a jackass. "Not because you cannot act like you fit in,
but because after couple years, you gonna wanna kill them."

It took more than a couple, but Joe, who's nodding right now
as he repairs the reels, was right all along.

"We can go Big Island," says Joe. "Maybe give Captain Cook's
big toe a proper burial. And bury a bunch of other shit there
while we're at it."

The Big Island. Bigger than all the other islands combined.
An active volcano making it even bigger every day. One-fifth the
amount of people than on Oahu. How long will that last? Boi
wonders. "Sooner or later," he says, "they'll come there, too."

Joe laughs. "Shit, they're already there. Some of the richest
men in the world got houses up in Kukio. They get their own
airport, hospital, everything."

Of course.

"But Big Island is good. We can live Puna side. If we lucky,
maybe you'll be old and I'll be dead by the time they infest over
there."

Boi thinks about Nina. His Waikiki plans were supposed to
have given The Gov a real problem to deal with during the rest of
his last term and turn his head away from his people-killing law. It
could have woken people up. And the flood would've made Nina
proud. He'd be like Moses, arms out, staff in hand, watching walls

of water crush those bolohead Egypt motherfuckers. But that's
not going to happen. He's spent. He wants to leave Oahu. Some
country-ass, Big Island living would hit the spot now. He wonders how the schools are in Puna. Terrible, he imagines. Crumbs
up the ying-yang. He thinks about the private school options,
about commutes and dangerous, two-lane highways. He wonders
how much aina he can buy with two million. Aina. He laughs.

"What?" says Joe.

"I was thinking about Nina."

"And what?"

Despite all the hate and rage he feels for rich people, with
their gated-communities, their food and wine festivals, their lin-
en-clad barefoot walks on the beach, and their acres and acres of
unused land, on this island or on any island—could be the Carib-
bean, the Bahamas, the South Seas—and despite the fact he'd like
to burn them all down, he's thinking exactly like them now, how
much aina (he didn't even use the word "land" in his head) he can
buy, what kind house he should build, what private school should
he send his kid to, what kind of local punks he's going to have to
deal with Puna side, the cost of more seclusion and privacy. He's
thinking like the haole he beat up in Waialua, he's thinking like
Charles Knotting's shipwrecked ancestor. And Shane, he never
thought like that. Glory never did either. Right now, he's worse
than both of them combined. He took them out. He took out two
crumbs. He's like the Helen Knotting bill personified.

And even though he's thinking like those private-jet Kukio
motherfuckers building mansions north of Kona, he knows he
doesn't want to be them. Or maybe he does. Maybe he did all
this time. The Waikiki flood was supposed to make him. It was
supposed to make the name Boi No Good ring out loud enough
to reach ears generations away. But no, he doesn't want wine cellars, yachts, and sunsets to watch every night. He doesn't want his
name on buildings or to sit on trusts. It's even worse than that.
He wants his daughter to be one of them. He wants Nina to own
wine cellars, yachts, and watch sunsets every night. He wants her

name to be on buildings and for her to sit on trusts. He wants Nina to be Knotting. He wants Nina to lord over aina.

Boi laughs.

"What?" Joe asks.

"I just realized, 'Nina' and 'aina' have the same letters."

Joe nods.

"I missed Glory's sentencing," says Boi.

Joe looks up from the reel he's working on. "She eating Shane, too?"

Boi shrugs. "You know what? I don't even give a shit anymore. They come, they come. I'm hungry."

Joe nods. "We go Haleiwa. Grab lunch."

Boi looks around Joe's place. The computer. Still broken. No case. The motherboard and hard drive naked except for dust-covered multi-colored wires coiled around them. The hundred-pound television with rabbit ears and no reception. The kitchen sink a receptacle for all things dirty, not just dishes. It's filled with tools wrapped in two-day-old cake noodles. The floor, hard, cold laminate stained yellow and caked with flecked food and onion skins. Can't walk into a kitchen like that without taking some-thing out stuck on the bottom of your feet. Boi doesn't want Nina living in a house like this. Not ever. All this time, he told himself that rich and powerful people are no better than he is, no better than Joe is, no better than Patricia, Nina, and even Glory. And maybe they're not, but he was lying to himself all that time. Be-cause to this day, he *believes* they are.

Was that what this Waikiki thing was all about? To show them that a local kid, raised on a broken-down bus, then a farm in Kahuku, a boy called Boi No Good, is just as powerful as they are. That not only can he kick their asses—the consola-tion creed of any haole-hating local—you might have all kind money and property, but I can still kick your ass—but that he can do one better. He can also call upon the gods and destroy the tallest things they build and force them scrambling off island.

Now all he's thinking is that they win. They are *better* than him. They crawled into his ears while he was sleeping like those golden centipedes. They burrowed there and whispered things that he didn't even think he heard. They whispered, "You're just like us. You want people island-wide, maybe even world-wide, to know your name." They whispered, "Look at you, will sell out your sister and get your own brother killed to get what you want. Look at you, you even want your kid to be just like us, too." Boi, whose ears are no longer filled with buzzing, ticking, static, and squid-god voices, is just now finally hearing all this. Colonization of the mind. He grabs the jar holding the centipedes stuck in ear wax and dumps the wads in his palm. He turns his head. Joe is busy brushing old cut toenails off the bottoms of his feet.

Boi pops the centipedes in his mouth and chews. He forces himself to swallow as wax gets stuck on his jagged, silver-filled back teeth.

6. _____

As Boi and Joe head into Haleiwa, they pass a spread-out fleet of lunch wagons nestled in front of restaurants going out of business. Boi had heard the stories before, about these steak and shrimp buses, not abiding by health codes, pulling up beachside to meet hungry tourists. These wagons, with their mobility and low overhead, put many a North Shore restaurant down for the count. One guy, owner of some thirty-year-old Mexican joint, got drunk on margaritas one night, worked himself into a rage, and started whipping Molotov cocktails at the parked and closed buses in the middle of the night. It was all funny to Boi, because the restaurant owners, the lunch-wagon owners, pretty much all of them were haole. And it was rare to see haole-on-haole action. Acting hot-tempered like a local. Acting like Boi. Boi rooted for the restaurant owners after he'd heard that story.

But as Boi and Joe drive by looking for lunch, the restaurant guys are losing. Now it's the wagon owners beefing each other over turf. Two of them scream at each other on the side of the road while a few tourists, less than usual for lunch-time Haleiwa, stuff their faces with Kahuku corn and Kahuku shrimp, food actually from the mainland, just like them. Joe laughs as they pass.

Civil defense sirens go off. Boi's relieved when Joe looks up and detects the sound, too. He's not hearing things. "What's with the siren? The hurricane didn't come."

Joe shrugs. "Dunno. Practicing for the next dud." He smiles.

"What?"

"No more siren by my house."

"Why?"

"I went vandalize um. Fricking siren makes Grover crazy."

Boi shakes his head. Beaches are empty. More restaurants, closed, closed, closed. Boi didn't think the restaurant guys were losing the war this bad. Even some of the wagons are closed. When they finally spot an open restaurant, a burger joint advertising that it sells real Big Island beef, Boi, figuring it's an omen or something, even if it's probably bullshit, pulls in. They get out of Boi's truck just as a wagon pulls up in front of the restaurant. The owner, an actual local, a Hawaiian even, by the looks of it, steps out of his restaurant. "Eh!" he yells. "Better move that bus before I broke your ass!"

The lunch-wagon owner, a scrawny middle-aged haole woman in a tank top with more ribcage than tits under her leathery, turkey-gobbler neck, yells back. "I'll call the police!"

Boi remembers he's a cop. Seems like ages since he's upheld the law as opposed to breaking it. He pulls out his badge and shows it to the woman. "Better go, ma'am, or I will have your bus towed."

She asks for a name and badge number. Boi tells her that if she does not leave now, he will not only give her his name, but he will also give her his badge number if she can actually stick her head far enough up her ass to read it because he's about to cram it in there. As she heads back to the bus, she mumbles something about violent locals. Wondering out loud why locals always resort to violence. The answer is simple: It works. The rich have lawyers, the poor have fists.

"Thanks," says the burger joint owner, who wipes his oil-spatter scarred hands on his apron. He's got a black local-boy mustache and lines and cracks on his shaved, pock-marked face, the face of a crumb trying to turn his life around. It happens more often than most people think.

Boi eyes the restaurant. A woman, with her hair clamped in a bun and her tee-shirt sleeves rolled up like a local chick in junior high PE class, stands on a bar stool and stretches a long line of electrical tape across the window. Boi looks across the street. Electrical tape X's on the windows of the houses across the street, too.

"What you guys need?" asks the restaurant owner. "I get some extra canned goods, bottled water, and batteries if you like."

Boi has forgotten how nice some people can be. He knows there's people like that on the Big Island. He needs to find them. He needs to surround himself with them. But now he's just wondering why the hell this guy is offering him canned goods, bottled water, and batteries. Just as he's about to ask, he watches the woman with the lunch wagon park across the street in front of the houses with the taped up windows. He watches her put up signs in front of her open counter. She's not selling food. She's selling bottled water for five bucks a pop.

Boi looks over at Joe, who appears just as puzzled as he is. Boi turns to the restaurant owner. "Sorry braddah, we've been out of it for awhile. What we missed?"

The restaurant owner shakes his head. "Hurricane," he says. "The fricka turned."

"What you mean, went turn?" Joes asks.

"It grew and stay coming back," the restaurant owner says.

Joe looks at Boi. "They can turn?"

"I guess no more hurricane roads out in the ocean, yeah?" the restaurant owner says. "Get wind, warm water, cold water, and other storms out there. Who knows what else. I close, but the storm going hit southside, and I need the money, so, you know?"

Boi's grinning. All he's picturing is a giant Kanaloa out there swinging wrecking balls with all eight of his arms. All that flailing weight, and it's hard for him to keep his footing.

The restaurant owner looks up at the sky. "Yeah, they get all that weather satellite stuff. But you know... Even haoles cannot be right hundred percent of the time."

Joe turns to Boi and slaps him on the back. He smiles, yesterday's meat still stuck between his teeth. "I told you! How many times I told you!"

Red Roof Joe is a prophet in his time, after all.

Boi hands the guy a twenty and starts walking back to his truck. Joe follows. The restaurant guy is yelling something, but Boi isn't listening. He pulls his cellphone out of his pocket. It's still turned off. What, almost three days now?

Fuck.

He steps in his truck and turns on the phone. There's a ton of messages. He deletes all the ones from Charles and his sergeant, even the ones from Patricia. With her hurricane preparedness, she'll be fine. He's searching for at least one from Chastity. He finds it.

She and her friends have decided to throw a hurricane party. The Gov told her personally that the hurricane was probably not going to hit. They're gonna hole up in Cheyenne's apartment. Cheyenne's apartment is in Waikiki.

Nina's with her.

He dials Chastity's number. No answer. Joe tells him they should go to Patricia's. Boi ignores him and dials again. "Fuck, fuck, fuck," says Boi.

Joe asks him what the problem is. Boi tells him.

"Auwe," says Joe.

Finally, in the right fucking context.

7.

The island in scramble mode. Gas lines. Shopping lines. Many who live on the coast head for emergency shelters, in most cases, their nearest public elementary school. Some bring two days' supply of food, water, toiletries, and bug spray while others come armed to the teeth—shotguns and semi-automatic assault rifles. These normally also arrive with first aid kits, gasoline, water purification tablets, and fatigues. They refuse to take orders from National Guardsmen, who demand that they put their hunting dogs in carriers—carriers that none of them have.

Others arrive with pets without carriers as well, at schools not even designated as pet friendly. They assure the Guardsmen and police that their dogs and cats are well-behaved. But the hunting dogs wearing choke chains are already barking at the cats as the house dogs wag their tails and tug at their shoulder harness leashes.

The Adjutant General, Manny Torada, is telling Charles all of this at Hawaii State Civil Defense Headquarters. As Adjutant General, Manny heads the Hawaii National Guard, and commands some 5,500 weekend warriors. Those assigned to the emergency shelters are reporting in.

"Little do all of these survivalists know, the meth-heads and home invaders are looting their houses as we speak," whispers Police Chief Holmes. Charles is not sure if the Chief is joking or not.

Many others are here underground with The Gov as well. There's the City and County Fire Chief. The vice-director of Civil Defense. The branch training Chief. The logistics planner. Rich Kato, head of the Waikiki Safety Board. The Hawaii Electric Company rep. The Mayor and his cabinet. The Gov's cabinet as well. The Governor is in charge of all of them. But like every other time he's been up here, all he's thinking is who came up with the idea to place the Civil Defense headquarters underground in Diamond Head crater? An HQ in a volcano. Charles suspects someone watched one James Bond movie too many.

At the moment, there's not much Charles can do. The hurricane is on its way, its outer edge some seventy miles east. There are Guardsmen and police assigned to Waikiki helping with the evac, but reports indicate that a number of them have started to disappear. They all face the same choice: help thousands of uncooperative tourists who decided to stay in Waikiki despite all preliminary evac attempts or go home and care for their families. As Kikilia nears, and impossible gridlock builds, some are opting for door number two.

The vice-director, a retired Navy general, suggests that they roll in the tanks that are parked outside the bunker. Where or for what, Charles is not sure. "The hotels will hold up, correct?"

Charles is looking at Rich Kato as he asks it. Kato nods. "It's a Category 3. The fear has never been whether the hotels will hold. The fear has always revolved around evacuation difficulties, as we are seeing now, and debris decapitating whoever is left."

"And the debris?" Charles asks.

"The hotels were actually cooperative," says Rich. "Everything seems to be locked up nice and tight."

Charles turns to the Adjutant General. Manny, an Air Force major general, perhaps the leading advocate for hurricane preparedness in the state, nods as well. "They'll hold. But boy, like I've been saying for years. We've been due."

It's true. He's another one who has been saying that. In fact, a few years back, he'd shown Charles a news story that called Honolulu the U.S. city most overdue for a hurricane. San Diego was second. N.Y.C. was third.

"The hotels should be fine," says Manny. "It's the storm surge that's scary. That combined with rain water coming in from the mountains. There will be flooding even if we don't get hit directly. We may need to declare martial law after the storm passes. Remember, sir, this island has about five days of food. People may go feral without electricity or water. That's the worst case scenario, anyway."

Charles nods. All this has been said to him many times before. No one is mentioning what will happen to single-family homes. They all know. If the hurricane hits then passes west of town, houses are going to take a beating. Some people in this room live in such houses. They don't want to jinx things.

Charles feels the satellite phone in his pocket. He wishes Boi still had his. Last time he looked, Nina was in Waikiki. What the hell is she doing there?

"Are the lifeguards briefed and mobilized?"

Manny nods. Though Charles respects the police, firefighters, and National Guardsmen, he wants watermen around him in case things go to hell. The people he trusts most in a water crisis are his fellow surfers and divers. He wouldn't choose them for companions walking into a gun fight or high rise inferno, but for this, they'll be perfect if things get bad.

"Remember, General. I want rescue teams on standby. Once this thing passes, we need to get in there."

"I wish you wouldn't keep saying that, sir," says Manny.

"You're not planning on going, are you sir?" the vice-director asks.

Charles glares at him. "You're damn right I am."

"But we need you here," says Manny.

Charles looks around the room. A fifty-man-long chain of command. He's never felt so unneeded in his life.

"Who's that kid with the video camera?"

Manny looks over. "That's the documentary fimmaker."

"He's coming with me."

Alarmed, Charles's chief-of-staff tugs on the governor's sleeve. Charles pulls his arm away. The Mayor and Fire Chief are off in a corner looking up at one of the screens, shaking their heads.

The walls in here are almost completely covered with televisions, maps, and white boards. The screens broadcast the local news or show live camera footage of beaches along the coast. Evacuation maps line other wall areas, each one showing the various small towns of Oahu. A professor sketches a red line on a whiteboard. He's been tracing the storm's path for hours now. The red line is pointed right at Diamond Head.

"Looks like a direct hit," says Charles. "Us, here."

Manny nods. "We'll be fine. We're in an underground bunker."

"Water flows downhill, last I remember. Who was the genius who decided to put a crisis headquarters right below sea level? Dr. No?"

Most in the room laugh. At least he can provide a bit of levity. But his hand is wrapped around the phone in his pocket and he's squeezing.

An aide stands up from behind his computer. He whispers in the professor's ear. The professor puts down his red pen and walks toward Charles and the Adjutant General.

"The eye is going to pass through Waikiki."

Charles feels a slight quiver in his lip. "You sure?"

The professor nods. "It may veer off before it hits downtown, but it will hit."

"Water will run down from the mountains," Manny says. "The storm surge may bring waves that run all the way up to the Ala Wai. Waikiki could flood all the way up to Moiliili."

"We have the tanks ready," says the vice-director.

"Keep your tanks," says Charles. "I want the jet skis."

"It won't be that bad," says Rich Kato.

But these men don't know the ocean like Charles does. The thing about the ocean is that every single time he's been told that it would be bad, that the waves would be gigantic enough to snap his board and him in half, or that the undertow would be strong enough to snatch him from the surface and pull him to the bottom of the ocean so deep that he'd scrape against black coral, every single time he's been told it would be bad, they were wrong. It was worse.

Charles looks up at the television screens. The sky is clear blue to the west. However, to the southeast, a wall of gray flickering with lightning bolts looms. He wishes Helen were here to see this. The insurance agent in her would turn as white as a ghost. He'd tease her and she'd punch his shoulder. He never showed pain, but that woman could hit hard enough to leave bruises.

Charles wishes Shane were here, too. But those wounds are too fresh to think about now. What was it that his guard said earlier that day?

College seemed like a far away place, like Paris or something. Charles is thinking about happiness in the same terms. Something that's foppish, in a foreign language, and thousands of miles away. Water drops pelt the camera watching for the hurricane. Charles grips the phone in his pocket.

He won't wait for the storm to completely pass the island. Once it passes Diamond Head, he will lead the rescue team into Waikiki.

8.

Boi races down the smooth asphalt skidmark called the Veterans Memorial Freeway. He'd dropped Joe off at the house and hitched Grover's trailer to his truck before starting his thirty-plus mile trip to Cheyenne's zoo-side Waikiki apartment. He packed the horse because he expected gridlock armageddon. Joe wanted to come, but Boi left him. He didn't want the old man slowing him down.

Thankfully, right now, there is zero traffic, and as Boi passes Mililani, he imagines all those middle-management middle-classers huddled in their garages, feeling safe and secure that they live in the center of the island a thousand feet above sea level. Maybe they are even laughing with each other now, thinking of all the friends they have who refused to live too far from town or the beach, who paid too much for the privilege of one day having their homes demolished by a natural disaster.

As Boi passes Waipio and Waipahu, and the Veterans Memorial Freeway merges into the H-1, he feels the wind picking up. Rain pelts his wind shield, and Grover stomps in the trailer. When he gets to Waimalu, traffic halts. Boi pulls onto the shoulder lane and punches the gas. To his right, electrical wires rattle. The rain is coming down harder now. Up ahead, there's a stopped SUV, hazard lights blinking, with a dead baby memorial sticker plastered on the rear window. Boi slams on the brakes. A woman, both arms shackled with gold bracelets, holds an infant outside her SUV and argues with an old haole man. She's got the look of a high school mother threatening lawsuits because a teacher didn't accept her son's late assignment. Boi honks his horn.

The woman faces him, her face ugly and twisted, her thinning curls and running mascara soaked by rain. Boi slams his horn again and forces his way off the shoulder and into the right lane behind a line of rubberneckers. His truck crawls past the woman who is still glaring at him as the haole man taps her shoulder. He's holding insurance papers. A hurricane's coming and both of them are out there haggling over a fender-bender. Boi wants to smack this woman and tell her to get her kid indoors or she'll be putting another memorial sticker up on her car, but he's short on time. The pace of traffic picks up as he passes her, and he races down this underwear stain of a freeway. Boi looks toward the horizon at the blanket of dark gray flickering with tiny, almost imperceptible flashes of electricity. And as he passes Halawa Valley, which contains the men's state prison where he and Joe will spend the rest of their lives if anyone learns the truth about Shane, he has this strange feeling that he's not going to make it out of this alive. But he doesn't care. He just has to get to Nina. He keeps his eyes locked on ahead, waiting to be close enough to see Waikiki ahead in the distance as if once he spots it, he knows he can get there.

It's raining harder now as Boi, his hands clenched around the steering wheel, guns up to ninety-miles-per-hour on the shoulder lane. Grover is in panic-mode now, kicking at the trailer's aluminum walls. Boi's heart races. He passes the airport—no planes on the tarmac, the place probably shut down. The wipers are on max, but Boi can barely see. He squints and it's by the airport where he finally spots the Waikiki skyline far up ahead. He glances to his left and whizzes past blurry red brake lights. He slows down, truck and trailer momentarily hydro-planing across asphalt. He gets off the freeway, heads down Nimitz, and hits more gridlock. Boi can't see Waikiki anymore and he panics. He stops before Sand Island, gets out, and braces himself in heavy winds and pouring rain as he opens Grover's trailer.

Grover looks down at Boi with wild eyes. Boi grabs the reins as the horse bolts out. Boi dangles from the harness and barely manages to pull himself on the horse. Grover tries to throw him, but Boi's got his feet in the stirrups now. The horse is breathing hard. Boi yanks on the reins, turns the horse around, and heads east. They race past the bottleneck, but the street is narrow. Boi turns right and cuts through auto-body back streets. The aluminum warehouse doors rattle as the wind whistles through Kalihi. Boi and Grover push on and fly by red and white Matson cans stacked three high. On any given day only five days of food in Hawaii, Boi thinks. Getting to Nina might only be the start. This hurricane is hitting hard enough to stop the ships from coming in.

Most people, they don't make decisions. They make just one. And that's to live each day like the one before it. The island isn't ready for a storm like this.

And Boi feels like an idiot because this thing, this swirl of wind power and black thunder that he's heading into now to save his daughter, this deaf monster he tried to copy with his pathetic bombs, it'll probably end up killing him. Yet he wished for it to come for most of his life.

9.

When a hurricane hits a small island, there's no 2,550-mile Highway 10 stretching from Santa Monica to Jacksonville, there's no cross-country haul beyond state lines. The sensible islanders pack up and mule their valuables to the central Oahu suburbs, where their brothers, sisters, and cousins diligently pack their garages with bottled water, toilet paper, and gasoline. The ones with no central Oahu relatives search for public shelter or they hunker down in coastal single-wall-constructed houses with flashlights, candles, and first aid kits. The National Guard is scrambling to get the over one-hundred-and-twenty-thousand tourists out of Waikiki. Sixty-thousand have been moved to high school gyms and churches, but some are still stuck in idling, packed tour buses that lock up Kalakaua Avenue, Ala Moana Boulevard, McCully, Monsarrat, and Kapahulu Avenue, the only five roads out of Waikiki. Hotel workers, also trying to high-tail it out of Waikiki, stand around outside their cars behind the tour buses and swear at themselves for taking double-time pay to help herd the sheep onto the buses. Now they're stuck here, too. One million people on a six-hundred-square-mile island, and half are sitting in their cars. So in a way, even though the air is being sucked out of the ominous, birdless weather by a one-hundred-and-fifty-mile wide swirl of rain, clouds, and screaming winds, it's business as usual. Until some, stuck in traffic for over ten hours, eying the same make-shift Waikiki storefront signs advertising disaster profiteering prices, get out and decide to loot the locked-up stores. The police, most of them, are at home with their wives and kids.

But Not Boi.

Boi is weaving through the Ala Moana Boulevard gridlock on Grover Cleveland's back, the only person heading into Waikiki.

He's never been in a hurricane before, and he's thinking, so far this isn't so bad. Strong wind and rain, but nothing that slows Grover down. Maybe that's why the newscasters kept calling it a midget. Boi approaches the Hawaii Prince and the Ilikai. The traffic lights blink red. A sudden gust blows from his left. Plumeria petals pelt him as he approaches the Waikiki towers that loom ahead. How did he convince himself that he could bring any of these buildings down? All that concrete, glass, and steel—unmoved by the Cat 3 storm. He will grab Nina and either hunker down in one of these indestructible buildings or haul ass out of Waikiki.

It's not until he nears Kalakaua Avenue that he sees it. A wall of darkness a few miles ahead. Lightning flickers, illuminating the endless tower of smoky gray. At first, it looks as if it's just fixed there, dwarfing Diamond Head. But when Boi squints and peers though the rain, he can't believe what he's seeing. Things this big don't move. But it's moving. It's rounding the old volcano and is headed this way.

People in the convoys must see it move too because they start to panic. The wide-eyed ones standing outside get back in their cars and buses and futilely honk their horns. One bus is so packed, shoulders and faces press against windows until they shatter. Boi kicks Grover's haunches, grips the reigns, and clenches his jaw. Between him and that swirling wall of squid-ink-colored storm surge is Nina. She's in a three-story walk-up near the zoo. Boi decides to head inland and take the path as far away from the ocean as possible.

When Boi gets to the Ala Wai, thunder booms overhead while street lights blink off and on. The wind picks up, and raindrops, firing horizontally now, pelt Boi's face. Grover stops and rears his head. He staggers a bit to the right, then to the left. Up ahead, the hurricane wall reaches the far end of the Ala Wai. Brown water bursts up as high as the hotel towers. It's as if there's a gigantic propeller motoring through the canal toward them. Boi kicks Grover, but he won't budge. Boi steers the horse around. Maybe Grover is right. Taking the Ala Wai Canal route is not a good idea. They dash back to the bridge. Brown water gurgles from the underground near Hobron. It's where Boi planted the sewage pipe bomb. He pulls on the reigns and Grover Cleveland stops on the bridge. Boi watches the brown water spread.

Boi races down Hobron and heads back toward Ala Moana Boulevard. An armada of abandoned yachts and sailboats rock over waves and pull on tethers like tied-up attack dogs. The wind blows harder and a couple of boats get loose. They charge a twenty-eight-story pink hotel with copper-colored windows and shatter. The wind picks up splinters of hull and mast and hurl them at hotel windows. But the windows don't break. Boi glances to his left again. More sewage seeps from underground. Hobron is now covered with ankle-deep water. Boi and Grover move on.

They pass the Ilikai and the Hilton. They pass a hotel under construction with a giant yellow crane perched on its top floor. The crane sways and rattles but holds for now. They pass Fort DeRussy. They race past Cheeseburger Waikiki. Where Aloha is

Served Daily. The closer they get to Kalakaua Avenue, the deeper the water gets. And when they get to Beachwalk, Boi sees why. The Blue Pearl Hotel gushes water from underneath like it's sitting on a giant fountain. Boi's bombs did some work after all. But Boi doesn't care right now. He needs to get to Nina.

High wind rattles coconut trees. The rain falls in sheets and pummels Boi and Grover from all directions. The wind howls, picks up twigs and leaves, and hurls them at taped-up display windows that contain mannequins holding purses and tennis racquets. But twigs and leaves aren't going to break glass. Rain stings Boi's face as he tries to out-race the Blue Pearl flood behind him. He rides as fast as Grover Cleveland will go down Kalakaua Avenue. A handful of optimistic faces peek out from lighted apartment towers above. One tower with a lobby full of tee shirt and watch stores tilts and springs leaks from its base—the location of bomb number two. Boi and Grover give this hotel a wide birth. They head further down Kalakaua.

One-way signs vibrate and palm trees bend. The wind tries to pick up bigger things than sand, twigs, and palm branches, bigger, sharper, and heavier things. But it's having a hard time finding them. People aren't dumb. Everything that could be carried indoors was carried indoors. Trash bins, trash in general. Plant holders, bellmen carts, chairs, tables, umbrellas, and tiki torches—all safely inside. Boi passes the Grand Pacifica Hotel, the location of the last hotel bomb. It looks like it's holding up.

Grover rears again. Boi no longer sees the hurricane wall. But when he looks to his right, he knows it's coming. More giant propellers in water—oceanside this time. A near two-story mountain of cresting water rumbles and races toward the shore. The speeding wave slams the beach. Grover screams, throws Boi. The horse looks left and right, for a moment not sure where to go. Then Grover races inland through a haze of frenzied moisture.

Boi gets up and heads for the nearest building, the Grand Pacifica lobby, but the taped-up glass door is locked with chains twisted through its metal door handles. Boi pulls out his gun and fires at the glass. He kicks through the spidered door and stumbles in.

The lobby is empty, but oddly, Hawaiian elevator music full of ukulele picking still plays. Things feel calm for a moment. Boi stands and looks around. Without even thinking, he steps toward the front desk. Then water slams the beachside wall of the hotel and shakes it. Boi waits for the wave to pass, but it doesn't. It's an endless roll of water that bursts past Kalakaua Avenue, past the high-class art store across the street. The wave is probably pushing its way all the way to the mountains several miles away. The lights and music snap off. As water seeps into the lobby, Boi knows he might be beat.

You did this.

Boi sticks his fingers in his ears and tries to concentrate. He has to get to Nina, but he doesn't know how. The building creaks then tilts slightly. The entire structure is vibrating now as the hurricane wall passes through. The lobby doors rattle. Boi can barely see the bending trees outside as he steps closer to the exit. The wind sucks the broken glass from the doors. It's sucking Boi now as he grabs hold of a pillar. Somewhere, on the other side of Waikiki, he prays Nina is doing the same. The hotel creaks and tilts again. Boi has to laugh. This building is about to fall on him, and it probably would have held up if he didn't try to blow it up. The water in the lobby rises. Boi's shaking but not cold. It's a foreign feeling to him, but he knows what it is. He's scared.

Just as he's certain the hotel will collapse, that twenty-eight stories are about to drop on his head, everything stops. No more building rattling and waves crashing. Boi lets go of the pillar. The howling wind dies down to a whistle. Boi takes a deep breath and heads outside.

What he sees is beautiful.

Swirling walls of gray lit up by lightning strikes flashing thousands of feet high. Way up top, a patch of clear, blue sky. Baby tornadoes swirl at the edge of the eyewall.

Boi is inside the eye of Kanaloa.

He falls to his knees. He wishes he could chant something to pay homage to the god. He prays that the squid god kept Nina safe.

Boi looks to his left. One of the tornadoes lit by lightning jerks side-to-side and bounces off hotels like a pinball. It hits the Blue Pearl Hotel. It springs off and slams into it again. The hotel falls. Boi stands up. The tornado, the god's swirling arms, hurls debris in the distance.

Now watch. What was once smartly packed inside is now outside.

Boi has to move now. He decides to get off Kalakaua and more inland. As he struggles through the waist-high water, he hears creaking behind him. A crash and the ground shakes so hard, it tosses him a half-a-block.

Boi flails in the water, gets up, and turns around. What was once the Grand Pacifica Hotel is now a pile of rubble. Underground sea-water spews from the cracks of the concrete, glass, and steel pile. The perimeter asphalt cracks and sinks. A wave of water large enough to surf barrels toward him. Boi braces himself. After the wave slams him against a building, Boi looks up.

"Nina's here! Did you know?" Boi yells, as if the squid god can even hear him over the howling winds. But then it answers by slowly shutting its eye. The darkness surrounding the blue sky above squeezes it out of view. The winds and rain picks up. The walls begin to close.

As Boi wades through water toward Kuhio, tiki torches blast through windows like spears. The wind launches bellmen carts, mattress frames, lamp stands, lobby river-rocks, and Bibles at sliding-glass doors and windows. The contents of one fifteenth-floor-hotel room crash through the window of another fifteenth-floor-room. The wind also picks up the debris from that freshly cracked room and chucks it at the next hotel. All manner of hotel room furniture, aluminum balcony poles, and banquet flatware is picked up from one hotel and fired at the next. The west side of the wall is quickly heading toward him. Boi scrambles for Nina.

An outboard-engine cover flies above Boi, missing him by a couple of inches. Lightning flashes white on fast-moving, waist-deep water that appears to be frantically searching for a place it can sit and rest. Boi trudges on through strengthening winds. He refuses to look back. It'll just slow him down.

Up ahead, water has already flooded gutters, parking garages, and streets. Boi is halfway down Kuhio, heading toward Diamond Head and the zoo as cars float out of underground parking lots. Boi veers left and heads to Ala Wai Boulevard. He wobbles, fighting the wind, fighting the water that is now chest-high. *Let go already. You're going in circles. You won't save her, and she's just another future crumb.*

"You sound like him," he shouts at Kanaloa. "You sound like Knotting."

Boi swims as hard as he can. When he finally gets to the Ala Wai, the canal is gone. It's all water now, stretching all the way to the mountains. Up ahead, the moving water pushes a floating sedan across Boi's path. Then another. Then another. Some are occupied and hotel workers leap from their sinking cars. Others don't. Boi watches as their cars reach the edge of the submerged canal and flip, trunk-end up. He thinks about diving down into the canal and trying to pull occupants out, but he can't. He has Nina, and the hurricane wall closing in behind him.

Boi's in full freestyle now, charging ahead, as a vacuum of water chases him. He strokes so hard that at first he doesn't notice that the water is getting more and more shallow. By the time he makes another block, the depth is too low to swim in. Boi stumbles to his feet and looks forward. What's left of the eye pushes and parts the water in front of him. He knows he doesn't have much time. He sprints as he imagines howling, chariot-riding Egyptians chasing him.

They catch up to Boi, scoop him up, and hurl him forward, ten-feet in the air, into a lightpole. His muscles burn and he barely hangs on.

You alone now. Give up.

Boi shimmies up the pole and spots wide-eyed honeymooners looking out their second-story window. He strains to hold on.
Rain and grit pelt his eyes.

You did this.

If he can't make it to Nina, yes, it's his fault.

Let me take her.

"No," says Boi.

The second-floor honeymooners open their sliding glass door,
jump off the balcony, and fall into the water below. Boi looks
down. They're treading water as they float toward Kuhio Avenue. Others jump off their low-level balconies, too. They think
they get it now. If the brown guy hanging onto the light pole can
handle it outside, they can, too. They leap from their hotel rooms.
They'd rather face the winds and water down below than be stuck
in a hotel about to drop. Wind and torrents of water snatch them,
and they hold their hands above flood surface as they're dragged
toward Kuhio Avenue by a raging river.

Boi struggles to hug the light pole as his arms and legs shake.
The wind shakes his legs loose, and for a moment he's suspended
parallel to the water below. The wind gusts again and slams his
ankles into the metal pole. *You're beat. No way you can get to her.*
Boi looks around at the devastation. He wonders if after all this,
Waikiki might still hold up, the infrastructure might still be intact, and the body count might still be low. Maybe as long as Nina
and Chastity stay inside, they'll be fine. Chastity was never much
of a swimmer, so he'd be surprised if she took the plunge.

A stanchion bashes Boi across the back. A chef's knife cracks
his temple, handle first. The wall is almost on him. He has to let
go. A sofa frame snaps in half across the light pole right above
him.

Boi's in the water now, being dragged down the street by the
flood. He flails and grabs at anything that will help him float. He
grasps onto a banquet serving tray. The flowing water lacks con-
sistent direction. At one moment, the current pushes Boi toward
Diamond Head, toward Nina, at the next moment, he's skipping

across the water, legs flailing, in the opposite direction. Mattresses and minibars and toilets crash around him like artillery. He spots a gaff floating by him and grabs it. He hooks it around a street sign. The water pushes hard and as his arms strain to hold on, he feels like he's water skiing.

I never wanted to take you, too.

"You aren't taking shit," he growls.

Boi hopes Kanaloa didn't hear the doubt in his voice. He looks up at the street sign. He's only a couple blocks away from Nina now. He watches the debris up ahead. Some of the debris is people. A woman floating face down in water slows at the intersection ahead then shoots across the street. Hollywood stop. A man with a surf leash wrapped around his neck zips past Boi. *You killed these people.*

The current shifts. In fact, Boi realizes it's all currents down here, and he watches the debris more closely, planning a path to take two blocks ahead toward Nina. He nods and lets go.

He's flung across the street. He misjudged the speed of the water and loses his serving tray. He hooks a stop sign and spins around it. He looks for something else to float on. A longboard, snapped in half, heads toward him. He grabs it. *The new state seal: A banquet serving tray and a longboard snapped in half.* Kanaloa laughs and laughs. Boi watches the water like a surfer waiting for the next set. He spots a strong current pushing in the direction he needs to go. Again, he lets go.

Boi zigzags and pole-hooks to get to the block with the two-story walk-up on Cartwright Road. And Boi's feeling it now. His ribs ache, his head throbs, but the waters and wind, partially boxed out by four broad hotel towers, are calmer on this side street. There's an old house ahead, water up to its asphalt shingles. An old Chinese woman is on the roof, her hands wrapped around a thick electrical cable. She spots Boi and mouths something, but Boi can't hear her. She's probably pleading for help. He heads in her direction. *Leave her. Chinese, Japanese, Filipino, Korean, haole, hapa, whatever. They all part of the problem, too.*

Just as Boi gets to the flooded house, the cable snaps. The woman, still holding onto the wire, is slammed through a window across the street, three stories up. Other cables snap. And now the spark-tipped wires flail in the howling wind like furious kraken tentacles.

Boi shudders. It really is Kanaloa.

Boi has to get by the squid god to get to the walk-up, to get to Nina. He swallows hard and pushes ahead.

Don't make me take you. If I take her, the rage will make you stronger. You will be stronger than him.

Boi now wishes the water and wind flowed more swiftly like the block before. But Kanaloa controls those things, too.

Kanaloa flails. The electrical tentacles overhead shatter windows and snap aluminum balcony railings off their hinges. One leg comes crashing down toward Boi. He jumps off the longboard right before it's smashed to bits. Boi dives down and gaffs a no parking sign. He's underwater now, and the current works against him as he grasps onto walls and partially uprooted trees, anything that will help him push forward as, over him, the tentacles cut through water. He lets go off the gaff and uses both hands as he works his way upstream out of the squid god's reach.

Kanaloa doesn't speak. Instead he unleashes a howl that drowns out the hurricane wind.

Boi breaks through to the surface and sees them. Chastity, Nikki, and Cheyenne screaming silently as they hang onto second-floor-balcony rails. Nina's in tears, sits in a cooler tied to a post. They all spot Boi at the same time. Nina stands up, holds her arms out toward Boi. It looks like she's about to jump, but knows better. Then thunder crashes like a starter pistol. Nina jumps in the water. The current takes her.

10. _____

After the eye passes through Waikiki, Charles is already wearing an official orange flotation jacket and shouting orders. A fleet of white pickups towing trailers mounted with jet skis are parked outside. Charles's team of lifeguards, all experienced watermen who grew up around some of the most dangerous surf in Hawaii—Makaha, Sandy's, Waimea, Pipeline—quickly pile into the trucks. They don't want to stay out in the one-hundred-and fifteen-mile-per-hour winds longer than they have to. They know it's a suicide run, but as the bumper stickers say, "Eddie Would Go."

Charles, sitting passenger side while a lifeguard drives and the documentary filmmaker shoots from the back seat, puts a hand on the dash while the truck speeds through Diamond Head Tunnel. As they exit the crater, they run into a gray haze and rain splatters against the windshield. Water has already puddled on the road, and they're on a volcano slope. Electricity is down. No flashing traffic lights. As they descend, the driver, a Hawaiian kid about Boi's age, wearing sunglasses while driving through the storm, calmly dodges tree branches flying across the street. Charles wishes he'd take those damn glasses off.

When they hit Diamond Head Road, the driver jerks the wheel, and the truck hydroplanes left. "Oww!" the filmmaker yells. He cracked his head against a window. Charles looks back and pushes the filmmaker's head out of the way so he can see behind him. He can barely make out the jet ski still hitched to the trailer being lashed with wind and rain.

The driver regains control and races past Kapiolani Community College. "I used to go school here," he says. He takes off his orange parka while holding the wheel one-handed. He's wearing his yellow, longsleeve lifeguard shirt underneath. Charles wants to reach over and strangle him. But the kid is a terrific driver. He guns down Monsarrat and lets the truck glide across ankle-deep water. It's asphalt shingles and guava tree-twigs pelting the truck now. The kid's humming and acting as if he doesn't even notice. Charles can barely make out the Waikiki skyline to the right. The truck engine gurgles then the vehicle slows. The water outside is now almost up the truck's undercarriage. This is a Cat 3, thinks Charles. Should the water be this deep? He looks back.

If it weren't strapped down, the jet ski would have floated away by now.

"Holy shit," says the driver. He's pointing at the Waikiki skyline.

Charles is almost afraid to ask what has this kid rattled. "What?" he says.

"The Grand Pacifica not there."

Charles peers at the skyline. He doesn't see anything especially alarming. Then again, he's looking at a hurricane, beyond rattling walls and bending trees, so he has no idea what's especially alarming in a storm like this. "You think it fell?" he asks.

"I dunno. I worked that beach. It's just not there."

"He's right," the cameraman says, shooting footage of the skyline. Charles suspects the cameraman doesn't know what he's talking about. This hurricane is not strong enough to knock down a high-rise hotel. But Charles pulls out his sat phone to alert the Adjutant General just in case.

The lifeguard hits the brakes. The cameraman's head jerks and hits the back of Charles's seat. He's bitching and moaning back there as he secures his camera on his plump shoulder. The lifeguard ignores the camerama, turns to Charles, and grins. "Time to get wet," he says.

Charles, the cameraman, and the lifeguards, now wearing army helmets, exit their trucks. Wind bellows and thunder cracks overhead. A powerful gust blows, and Charles grabs on to the truck's bed and waits it out. The flurry weakens. Charles and the lifeguards jump on the jet skis. Charles rides behind the same kid who drove the truck. After about ten seconds of trying to drive and hold his helmet on his head at the same time, the kid unstraps his helmet and tosses it. It flies back toward Charles. He actually has to duck.

Charles looks back. The other lifeguards have tossed their helmets, too. The filmmaker is still holding his on with both hands.

They gun through Monsarrat. Except for the fact that they're flooded, the fish taco joint and the church to the right, and the baby strip mall to the left, all seem to be holding up. The houses are not faring as well. Some have half their shingles ripped off. The roofing that remains clings and flutters, sometimes in large pieces, like laundry line bedsheets clamped down with wooden pins. One house has lost its screen door and window. The house has been speared with so many branches that it looks like an enormous tree is growing from somewhere inside. Charles knows that only a tornado could do this. Lucky for them, the eyewall has already passed. If a hundred or so impaled houses is the extent of the damage...

Once they clear the houses and hit the wide open spaces of Kapiolani Park, Charles knows that it isn't. What was once a jogger's paradise is now a three-hundred-acre lake littered with debris, so much debris that it's as if thousands of dresser drawers were up-ended and dumped into the water. Again, Charles thinks, there should not be this much water this fast. Something else besides the storm surge is pooling here. The smell seems to point to sewage, but that could just be the Ala Wai Canal. Could a collapsing hotel drive down with such force that it breaks Waikiki's underground water table? Maybe, Charles thinks, because what he's seeing is not Cat 3 middleweight damage. Whatever passed through here had heavyweight, brain-bleeding, knockout power.

The lifeguards try their best to dodge the debris, but the water's brown surface is slicked over with all manner of leaves, branches, clothes, and paper products. As Charles peers ahead when the jet ski is nearly flipped over by a gust, he sees the shadow of something big through all the rain and haze. It's the dome of the Waikiki Shell, looming, intact.

He looks over to his left. Abandoned cars submerged in brown water. Then he spots what appears to be a floating body dressed in white. The jet ski begins to stall and the lifeguard yells something.

"What?!" screams Charles.

"The intake!" the lifeguard yells. "The jet ski stay sucking in debris!" Charles looks behind him. All the other jet skis, at least what's left of them, are stalling as well. According to Charles's count, they seem to have lost three already.

The boy-wonder lifeguard jumps off the jet ski and wades through the water to get to the body. He flips it over. It's a skinny woman wearing a wedding dress. Probably refused to evacuate because she spent over a year and a hundred grand planning her Hawaiian wedding, and she was not going to let a storm block her way down the aisle. Charles yanks a wedding veil from the jet ski impeller and tosses it. He turns and watches as the lifeguard lets the body float away and peers ahead. "More bodies!" he yells.

Charles can barely make them out. Heads bobbing on the surface like floating fruit. Charles's sat phone rings. It's Nina. He can't answer, not now, but he's coming.

The lifeguard heads to the floating corpses. "Wait!" Charles says.

The lifeguard turns around.

"The canoe club is a block away! We got canoes there! Let's go get them!"

Charles turns around. The other lifeguards nod. The rescue party heads for the private canoe club. Two lifeguards have to help the cameraman get through the water. Through the howling wind, Charles hears sporadic hollering in the distance. He turns back to the bride and watches as her body drifts away. He thinks of Helen. He thinks of Shane, too. And Nina. He powers through the water, wind, and debris and heads for the canoes.

11.

As Nina is wisked away by current, Boi reaches out and grazes her little, pruned hand. She slips by and is whisked toward a clot of shattered wood, suitcases, and sneakers. The dark gray clouds above light up like strobe lights, and Nina's face flickers with terror.

Boi strokes after her, but Nina's already going under. She reaches up as the current pushes her to the wood, shoe, and suitcase pile-up. She manages to grab a suitcase handle, but the water is pushing her under the wreckage. Once she's underwater and lets go, Boi knows she's gone for good.

The pile of debris breaks up. Nina is still hanging on to the floating suitcase that now bullets aross the surface. Boi can't swim fast enough with his head above the water. The water is too dirty for him to be able to swim underwater and see. Boi guesses where she'll end up, takes a deep breath and strokes with everything he's got.

He bursts from the water and swivels his head. A skinny arm banded with a gold bracelet heads right to him. The current pushes Nina right into Boi's arms. His entire body goes so electric and the inside of his mouth tastes like batteries. A blubbering Nina hammer-fists Boi's face and wails, "What took you so long?!"

Boi kicks back to the nearest apartment building. Furniture covered with wind-puffed trash bags sail across the choppy brown surface. Boi tells Nina to hold her breath. She's protesting, but he pinches her nose and dives into the water anyway. She's pounding his chest as he swims as hard as he can. It's no good. He's too exhausted, and the current is too strong. Boi grabs onto a traffic light pole. He searches for something, anything, that can help get them back before the rushing water pulls them further away.

There's a tree up ahead. A line of wind-stripped trees half-submerged, roots dug deep somewhere next to the sidewalk below. Nina's pressed against his chest and her arms are wrapped around his neck. She's practically choking him. Boi takes a deep breath and kicks off the light pole. He charges the first tree. His fingers grasp at branches as the current pushes against him. Some snap in his right hand, but the ones in his left hold up. Nina's coughing up water. Boi turns her face to her. She nods and her grip tightens. He pushes off the tree, and they make it to the next one. Boi takes a breath then continues on, frantically kicking off trunks and freestyling from tree to tree. He must look like a mommy monkey, baby wrapped around him, swinging through forest canopy in slow motion.

On land Nina's light, so light that he can easily press her over his head, one-handed. But here in the water, her arms wrapped around his neck, she's a ton. By the time they're at the last tree, Boi and Nina are only several feet away from the apartment balcony. Lungs stretched max and muscles on fire, Boi kicks off the last tree, strokes against the current, and grabs hold of the apartment railing. The three women, bodies underwater and on their last legs, scream at him from the balcony. Boi climbs over the railing and ignores them.

Boi kicks open a door. He heads for the bathroom. He falls flat on his back in the tub with Nina, whose arms are still wrapped around him. Both are breathing hard. Her little heart is pounding so fast, Boi's afraid she'll be the first seven-year-old in history to have a heart attack. Since she'd entered his life, she was reason enough to breathe. But something happened when she got older and could dress, shower, and feed herself, when she could read, argue, write, and make up silly songs like "The Dancing Cactus" and "Blood on the Lip"—the grungy, hard rock ballad she'd sing in a gravelly, high-pitched voice (were these songs about him? He isn't sure). Something happened when she could make him laugh, not by being cute, but by being funny. She became a person. *And people were the problem, weren't they?*

All this time he'd been afraid of what she would do without him. But now he sees he needs her more than she needs him. And all he's wishing now was that he'd witnessed her birth instead of being locked up in the boys' home. Her birth—wow—that must have really been something.

Boi squeezes her hard. Nina pushes away and looks down at him. "Go get Mom," she says, shivering.

The winds howling so loud that he barely hears them screaming outside. He thinks. He can't leave Nina and risk his neck and go out there again. And life would be so much easier without Chastity. Having to kiss her ass or get ROPA'd. Having to kiss her ass or lose Nina. But Kanaloa stays quiet. No question what the squid god would tell him to do.

"You have to help them, Daddy," says Nina.

Boi doesn't say anything.

"They're all going to be mommies."

He looks at Nina. "What?"

"They all got babies on board."

Boi has to laugh, which sends a sharp pain to his ribs. Of course. The impending Helen Knotting Law. Like gun freaks who stockpile ammo whenever a Democrat wins the Presidency, these welfare queens, they're getting knocked up one more time before they have to get sterilized if they want to collect their government checks. Suddenly, Boi likes them. Boi wants to save them, or their unborn kids anyway. Jab another finger in Knotting's eye.

"Be T-R-R-F-C-C," says Nina.

Trustworthy, Respect, Responsibility, Fairness, Caring, and Citizenship. It's her school's credo. It occurs to Boi that no elder of his ever asked him to be any of these things. Makana, no. Charles and Helen, they asked him to lie, then be loyal and ambitious. Joe and Kanaloa wanted him to be a goddamn terrorist. Maybe Patricia or his grandmother told him to be such things, but he doesn't remember because their voices, even back then, were drowned out.

But Nina's telling him to be good.

"Fuck," says Boi. "Okay, sweetie."

He tells Nina to stay in the tub no matter what and heads out. The wind's gotten stronger. Boi goes for Nikki, the one who's screaming the loudest, first. He leans over the rail and grabs her arm. She's fighting him, so he grabs two fistfuls of hair and yanks her up. She slaps at his arms as he drags her to the apartment and throws her inside. Something blue and slimy heads for Boi like a curveball. Boi ducks. Jellyfish splatter against the window. Box kind, could paralyze him.

Boi grabs Cheyenne next. After she saw what he did to Nikki, she's more cooperative. She latches onto Boi's hands and he pulls her over the railing. She asks him what if the water rises even higher. Boi ignores her as he heads for Chastity.

Chastity. Skank Fu. Sixth grade cock sucker, community college drop-out, mother of his child, maker of Hawaiian salt blends. She's looking up at him now, her eyes wide and wondering, wondering if he'll save her, wondering if he'll grab her hands, pull her up, then let go, and let the currents take her. He looks around. Shopping carts, televisions, and a trishaw tangled in treetops. The wind blowing and headless mannequins in pink tee-shirts across the fishy-smelling water. He did all this. Boi reaches down to Chastity. She doesn't reach up at first. "You better not fucking let go!" Reading his mind.

Boi laughs. His ribs hurt, which makes him just laugh harder. He closes his eyes and laughs and laughs. He feels Chastity grab his hands. Eyes still closed, he pulls her up over the balcony.

This is why he doesn't see it coming at first. An aluminum sign coming at him like a giant, flipping coin. But he sees it when he opens his eyes. It smacks him across the head and sends him flying into the glass window. The window shatters. The powerful gust shoves a dazed Boi over the window sill, head first, and he feels a sharp, stabbing pain in his stomach as his feet leave the ground. He's stuck there for a moment, like a see-saw plank bolted to a playground fulcrum.

He pushes himself off the sill and falls to the balcony. Chastity's screaming something, but he can't hear. He can hear Kanaloa fine, though.

I didn't want to take you.

He looks down. Dagger-sized shards of glass stuck in his belly. Chastity grabs Boi's arm and drags him into the apartment. He turns around and takes a last look at all the horrible tree-bending, street-flooding, debris-swirling damage he and Kanaloa have done.

When Boi stumbles into the apartment, he looks down. The sign that hit him is on the floor inside, a stick-figure man holding one arm out of the surface of the water, slightly bent like a synchronized swimmer. The last thing he sees is a caption on the sign, words of wisdom to live by: When in doubt, don't go out.

Boi collapses to the floor. He must be in hell because all he hears are chicks screaming. Sent to hell because of Shane. Because of Glory. Because of what he did to Waikiki. And he hopes hell exists, he hopes he's headed there now, sent down straight into the brimstone and fire, because that devil, the one who brought the white man to Hawaii, the one who killed off all the natives, the one who's working on turning this island into a six-hundred-square-mile tropical resort donut built on the bones of past people, the one who's trying to take Nina, when he sees that red-pointy-eared mother-fucker, he's going to smoke that fool. And while he's down there, he's going to clip Kanaloa, God of the Underground, too. Hate this strong, you even feel it when you're dying, even when you going moemoe, even when you sleep.

Nina's tapping his shoulder. He doesn't move, so she stops tapping and shakes him. He barely manages to turn his head, face her, and open his eyes. With both hands, she's holding something the size and shape of a Costco garlic salt container. What's she trying to do, feed him? No, his daughter is smarter than that. Boi shuts his eyes tightly, opens them, and looks closer.

"Don't worry. Uncle knows where we are," she says.

Boi makes it out. It's a satellite phone. The Gov must have given her one, too. So he'd always know where she was, know what she was doing—and will be in her life as long as she has that damn phone. Boi can't do a damn thing about it. He struggles to reach for it, but can't. He feels himself taking, quick, short breaths.

Boi reaches for the phone once more, but Nina, looking alarmed, pulls it away. He closes his eyes and tries to breathe. He imagines Nina's confetti dolls flittering above, the drawer full of quarter-sized, balloon-fingered red-haired girls smiling as they shower his face. He doesn't want to lose them, so he snatches at them, but they slip through his fingers. Crawling and gasping, he's on the floor now stuffing them in his pockets, but there are too many. His heart pounds as he tries to save them all. At least he can smell the ocean from here.

III. The Great Aloha Telethon

1. _____

Koolina. West side. A field of freshly laid sod. A chapel with blue-tinted windows fronted by white plumeria trees. White tents, white table cloths, hundreds of white plastic chairs. Floodlights clamped on hurricane-stripped coconut trees. A JumboTron. A thoroughly sound-checked stage. Two boats on the near horizon, the ocean, still hurricane brown. Off to the side, a cigar lounge tent for douchebags.

Two weeks and three surgeries after Hurricane Kikilia, Boi, with Joe and Nina bedside, is watching the telethon from his hospital room. Unable to talk and doped up on painkillers, Boi reaches for Nina's hand. A wave of relief fills him as he touches her fingers. Every time he wakes up, he's surprised she's alive and glad that sleep did not send him to an alternate reality. Nina pats his hand and points at the TV.

The thousand-dollar-a-plate seats fill. Men and women in aloha attire and earthy linens. A few forty-year-old chicks in high-heeled black boots. Looks like they're congratulating each other on how young they look. Brown waiters and waitresses, lucky to have a job at a time such as this, pour water. A band onstage fronted by three Hawaiian girls plays a song called "Do the Hula." The crowd applauds and whistles as a middle-aged hula dancer with loose belly skin steps onstage wearing a plastic green skirt that looks like it went through a paper-shredder. Her neck, her wrist, and her ankle are wrapped with polyester orange leis. The band leader introduces her. Her name is Patricia Bolosan. On the whole, the dance looks like a three-minute-long blown kiss.

"Is that grandma?" Nina asks.

Joe nods. The music shifts from plucked strings to synthe-sized beats. Patricia gyrates to what the band leader calls hip-hop hula. She moonwalks into a holo. "Wow, what the fuck," says Joe.

Boi doesn't want to watch. He strains to wrap his hand around the remote. He barely manages to pick it up then drops it on his freshly scarred, swollen stomach.

Nina grabs the remote. "You want it louder, daddy?"

Boi tries to shake his head but only manages to flop it once on the pillow. Nina turns up the volume.

When the song's done, there's a dramatic moment of silence, of darkness, before the JumboTron lights up. Images from the hurricane that blew through the entire island coast two weeks ago intercut with national news reports listing numbers—the loss of life, the loss of cash, and the speed of the wind. Then images of Waikiki. Images of Kry-lua. Images of the North Shore. Images of Hawaii-Kry. Images of the airport and the capsized Arizona Memorial. No images of Ewa Beach. No images of Hauula. No images of Kahana Bay. No images of Nanakuli, which is right down the road. No images of Kualoa, except for one taken from a distance of Chinaman's Hat, the most photogenic islet in the state. But there's an odd image or two once in awhile. The im-age of local looters shattering supermarket windows with baseball bats. The image of female prisoners in red smocks abandoning the flooded correctional facility in Olomana and heading toward the mountains.

Glory. He waits to hear confirmation from Kanaloa. But Kanaloa hasn't talked to him since he arrived at the hospital. Over forty blood transfusions, the doctor had said. Half the blood in his body is no longer his own. Right before the second surgery, when Boi could talk, he'd called out to the squid god. The doctor told him that it's the twenty-first century. We kill gods with pharmaceuticals now.

When the images on the JumboTron are of places recognizable, places seen in movies and on television, the crowd gasps at the devastation. The pink hotel with cracked windows and caked in mud. A dead horse on a pyre of broken outrigger canoe hulls. Duke's bronze feet dangle out of a second story artisanal cheese shop-window. Beaches muddy and white-sandless. McMansions destroyed. Three hotels reduced to crushed concrete and rebar. All the while, Iz's haunting rendition of "Somewhere Over the Rainbow" blasts from the state-of-the-art sound system. Teary-eyed second wives dab at their mascara eyes with white cloth napkins.

Boi looks at Nina. She is crying, too.

Then the images turn more optimistic. Nina claps. People helping people. Famous people at that. And not just flavor-of-the-month reality TV stars, too (though there are some of those sidling in front of the camera), but Grammy Award winners, Academy Award winners, stars whose movies net over a hundred million on a regular basis. There's a particular group of A-listers who, according to the caption, call themselves The Justice League of Aloha. Pictures of them starring in superhero movies intercut with them in real-life providing Hurricane Kikilia relief. Batman ladles soup into bowls for the suddenly homeless. Wonder Woman carries a crying brown baby with makapiapia in his eyes into a helicopter. A sweaty Flash shovels rubble into wheelbarrows with firefighters. He's the only one not wearing a surgical mask. Gotta see his face. They all have homes in Hawaii, they say. They all were overcome with the desire to give some aloha back. The spokesman, an actor who plays The Mudwrestler, a former accounts payable beancounter who finds one morning he has the ability to turn himself into mud, and finds all sort of imaginative ways in which this is a benefit (mostly in female mud-wrestling rings), he visits a hospital and makes kids laugh. His name is Peter Patrino.

Joe shakes his head. "Auwe," he says.

Then other images appear. These of other real, everyday heroes. First responders. Doctors and nurses. Cops Boi either knows or recognizes. Social workers like big-haired Lisa Akamine, who's working hard finding temporary shelter for displaced people. Construction workers like Clyde Sanga, who sits in an excavator working overtime to help in the Waikiki clean-up efforts. Wealthy private citizens like Rich Kato, whose family is donating a million dollars in the effort to bring sand from Iraq over to Oahu to replenish the beaches.

"Wow, those people are TRRFCC," says Nina. Boi wants to talk, to tell her they are not. He wants to tell her they are JERKOFF's. He reaches for the feeding tubes snaking from his nostrils to his stomach. Joe grabs his hand. Maybe he's right. They both need to watch this.

Holding a mic, Peter Patrino himself appears on stage to wild applause. Low-key and dressed in khaki shorts and an aloha shirt, the same vintage orange one Elvis wore in *Blue Hawaii*, he's here to introduce the truest hero, he says. He's here to introduce the man who organized a group of lifeguards to go into Waikiki and bring people out, not after the hurricane hit, *during* the hurricane.

Boi closes his eyes for a moment to prepare himself. He knows what's coming next.

Low pixel smartphone video footage. Lifeguards paddling outrigger canoes into Waikiki. They toss tourists ring buoys and pull them onboard. They climb up hotel balconies and pull tourists from flooded hotels. They pull each other into boats when one of their boats goes down. But none of them are as brave or crazy as the one who jumps into the water with a surfboard and paddles toward three pretty young ladies trapped on the second floor of a Waikiki walk-up. None of them swim as strong as this man, who is paddling back with a little girl wrapped around his neck. And this man, who is now carrying the body of a young man impaled by shards of glass out of the apartment, this man, big, tall, skinny long legs, and broad at the shoulders, what little hair he has left on his head thrashed by wind, this man, he's more than twice their age. Even Kanaloa's flailing electrical wire tentacles go limp when this man passes.

The real hero, says Peter Patrino, the true hero, he says, not a movie hero, but a hero of flesh and bone, is Governor Charles Knotting.

The Gov steps on stage, wearing a baseball cap, humbly bowing his head. The applause register at twice the volume of Peter's entrance. Everyone's heard the stories. Everyone knows what this poor man has been through. He just lost his wife to cancer, his son to murder. But the sorrow didn't stop him from being a real leader, like the generals of old who would ride into battle with their troops. He isn't like the typical twenty-first-century leader who arrives on the scene later to commemorate and speechify. No, this guy is old school. Custer at Little Big Horn. Roosevelt charging San Juan Hill. That's when the chants start. One table, full of Republican party bigwigs from the mainland, they start it. Knotting for President! Knotting for President! Make it work! Make it work!

Nina claps. "Knotting for President!" she says. "He saved you, daddy!"

Boi did this. Every time he tried to chop the big man down, The Gov just got bigger. Shane, Waikiki, all of it. It was because of Boi Shane had died. And The Gov just got bigger. It was Boi who had shaken Waikiki loose enough for the hurricane to do all that damage. And The Gov grew again. It was Boi who Charles risked his life to save. Boi has made Charles Knotting a fucking national hero.

Charles waves to the crowd. The chants get louder. And as Boi watches, he knows it's a done deal. Charles will get his bill passed. Hell, Charles will probably become President of the United States.

Peter steps next to Charles, and The Gov puts an arm over his shoulder. The crowd cheers and cheers. Boi imagines the millions across America cheering from their living rooms as well. Peter Patrino tells them to pick up their phones and give. He tells them to pick up their phones and show aloha. He says it in his terrible pidgin for good measure. "Brah, no be all stingy liddat. Spread da aloha spirit!"

Joe groans. "What's wrong, papa?" Nina asks.

Boi sees it clearly now. He grabs Nina's hand to brace himself. The crowd and the folks at home across America, Canada, Japan, China, Europe, and South America, they will remember their three-day vacation junkets and pull out their phones. They will remember being greeted with flower leis at the airport and dial the number on screen. They will remember the beaches and hikes and fishing and surf lessons and they will pull their credit cards from their wallets. And others with timeshares, the ones who loved Hawaii so much they decided to spend a month out of a year here, they will give even more. And the ones who bought for eventual retirement and wait for tear-downs and new construction and age sixty-five, they will give the most. They all will give so that their beloved Hawaii can be built whole again.

Glossary

ahaaina: a banquet or feast.

aina: land.

ai-no-kea: "I don't care" in Hawaiian pidgin. Seen on tee shirts and bumper stickers across the state.

alii: the ruling class of ancient Hawaii.

Aliiolani Hale: located in Downtown Honolulu, originally intended to be the royal palace, it served as a judicial building for over a hundred years. Its exterior now serves as the headquarters in the *Hawaii 5-0* television series.

aloha aina: love of the land.

aweoweo: a red, big-eyed nocturnal reef fish.

babooze: an intellectually-challenged individual.

batu: crystal methamphetamine.

Bayonet Constitution: the 1887 Constitution of the Kingdom of Hawaii, signed by King Kalakaua under threat of armed militia, it stripped the monarchy of most of its authority, greatly diminishing Native Hawaiians' voice in government.

Big Five: The five large sugar industry companies that controlled Hawaii for over half a century.

Bishop Museum: the state's largest museum. It houses an extensive collection of Hawaiian artifacts and heirlooms.

Black Point: a gated community on the southeast side of Oahu.

bobora: a Japanese national.

borinki: someone of Puerto Rican descent.

boroboro: worn down (usually in reference to clothes)

calabash: a term for an extended family that includes long-time friends.

Captain Cook (1728-1779): The British explorer who was the first westerner to Hawaii. After attempting to take Kalaniopuu, the ruler of the Big Island, hostage, he was stabbed to death by Native Hawaiians at Kealakekua Bay.

Democratic Revolution of 1954: Backed by unionized plantation workers, the Democratic Party of Hawaii took control of the state legislature (22 seats) from the Big Five-backed Hawaii Republican Party (8 seats).

Duke Kahanamoku (1890-1968): famous Hawaiian surfer who won five Olympic swimming medals. A restaurant chain is named after him including one in Waikiki.

ehu: red-brown.

Great Mahele: the 1848 land re-distribution act that allowed foreigners to own land and ended up drastically reducing ownership by commoners.

Green Harvest: a police crackdown on marijuana growing that started in the late 1970s.

Grover Cleveland (1837-1908): President of the United States during the overthrow of the Kingdom of Hawaii.

hale: a simple thatched-roof dwelling.

hanai: child adopted by other relatives.

haole: a person of Caucasian descent.

hapa: a person of mixed racial heritage, today typically Caucasian and Asian.

hapai: pregnant.

hauna: stink.

hee: octopus in Hawaiian.

Hokulea: the double-hulled voyaging canoe that sailed in 1976 from Hawaii to Tahiti without the use of navigational instruments.

heiau: an ancient Hawaiian temple, most of which were destroyed when Christianity and sugar plantations entered the picture.

Hilo Hattie: Named after a famous Hawaiian entertainer, a retail chain that sells Hawaiian print clothing and Hawaiian-themed souvenirs.

holo: a running side step in hula.

hoolaulea: a Hawaiian celebration or festival.

hui: a business partnership or syndicate.

ili ili: smooth, water-worn rocks, once employed in religious rituals, now used for hot stone massages at high-end spas.

immersion school: Hawaii's, charter schools where all subjects are taught in Hawaiian language.

imu: Hawaiian underground oven.

ipu: a percussion instrument made from gourds.

Japanee: pidgin phonetic for "Japanese."

Kahala: a neighborhood on the southeast side of Oahu where rich people live.

Kahaluu: a small, rural neighborhood on the windward side of Oahu where gentrification has gone slowly here due to its brackish, muddy coastline.

Kahekili II (1737-1794): a great chief and ruler of Maui who also conquered Oahu. He tattooed half his body from head to foot. Highways are named after him.

Kailua (or Kry-lua): a residential community on the windward side of the island, named one of the best places to retire by *US News and World Report.*

Kaimuki: a Honolulu residential and small business district where ostriches once roamed its mountain side.

Kalaupapa: once a leprosy colony on the island of Molokai.

Kam Schools (Kamehameha Schools): a private school founded by Princess Bernice Pauahi Bishop (the last descendant of the royal Kamehameha family) for children of Native Hawaiian ancestry.

kamaaina: a long-term resident of the Hawaiian Islands. Some newcomers designate themselves as kamaaina way too quickly.

Kamuela: official post office designation for the Big Island's Waimea area. Translated "Samuel" in Hawaiian, it is named after either postmaster Samuel Spencer or Parker Ranch heir, Samuel Parker.

kanaka maoli: a person of Native Hawaiian descent.

Kane: the god of creation and light is one of the four major gods of old Hawaii.

kanikapila: a gathering to play music.

kapuna: honored elder or ancestor.

Kaunakakai: the largest town on the island of Molokai.

keiki: child.

Kewalos: a popular surf spot next to Ala Moana Beach Park.

kiawe: a mesquite tree.

King Kalakaua (1836-1891): the last king of the Kingdom of Hawaii whose last words were: "Tell my people I tried."

King Kamehameha I: the warrior chief who conquered the Hawaiian islands and formally established the Kingdom of Hawaii in 1810.

koa: wood from the acacia koa tree, which is endemic to the Hawaiian islands.

Kohala: the northwest area of the Big Island.

kokua: extending help and love to others.

Kuliouou: a neighborhood on the southeast side of Oahu with many million-dollar homes.

kumu: teacher/source of knowledge.

kumu hula: a source/teacher of hula.

Laie: a small town on the northeast shore of Oahu. Once a sanctuary for ancient Hawaiian fugitives and the site of two Hawaiian burial grounds (heiau), it is now known for its high Mormon population and the location of Brigham Young University Hawaii.

Lanikai (or Lani-kry): a beachfront neighborhood within Kailua.

loi: pond fields used to grow taro.

loliana: evolution or transformation from one state to another.

lolo: stupid.

Lono: Hawaiian deity associated with fertility, agriculture, rainfall, and music.

luau: a Hawaiian meal normally prepared for special occasions.

luna: a plantation foreman.

mahu: a homosexual male.

makuakane: father.

malama: to care for or preserve.

mana: a spiritual force that flows through all things.

manini: a striped reef tang common to the islands. Word is often used as a synonym for "small."

Manoa: a valley and residential neighborhood on Oahu, once the site of early sugar cane and coffee plantations.

Mililani: a suburban neighborhood in central Oahu named an "All-America City" in 1986.

moemoe: to sleep.

moke: a large, tough-looking Hawaiian male.

Mokolii: an islet also known as Chinaman's Hat.

Mokuleia: a community on west end of North Shore, Oahu with an over-fifty percent Caucasian population, a sky diving center, and a polo field.

mon: Japanese emblem, like a coat of arms, that identifies an individual or family.

moo: lizard water spirits, almost always female, that often take human form.

obake: ghost.

ohana: family.

olapa: one of Hawaii's most common forest trees.

Olomana: three mountain peaks on the Windward side of Oahu. Also the name for the island's youth detention center in the area.

olona: a fibrous plant once used as tying material by ancient Hawaiians.

opihi: a saltwater limpet.

pake: a person of Chinese descent.

palaka: a Hawaiian checkered denim typically worn by sailors, lepers, and plantation workers, now worn by wannabe kamaaina (see kamaaina above) to show that they belong.

Pali: a Koolau Mountain lookout a thousand feet above sea level that was the site of The Battle of Nuuanu. There's now a golf course named after it.

Palolo: a neighborhood on the southeast side of Oahu known for its lush valley and public housing project.

paniolo: Hawaiian cowboy.

Papakolea: a twenty-seven acre Hawaiian homestead residential area in Honolulu.

pau hana: after work.

Pele: Hawaiian goddess of fire, lightning, wind, and volcanoes.

pepito: a card game also known as Chinese poker.

pikake: a fragrant jasmine often used in lei making.

pilau: stink or rotten.

popolo: black

Portagee: pidgin phonetic for "Portuguese." Ethnic stereotypes include: dim-witted and likes to talk a lot.

Princess Kaiminaauao (1844-1848): adopted daughter of King Kamehameha III and Queen Kalama., whose siblings, David Kalakaua and Lydia Liliuokalani, were the last two monarchs of the Kingdom of Hawaii.

Punaluu: a black sand beach on the island of Hawaii where endangered species such as the Hawksbill turtle can occasionally be spotted. Developers have been trying to build here for years.

Puuopelu: a ranch estate on the Big Island of Hawaii.

shaka: a hand gesture greeting.

tita: a very tough female.

tutu: grandmother.

UH: the University of Hawaii.

ulua: a trevally over ten pounds.

vog: a type of air pollution from the Big Island created when volcanic gases react with oxygen, moisture, and sunlight.

Wahiawa Circle Island: the #52 city bus that travels west from the Ala Moana Shopping Center to the Turtle Bay Hilton on the North Shore.

Waiahole: a small, rural neighborhood settled in an east Oahu valley where houses are often fronted by anti-development signs.

Waialua: once one of the six original districts of ancient Oahu.

Waianae: rural neighborhood in west Oahu. One of the first areas populated by the ancient Hawaiians, it is now known for its relatively high Hawaiian, homeless, and four-wheel drive population.

Waimanalo: a small, rural neighborhood in east Oahu separated from Waimanalo Beach by Bellows Air Force Station, a training and recreational area used by current and former employees of the Department of Defense.

Waimea, Hawaii: largest interior town on the Big Island that once supported thousands of native Hawaiians. Site of massive sandalwood deforestation, it becamse home to one of the largest cattle ranches in the country.

Waipahu: once considered the ancient capital of Oahu by ancient Hawaiians, it became a sugar plantation town at the beginning of the twentieth century. Now a relatively impoverished community with a higher than average Filipino and Pacific Islander population.

wana: a venomous sea urchin.